P9-DWT-096

THE SWEETEST CHASE

CALGARY PUBLIC LIBRARY

MAY   2016

Also by Sharla Lovelace

The Reason Is You

Before and Ever Since

Just One Day

Stay With Me

Don't Let Go

Heart of the Storm series

Loving the Chase

THE SWEETEST CHASE

SHARLA
LOVELACE

Montlake
Romance

This is a work of fiction. Names, characters, organizations, places, events, and incidents are either products of the author's imagination or are used fictitiously.

Text copyright © 2016 by Sharla Lovelace Scroggs
All rights reserved.

No part of this book may be reproduced, or stored in a retrieval system, or transmitted in any form or by any means, electronic, mechanical, photocopying, recording, or otherwise, without express written permission of the publisher.

Published by Montlake Romance, Seattle

www.apub.com

Amazon, the Amazon logo, and Montlake Romance are trademarks of Amazon.com, Inc., or its affiliates.

ISBN-13: 9781503953963
ISBN-10: 1503953963

Cover design by Eileen Carey

Printed in the United States of America

To my mom, who never doubted that I could fly.

Author's Note

Cutting to the chase here, as I'm busy writing, writing, writing the next Heart of the Storm book . . . *chase* . . . did you catch that? (Snicker.) But I wanted to wave and say thank you for reading, and I hope you are enjoying the Chase family so far! I adore them, and I'm so excited to share the next sibling with you.

This is Simon's book, if you haven't already gathered that from the blurb, and I love Simon so huge. I had a crush on him in the first book, and writing his book was a dream. So, you know Simon had a little thing for Quinn, right? Even though she was kind of spoken for? Well . . . all I can say is, hold on. Things are about to get crazy, and I hope you like a little steam with your crazy!

Quick thanks again to the Montlake team of superheroes, my editor Maria Gomez, and my agent Jessica Faust. I'm a lucky girl.

Hugs and forever kisses to the loves of my life, my husband Troy and my kids Amanda and Ethan (who are all grown up and probably cringe when I call them kids, but hey, I'm old and I can call 'em whatever I want). Y'all are my rocks, my home base, and my air. Lovessssss.

As usual, stay tuned in to the end of the book . . . Quinn has a certain something she's dying to have at her wedding, and the recipe for it is at the back.

I love hearing from my readers, so please shoot me a line on Facebook or Twitter (@sharlalovelace) and tell me what you think!

Enjoy Simon and Quinn's journey! Love is dangerous—stay strong in the storms, my friends.

xoxo
Sharla

Chapter One

Quinn was getting naked back there. Jesus Christ.

The windshield wipers were slamming out a rhythm, the windows were back up, and the hottest woman Simon had ever known was buck-naked two feet behind him.

"That camera isn't on, is it?" she asked, pointing at the small camera sitting on the console between Zach and Simon. "Crap, what about the mobile cams?"

"Relax," Simon said, pulling off his soggy ball cap and scrubbing his fingers through his hair. "I turned them off the second you said you were stripping."

There was a sentence he never expected to say.

"Oh, my God, I knew better than to come on this run," Quinn said, her voice strained—it sounded like she was wrestling something over her head. "*Come on, Quinn,*" she said, deepening her voice. "*Just a couple of hours*, they said. *Think of the cloud formations,* they said."

"It *was* just supposed to be a couple of hours," Simon said.

"There *were* some great cloud formations," Zach chimed in.

Quinn responded with a thwack of a soaking-wet T-shirt against the side of Zach's neck, and Simon crammed his hat back on, shaking his head.

"Sounded just like you," he said, looking at Zach.

"I don't sound like that," Zach responded, peeling Quinn's shirt off his skin and dropping it in Simon's lap.

"You're no better," Quinn said, kicking the back of Simon's seat. *"Please, Little Bit, we need you,"* she said dramatically, her voice muffled.

"Now *that* sounded like *you*," Zach said, pointing at his brother.

"Need some help?" Simon called to her, ignoring him.

"I'm good," she grunted. "Damn it. Thought this might happen, so I brought clothes—ow—but a towel would have been nice. God, my mother is never going to let me hear the end of being late to Phoebe's baby shower."

"We did need you, for what it's worth," Zach said, glancing in the rearview mirror. "We—"

"Eyes on the road, Mr. Getting Married in Two Days," Quinn said, kicking Zach's seat in turn.

Zach lifted a splayed hand. "Hey, I'm being a total gentleman here. I'm just saying thank you. We did need you. The Infinity van filming *us* was great, but we needed an inside eye filming the weather."

"Or an outside eye," Simon said, looking at his brother's profile without caving to the peripheral vision that wanted him to follow. "Since she hangs out the window."

"Can't get across what it feels like to be in a storm unless you're in the storm," Quinn said.

"Good thing Simon doesn't mind groping your leg while you anchor down, huh?" Zach asked, grinning at Simon.

Simon gave him a look. "Hey, as long as she doesn't kick me in the face or strangle me with it, I don't mind making sure she doesn't fall out the window."

And yes, holding on to Quinn's smooth calf every time she needed to anchor herself around the front seat to lean out and film . . . wasn't a sacrifice.

Just months earlier, the Dallas-based Internet network Infinity had dangled a carrot. They'd heard of the storm-chasing Chase family of Cody, Texas, and wanted to design a new reality show around them. What started out a little rough and chaotic was now starting to find its footing, and the original contract for the pilot and three episodes had now expanded to ten.

A film contract did not guarantee optimal weather or crew, however, and today was one of those times. Eli, the oldest, was doing a storm-safety guest spot at the station—one of the few things about the show that he conceded was valuable. Hannah, who normally handled the filming and photography on the storm runs, was helping Zach's fiancée Maddi with last-minute wedding preparations. Therefore, they'd gone out with the minimal team of Zach, Simon, and Quinn at the prospect of some heavy waterspouts over Lake Grapevine. Zach had the storm-sniffing instincts of a wild animal and always drove. He could get them in and out of places that no one else dared. Simon, who was the team's weather guru and meteorologist at Channel Four News in his nonchasing time, had seen the cells build up, and the numbers looked good. Good enough to give it a shot. Hannah's photography assistant Quinn was filling both their shoes in Hannah's absence, despite having her little sister's baby shower to go to—but Zach had assured her he'd have her back in time.

Then the clouds had pulled back, doing a little seduction dance with Zach, dropping a ton of rain but no funnels and yet teasing with cloud formations and possibilities. Simon knew his adrenaline-chasing brother wouldn't be able to resist following that shelf cloud a little longer. It was in his blood.

"Well, you come in and explain that I'm late to a Parker formal function because you were waiting for a cloud to drop a rope for you," Quinn said, her voice going muffled again. "On second thought, scratch that."

"Whatever," Zach said.

"Whatever, my ass," Simon said, laughing. "You wanted a big one while Eli's in Dallas and couldn't fight you on it."

Big brother Eli was all about family, safety, and going by the rules. He'd witnessed their father die at the hands of a tornado, and was always the one trying to rein in the adrenaline rush that went hand in hand with their line of business.

"No, actually, I wanted a big one before I leave for a week," Zach said. "I promised Maddi a honeymoon free of all things storm-related."

Simon knew the memory Zach always kept in the back of his mind. The one from seven years ago, when a tornado ripped into their apartment complex and buried Maddi in the rubble. On what was supposed to have been their wedding day. It had been a long journey back, but there they were again, and he'd promised her a sunny-day wedding with no drama.

"God help you if it rains—"

"It's not going to rain, Mr. Weatherman," Zach said, raising his fist in Simon's direction. "You said there is nothing else brewing all week long, and if you're wrong—"

"Back it up there, Rocky," Simon responded, pushing Zach's fist away. "I've barely been at work to do any real research thanks to the film schedule. I've had to scam off my connection at the National Weather Service."

"Just saying," Zach said, raising his eyebrows.

"*I'm* just saying," he said, holding up his hands. "I report it, I don't make it—"

Simon's words died in his throat as Quinn's feet landed on either side of his seat. He and Zach both looked at the foot between them.

"What are you doing, Quinn?"

"Pulling up my leggings," she said, lifting herself with another grunt.

"Shit," Simon muttered under his breath. Now she had her legs on either side of him with her pants down. It was too much for one man to take.

"Breathe," Zach whispered on a laugh as he backhanded Simon in the chest.

With a last *oomph*, Quinn swung her legs down and turned her back to them. "I'm so sorry, but I need help," she said, making both Simon and Zach look back.

Where Zach brought his amused gaze back to the rainy stretch ahead, Simon stared at Quinn's bare back. Bare except for a red bra strap, exposed by an open zipper that she'd wrestled up to just above the small of her back.

"What if I go the wrong way?" Simon asked, teasing in order to prolong the view.

"Then you'd be Zach, not you," Quinn said over her shoulder.

"Hey!" Zach said. "Nearly married man over here!"

"And what, I'm Saint Simon?" Simon grumbled, pulling up her zipper as slowly as he could without making it a sexual overture.

"Almost there," Zach said, turning into a gated community and waving at a guard who barely even glanced up. "Tell you what—we'll swing by your apartment and get your car and drop it by here so you can leave when you want."

Quinn whipped around. "Really?"

"Least I can do," Zach said.

She blew out a breath. "That would be great, thank you." She groaned as she caught sight of herself in the rearview mirror. "God, my hair looks like—" Quinn began twisting her soggy blonde pony-tail into a bun. "Have anything up there? Paper clips?"

"Seriously?" Simon asked.

"Any port in a storm," she said, gesturing impatiently. "C'mon, I need something. Anything."

Simon dug through his battered leather computer bag and closed his fingers around something. "I have a binder clip," he said, holding it up.

Quinn sighed. "Sold." She snatched it from him and somehow fastened her bun with it, tucking in the levers.

"I can't believe you just made that work," Simon said.

"It's not a sure thing yet," she said, scrubbing at wispy wet bangs and fanning them. "Say a little prayer that it will hold." She tugged at the red-and-black dress-turned-smock over her leggings, looking for wrinkles. "How do I look? Like an urchin?"

Quinn could look hot clad in a paper bag, but Simon was biased.

"Nah, I've seen urchins," Simon said with a wink. "You've got 'em beat."

"I'll pinch your ear with this clip," she said, closing her eyes and shaking her head.

"Not while it's the only thing holding your hair up, you won't," Simon said, reaching back to pat her knee. "Relax, it's your fam-ily, not a firing squad. And it's just a shower. I've never seen you so keyed up."

"It's my mother," she corrected. "And nothing is ever *just* any-thing with Adelaide Parker. You've met her—" Quinn stopped, gasp-ing, tearing through the duffle bag and nearly crawling onto the floorboard. "Oh, shit!"

"What's the matter?" Zach said, pulling up in front of a large, gated Tudor-style house. A line of high-end SUVs with various baby-themed bumper stickers crowded the curb.

"Shoes!" she cried, slapping her hands over her face. "I forgot shoes."

"You have your boots," Zach said, chuckling.

"No!" she said, her voice quavering. "They don't go and they're covered in mud."

"Hey," Simon said, turning around. Her tone wasn't right. Quinn wasn't one to rattle easily; in fact, she was probably the most levelheaded, quick-thinking woman he'd ever met. And right now, she was rattled. "You okay?"

Her deep-green eyes met his briefly before she blinked away, and he saw trouble in there.

"Yeah," she said softly. "Just—" She stopped and shook her head. "Just a little too much family lately."

"Wedding planning will do that," Zach said.

"Come on," Simon said, getting out and opening her door to avoid further talk about Quinn's upcoming knot-tying. "Go explain and make them all laugh about it. You're good at lighting up a room."

Quinn climbed out and straightened clothing that looked pretty damn good, considering how it had made it onto her body.

"You look beautiful," Simon said.

She gave him a grateful smile that didn't quite reach her anxious eyes. "You always say that."

He shrugged. "Well, it's usually true."

She chuckled wearily. "And today I look like a drowned rat," she said, holding up a hand. "Don't say you've seen those, too." She took a deep breath. "All right, I'm going in," she said, handing Simon her keys. "Thank you for doing that."

"Good luck."

"Break a leg!" Zach yelled.

"My luck, I will," she muttered, turning and heading up the long wet sidewalk on bare feet, a big purple box under her arm.

Simon watched her turn back and mouth *Save me* as she made a face and disappeared behind a gate. He chuckled as he got back in the vehicle, then did a double take at Zach's look.

"Shut up," Simon said.

"Haven't said a word," Zach said, pulling away from the curb.

"You don't have to," Simon said. "You have Mom's eyebrow-raise down."

"You've got it bad, bro," Zach said.

Simon fastened his seat belt. "I don't have anything," he said. "Just drive."

"You're ate up."

Simon rubbed at his face, exhausted. "Thanks for the observation."

"And you're running out of time," Zach said. "Her big day is right around the corner, too."

"I'm aware."

"When is it?" Zach asked. "Maddi knows, but I'm—"

"Clueless, I know," Simon finished for him. "A month," he said then, feeling the kick to his nuts he'd been experiencing lately every time he heard the words. "Quinn gets married in a month."

Chapter Two

Quinn stood outside the big wooden double doors, looking up at the knocker as if she actually had a choice. She rolled her head on her neck to hear the satisfactory popping of stress relief and took a deep breath.

"Get on with it," she said under her breath, adjusting the big purple and silver wrapped package under her arm. "No time to mess around."

The door opened as she reached for the handle.

"Quinny!"

Quinn widened her eyes and stretched her mouth into a smile, then dropped her gaze to her sister's feet.

"Phoebe!" she cried through her teeth. "I'm so sorry I'm late—give me your shoes."

Her sister's eyebrows lifted in question. "What?"

"Say your feet hurt," Quinn whispered in a rush, pointing to her bare feet. "I changed in the car and I forgot to pack shoes."

"Why did you change in the car?"

Quinn sighed and worked to dial back her impatience. "I had to work, that's why I'm late. We were filming on the other side of Fort Worth and it ran over, so I changed in the backseat going down the highway. Please?" Quinn begged. "Don't make me go before that pack of wolves like this."

"Jesus, Quinn," Phoebe said dramatically, kicking off the black Manolos. "Just so you know, I love these shoes."

"And I'll love them, too," Quinn said, rubbing her sister's belly. "Besides, aren't pregnant women supposed to wear flats or something? Lord, you're huge."

Phoebe's mouth dropped open and she swatted at Quinn's shoulder. "Don't you know better than to tell a hormonal pregnant woman how big she is?"

Quinn smirked and slipped on the probably-eight-hundred-dollar shoes. She'd forgotten how comfortable money could feel.

"Sorry," she said, blowing her an air kiss. "Can hardly even tell you're pregnant."

Phoebe laughed and looped an arm around Quinn's neck and pulled her into the foyer, steering her toward their mother's sitting room. Cackles and diva giggles could be heard.

"Is your hair wet?" she whispered, pulling her arm back.

"It was raining," Quinn whispered.

"Y'all!" Phoebe called out as they entered the room. "Look who's here!"

The crowd didn't exactly erupt into applause, but there were some respectable *ohs* and polite *yays* and broad smiles. There was one *Who's that?* mumbled within Quinn's hearing, but nothing unexpected. It wasn't her crowd. It never had been. She'd gone to school with most of them and didn't remember half of their names, either, so the admiration level was mutual.

Phoebe squeezed her neck in another hug before she let go, and Quinn took a cleansing breath as she smiled at all the camouflaged sharks in the room. It was worth it for her sister. Even the dropped gazes as many of them did the head-to-toe assessment. That was okay. She had good shoes.

"Hey, Quinn," said a soft-spoken woman she remembered from Phoebe's wedding two years back. One of the few of her sister's friends at whom Quinn hadn't instantly wanted to throw her champagne glass.

"Hi," Quinn said, smiling, unable to recall her name. "Good to see you. Sorry I'm late, y'all. I had to work."

Yep. There was the look. Work wasn't something most of these women had a clue about.

"What'd you bring me?" Phoebe whispered loudly with a wink at the others. She took the box from Quinn's hands and tilted it back and forth. "Feels like the new baby playtime station—y'all know the one? Attaches to the car seat *and* the stroller?"

"And it has the baby-to-mommy talk button on it, like a baby cell phone!" cried a redheaded woman with a perfect chignon. Quinn remembered her being a cheerleader in school and getting mono. That's all she could come up with. "Carter loves that!"

"Megan does too," said a brunette in a red dress who looked ready for a whole other kind of party. "She can entertain herself for *hours.*"

"Probably does," Quinn mumbled to herself.

"What?" Phoebe asked.

Quin thought quickly. "Oh, I was asking, where's Doug?"

Her sister waved a hand. "He's in the kitchen," she said. "Probably eating all the hors d'oeuvres."

"Sounds like the place to be," Quinn said, chuckling. Alone. No one else found that funny.

"Quinn," said a voice behind her that sent her hands in search of each other. She clutched them together as she turned. "I didn't hear you come in, honey."

"Mom, hey," Quinn said, moving to hug her carefully so as not to mess up her blouse. Adelaide Parker didn't do *messed up*. "I know I'm late, we had to work, and I had the guys drop me off—"

"Drop you off?" Adelaide asked, pulling back.

"—so I could give Pheebs her present," Quinn finished.

"Looks like the playtime station," Phoebe said, widening her grin like a child at Christmas.

Phoebe *was* a child at Christmas. All her life, Quinn's younger sister was the epitome of the sweet, naive, helpless rich girl, and everything made her happy. Gleefully happy. And why wouldn't it? She had a beautiful home, a beautiful man, and a beautiful life unencumbered by things like financial worries or stress. Now she would have the beautiful child, too.

And Quinn wouldn't have it any other way. She adored her little sister and had spent her life looking out for her, more than Phoebe even knew. Consistently hearing from her mother how she herself fell short, however, did wear on the occasional nerve.

On that thought, she noticed her mother's mental note-taking of her outfit. She knew it didn't measure up, but—

"Lovely shoes, Quinn," her mother said.

"Thanks," Quinn said. "Phoebe, why don't you open your gift."

"We've already done the gifts," her mother said. "The guests are eating."

"I don't think anyone will be offended if she opens another one while they eat," Quinn said softly. "It's okay."

"Works for me," Phoebe said, maneuvering her body down onto a chair and balancing the package on her knees.

"Phoebe, where are your shoes?" her mother asked.

Crap.

"My feet hurt," Phoebe blurted.

"Well, you can't just walk around in your bare feet," her mother said under her breath.

"Sure she can," Quinn said. "She's pregnant and home and among family and friends. Who cares if she has shoes?"

Phoebe glanced up at Quinn as she ripped into the purple paper, an eyebrow cocked as if to say, *Listen to your own words.*

"And pregnant," Quinn repeated, for her benefit.

"So you had to work at that place?" her mother asked. "You couldn't ask off? I mean, this has been planned for months, honey."

That place. It was bad enough in her mother's eyes that Quinn chose to work after getting her fine arts degree. The least she could have done was take a respectable position as a media consultant or something in her father's company if she was hell-bent on working. But choosing to forego that route and struggle with a job search on her own—taking some business courses and settling for a management position at a big-box media store like Snap Depot—was tantamount to treason.

If Quinn didn't favor her mother so strongly, she was pretty sure there might have been DNA testing done around age nine.

"Wasn't there today, Mom," Quinn said. "I told you, they dropped me off. We had a shoot today on the other side of Fort Worth, and it ran long."

"Ah, your little show," her mother said, picking up an abandoned plate. "Have you ladies heard about Quinn's TV show?"

"Um, it's not *my*—"

"I've seen it," a pretty blonde said, raising her hand. Quinn remembered her. She'd been the valedictorian—or the class president or something in Phoebe's grade, two years behind Quinn. She'd given the speech at their graduation. And then ditched college to marry her boyfriend and be a soccer mom and society wife. How hideous could that be? "Very exciting! Feels like you're right up in it!"

"How much of that is real?" the redhead asked.

"All of it," Quinn said. "What you see is what we're doing."

"Seems a crazy way to spend a rainy day to me," the redhead said.

"I'd be terrified," the blonde said, smiling. "That first episode where y'all nearly got taken down? The one with the cell phone video? Oh, my God, I couldn't breathe through that."

Quinn's stomach still tightened at the memory. She'd been in the other vehicle with Eli while Zach chased down Maddi in the Infinity van, but when they reached them and Simon was missing? Quinn swallowed hard against the sour taste that filled her mouth. She'd never felt fear like that before. The absolute devastation of thinking someone you care about might be—

But he wasn't. He was okay. She'd latched on to him that day like never before. Quinn was normally careful around the Chase brothers to avoid any impropriety. She did have to work with them, after all, and they were her best friend's brothers. But Simon was different. He was a best friend in his own right. And on that day, in that moment, nothing had mattered except feeling him alive and breathing.

Nothing inappropriate about it. Celebrating a return from the dead warranted a little boundary-crossing.

"But you don't have kids to worry about coming home to, I guess," the blonde woman continued.

Quinn pasted on a tolerant smile. "Yep. No kids. If I die, no one cares."

"Quinn!" her mother admonished. "That's not—"

"Oh, my God, this is better than the playtime station!" Phoebe squealed. She held up the box for the room. "A foot massage kit!"

There were some definite *oohs* that time around as the spoiled genes poked their selfish little heads out.

"Thank you, Quinny!" Phoebe said, leveraging herself to push out of the chair. "I will use it every night!"

"What are you using every night?" said Doug, Phoebe's husband, as he entered the room with a smile and a plate of hot, steaming crab, drizzled in butter.

The way all the women's heads swiveled, Quinn figured they were picturing *him* drizzled in butter. Doug Blackwell was quite the eye candy. But Quinn hadn't eaten anything more than half a bag of Fritos all day, and her stomach grumbled at the aroma.

"For me?" she asked, putting on a cheesy grin.

Doug's face fell. "No."

"But you love me," Quinn said, reaching out and gently tugging the plate out of his hand. "And I'm starving. I've been out in the rain all day."

"Fine," Doug said with a wink, huffing and pretending to be put out as he turned around and headed back to the kitchen. The longing sighs were heard around the room, and Quinn had to restrain herself from rolling her eyes. Doug said over his shoulder, "You Parker women, your powers of evil know no boundaries."

"Just think if the baby's a girl," Quinn called after him with a mouthful of crab. "You'll be voodooed in your sleep."

"Won't be long and you'll be having some little voodoo-ettes yourself, Quinn," Phoebe said. "Wouldn't it be wonderful if you and Eric got pregnant right away and we had back-to-back babies?"

Quinn stared at her. She couldn't imagine anything less wonderful. Yes, she wanted kids. Eventually. Maybe. She was thirty, so it was . . . kind of . . . time to start thinking along those lines probably. But being someone's mother? That thought was terrifying. And looking at these women—a few of whom maybe had a path of their own at some point, who now lived and breathed everything baby couture—Quinn felt a little ill.

"Let's just get through the wedding for now," Quinn said, her smile weakening. "And work all the bugs out with *your* kid."

That brought some laughs, and Quinn felt the tension ease up in her neck.

"Speaking of," her mother said quietly. Oh, hell, she had spoken of it. "Are those invitations in the mail yet?"

Sigh. The crab no longer tasted appealing. "No."

"Quinn Elizabeth Parker," her mother hissed. "Six weeks! Those were supposed to go out six weeks before the event!"

"Well, I happen to think that's—ridiculous," Quinn said, setting her plate down. "I throw things away if they're on my counter or fridge that long. I'll send them out this next week. I've been busy."

"I hope with something more important than those silly jobs of yours," her mother said. "Thank God that's about to come to an end."

Quinn frowned. "What's coming to an end?"

"That Snap place job and the running around chasing tornadoes with the Chase family," she said, gesturing with her hands.

Quinn laughed, a quick sound that sounded more acidic than humored. "Yeah, that's not likely. Snap Depot may not be sexy, but it pays my bills. And we have a contract for the show."

Her mother looked at her with a patient smile. "Eric may have something to say about it once you're married," she said.

"Eric is fine with it," Quinn said. "We've been together for three years, Mom. He knows me. He knows what's important to me."

"So have you been packing?" her mother asked, clearly deciding on a detour.

"Oh, where are you going on your honeymoon?" the redhead asked. "A cruise, maybe? Bonnie went on a couples cruise for theirs and she said it was sooo hot."

"No," Quinn quipped, pasting on a smile. "We're going to the mountains, to a cabin resort and—"

"The mountains?" a tiny brunette said, looking appalled.

"I like mountains," Quinn said. "Nature."

"The ocean is nature," the redhead said, laughing. "And a hell of a lot sexier. Naked swimming—"

"Quinn's not a water person," Phoebe said quickly. "And I think a week cuddling in the mountains sounds divine."

Quinn smiled at her. Phoebe might be the little sister she always looked out for, but she sure knew how to come to her rescue today.

"Not a water person?" the brunette asked, shaking her head and nudging the woman next to her. "I can't even imagine. I love the sun."

"They have sun in the mountains," Phoebe said. "It's not a beach exclusive."

"So anyway," Quinn said, widening her eyes with her smile and hoping to bring an end to the circle of hell. "That's what we're doing."

"Not important," Adelaide said, tapping out on that subject and bringing the attention back to herself. "You didn't answer my question."

Quinn shook her head, consistently surprised that she could be surprised. The pool accident when she and Phoebe were little was a subject her parents avoided talking about their whole lives, assuming it would traumatize them more. There was no reason, really, as Phoebe was only four and didn't remember, and Quinn, although deeply terrified of water afterward, learned early on that avoidance was a Parker heirloom.

Much better to have the pool filled in and made into a ten-foot-thick patio that they could have parties on than actually talk about anything.

"I'm sorry—what was the question?" Quinn asked.

"Packing?" her mother said.

"For the honeymoon?" Quinn said. "No, that's still a month away—"

"Not for the trip, honey," she said. "To move into Eric's house."

She gestured as if that were the grandest plan on the planet. Darting a glance around to ensure the guests were talking amongst themselves and not listening, she continued. "Honestly, honey, in this day and age, with everyone living together first, I'm surprised you're still batting about that dingy little apartment."

Quinn absently ran a hand over her hair and then pulled her hand away as her fingers landed on the precariously placed clip.

"I like my dingy little apartment," she said. "And you know, most parents don't want their daughters shacking up."

Her mother gave a sound of disgust. "Quinn, don't be crude."

"Just saying."

"Eric's house is in a better place. Here in Clayton, more suited to you, is all *I'm* saying," her mother said, holding up a hand to signify the discussion was over while others might overhear.

More suited to you, Quinn thought.

"Well, I called everyone yesterday to confirm everything," her mother said. "The florist, the caterer, and the band—"

"I told you I'd already done that," Quinn said, patting her face. Was it warm in there? It felt warm.

"Can never be too careful," her mother said. "And good thing I did, too. The florist said the paperwork mentioned daisies at the reception and on the end caps at the church?"

"Yes, that was my idea," Quinn said.

Her mother laughed as if she'd suggested live pigs. "Daisies, Quinn? Honey, you aren't hosting a picnic in a barn. This is a wedding."

"It's *her* wedding, Mom," Phoebe piped in, earning their mother's pointed look. Phoebe held up a hand to deflect the invisible darts. "I mean, you made me have roses."

"And it was beautiful."

"I hate roses," Phoebe said, squinching her nose a little. "They remind me of funerals."

I love you, Phoebe.

"Which is precisely why I went a different way this time," Adelaide said, widening her eyes as if her daughters wore her out. "Orchids are just as classy."

"When you're sixty," Quinn muttered.

"Or dead," Phoebe quipped.

The doorbell rang, and Adelaide's forehead creased. "No daisies, Quinn," she said, heading toward the door. She stopped and wheeled back around, holding up a finger. "Or how about this? Little individual guest gifts at the table with a daisy motif?"

Quinn felt the heat rise to her neck. "Daisy motif," she echoed.

"I can have something designed for you to look at in a few days," she said. "We'll mix it up to match your invitations, but with your little touch," she added, backing out of the sitting room and toward the door.

Quinn shook her head and blinked hard to shut out the impending burn. Her little touch? It was her little effing wedding—in theory. In reality, neither she nor her sister had any say in their nuptials. Adelaide Parker had designed, produced, and directed Phoebe's wedding like a premiere event, and Quinn's promised to be the same. Something *for her to look at*? Please. Like it mattered.

Her phone buzzed in her hand, and she hit the button.

"Hey, babe," she whispered.

"Hey, lovebug," Eric said in her ear. Her lip automatically twitched at the nickname she'd never particularly cared for, but as usual she just smiled into the phone. "What's up?"

"At Phoebe's shower," she said, walking a few steps away from everyone.

"Good," he said. "I was just checking to see if you made it okay."

"Yeah, the filming went long," Quinn said, leaving out the parts about Zach just wanting to wait for more weather and changing in the back seat with two men just a foot away. He didn't need to know that. "But I managed. They dropped me off."

"Oh, do you need me to come pick you up?" Eric asked, his voice sounding hopeful. Only Eric would be interested in making an appearance at something most men would beg to get out of.

"Nah, it's okay," she said. "Zach and Simon are going back for my car. They'll drop it by."

She heard the judgment in his silence. "I wouldn't have minded, Quinn. I'm right down the road."

And then she would have been at the mercy of when he wanted to leave, when he was done visiting and making a big show, when he was ready.

"I know," Quinn said. "I just wanted my car. It's not a big deal."

There was a slow sigh. "How do you think that looks?"

"To who?" she asked, frowning.

"To the house full of people there," he said.

"Who are also all driving their own cars?" she said. "Come on, Eric. It's not 1950."

It wasn't about that. She knew it wasn't about that. It was about two other men dropping her off and then bringing her car over, and that she didn't consider asking Eric to be her saving grace instead. She could feel it through the phone.

"All right," he said finally. She knew he was rubbing his face in frustration. What he always did to avoid arguing with her. "So I'll see you tonight?"

"See you tonight," she said. "I love you."

"Love you back, lovebug," he said.

"You're engaged to Eric St. James, right?" the blonde asked when Quinn hung up and turned around.

"Oh, God, he's hot," the redhead said, clapping a hand over her mouth and laughing. "I'm sorry, was that out loud?"

Quinn chuckled and welcomed the feeling the laugh brought on. "It's okay," she said. "I happen to agree."

"Didn't he make one of those Most Eligible Bachelor lists one year?" the brunette piped in. "One of the Dallas periodicals, wasn't it?"

"The Dallas Observer," Phoebe provided, winking at Quinn when she gave her a look. "Yep, my new brother-in-law to be is eye candy, that's for sure."

Quinn narrowed her eyes. "Really?" she said.

Phoebe snickered. "Pregnant brain."

"Does Eric's family still have that big beach cabin on the coast?" the redhead asked. "I used to hear about that all the time when he was dating Cheyenne Miller." She blinked at the pause in the room. "Years ago, of course," she added quickly. "Like right out of high school."

"I think they do, yes," Quinn said, tilting her head politely.

"Oh, I would be there all the time," the brunette sun worshipper said.

"Simon," she heard her mother say in surprise, opening the door. Quinn snapped out of the odd conversation about her fiancé and propelled herself toward them.

"Hi, Mrs. Parker," Simon said, standing there with his cap in his hand and Quinn's keys in the other. His clothes were still damp and one leg of his jeans had a mud smear, but somehow, even with hat hair, he looked as charming as ever.

Quinn felt some of her knots melt away as his smile blanketed her. He could have stuffed the keys into a plant or under a brick and just texted her. But he didn't. He came to check on her sanity.

"Your keys, m'lady," he said, holding them out. His gaze dropped to her feet before he met her eyes again, nodding with a grin of approval.

She laughed and took the keys from him. "Thank you, sir," she said, attempting a mock curtsy.

"How are you doing, Simon?" Phoebe asked, waddling up beside Quinn.

"Perfect," he said, smiling at her with that incessant Chase charm. "Phoebe, you look gorgeous as usual." He did a little head bow. "Ladies, I can't stay, but have a good rest of the day. Quinn?"

Quinn tilted her head, amused. "Simon?"

"Drive safe."

She gave him a little salute as he turned and sauntered down the sidewalk. She closed the door and nearly ran into her mother.

"Jesus, Mom," Quinn exclaimed. "Back up a step, will you?"

"You're splotchy," she said, glancing down at Quinn's neck accusingly.

Quinn's hands automatically went to her chest and neck. "Well, you flustered me," she said. "All that flower drama."

Her mother walked back into the sitting room, but Phoebe stayed where she was, chewing a corner of her lip and eyeing Quinn.

"What?"

"You're splotchy," she said.

"We just covered this," Quinn said.

"Uh-huh," Phoebe said, glancing from the door back to Quinn as she passed her. "I heard. Flowers."

Chapter Three

Simon needed a shower in more ways than one. As he trudged up the sidewalk to his condo, clothes still damp, hat making his head itch, he decided a hot shower had to trump the cold one. Shower, nap, maybe a shelter visit before work.

Work. Everything in his soul died a little when he thought about the place. It was depressing how a place—a building, the people inside it—could suck the living breath out of something he loved so much. Simon loved weather. The puzzle of it. The predictable unpredictability of it. The thrill that made his skin buzz when he saw something—a pattern or telltale sign that others didn't catch. And the rawness. The gritty, unforgiving power of nature when it looked you in the eyes and said, *You can't control me.*

It's what made him good at it. And what frustrated the hell out of him when the powers-that-be above him at the station slung him around like an unpaid intern. The chief meteorologist, Raymond Nance, was the next-door neighbor and card-playing buddy of Barry, the news floor producer. And neither Raymond nor Barry cared much for Simon. He didn't know why, but the situation definitely took a turn for the worse once the reality show came into being. Therefore, it didn't matter how good a job he did or what he found in his research. Raymond took the glory, and Simon had no leverage to battle it. As it was, Barry was giving him more and more grief over his frequent time off for filming and runs.

Every night that Simon walked into that station, a prickle of unrest settled over him. He shook it off, told himself it didn't matter what Barry and Raymond thought or said. Not really. Yeah, they could mess with his career, but he knew he was doing a good job. He knew that in his core. So he went through the motions, smiled for the camera, reported what he knew, and went about the rest of his life. Home. Chases. Shelter. Work again.

The homeless shelter/soup kitchen in Trinity was the one place that kept things real. He led a television lifestyle—not that being a late night news meteorologist was anything glamorous, and the storm chasing reality show *The Chase* was still in its infancy—but living his life in front of a screen did tend to make things glossy. Lending his time to the Trinity Outreach Center gave him balance. Reminded him that real life is anything but glossy.

That had been something near and dear to his dad's heart. Josiah Chase had gone to the Trinity shelter every Saturday evening for as long as Simon could remember, frequently bringing him along. He'd plated food in many a serving line while his dad meandered among the crowd, shaking hands, gripping shoulders, laughing at jokes. Making them smile. Reminding them of the people they'd forgotten they were.

His dad was good at that. Better than most, and certainly better than Simon could ever hope to be. It was all he and his father really had in common, after storm chasing. Zach had the carpentry gene, Eli and Levi were into sports, and Hannah was just his baby girl. That was enough. Simon was always a bit of an outlier. Tough and buff but not big like his brothers, he turned more toward science than sports. And more toward the white-collar world than the blue-collar one he'd grown up in.

So if hanging out at a homeless shelter with his dad gave them a connection, then that's what he did. And after his dad's death, he felt it only fitting to try to carry on that legacy. A legacy that was barely limping along now, regardless of how much Simon kept splinting it together. What he gave was just Band-Aids. The place needed surgery.

Before Zach took the scenic route home, Simon was planning on stopping by. Now all he wanted was sleep. He was exhausted, having come right off the night spot at Channel Four to go on that morning's filming, and he felt like the grime quota of Texas had landed on him.

Simon tossed his hat on a hook as he went inside and went straight to the fridge. Grabbing a root beer, he popped the top and downed it, looking around. Everything in its place and neat. Dusted. Swept. His dry-cleaning bag with his work shirts the only thing out of place, hanging where he'd left it on the back of a barstool when he'd run in to change clothes.

Neat. Orderly.

Empty.

No one else there to mess it up. To leave stuff around, not pick up their dishes, leave the cap off the toothpaste. Simon hated those things, but lately he'd come to feel that too much was missing. Life was missing.

Quinn was missing.

How he could feel that way when she'd never been his—he didn't understand. But there it was. And she was about to officially belong to someone else.

He leaned on his hands against the counter, blowing out a breath. Day after tomorrow, his little brother was getting married, and then Quinn was next. Zach getting married first wasn't the problem. Hardly. Simon never even really saw that in the cards for himself—a wife and kids and all that. It never felt like a direction he needed to go. He'd had relationships here and there, and found them constricting. Not because of just being with one woman; that part was fine. It was more about being accountable to another person. That need to tell someone your every plan and know theirs in equally mind-numbing detail just because that's what couples do— that wasn't him. So Simon was always honest with the women he dated. He didn't do love. He didn't do commitment. But he *would* show them a damn good time while they were together.

So what was his problem?

Quinn Parker was his damn problem. She'd always turned his head. Had since the moment he met her, back when she and his sister were college roommates and she first came over to meet the family. She was stunning. Long blonde hair that looked like silk, green eyes that never needed makeup to look gorgeous, and an infectious laugh that got under his skin.

He'd had a crush that wouldn't stop, but she was Hannah's friend, and that was a line he wasn't going to play with. Then she started working with them and became a friend he couldn't imagine losing, and it never seemed the right time to go there. And then she met Eric.

And that was okay, he always told himself, because once again, he didn't do relationships. And she didn't do friends-with-benefits. So there. She was where she should be.

So why, then, as the time neared for her to make that oh-so-okay relationship a permanent one, was Simon walking around in a constant twitch?

You're running out of time on that.

Simon yanked his shirt over his head and walked to the bathroom. He had to let it go. She was about to walk down the aisle and seal the deal with someone else, and like it or not—it mattered. And that was new territory for him. The memory of her eyes, scared and devastated and crying when he'd climbed out of that ditch some months back, how she'd screamed his name at the top of her lungs until he answered. How she'd flung herself into his arms and clung to him like she never wanted to let go—that had flipped a switch inside him he didn't even know he had. That moment never left him. Ever.

It was a moment between them that might be all he'd ever get. And it was his own damn fault for never speaking up.

Simon got in the shower and turned on the water as hot as he could stand it, letting the steam take over. He needed to think about something else. About work. About his boss Barry being a dick. About Raymond being up Barry's ass and making up complaints about Simon not having his head in the job like he used to.

Maybe he didn't. Maybe he was spreading himself too thin. Or maybe after Quinn Parker was off the market once and for all, he could go back to normal.

Quinn sat cross-legged on her couch with a lap tray full of stuffed envelopes, a list her mother had given her, and a pen. *Save the date.* She closed her eyes and rolled her head on her shoulders, trying to work loose a kink in her neck from yesterday's backseat gymnastics.

She giggled a little to herself on that thought. God, she was getting old if just leaning out a window and then changing clothes in a vehicle made her sore. She could remember much more interesting backseat contortions in her younger years that never made her hurt the next day.

Yeah, well. Thirty did that.

Quinn looked around the little brownstone apartment she shared with Hannah, feeling like a giant hand was hovering somewhere.

Waiting to snatch it right out from under her. Okay, so in the grand scheme of things, in all the little cluster of small towns that backed up to each other, her little section of Shelby, Texas, might not be the greatest.

The Chase house was in sweet old Cody, probably the prettiest of the towns with a few hills and trees and that creek that ran through it. Quinn's parents, sister, and fiancé lived in Clayton, a town created with old money and sustained with new. Nearby Trinity, with its big old rambling homes and ancient old clapboard church, could have been quaint once, but trouble seemed to follow trouble, and over time that town seemed to be choking itself out. Shelby, where Quinn and Hannah and Simon lived, rode the fence. Some parts were nice, some parts were not, and then there was where she currently sat on her couch, in her slightly bohemian little brownstone, feeling gloomy. Not quite needing-six-deadbolts-on-the-door-like-in-Trinity kind of bad, but not a leaving-your-car-unlocked-like-in-Cody kind of good, either.

But it was hers. And Hannah's. They had made it home.

When they'd finished college and left the dorm life behind and found this place, they'd jumped on it. It was artsy. It was retro. It was so them. So what if that was eight years ago and they were still there? It was awesome.

Exposed beams and glass bricks and mismatched furniture in an open concept, along with open-fronted cabinets and thick wooden countertops. They had their candles everywhere, their favorite shots framed and adorning the walls, even a few of them in hanging frames like giant wind chimes.

The place spoke to Quinn. It fed her soul. She couldn't imagine leaving it.

She had to leave it.

For Eric's oh-dear-God-uptight-perfect house. Yes, he had a house. A two-story stucco-and-glass modern creation that Quinn was nervous to even walk in with her shoes on, much less live in. It was pristine and gorgeous and minimalistic and Quinn hated it. She had tried to convince him to sell, for the two of them to find a new house together that they'd both love, but he was attached to the charmless, colorless piece of "art."

Eric was a *grown-up*, according to her mother, having bought a house before the age of thirty instead of still paying rent. Not that everyone automatically made that choice. Hannah, for one. Simon, for another—although technically his was a condo, so maybe that rounded him up on the "adulting" scale.

She had to stop this. She was obsessing over the wrong things. She'd managed to fight off the move-in-together arguments from both her mother and Eric thus far, but it was coming up on the moment of no return. She was about to be Mrs. Eric St. James— which was good . . . she was good with that. She was more than good with that—she was fantastic with that. She was marrying the love of her life, a gorgeous, successful, witty, funny man who loved her. She had the friggin' save-the-date cards in her lap to prove it.

And marrying him did require this quirky little point of living in the same house. And leaving her best friend and her haven behind. Not much way around that.

Although, she needed to quit throwing Hannah into that weepy self-indulgent mix, because Hannah was really fine with it. Hannah had given her blessing the day they'd gotten engaged, and she knew she'd either have to find another roommate or cough up the whole rent on her own. She would be okay. She kind of came and went anyway, depending upon where she and Jonah Boudreau were in their unhealthy on-again, off-again not-so-secret dance.

Quinn was the one with the issues.

And no, she hadn't packed a thing yet. Even though the words had come from her mother's mouth, Quinn knew damn good and well they were on the mark. She had been there in the brownstone for eight years—she had a lot of crap. She should be culling and discarding and organizing, casing out Eric's place to plan where her things would go and figuring out what she was bringing with her to her new life.

Except every time those words crossed her brain, she got a twitch and turned on the TV instead. *None* of her things were going to fit in her new life. Eric's house would thumb up its snooty stucco nose at them and relegate them to storage in the attic. Which was bigger than her apartment.

What was wrong with her?

"What the hell is wrong with you?" Hannah said, blowing through the door at a near jog.

"What?" Quinn said, blinking at the sudden turn. She picked up the pen on reflex, like a kid getting busted for not doing her homework. "Um, I don't know, you'll have to narrow it down."

"Dinner with Maddi?" Hannah said, palms up, eyes wide to drive a point of some sort. At Quinn's blank look, she added, "In lieu of a shower? At Carmichael's?"

Quinn blinked. "There was a dinner?"

"*Was*. The key word there," Hannah said, landing in the big chair across from Quinn. Quinn loved that stupid chair. "I texted you a reminder this morning."

"I—" Quinn shook her head and held her hands up. "I missed it. My brain skipped over it—something. I'm sorry. Gah!" She rubbed at her eyes. "I feel bad now. Did she have a good time, at least?"

Hannah narrowed her eyes, and Quinn looked away before she read her like a book. "Yeah, it was good," Hannah said. "I tried calling you too, but—"

"Crap," Quinn said, looking over her shoulder at the counter-top. "Phone must be in the bedroom on vibrate. I turned the ringer off last night when we went to bed."

"Eric came here?" Hannah asked, looking surprised.

"He did," Quinn said, smirking. "We went out to eat, went to a movie, then came back here to hang on the couch and watch more movies."

Hannah's gaze was unblinking. "Wow, I wasn't sure he knew the address."

"Quit."

"Seriously, y'all never come here, you always go to his place."

"And I'm about to be there all the damn time," Quinn said, hearing the acid in her tone. "So I'm trying to milk a little time here. And where were you last night?"

Hannah flipped a hand nonchalantly. "Out."

"Mm-hmm."

"Finished addressing all those envelopes yet?" Hannah asked.

"Nice."

"I try," Hannah said. "So you need some help?"

Quinn blew out a grateful breath. "Please? I don't know why my mother won't let me import this list into label software and print them."

"Because it's tack-ehhh," Hannah said, putting on an extreme snooty tone and making Quinn laugh as she handed her a stack of envelopes and a page of names. "So what's up with you?"

Quinn looked at her. "What do you mean?"

Hannah set up a pillow like a table and reached over the arm of the chair for another pen on top of a stack of books. "You're all weird and withdrawn and pensive, lately."

Quinn frowned and concentrated on the first name. *Carter and Constance Aversteen*. "I'm not pensive."

"Please. You're channeling Ernest Hemingway."

Carter and Constance Aversteen. Quinn positioned her pen and wrote neatly. *Carter and Constance—*

"I don't know what you're talking about," Quinn said. *Averst—*

"It's like you don't really want to get married," Hannah said, picking up an envelope.

Quinn dropped her pen and sat straight up. "Of course I do," she said defensively. "How can you say that?"

"Because you're acting like a puppet being yanked around," Hannah said. "Not like someone excited about what's to come. People are usually happy when they're about to get married."

Tears sprung to Quinn's eyes, and she blinked rapidly. "I am happy."

Hannah tilted her head with a look that suggested otherwise.

"I truly am," Quinn insisted. "I love Eric. He loves me. We're perfect together, and I've known that since we met."

"Uh-huh," Hannah said. "Why did that sound like an infomercial?"

"It's the truth."

"So why the hair-pulling?"

Quinn blew out an impatient breath. "I'm not pulling hair."

"Sister-girl, you're gonna be bald if you keep stressing like you are," Hannah said. "What's going on?"

Quinn leaned back on the cushions and chewed on the inside of her lip. It was just Hannah. She could always tell Hannah anything. Almost anything.

"I don't know," she said. "It's just been—*later* for so long. Now it's here. Like barreling-up-on-me kind of here. And I know I have to leave this place and go live in the bubble."

One of Hannah's eyebrows lifted. "*That's* what has you so frazzled?"

"This is our home," Quinn said. "I mean, I know you've moved out a few times—"

"Never out," Hannah corrected. "Just detoured a little. Like a vacay. My stuff was still here."

"See?" Quinn said, pointing. "You couldn't do it for real, either!"

"I wasn't getting married," Hannah said, pointing back at her. "And I don't see Eric selling the bubble."

"No."

"Or moving in here with us."

"Definitely no," Quinn said.

"Your coffee mug assortment alone would do him in."

"Hey, they're coming with me," Quinn said matter-of-factly.

Hannah laughed. "Oh, right, they'll go great with the matching stoneware."

"How did you know he has—"

"Seriously?" Hannah said, snorting. "He has matching stoneware? Where the hell is his grungy bachelor side?"

"I don't think they allow those in Clayton," Quinn said, giggling.

"You just need to relax," Hannah said. "Remember, it's not about where you are, it's who you're with."

"Thank you, Mrs. Hallmark," Quinn said.

Hannah put her pillow with the envelopes on it on the floor, then pulled up a knee and wrapped her arms around it. "Shut up and listen," she said. "You're marrying the man you love, Quinn. You're starting out a whole new journey of your life."

"My mother thinks my new journey involves quitting both my jobs to stay home and plan luncheons," Quinn said, picking at the corner of an envelope.

"Oh, the hell with that," Hannah scoffed.

"And I can't have daisies at my wedding."

Hannah frowned. "Um."

"Just saying."

"Is that relevant?" Hannah asked.

"Clearly not," Quinn said on a sigh, pushing her tray aside and leaning sideways to lie on the couch.

"You just need to get out of your own head," Hannah said. "You're driving yourself crazy in there."

"I'll say," Quinn muttered.

"You should do something spicy to kick things up a notch," Hannah said. "Get the two of you all excited to become husband and wife."

"We're spicy," Quinn said defensively. "Sort of. Or we used to be." Weren't they? Lately they'd been so busy or tired that getting their clothes all the way off wasn't even a priority. "What kind of spice are we talking?" Quinn asked.

"I don't know," Hannah said, shrugging. "Be abstinent till the wedding—but—"

"He'll never go for that," Quinn said, already shaking her head.

"But—" Hannah repeated, eyes wide, hands held out to hold off argument. "Tease him with it. Flaunt what he can't have. Walk around the house naked." She scrunched her nose. "Oh, sorry, that would only work if you lived together."

"Don't start."

"Just saying."

"I would never be able to land anywhere over there," Quinn said, flailing a hand. "It would taint the furniture."

Hannah pulled a look. "How are you ever going to have kids there?" she asked. "Kids are filthy, creepy little beasts."

"I know!" Quinn said. "It terrifies me, just thinking of Phoebe bringing her baby over. What if it pees on something?"

"Come to Zach's wedding commando in a knockout dress," Hannah said, laughing, palms up. "Tell him when he gets there so he has to think about it the whole time."

Quinn sat back up and wagged a finger at her. "That's actually pretty good."

"And then keep crossing and uncrossing your legs," Hannah continued, demonstrating with a melodramatic flare.

"You've done this before, haven't you?" Quinn asked.

"Possibly."

It was always the same—the déjà vu that washed over Simon every time he pulled up to the old Trinity Outreach building. That sense that this day was just like the last, and the one before it.

Because for the people on the downtrodden east end of Trinity that frequented the shelter for a dry bed or a hot meal, every day was the same. Their lives didn't change, and neither did this place. It was always there, limping along some times more than others, dependent on donations and divine intervention most months, but still holding on. The building wasn't pretty, and it wasn't big enough for the need, and Simon and the other volunteers had heard the griping from the residents on the neighboring streets for years. Paint it, rebuild it, cover it up, tear it down—he'd heard it all. He'd personally repainted the whole building twice, and it did little more than dress up a troll, but he knew that wasn't the real issue.

As much as the area appreciated having a place to take care of the needy, no one wanted the needy in their neighborhood.

Simon approached the metal door with the rusty edges and reached above it to touch the faded wooden sign bolted to the building. Déjà vu hit him again.

"Tap that sign, son," Simon's dad said.

Simon's feet left the ground as his dad lifted him higher and higher. His hand stretched out over his head to touch the wooden sign with the burned-in letters. LUKE 6:31.

"I made that a few years ago to remind people of what's most important

when they come here," his dad said as Simon's fingers touched the wood. "I put my hands on it every time I come, too. To remind myself."

"What does it mean?" Simon asked when his feet landed back on the pavement.

"Go look it up when we get home," Josiah said, looking down at him with the hint of a smile in his eyes. "The curiosity makes people do that, too."

"It's gonna be something major, isn't it?" Simon asked with all his seven-year-old wisdom. "Something like 'May the force be with you.'"

His dad laughed, tickled from deep in his chest as he rested a hand on Simon's head and reached up to touch the sign with the other.

"Something along those lines," he said, pulling open the metal door. "Remember to be kind, son," he added. "These people aren't less than us, just less lucky. We're here to share a little of ours."

"Of our luck?" Simon asked.

"We have extra," his dad whispered with a wink.

Simon nodded seriously. "I'll share."

"That's my boy."

Simon's eyes burned a little at the well-remembered words. In those days, and in this place still, he was his father's boy.

"Let's go share some luck, Dad," he whispered, pulling open the creaky door.

"I always get double meat," whispered a grizzled elderly man with a painter's cap. "Robert always gives me double."

"Well, that's nice of him," Simon whispered back as he handed the man his plate. "You must be one of his favorites."

The old man smiled and eyed the Salisbury steaks in the pan.

"I tell you what," Simon continued. "We're running a little scarce today. Why don't you check back for seconds after everyone has a plate, and I'll see what I can do."

The old man nodded sadly and ambled on, glancing back once at the pan.

"We don't have a Robert working here," said the pretty brunette next to him under her breath.

"I know," Simon said, handing out the next plate.

"And we can't afford to give them seconds," she said even lower.

"I know," he repeated. "But it gives him something to hope for, and maybe he'll be full after the first plate."

"They're never full," she said. "They never get enough. I can't give them enough."

"You do plenty, Stacey," he said, nudging her with an elbow and pulling a small bag of beef jerky out of his pocket to palm off to an old man with gold teeth.

"You know what makes me smile," the old man said, grinning from ear to ear as he walked away.

Stacey stared at him. "You're such a pushover," she said.

Simon smiled at a young mom in line who was probably twenty-five and looked forty. "No, Stacey, I just know how to work people."

"You're saying you're a player?" Stacey asked, chuckling, handing her tongs to the woman next to her. "What am I saying? Of course you are."

"Such labels," he said.

She laughed. "Such bullshit. You know, you start doubling up portions and giving stuff away, Miss Ava in there will come out and whack you with her spatula."

"Sshhh," Simon said. "Don't sell me out."

"I heard that!" yelled a heavyset old woman through the kitchen window behind them. Her head was wrapped in a scarf and a hairnet, and one unruly gray curl still poked through. She was flipping more meat on a fryer and stirring a big pot of something with the other hand. "Don't make me come out there, Simon Chase."

"You love me, Miss Ava," Simon said. "What do you have going there for tomorrow?"

"Chicken gumbo," she said. "As if you couldn't smell it."

Simon laughed and filled another plate. "Always better the second day, right?"

"Damn straight," she said.

"Y'all got this for a bit?" Stacey asked, brushing off her hands. "I need to go check tables."

"You look like the walking dead, Stace," Simon said.

She widened her eyes at him. "Wow, Simon—be still, my heart."

Stacey March was not only in charge of running the shelter, but she was also an ER nurse for a small charity-driven hospital there in Trinity. Simon had met her a year earlier, right after she'd taken over the shelter from the previous manager, when their decision to have drinks after serving a holiday meal led to a rush of carnal frenzy.

With their mutually odd hours and neither seeking anything deeper, spontaneous hookups worked for them—in a friends-with-benefits sort of way. For a while, at least. As time went on and especially after that last big tornado Simon and his family chased had taken him for a private ride, the keeping-it-simple plan started feeling a little too simple. A little too hollow.

It had been two or three months since their last time, and that had just been a fast and furious shower rendezvous. His head just wasn't there lately.

And now . . .

Simon pushed that thought away and grinned at Stacey. "I know. I have a way with words."

"I just got off a double," Stacey said, doing a little mock bow, still in her pink scrubs that he always felt were a huge contrast to her scrappy no-nonsense personality. "So yes, I probably do look like the dead. I'm doing good to stay upright." She paused and smiled with tired eyes. "Too wiped out for any angle," she said pointedly, and he knew what she meant. It was their code—asking how tired the other one was.

Actually, he'd just been teasing—she still looked adorable, her dark hair falling down from her bun in wispy little pieces. She was hot, and she was a firecracker in bed, but he did have a rule. They might not have strings, but he at least had the respect to be *with Stacey* when he was with Stacey. Today, he wouldn't have been. For the last few *months*, he wouldn't have been. A certain blonde was taking over more and more of his thoughts of late, sexually and every other way. Especially after her wardrobe change in the backseat earlier.

Simon grinned and handed her the next empty plate. "Here," he said, guiding her to his spot. "You do this—" He turned and spotted a stool in a corner and jogged to it, bringing it back with him and placing it directly under her bottom. "Sit, and serve. I'll check tables."

The look she gave him was priceless. Gratitude and relief and amusement all wrapped into one. "You know, I kinda like you today, Simon," she said. "Even if you did tell me I look like crap."

He chuckled as he kissed her on top of her head. "All part of the complicated Chase charisma," he said.

"Oooh," crooned a little old lady with only a bowl of salad. Free food, and all she went for was the salad. He'd never understand it. But that was okay. More meat for the others. "Y'all are too cute."

"Yeah, you gotta watch this one, Mrs. Tanner," Stacey said, pointing at him. "He may be hitting on you next."

Mrs. Tanner laughed and blushed on her way to a table, still giggling when she sat down. Simon smiled at Stacey as he headed off to ask if anyone needed anything, clear off tables, and shoot the shit with old men who sometimes came there just to escape being alone. Some nights, his biggest fear was becoming one of those old men.

It was a shame, he thought sometimes, that he and Stacey never clicked on a deeper level. It was easy with her. She was snarky and a little bit badass and didn't put up with much. They might have been perfect together in another lifetime, without her ex twisting her attitude toward men and his need for a woman he couldn't have. Then again, with complications and rules, they might have killed each other, too.

A white-haired man, who had been volunteering there as long as Simon had, was putting out a few more folding chairs as he eyed the food line snaking out the door. He was a big guy, probably in his midsixties—and Simon had maybe had four or five total conversations with him in the past twenty years. And that was okay. The guy wasn't much for talking to the clientele, but he was a workhorse.

"Hey, Daniels," Simon called, getting his attention.

"Chase," he said, acknowledging Simon with an upward nod.

"Has Harry been by lately?"

Daniels shook his head slowly and left to fetch more chairs while Simon muttered under his breath and headed back to the serving line.

"What's with the sour face?" Stacey asked.

"Harry," Simon said. "Daniels said he hasn't been by."

"I haven't seen him," Stacey said. "I brought a box of canned goods out there last weekend, but he wouldn't come to the door. I left it there and watched from my car till he came out to pick it up."

Harry was a recluse that Simon had known as long as he could remember—*known* being a loose term when it came to Harry. He was a former Special Ops soldier from a time before television and the internet glamorized them. Back when "unconventional warfare" truly meant that no one knew what they did. He'd taken up residence in an old abandoned warehouse a few blocks from the shelter years earlier, preferring the company of rats to people and the sound of the nearby creek to traffic.

Simon's dad had brought Harry food once a week from the shelter, and Simon arranged for the same—whether it was someone else bringing it or himself. As finances got steadily worse at the shelter, Simon usually bought Harry's food himself, not wanting to take food away from someone else.

There was something about the old man that always got to Simon. Maybe because Harry was a carpenter by trade like his dad, or because Josiah always had showed such interest in him. Maybe because he had cried openly when Simon came to tell him of Josiah's death. Whatever the reason, Simon had a soft spot for the cranky old eccentric and was one of the few people to whom Harry would even speak.

Harry was always a bit paranoid, storing away more than he ate, hiding his meager belongings for fear of a looming apocalypse and everyone coming for him. He used to at least show up for an occasional shower or on Sundays for Miss Ava's famous blackberry cobbler. In recent months, however, he wasn't even doing that, and Simon feared he might be spiraling downward.

"You don't need to go over there alone," Simon said. "Wait for me, or bring Daniels with you."

"I'm good," Stacey said. "I can take care of myself." At the look he gave her, she continued. "I make lots of racket, okay? And I'm bringing him food, he isn't going to go off on me."

"Just bring someone next time," Simon said. "Make me happy?"

"Yes, Dad."

"Miss Stacey?" a little boy asked, approaching the food table and poking his head in between two old women. "My mom told me to come tell you the two back shower stalls are both broken now. There's just the one, and—well that's the one everybody can see into."

Stacey sighed. "I know. I figured that last fix wouldn't hold. I'm sorry, Cameron, y'all might have to sponge bath it tonight if you don't want the front stall."

The little boy twisted his mouth in deep thought. "We can take turns standing in front."

"There you go," she said, pointing her tongs. "Way to think through a problem."

He grinned as he walked away, actually feeling good about having to go shower in a grimy, half-exposed public shower area, because Stacey had made him feel that way. The look of despair on her face afterward, however, told volumes.

"I'll get someone to work on the showers, Stace," Simon said. "Don't sweat it."

"I have to sweat it," she said in a low voice. "It's one thing after another. Showers. The pantry is getting low. The roof leaks, and the plumbing sucks. The yearly inspection is coming up, and the wiring in this place is seriously held together with duct tape and tie wraps."

"I can look around for an electrician, too," Simon said.

"And then the ceiling will fall on us," she said, gesturing at the stained-asbestos-square ceiling. "And kill us all with the fibers. What are you going to find for that?"

"A ceiling guy?" Simon said. "I don't know, Stace, but we'll figure it out."

"Before or after we get shut down?" she said.

Simon moved behind her and worked his fingers on the hard knots of her neck.

"You're working yourself up into a frenzy," he said.

"Oooh, God, you can do that for another hour," she said, her head falling forward and the tongs banging on the pan. "Maybe three."

"It'll work out," he said. "I'm still thinking on a plan."

A plan he kept circling. And circling. A plan that involved doing the one thing he swore he'd never do.

A certain grandmother of his had slyly paid off his college loans years earlier and, with her connections to every conceivable institution in the state of Texas, he suspected she'd also had a grade or two fixed for him. At the time, when he was proudly living on ramen noodles and attitude, wanting to do everything himself, he could have spit fire over her interference, but that had fizzled with time. Simon shared his siblings' need to be independent in spite of their grandmother's wealth, but as he got older, he began to see her less as the sharp-tongued manipulator she liked to portray and more of the frail old woman that protected her family at all costs. Annabelle Chase would never be the warm-and-fuzzy grandma. So she showed her love the only way she knew how. With money.

She'd even manipulated her funding into their reality show with Infinity, but Zach had managed to forgive her for that. And Simon was gearing up to ask for a favor. One he would rather pull his toenails off than ask. Because Granabelle was shrewd. She loved her family fiercely, but she didn't do anything for nothing, and Lord only knew what she'd want in return.

"Your plan better come with a miracle," Stacey mumbled. "This place can't take too many more patches. You work tonight?"

"Yeah." Simon felt the familiar dread in his gut. "I'll probably head over to check on Harry beforehand," he said over her ear as he moved his thumbs up the nape of her neck. "Maybe bring him some cobbler on Sunday."

"Sunday," she murmured. "Cobbler."

He chuckled. "Don't fall off the stool," he whispered.

"What are you doing on Saturday?" Stacey asked, tilting her head back with sleepy eyes. "I'm off."

Simon met her pretty, dark eyes and saw the question. *Damn it.*

"My brother's getting married," he said.

She nodded. "Ah."

He wished he could do what most normal people would do and ask her to come with him. Be his date. Have a good time. Actually have someone on his arm for a change while Quinn paraded around on Eric's.

Then again, why the hell not?

He took a breath, opened his mouth to speak, and then narrowed his eyes. *Complications.* This could trickle over into that world. This could—

"What would you think about coming with me?" he blurted out, squinting further, as if he might need to brace for it.

Stacey's eyes widened in surprise, then amusement. "To a wedding?"

Simon shook his head, her body language bringing him back to reality. "Yeah, I know. Dumb question."

"No, hang on," she said, chuckling. "Don't go dangling carrots and then yank them away."

He stepped closer so that the gossip that was bound to run rampant would maybe be lessened. "I'm just saying—"

"That you and I don't do dates," she finished.

"Exactly," he said, letting go of a breath.

"So why'd you ask me?" she said, tilting her head all cute to mess with him.

"Temporary insanity?"

Stacey laughed and poked him in the chest. "No big deal, Simon. I've had family functions before, too, and filling that plus-one is sometimes worth the insanity."

He pulled his head back in surprise. "So you'll go?"

"If you still want me to," she said with a shrug. "I don't get to dress up that often. It'll be fun." She stood up and raised an eyebrow. "As long as there are no misunderstandings while I'm meeting your family."

Jesus, what was he doing? Bringing Stacey to meet his mother? *Complications, much?*

"I'll introduce you as a friend," Simon said, holding up a hand. "And make it business, too." He paused, thinking about whether to bite that particular bullet. "I might introduce you to someone."

Her eyes widened in question. "Someone?"

"Someone with purse strings," he said.

The question turned to curiosity. "I'm intrigued," she said. "Business. You'll feed me, of course."

"Of course."

"And then you'll owe me a really hot night," she whispered, leaning forward. "So it's a win-win."

Quinn flashed through his mind. As did the be-with-Stacey-while-with-Stacey rule. Quite the corner he'd talked himself into.

"Absolutely."

Chapter Four

Simon pulled up outside the warehouse, such as it was. A pile of crumbling stone and wood, with no glass left to speak of, rose three floors from the ground in front of a rushing creek. Same creek that ran behind his mom's house, but looked nothing like it.

The creek here was alive and full of vigor, wearing down stones and pumping oxygen into the water. In Cody, it was sleepy and barely bubbly, as if just the act of passing through Trinity wore it out.

Simon let his gaze scan the building as he got out and retrieved the cardboard box of cans and the small foil pan of hot food Stacey had put together. He looked at the door, the windows, any opening, any sign of movement, any show of Harry lurking. He'd learned long ago not to just sneak up or walk in like it was the abandoned building everyone else saw it to be. Harry saw every square foot of the sprawling structure as a stronghold. His stronghold.

Simon found out the hard way once that Harry took that idea very seriously. He'd just walked through the open door one evening right at dusk, carrying a big sleeping bag he'd picked up at a garage sale. It was getting cold, and he wanted to be sure Harry was staying warm at night. It was odd that the door wasn't locked, but Simon knew Harry would leave it open if he was working on something outside, and nearby enough to see it, so Simon didn't think anything of it.

Walking in unannounced in low light with a large bulky object was a bad idea. And for that, Simon found himself slammed against the wall with the sharp tip of a number 2 pencil pointed at his jugular. He was careful to make his presence known after that.

"Harry!" Simon called out as he carried the box to the main door. "Hey, bud, it's Simon! You here?"

It was a rhetorical question, and he knew it, since Harry rarely left anymore, but Simon recognized he needed to show the old man some respect. And make some noise. He laid the box on the dry gravel and banged on the heavy metal door.

"Harry?" Simon called out again, the familiar feeling of dread creeping in. He was always afraid of finding the worst. That Harry would have a heart attack or fall or something, or that any of the other younger, more violent vagrants would break in and take down the older man for his stash and his shelter.

Not that Harry was just any old man.

"Harry!"

"I'm here!" came the responding disgruntled and raspy voice, hardened by life and a rumored punch to the throat some four decades earlier. "Enough with all the hollering."

A latch clicked on the other side, followed by heavy items sliding away and what sounded like a metal pipe being pulled from the door handle.

"You're letting everything within five miles know I'm here, too," Harry grumbled, tugging open the rusty, squeaking door only about a foot when he stopped.

"You specifically said to make noise," Simon said, picking up the box and nudging the door open a few more inches. It wasn't a new conversation. They had nearly the same argument every time. That was okay, though. The way Simon saw it, the day Harry stopped bitching about things or lost his famous paranoia, he was either on his way out of this world or they all were.

"Noise, boy," Harry said, running a dirty hand over a dirtier gray-and-brown beard. "Not a ten-gun salute."

Simon blinked at the stench that reached his nose. "Gonna let me in?" he asked. "Or are we gonna argue through the door all afternoon?"

"You can leave it all right there," Harry said. "I'll bring it in."

"You're welcome," Simon retorted.

"Thank you," Harry shot back. "You know I appreciate it."

"Then show me some hospitality and invite me in," Simon said.

"Don't play me, boy," Harry said, his light-blue eyes crinkling in the corners as he narrowed them. "I'm not crazy and you aren't stupid, so quit pretending we're either." He pointed at the box with his chin. "Put that shit down. It looks heavy."

"Why are you being a pain in the ass, Harry?" Simon asked, setting the box back on the ground. "I thought we were buds."

"Me and your dad were buds," he said, his voice softening. "You get points by association."

Simon smiled. "I'll take that." He cast an eye over Harry's appearance. "I heard you aren't coming in for meals anymore. Not even for the cobbler."

Harry shrugged. "No time."

"Really?" Simon asked. "Your schedule is that tight?"

"Don't presume to know what I do," Harry snapped.

"I'm just saying," Simon said, holding up his hands. "My schedule's packed too, but I don't pass up food." He gave the old man another once-over. "Or a shower."

"I clean up in the creek out back," Harry said.

"Well, I think you might have missed a few days," Simon said. *Or weeks.*

"Nobody here to impress," Harry said, gesturing around him to a room largely hidden from view with pieces of tarp. "So feel free to be moving along if I'm offending you."

"All right," Simon said. "I'll go. Have to get ready for work in a bit anyway."

"How's the weather?" Harry asked, finding the one topic he actually found Simon useful for.

"Nothing for a few days," Simon said. "Did you take care of the leaks you were having?"

"I guess I'll find out when it rains again," Harry said, widening his eyes, making them stand out in contrast with the dirty surface of his skin.

"Guess so," Simon said.

"So I'll see you next time," Harry said, leaning all his slight weight against the door, pushing with all he had to get it shut again. Simon had given him some oil to loosen it up but knew he wouldn't use it. Harry liked it that way. Harder for unwelcome visitors to get in, and easier for him to hear them if they tried. "Thanks, Simon."

Harry's eyes met his and for a two-second stretch, the grumpy old ex-soldier dropped the armor, and the shame and insult of accepting handouts to survive was burning in his face.

"Anytime," Simon said, sticking his fist through the gap before Harry could close it.

As usual, there was the requisite pause, then a quick fist bump before Simon was shoved back out and the door closed. Harry'd wait till Simon was in the car and headed down the street to open the door again and get the food, no matter what.

He'd once gone a week and a half with nothing more than a can of Vienna sausages and some crackers, and yet he was still too proud to dive into the hot roast and mashed potatoes while Simon was still there.

Simon backed up and assessed the building and the roof, as he always did. It had withstood its share of storms and even a tornado or two over the decades. But the last big one that had zeroed in on Cody had blown some big wind in Trinity's direction, and the whole roof didn't look much stronger than one of the flimsy tarps Harry had stapled over the holes.

Another bad one and the building itself might not even survive, Simon thought. Hopefully that wouldn't happen. But if there was one thing he had learned in both lines of business, it was that the weather was a fickle tricky bitch.

"Put all the chairs outside and then come back," Miss Lou called out.

"What's after that, Miss Lou?" a young man asked, loosening his tie and rolling up his shirt sleeves.

"I don't know yet, Casey," she said, chuckling. "I'm hoping it'll come to me."

"You got it," he said with a wink and a gesture toward three others. "Don't you worry about it. We'll get it set up nice out there."

"Y'all are so sweet to help out," Miss Lou said. "You and the crew came to see the wedding, not be put to work."

A low growl turned Miss Lou around, and she looked down at an ancient beagle who was staring down the strangers in the house. "Cracker, what are you doing out of that room? I just put you in there!"

Cracker wagged his tail like he'd just performed a trick, when the truth was he probably hadn't heard a word she said. The old dog was mostly deaf, but ruled that house regardless.

"What's the matter?" Quinn asked as she emerged from the back hall in shorts and a tank top, her hair in giant rollers, her favorite camera around her neck. "Oh, Cracker, how did you sneak out?"

"The boys are all getting ready at Zach's house and so some of the crew who arrived early are helping to set up chairs and things outside. Cracker's not thrilled." Miss Lou waved a hand. "Let him be."

"I can help them," Quinn said. "Maddi's ready. Hannah and I can—"

"Grab those lemon bars out of the oven," Miss Lou said, already moving to the next task at hand, tossing her the box of powdered sugar.

"Yes, ma'am," Quinn said, jumping into action. Her mouth watered as the baked lemon aroma wafted into her face. That, combined with the cookies, the double-layer chocolate cake, the banana pudding, and the pecan tarts. And all of that had to compete with the seafood gumbo simmering on the stove since early that morning.

One could walk into that house stuffed to the gills, and start drooling with hunger anyway.

"I can't believe you made all this for today," Quinn said, sifting sugar over the lemon squares.

"Well, it's what Maddi wanted," Miss Lou said. "A big gumbo and a dessert smorgasbord instead of a wedding cake." She laughed. "I figure she's due after missing the first one. Oh, thank you, Jesus, for this bright sunny day."

"I second that."

"Your day is coming up quick," Miss Lou said, stirring the gumbo. "You getting excited?"

Wasn't she? People kept asking her that. Quinn flashed on the previous day's conversation with Hannah. It seemed that she kept answering these questions with nods and *of course*, and *I can't wait*, but in all honesty all she could eat, taste, and breathe was panic.

She loved Eric. Had fallen in love with him in the first month they were dating, and had their kids named before they got engaged on their one-year anniversary. But it had all been in the future then. Something tangible she planned way out for a time they'd be truly ready. Two years later, Eric had decided they were ready.

I can't wait any longer for you to be my wife, Quinn. To start our family. What are we waiting for?

What *were* they waiting for? There would be no perfect time, no perfect moment. Only moments. Perfection was up to them. So she set a date.

A date that was now only a month away, bringing on questions about jobs and houses and babies and personal space. Okay, no one had asked about personal space. Maybe that one was all on her. Suddenly those hypothetical kids were strangling her, making her want to hide her ovaries.

And the silly crush she'd had for the past ten years—that had been niggling at her lately. It was just a crush. Everyone had them. That person you can't help thinking about, but know it could never be. She'd been thinking about him more than usual the last couple of months, but Quinn knew that was just because she was about to tie the knot. That what-if fantasy window was about to close. It was crazy, anyway. She was in love with Eric St. James.

Besides Hannah, Simon Chase was her best friend. And Hannah's brother. And someone who always took care of her just like he did his own sister. Simon never saw her as more than that.

"Of course I am," she said with a smile. "It's just all happening so fast."

"Fast?" Miss Lou said, chuckling. "Honey, it's been a couple of years, hasn't it?"

"So Maddi picked all of this menu?" Quinn asked.

Miss Lou looked at her sideways. "Yes, ma'am."

"Must be nice, getting the wedding you want," Quinn said, fingering her camera.

The kitchen was perfect, in a disorganized, tumbling sort of way. Martha Stewart might have a coronary in there, but Quinn delighted in the chaotic love that emanated from the haphazard stacking of cooling food. A bowl of bacon-wrapped peppers sat in a colander, balanced over the sink with a large trivet.

Her special camera lenses were lined up and ready on a side table in the living room, but this would do. She snapped an image of the food from an angle, with a partial of Miss Lou blurred in the forefront. Another of her pushing hair out of her face as she stirred the gumbo.

"Aren't you getting what you want?" Miss Lou asked.

Quinn let her camera hang back down and busied herself arranging cookies on a platter. "Sure. If I was my mother," she said. "There will probably be expensive delicacies and things requiring special little forks and desserts with names I can't pronounce."

Miss Lou laughed out loud. "And I'm guessing you don't want those?"

"I want cobbler," Quinn said. "Blackberry cobbler. With ice cream. And short ribs with potato salad. And your picante cream cheese dip. And a simple, pretty strawberry cake."

"Wow, you've thought it out," Miss Lou said.

"I have a lot of time to do that," Quinn responded. "Since I don't get to do any of the actual planning. I couldn't even have Hannah take the pictures, that wasn't as good as the photographer from *Ascot Imagery*. Who is four times the price, knows nothing about me, and has about as much creative thought as this spatula," Quinn said, holding one up.

"Aw, Quinn, I'm sorry," Miss Lou said, touching her cheek.

"Hannah is ten times better," Quinn said.

"You and Hannah are both amazing," Miss Lou said. "I'm glad the two of you are taking the pictures today. I would think you'd at least get to sound off on the photography decision for your own day."

Quinn smiled, an action that didn't connect to anything inside her. "You would think," she said softly. "It's okay, though. Hannah's going to take some shots on her own anyway, so I know she'll capture the good stuff."

She squatted to eye level with some of the desserts decorating the island, adjusting her focus to capture the sea of deliciousness that seemed to roll forever from that perspective.

Miss Lou sighed. "I'm afraid mothers get a little crazy with daughters come wedding time."

"You won't do that with Hannah," Quinn said.

"Assuming she ever puts up with any man long enough for me to find out," Miss Lou said.

"True," Quinn said, chuckling.

"And count your blessings, sweetheart," Miss Lou said. She held up an oven-mitted hand. "I know it may feel like jaded blessings at times, but your parents at least want to give you a wedding." Quinn looked at her. "You see who's giving Maddi hers?"

Realization settled over Quinn's skin.

"Hello?"

Quinn and Miss Lou exchanged a glance at the young female voice that was followed by the sound of the front door closing.

"Grammy Lou?" the voice called again.

Miss Lou's eyes went wide and she all but threw the oven mitts across the kitchen.

"Kinley?" she cried, running out. "Oh, my heavens, child!"

Quinn followed her out, laughing at the sight of Miss Lou

rocking a beautiful blonde girl back and forth. Her hands flew to her camera, letting the images go crazy.

"Let me look at you," Miss Lou said, holding the grinning girl at arm's length. "When did you get so ugly?"

"Grammy!" Kinley said, swatting at her.

"Wow, Kinley," Quinn said. "I haven't seen you in forever. Do you even remember me?"

She'd only actually met Kinley a handful of times. Simon's brother Levi didn't come home much—usually just at Christmas, and he only had his daughter for that holiday every other year. And Quinn had missed the last one.

"Oh, yeah," Kinley said. "I mean, yes, ma'am," she corrected, glancing at her grandmother. "I used to think you were a model or something when I was little."

"Oh, Lord," Quinn said, chuckling. "Not quite. Although my mother might have been happier."

"But you weren't wearing rollers then," Kinley added, with an eyebrow-raise.

Quinn laughed as a hand automatically went up to her head. "So how old are you now?"

"Eleven," she said, her blue eyes sparkling prettily when she smiled, matching the light blue of her dress. "And a half."

"Well, of course," Miss Lou said. "Don't be shorting yourself of that half! So where's your dad? Or did he just let you take the car?"

"Well, he tried, but I said no," Kinley said, a hand on her hip as she shook her head. "That truck of his would not look good on me."

Miss Lou burst out laughing. "Oh, you little minx," she said. "You are my son made over, that's for sure."

"He dropped me here and went to Uncle Zach's to get ready," she said.

"That boy," Miss Lou grumbled. "He knows better than to skip over the momma greeting."

"I think I'm supposed to soften that indignity," Kinley said, narrowing her gaze.

"Indignity!" Quinn cried, laughing as Miss Lou sputtered again. "You're a hoot, Kinley. You need to come hang with me." The crew started filing back in from the backyard, ties loosened, sleeves rolled up. "Come on, let's go check on the girls."

"Looks different," Kinley said, studying the living room.

"It *is* different," Miss Lou said. "Tree fell on the old room, so we had to make a new one."

Quinn thought the rebuild was even better than the original, which was already the living room of her dreams. Now the windows were bigger and brighter; the woodwork was custom designed by Zach with different types of inlaid wood and almost matched the table he'd made with his dad. The new room was gorgeous. And today was the perfect day to show it off.

The doorbell rang, and Quinn glanced at her watch.

"Yikes, I need to go get dressed or I'm gonna be attending this doodah in my shorts."

"You two go on," Miss Lou said, waving a hand on her way to the door. "I've got it out here."

"Aw, Cracker," Kinley cooed as the dog wagged its way to her, miraculously either remembering her from year to year or just liking how she looked. "Can we bring him in?"

"Absolutely," Quinn said. "It was where he was supposed to be anyway." Her voice dropped conspiratorially as she and Kinley approached Miss Lou's big master bedroom where Maddi was getting ready. "Now brace yourself. Crazy women in here."

The laughter was infectious as she opened the door, and three very different women sat cross-legged in their dresses on the king-sized bed. Maddi sat in the middle, looking like a princess in a simple white strapless dress, her dark shiny hair arranged in soft waves around her shoulders. The striking redhead at her right sat with her legs tucked to one side, since the painted-on green dress she wore wouldn't allow for Indian-style. To Maddi's left, in a deep royal-blue fitted sparkly stretchy dress that could probably allow for full cheerleader splits if she wanted it to, was most likely the instigator of whatever they were giggling over, tucking crazy stray dark auburn curls back into the clips they were escaping from.

All three stopped laughing abruptly, clutching their drinks to them as if they were kids who'd gotten caught doing something naughty. Quinn grabbed her camera and snapped two or three shots expertly, without even looking. Something would catch.

"I brought another girl to the party," Quinn said quickly. She stepped aside for Kinley, and Maddi and Hannah both gasped.

"Oh, my God! Kinley!" Hannah cried, vaulting off the bed like she was wearing gym clothes and still not spilling a drop of whatever was in her glass. Kinley had to put the dog down quickly before he got crushed. Maddi got up a little more carefully but was right on Hannah's heels as she hugged her niece. "You've grown so much!"

"I want your dress, Aunt Hannah," Kinley said, touching the material.

"Okay, you haven't grown *that* much," Hannah countered, laughing. "But wow, you are going to crush some hearts, little girl. You definitely take after your mom with all that blue-eyed blondeness."

"I don't know," Kinley said. "Dad says I have his mouth."

"Let's hope not," Hannah said on a wink. "But yes, there's definitely some Chase in that smile," she said, touching the girl's cheek.

"Grammy Lou is blonde and blue-eyed," Kinley said, tilting her head with an innocent grin. "Maybe the awesome just skipped a generation."

"Oh, yes," Maddi said, laughing as she hugged Kinley. "You certainly do have Levi's mouth. So where is the prodigal son?"

"With all the uncles," Kinley said. She focused in on the remaining woman in the room. "Hi. You have pretty hair."

Maddi laughed as she turned around. "Sorry, this is my boss, Nicole Brian."

Quinn bit back a smirk. Nicole did have pretty hair. She had pretty everything. But she was like a bipolar tigress. One moment she was wanting to paint your nails and be girlfriends, the next she was ready to scratch your eyes out.

Nicole slid off the bed in one graceful move, her eyes never leaving Kinley as she smiled at her. "And you have the face of an angel," she said. "A face for the camera."

Maddi pivoted in place, her smile never faltering. "No."

"Really?" Kinley said, her angelic camera-ready face coming to life with wide eyes.

"What?" Nicole said innocently, facing Maddi. "She's gorgeous! The screen would soak her up. The fans would love the family angle—"

"We don't have fans yet," Maddi said.

"Get more family in on this little shindig," Nicole said, under her breath but loud enough for the room to hear, "and you will."

"Levi would never go for that," Hannah said, knowing her twin brother would sooner throw himself under the wheels of the vehicle than let his daughter go on a storm run.

"I so want to go on a chase!" Kinley said, stepping forward, her expression eager. "I've heard about it my whole life! And now it's on TV!"

Quinn wanted to say so many things. Things that bounced around both sides of the fence. She agreed with Nicole's eye for what the camera would love. Kinley was a photographer's dream. Perfect lines, amazing colors, eyes that Quinn would die to get close-ups of. Innocence with snark that would totally bleed through. And the viewers of *The Chase* probably *would* love to see a little more family drama. Make it more personal and relatable. Eli always made sure they got no drama whatsoever, keeping to the subject at hand. Which she understood from a family standpoint, but reality-show ratings could only stand so long on subject matter. Human nature craved drama. Bullfights weren't to cheer on the matador.

Getting a few shots in of the long-lost son and his adorable little girl—that could play well. But Quinn had heard about Levi and his falling out with Granabelle and desire to get away from the family business that had taken his father's life. He'd probably whisk Kinley out of there as soon as the wedding was over if he caught wind of such an idea.

"Seriously, my dad is such a buzzkill about storms," Kinley said.

"A buzzkill?" Quinn said, laughing. The things that this kid said.

"He's told me all these stories," Kinley said. "And yet we do nothing when big storms come in. Nothing!" she said, throwing up her arms melodramatically.

"What are you expecting to do?" Hannah piped in, tilting her head with an amused expression.

"I don't know, go drive around?" Kinley said. "Look for funnels? Have a little excitement?"

"Excitement," Maddi breathed, shaking her head. "It's not all it's cracked up to be."

"I'm just saying, it's worth talking to her dad about," Nicole said. "They are only here for the wedding, right? We could even interview them at the—"

"No," Maddi said, hands on her hips. "No, no, a million times no."

Nicole rolled her eyes and smiled at Kinley. "Maddi won't let us film the wedding of one of the hottest storm chasers of all time to add to the show."

"Of all time?" Maddi said. "A little overkill, maybe?"

"Uh, excuse me?" Hannah said, throwing an arm around Quinn and doing a hand flourish between them. "*He's* the hottest? That's debatable."

Quinn snickered and then glanced at the eleven-and-a-half-year-old in the room. "Hey? Young ears over here," she said.

"I'm not that young," Kinley said. "I've kissed a boy."

"Sweet Jesus," Hannah said.

"Do tell," Nicole said, laughing.

"No, let's not," Maddi said, widening her eyes at Nicole.

"Oh, come on, drop me a bone today!" Nicole said. "The personal stuff is TV gold. Viewers love it." She rolled her eyes. "Okay, back to your Zach. You deny that he's a catch?" Nicole asked.

"*My Zach* is the key part of that sentence," Maddi said. "The storms get Zach Chase, the show gets Zach Chase." Maddi sat on the edge of the bed and smiled as she closed her eyes. "Today he's just my Zach. Just mine. Today, I'm not sharing."

"You're so calm," Quinn said, amazed at how peaceful Maddi looked sitting there. "I know I won't be. I'm not even calm now," she added, laughing.

"Oh, you will be when you're looking into his eyes," Maddi said, chuckling. "That's just nerves talking. I guess I'm calm because Zach's always been my one and only," she said. "Today is just a formality."

Quinn took a deep breath. God, to be that sure. "Well, you're right about today being about you and Zach," she said, stepping forward. "No show today. No *talk* of the show, even."

"Fine," Nicole muttered, winking at Maddi. "We'll focus on the *love*."

"Oh, gag," Kinley said.

"Oh, now listen to you, Miss-I've-Kissed-A-Boy," Hannah said.

"I didn't say I was in love with him," Kinley said, her cheeks going pink.

"Yeah, well, give it a few years," Hannah said, laughing.

"So Maddi," Quinn began. "I don't think I ever heard—where are you and Zach going to live? I mean, with you working in Dallas and all?"

Maddi darted a quick glance at Nicole, who just did a little shrug that neither looked comfortable with. "I'm just in a rental there," Maddi said. "So I'm going to move in here at Zach's, and—I don't know. Probably keep my rental for a while in case the commute gets crazy and I'm working late. Or maybe we'll stay there during the week and come here on weekends," she said. "Don't really know yet."

"I'm bringing in some help with the filming side, too," Nicole said. "To fill in the holes wherever Maddi isn't."

"I told you, I don't need my holes filled," Maddi said under her breath.

"That's your perspective," Nicole said, widening her eyes with a smile that asked for the conversation to be over. "Most projects aren't as all-consuming as this one. A little extra help won't hurt. Like an assistant."

"I *am* the assistant."

"An assistant for you," Nicole clarified.

"Good grief," Maddi said. "And what do you mean this one is more all-consuming than normal?"

"Case in point!" Nicole said, pointing two fingers at herself. "I'm attending the wedding of my assistant to one of our show's stars. A little out of the norm."

"She called Uncle Zach a star," Kinley snickered to Quinn.

"Don't tell him that," Hannah muttered.

"Okay, let's get back on track," Quinn said. "Sorry I asked," she mumbled to Maddi.

"Good idea," Hannah said. "So Quinn, you going casual today, or what?"

"Gah, give me fifteen minutes," Quinn said, snatching her dress off its hanger on the closet door and running for the bathroom.

Hannah shook her head. "Only takes her fifteen minutes."

"Quit griping and come zip me up!"

"I bet your mom makes you take four hours for a full makeover on your wedding day," Hannah said, following her and holding out a half-empty wine cooler. "Here, you left this earlier."

Quinn's hands faltered as she stripped and pulled the simple black dress over her body. She met her own eyes in the mirror, blinking quickly as Hannah appeared behind her. She took the bottle and set it down. . . . *a full makeover on your wedding day.* Another thing she wouldn't want and wouldn't have a choice about.

"You okay?" Hannah asked, pulling up the zipper.

Quinn smiled and started unrolling her hair. "I'm good."

"Want another drink?" Hannah asked. "Your weeny little wine cooler is probably warm now."

Quinn wasn't a big drinker, and when she did imbibe, it was rarely liquor. Beer and wine coolers were usually her meek method of poison.

"Nah, all I've had is carbs today," she said. "I'll be drunk before the party even starts if I have any more."

"Lightweight."

"Lush."

"So I see you took my advice, huh?" Hannah asked, gesturing to the dress Quinn had on. "All I saw was skin as I zipped that up."

Quinn sighed. "Why not? Might as well have a little fun with this today."

"Stepping out on the wild side," Hannah said with a smirk. "My little girl is growing up."

"Don't make me hurt you," Quinn muttered, finger-combing out her waves. "Good grief, all this hair."

"People would sell body parts for all this hair," Hannah said. "Don't complain."

"I hate it," she said. "It's in the way. For what we do? It's totally in the way. I so want to chop it off," she said longingly, holding her hands at a chopping pose at shoulder level.

"So do it," Hannah said with a shrug.

Quinn shook her head. "Eric would shit. He loves it long. Told me he wants me to have long hair even when we're old and it's silver."

"Eric's not the one carrying it around."

"True."

"So how are you going to tell him about the kink you have going on tonight?" Hannah asked.

Quinn inhaled deeply and let it go. "Not sure. Gotta come up with something seductive and sexy."

"Just don't tell my brothers," Hannah said. "Especially not Simon."

Quinn pulled a face. "Why on earth would I bring that up?" She blinked then as her brain caught up to the last words. "And why *especially* not Simon?"

"Because he's always had the hots for you," Hannah said, leaning into the mirror for a little eyeliner repair. "If he knew you were walking around like that, poor guy might stop breathing."

Quinn blinked again. "What did you say?" she asked, realizing the words were just air with enunciation.

"What?" Hannah asked, giving Quinn a double take in the mirror. "What?" she repeated.

"Simon has—" Quinn couldn't even say the words. It was preposterous. "He has what?"

Hannah gave a snarky face and went back to her makeup repair. "You knew that."

"Did *not* know that," Quinn replied. "Pretty sure I'd remember this conversation."

"Well I may not have said anything," Hannah said. "But good Lord, it's painfully obvious. You'd be a fool not to see it."

Quinn raised a hand as her heart sped up, feeling her scalp begin to sweat. "Fool."

Hannah looked at her and chuckled. "Well, anyway. Now you know. Don't go telling him anything—save his manly pride." She gave Quinn a once-over in the mirror. "You ready? You look a little pale."

Quinn looked in the mirror and reached absently for her lip gloss as she took a deep breath to slow her heart back down. *You'd be a fool not to see it.* Crap.

Chapter Five

"A cloudless sky," Simon said, looking up as he walked with his brothers down the gravel road that connected Zach's house to his mom's. "Fate shined on you today, little brother."

"Yeah," Zach agreed, kicking a rock ahead of him. "How often do we wish for good weather? I was a little nervous that karma might kick me in the ass."

"I could kick Levi in the ass for not driving us back," Eli said, tugging at the collar of his buttoned-to-the-neck black shirt. "All this black shit makes me wish for a few clouds."

"And an air conditioner," Simon agreed.

"You don't want to ride in the backseat of my truck in all this black shit," Levi said, running his fingers back through his short, slightly-spiky-slightly-just-messy light-brown hair. "You'd pick up everything back there, including most of a golden retriever."

"Man, it's good to see you, though," Simon said, hooking his suit jacket over his shoulder with one finger. "You need to get up here more often."

"I—" Levi began, raising an eyebrow.

"I know Granabelle ran you off, and knowing her she'll live to be a hundred and ninety—"

"At least," Zach added.

"But we miss you, bro," Simon said.

"I was about to say," Levi said, holding up a hand, "that there's a slight chance I might be moving back." Levi frowned. "And Gran didn't run me off."

"Seriously?" Eli asked, stopping midstep.

Everyone else stopped as well, and Simon rounded to study his perpetually AWOL brother. Growing up, Levi had been the golden boy, star of everything, bright lights in his athletic future, and Gran's favorite. Not that she ever admitted it, but everyone knew it. At least until he got Heather Walters pregnant right after graduation. He probably would have made a more clear-headed choice had Gran not swooped in with the *"She's beneath you, she'll ruin your life"* spiel, even going to Heather and her parents with a check.

Instead, still reeling from their father's death the year before and strung out on stress, young love, and anger, Levi bolted with Heather. Leaving the college scouts and the bright lights to die behind him.

And coming home only when he absolutely had to.

"Way to bury the lead," Simon said. "Kind of important news, don't you think?"

"More important than Zach's wedding day?" Levi said, moving his suit jacket to the other arm and clapping Zach on the shoulder. "Don't think so. It's the second time I've come up to see him marry the same woman. I think it's about him today."

"Don't jinx it, man," Zach said, slapping his back in return. "And you aren't using me to hide your shit. Spill."

Levi sighed. "This is why I don't talk."

"And yet you did, so go," Eli said.

Levi shook his head. "Heather has to move back to take care of her mom," he said. "Her dad's been gone a couple of years already, and her mom's terminally ill."

"That sucks," Simon said.

"Yeah, it does," Levi said. "They've never had much money, and she wants to be home for the duration but can't afford a live-in nurse." He rubbed at his eyes. "And I feel like a dick for thinking about myself, but Heather moving back here is going to make our joint custody of Kinley a damn nightmare."

"Oh, hell," Simon said. "I didn't think about that."

"So I started looking at coaching jobs closer to this area," Levi said. "Close, without actually *being* here," he amended.

Simon caught the look that passed through his brother's eyes. "And?"

"And the Briartown Bobcats caught wind that I was open and called *me*," Levi said, his jaw clenching through the smile he forced.

"Holy shit," Zach said. "That's—"

"Yep."

Simon started to laugh and swung an arm over his youngest brother's shoulders. "Come on, we need to be less sober for this conversation," he said. "We'll hit it back up after Zach says *I do*."

"Oh, hold up," Zach said, holding out a hand as the house came into view. "Gran just got there. Let's let her make her entrance."

"Please," Levi said dryly.

"Dude, you're about to spend an afternoon with her," Zach said. "You need to learn how to fake it and move on."

"She means well," Eli said. "The outcome isn't always ideal, but—"

"I know," Levi said. "And I fake it every time I come, so I'm not new to that. It just—"

"Reopens everything," Eli said.

"Burns my ass up," Levi said, shaking his head. "Hey, Mom and Hannah don't know about the possible move yet," Levi said. "Neither does Kinley. I'd like to keep it on the down low till after the interview at least."

"Which is when?" Simon asked.

"Tomorrow."

"Oh, so you totally multitasked my wedding," Zach said as they rounded into the big open driveway of their mother's house.

"Do you always whine this much?" Levi asked.

"Yes," Eli said, a smirk on his face.

"Come on, big brother," Levi said, chuckling. "Enough about me. Let's go get you married. Be with family."

"Shit," Eli muttered.

"Comments?" Zach said flippantly.

"Family," Eli said. "It's never just family anymore. We have cameras following us everywhere. I'm surprised we don't have one with us right now." He looked up in the trees. "Hell, maybe we do."

"Yeah, that would drive me nuts," Levi said.

"You're not helping," Zach said, whacking Levi in the chest. "It's not that bad."

"Really?" Eli asked. "When's the last family dinner we had that didn't double as a filming or a meeting about filming?"

Zach put on a shit-eating grin. "I'm gonna go marry the hottest woman in town now, and then I'm gonna go have endless sex with my wife for a week." He laid a finger on Eli's chest. "You can't piss me off today."

Eli actually laughed at that and shook his head, spinning Zach around and pushing him forward.

"All right," Eli said, still looking amused. "Let's go do this. Cameras or not."

"First, I'm gonna go hit on that bride of yours and see if she's still the traffic stopper she used to be," Levi said.

"She is," Eli, Zach, and Simon said at once.

"Okay," Simon said laughing. "Coats on, guys. Let's show them how the Chase men clean up."

He opened the door chuckling at his own words, but what he saw standing in the hallway just ten feet away damn near closed up his throat.

Quinn stood there talking with Hannah, looking like she'd just stepped out of a magazine. A tiny black dress formed to her body, showing off sculpted legs that were accentuated by the simple black high heels on her feet. A cutout piece across her chest exposed creamy cleavage he'd honestly never seen before, as her blonde hair fell down in big tousled waves.

She was every sexual fantasy he'd ever had.

"Fuck," he muttered under his breath.

"What?" Zach said, pushing in beside him. "Oh. Holy hell."

"Understatement," Simon said.

"Are we going in, or just decorating the doorway?" Eli asked.

At Eli's words, both women turned, and Quinn's gasp and slightly parted lips did nothing to ease the growing discomfort in his pants.

There were other people milling as they came in. His mom was pushing Gran's wheelchair to the kitchen. Some of the show's crew was there, chatting within view. Nicole Brian came around the corner from the hallway, and her jaw dropped as the group of them walked in. "Sweet baby Jesus," he heard her mumble, but he only had eyes for the blonde that was looking at him as intently as he looked at her.

"Wow," Quinn said in a whisper when he got as close as he dared.

Simon opened his mouth but nothing came out, so he just smiled and forced his eyes not to drop to her chest.

She giggled and raised her eyebrows. "You're speechless?"

He cleared his throat and tried to swallow. "Evidently."

"Since when does Simon Chase not have something to say?" Quinn said, tilting her head.

"When he's looking at you," he said. *Shit.* He wanted to suck the words right back out of the air, but they were out there now. And he couldn't help it. She was—damn. "Sorry," he said, grinning, hoping he came off as chagrined. "You just look stunning."

The pink that rose from her exposed chest all the way up her neck just about did him in. It was gonna be a long evening.

"Wow," she said a second time, fanning herself with a free hand. He noticed for the first time that she held a camera in her other hand, cradled to her body as the strap hung freely below.

"Sorry," he repeated.

"No, I just don't embarrass easily," she said, chuckling. "You took me off guard. And you—" She made a cute little show of doing a once-over and then fiddling nervously with her hair. "Wow."

"You're on with that word tonight," he said, a mischievous grin pulling at his lips.

"What can I say?" she said, patting her forehead. "Maybe you've taken my mouth away, too."

"Come on, you see me dressed up for work all the time," Simon said. "But you—this is—" Shit, he was babbling like a girl. *Get it together.* "I've never seen you look like this."

She put a hand on her hip, which only somehow managed to pronounce her boobs. "You know I do have a life outside of rain-drenched shorts and muddy flip-flops."

"I suspected as much," Simon said, narrowing his eyes, needing to lighten the sexual charge that he was probably the only one feeling. "But I can't remember the last time I even saw your hair down."

She touched it, close to her chest, and he felt his dick twitch.

"Well, you may dress up for work, Mr. Chase, but not like that," she said, pointing up and down at the black suit over a buttoned-up black shirt with no tie. Zach's request. Even though there were no groomsmen for this event, he suggested his brothers all go in style. "This black on black thing y'all have going on is—" She stopped and fanned herself again. He knew it was done in fun to be cute and complimentary, but the flush of her skin gave her away.

She was flustered. *She was flustered?* This was different.

"You like?"

"I like."

"You two do realize I'm still standing here, right?" Hannah said from his right, and it might as well have been from a bullhorn.

Quinn started, going even rosier as she laughed and glanced at Hannah. "Of course," she said. "We're just being silly."

"Probably the next time we'll be this decked out will be next month," Simon said. "Although I'm pretty sure you'll be trumping us all on your day."

Quinn smiled as Hannah ditched them to shriek and throw herself at a laughing Levi, but the color faded from her cheeks. "I guess. You'll have to ask my mother."

"Your mother?"

"She took the dress to her own seamstress to enhance things," Quinn said, her eyes going unfocused. "It wasn't good enough."

"You gotta step up, Little Bit," Simon said, leaning into her field of vision. "Stop letting her run everything. You're one of the toughest women I know. Why do you let her mow you down?"

"Because—she's the Granabelle of my family, Simon," Quinn said with a defeated sigh. "People let her do what she does because it's easier and more self-preserving than firing her up."

"On day-to-day things, I get that," Simon said. "Although having a mental break because you didn't have shoes—"

"I totally scored on that, by the way," Quinn said, laughing, grabbing Simon's arm.

"I saw."

"Had to sell my sister down the river to barefoot-and-pregnant-ville, but hey."

"But your wedding day, Quinn—"

"Phoebe didn't get what she wanted either," Quinn said. "It's not a big deal."

"Not a big deal?" Simon questioned. "It's supposed to be the greatest day of your life."

She met his eyes for just a second and then blinked away. "It will be," she said. "That's just stuff. Food and flowers and . . . dresses— that's not what a marriage is about."

"True," Simon said. "It's about being with your best friend."

Those green eyes shot up to his again, and the weird bubble that had isolated them earlier was back. Like they were the only two people in the room and his words bounced between them.

Another squeal echoed through the foyer, however, breaking the moment as his mom cleared a path to get to Levi. The foyer had actually come to life with noise while Simon and Quinn had been temporarily captured in their odd little space. Odd in the sense that it hadn't felt one-sided. Had he imagined that?

"Oh, who's that?" Quinn asked, pointing. "Maybe a friend of Maddi's?"

Simon turned to follow her gaze and felt his head explode.

Stacey stood in the doorway looking like a runway model. Holy hell.

"That's my d—" Simon began, swallowing the word. "A friend of mine from the shelter, I asked her to be my plus-one for this thing."

Quinn's eyes widened just slightly. "You have a date?"

"Not a—" Simon held up a finger. "Hold on, let me rescue her from the doorway. Be right back."

"Take your time," Quinn said. "I'm gonna—" She pointed toward the restroom.

"Take yours," he said with a wink.

Really? *Take yours?* He was slipping.

Quinn entered the bathroom and locked the door behind her before her knees could give way.

"Shit," she whispered, resting her back against the door and looking skyward. She didn't know whether to laugh at the lunacy of it or cry over the irony. "Shit, shit, shit!"

What the living hell had that been out there? The second— the *very second* Simon had walked through that door looking like friggin' James Bond, everything had turned. Quinn had felt it. In that second, she belonged to him. What the living hell? *She couldn't belong to him!*

But his eyes had locked in on hers with . . . that look—God help her, that look—and she couldn't have moved if she'd wanted to. It was like everyone else disappeared and it was just the two of them. Every inch of being naked under that dress had raised hands and waved. She'd half expected her ovaries to fall out on the floor and beg. And then—

Quinn pried herself off the door and met her own eyes in the mirror.

Since when does Simon Chase not have something to say?

When he's looking at you.

"God, Mary, Jesus, and Joseph," Quinn muttered, trying to channel Miss Lou instead of the string of curses dancing in her head. "Or something to that effect."

He's always had the hots for you.

"Why?" Quinn asked the mirror. "Why now? Why do I find this out now?"

She turned the cold water on full blast and placed her wrists under it. She needed to cool down, cool her blood, cool her jets, cool her hormones, whatever the hell it was that was raging through her like a bullet. It was Hannah's words, that's what it was. Quinn would have still been tweaked by Simon's actions, by his words, by his unbelievably sexy appearance, but it was Hannah's innocent little admission that wrapped itself around all of those things and lique-fied. Oozing like hot honey into all the cracks, bringing everything to a heightened awareness.

She looked at herself again, cheeks flushed, chest flushed, eyes shiny like she was coming off a bender.

"It doesn't matter. You can't do this," she said to her reflec-tion, turning off the water and resting her weight on the sink. "You can't—" She bit her bottom lip as something that felt less like silly attraction and more like the gavel of hell came crashing through her body. Looking up at the light fixture, she blinked back what she refused to let come. "You're being ridiculous," she whispered. "Stop this."

Eric was going to be there any minute, and where was she? Locked in the bathroom acting like a hormonal twit over another man. Another man who was here with another woman. Yeah, explain that one.

His date. Simon never brought a date to anything—not that there were usually things to bring dates to. They didn't really talk about that part of their lives much, so maybe he did go out with women. Maybe he had relationships she didn't even know about. Oh, shit, what was she thinking—Simon Chase was a hot eligible single man, with a fiery wit and eyes that could melt the pants right off a woman. *Of course* he dated. And probably most of them looked like *her.*

Quinn inhaled deeply and let it go slowly, willing her heart to slow down. Drying her hands on the hanging towel, she continued to take slow breaths as she dabbed at her eyes and face.

It was fine. It had to be fine. No more crazy, regardless of how damn good Simon looked. He wasn't hers to feel this way about. Meeting her own gaze in the mirror again, she let those words sink in.

He's not yours.

"He's not yours."

Weaving through the crowd of his family as well as a few friends trickling in, Simon made it to Stacey.

"Hey," he said.

"Hey, yourself," she said, smiling at him appreciatively. "You look—really good in that suit."

Simon took the moment to take her in. A red dress that could stop time set off her dark hair, and she looked like a million bucks. He should feel like the luckiest man alive to have her on his arm, and he did, but . . .

"You look amazing," Simon said.

"Thank you," she said, doing a little mock curtsy. "Been a long time since I had an occasion to wear something hot."

Simon chuckled. "Well, you've succeeded. I'm the luckiest guy here."

"And there's an added little bonus for you to think about all evening," Stacey said, pulling his thoughts back to her as she leaned up to whisper in his ear.

"What's that?" Simon asked, forcing his mind away from glancing around for Quinn. *When you're with Stacey, be with Stacey.*

"There's nothing under this dress," Stacey said against his ear.

Simon met her eyes. She was good. She wasn't messing around with the you-owe-me-a-hot-night part of the deal. And certain parts of his anatomy definitely knew they were being summoned.

"So maybe you *will* be the luckiest guy tonight," Stacey said, giving an innocent shrug as she batted her eyes. "Hopefully not luckier than the groom," she amended. "That would suck for him."

Simon grinned. "I'm not too worried about Zach."

Eric appeared in the doorway then, and Quinn breezed past Simon on a fresh scent of vanilla and berries, laying a hand against Eric's chest for leverage as she reached up on her toes to kiss him. Simon's jaw muscles twitched as he looked away.

Eric St. James was Quinn's perfect match. Successful. From a wealthy family much like hers. Their dads played golf together. What was it about rich people that made golf mandatory? He was even blond like her. They'd certainly make some shiny children.

Simon tucked Stacey's hand into the crook of his arm, wondering if he was going to survive the evening. "Well, come on, Miss Not a Date," Simon said, her husky laugh making him chuckle, too. "Let me introduce you to my grandmother."

"Wow, the big guns right out of the gate?"

He smirked. She had no idea. And he still wasn't sure how he was going to go about this. Everything in his being told him it was a bad idea to involve Gran in a financial issue. The shelter had always been his. Not his like it belonged to him, but just—his. Pulling her in, if she even went for it, would open all the doors.

But then all Simon really needed to think about were the faces he saw every week. Of the little boy and his mom worrying about where to take a shower. He smiled at Stacey.

"You brought the A game, sweetheart, I'm just playing along."

Stacey threw her head back and laughed. "Touché."

Chapter Six

"Hey, babe," Eric said, grinning down at Quinn as she pushed up on her tiptoes to kiss him. "My God, you look incredible."

"Thank you," she said, still trying to catch her breath, feel her extremities, anything. "So do you. Come on."

Quinn took him by the hand and walked into the living room, faltering for just a second at the sight of Simon introducing his date to his grandmother and Hannah.

With her perfect shiny dark hair and sexy eyes and . . . and a dress she must have been sewn into. A friend from the shelter? Quinn had never been to the shelter in Trinity, but she couldn't imagine this woman working there. And no one put on a dress like that to come be just a friend. That was a do-me outfit if she'd ever seen one.

But just moments earlier . . .

Quinn's breath caught in her chest just thinking about it.

No. It didn't matter. She wasn't that kind of woman, she had an incredible man of her own, and she had no business entertaining other thoughts. Hots, crushes—those were superficial things, not love. Not serious things like love and marriage.

"Get it together," she whispered under her breath.

"What's that?" Eric asked.

Quinn sucked in a little breath at Eric's voice and smiled at him. *Yes, Eric, your fiancé, remember him?*

"Nothing, babe, just thinking out loud," she said, putting an arm around him and pulling him closer.

"Thinking about our wedding?" he said, touching her hair softly.

"Of course," she said automatically. "Can't wait."

"Neither can I," Eric said. "God, your hair looks hot like this. You should wear it down more often."

"What would you think if I cut it short?" Quinn asked, tasting the rebellion on her tongue.

The look that crossed Eric's features told her volumes before he ever spoke.

"No!" he said, looking horrified, and then dialing it back. "I mean, of course you'd still look gorgeous, you always do, but babe, your hair is so pretty and sexy. I can just see you all in white with all this spilling around you."

"Maybe I should chop it off and make a wig out of it so everybody else can wear it for a while," she said, shaking her head.

"What?"

Quinn smiled. "Nothing. Just kidding."

She glanced around the room, and *bam*—there it was again. Simon's gaze landing on her with that—what? Force? Magnetism? *Desire.*

It pulled the air from her and she curled her fingers into Eric's belt loop for grounding. What the hell? No, there was something else, something different, something more. Had he always looked at her like that, or was she just now seeing it after what Hannah told her? He sure didn't appear to be looking at his little wonder woman that way. Or was that just wishful thinking?

Oh, my God, stop!

She was being tested, that's what it was. She was a month away from committing herself to Eric forever and she was going a little wiggy. That's all. *That was all.*

"Eric!" came Miss Lou's voice, mercifully breaking into her thoughts. "Good to see you again, baby!"

She enveloped him in her typical momma-bear hug, making him laugh.

"Good to see you again, too," Eric said, beaming as he looked back at Quinn. "You *are* coming to our little shindig next month, aren't you?"

"Oh, honey, I wouldn't miss it!" Miss Lou said, squeezing Quinn's hand. "This girl is just like one of my own. I'm so excited for the two of you. It's at the Clayton Country Club, right?"

"Yes, ma'am," Eric said. "Only the best for my Quinn."

Quinn smiled. "I wanted to have it outside under the gazebo, but—"

"You don't want the guests to be uncomfortable," Eric said. "Or us," he added, laughing. "Indoors is a more refined way to go."

Quinn stiffened, forcing her smile to stay in place.

"Well, I'm sure it's going to be spectacular," Miss Lou said, patting both of their arms. "I can't wait. Excuse me for a second, I have to go check on some things."

Quinn let go of a breath. "You realize *this* wedding is taking place outside, right?"

Eric blinked, then glanced out the windows, most likely taking in the chairs and the decorations.

"Oh."

"Yeah."

"Sorry," he said, wincing. "Do I need to go apologize?"

"No," Quinn said, patting his chest. "Just—try to hold in your highbrow opinions today, okay?"

Eric's head jerked back. "My highbrow opinions?"

"Yes," Quinn said, looking around, catching Simon laughing at something *his date* was saying. *God.* Quinn rolled her shoulders and popped her neck to shake it off. "The Clayton mandatory we're-better-than-everyone-else attitude. That's fine there among your own, but not here."

Eric laughed and gave her an odd look. "Among *my* own? I'm sorry, where did *you* grow up?"

Quinn met his eyes and sighed. "I'm sorry. I'm just—I don't know. That *more refined* comment you made just made me itchy, I guess."

Eric's gaze went a little less harsh and he took a deep breath as he studied her. Pulling her close, he rested his lips against her forehead.

"Forgiven," he said. "I love you."

"I love you, too," Quinn said, wrapping her arms around his torso and pulling him against her. Things felt better that way. Things made sense that way. And she desperately needed for things to make sense.

"You know you're still a Clayton girl, right?" he said against her hair. "Just because you choose to live a more blue-collar life right now, it doesn't change your roots."

Quinn swallowed and focused on the collar of his shirt. Shutting her eyes, she inhaled, taking in his cologne and his smell. The uniquely Eric aroma she'd loved for years.

"I know."

"But you always take up for the underdog," Eric said, pulling back and running a finger along her cheek. "And that's one of the things I love so much about you."

She nodded and frowned at the same time, unsure if that was a compliment or another dig. "The underdog," she echoed.

"Besides," he continued. "Once we're married and you're back where you belong, it'll all come back to you," he said on a chuckle. "Like riding a bike."

Gran was sparkly as usual, perched in her wheeled throne like the queen of the castle. Not that she had that designation, but Simon's mother had dutifully deferred that role to her mother-in-law ever since his dad died. It was easier that way—Quinn was right about that. It was certainly quieter.

"So, you're a nurse?" Gran asked, those eyes of hers zeroing in on Stacey, the focus belying her age. She looked a hundred, her body a shriveled raisin in designer clothing. Her hair was never out of the perfect knot she paid people to put it in, and wispy pin curls trembled around her face as if they were afraid to be alone out there. She *looked* old. But her eyes mirrored the ever-so-shrewd mind still ticking away inside.

"Yes, ma'am," Stacey said, smiling graciously. "ER at Trinity Medical."

Gran raised an eyebrow and folded her hands in her lap. "Which means you see a lot of crap, I can imagine."

Stacey chuckled. "More than I'd care to, that's for sure."

"And you run that shelter too?" Hannah asked. "Jesus, when do you sleep?"

Stacey nodded, the worry slipping back behind her smile at the mention of the shelter. "Every possible chance I get," she said. "And I have some awesome volunteers that help pick up the slack." She touched Simon's shoulder. "This guy for one."

"Daddy used to bring you there when you were little," Hannah said.

"Yes, he did," Simon said, wondering if Gran even knew that.

Suddenly he knew what card to play.

"My Josiah always had a heart for causes," Gran said. "He sought them out."

"I always wanted to go," Hannah said, pretending to sulk. "But he always said no."

"Wasn't the place to bring little girls," Gran said, winking at Simon. "Ratty smelly boys—eh, no big deal."

"I loved watching him work the crowd," Simon said. "He had a way. Made people feel like—" Simon paused for the right word.

"Like people again," Stacey finished.

"Exactly," he said. "They responded to him." He nudged Stacey's arm. "You have that, too."

She shrugged. "I try. It's sad, the things I see—in both my jobs," she said. "People fall down so far and for so long that they forget what living is. When you have to scratch and climb to just get one meal for the day, and get forced to stand in line after line to survive, you start feeling like cattle. You forget what dignity feels like."

Gran was catching every word with a curious gaze. "You sound like you have a little firsthand knowledge," she said.

Stacey pressed her lips together in what Simon knew to be a nervous tell.

"We fell on some hard times growing up," she said, darting a quick glance at Simon and looking away. "Enough to not want my patrons to feel like that in my establishment."

"That's honorable," Gran said. "You don't see much of that these days. My son was one of the few."

"Dad loved that place," Simon said. "It was very personal to him. And I guess it trickled down to me, because I sure seem to find myself plating mashed potatoes a lot."

Stacey laughed, her hand on his arm.

"Simon charms all the little old ladies," she said. "You should see the glow on their faces when they walk away."

"Aw, Simon," Hannah purred. "You breaking hearts over there, big brother?"

Simon gave his sister a look. "Yeah, well, let's talk about Mr. Palinsburg, shall we?" he asked Stacey. "Who nearly drops his plate every time you speak to him."

"He has arthritis," she said.

"In his *back*," Simon countered, actually making Gran laugh.

"Well, good for both of you, giving back like that," Gran said. "Stacey, it was nice to meet you, and I hope to talk to you again," she said, backing up her chair and ending the conversation in her usual abrupt way. "But I have to go find some decent food to take my medicine with, and that may be a challenge with the barn-dance menu Louella came up with."

"I don't know, it looks pretty good in there, Gran," Simon said.

"Hmm," Gran huffed, rolling away. "We'll see."

He didn't get to make a pitch, but the groundwork was laid. And Stacey had just about sold it on her merit alone, without even knowing she was doing it.

"She's a trip," Stacey said when Gran was gone.

"You have no idea," Hannah muttered.

Simon laughed and turned to his right, and *wham*, there they were. He bit back a curse as the feeling kicked him square in the nuts. Watching Quinn, looking like she was, smiling up at Eric as he spoke to her—fuck, it was torturous.

Shit, she took his damn breath away. And then those eyes—Jesus, those eyes damn near knocked him into the wall as her gaze burned right through him.

"Simon?"

"Yes?" he said, turning quickly, his voice cracking like a fourteen-year-old boy. "I'm sorry, what?"

Stacey snickered. "Where did you go?"

"I—I don't know," he said, passing a hand over his face. "Sorry."

"Hannah went to see about getting some pictures," she said. "I think I'm gonna grab some of that barn-dance food," she added with a wink.

"Go for it," he said, squeezing her arm. "I'll be out here waiting for you. Kicking sawdust around."

Simon couldn't help the path his eyes took as Stacey walked off into the kitchen, and shamefully they weren't on her. They should be on her. She was amazing. She was beautiful. She felt strongly about the same things that he did, and more important, she wanted no complications.

What did he want? The most complicated cluster of a maze there ever was.

A smoking-hot beautiful blonde-haired green-eyed maze that looked like a dream and could probably still turn his head if she turned troll and sprouted hair from her nose.

Zach was right. He had it bad. Shit, his stupid ass had it bad.

"Quinn, do you have your camera?" Hannah asked, appearing at her left. "Yes, you do," she answered herself, noting the apparatus in Quinn's hand. "Can you get some shots of the family real quick?"

"Yes!" Quinn said, spurring into action. *Get out of your own head and do your job.* "Have to do some work, Eric, be back in a bit."

That was exactly what she needed. Keep busy. Quit trading heated looks with a man she had no business doing that with. Let her instincts take over and carry her to that happy place where—

All four men were lined up along the long dining table, black suits on black shirts, with Hannah sparkling in the middle.

"Dear God," Nicole said under her breath, walking up beside Quinn.

"Right?" Quinn agreed, stunned in her own right. "They belong in a calendar."

Eli and Zach were on one side, looking like two versions of the same man. Dark hair and eyes, a hint of planned scruff that just made them look delicious. One looking mysterious and brooding, even through his smile. One looking like he'd caught the canary.

On the other side of Hannah was Levi, lighter haired and breathtaking, with a look of mischief about him that reminded her of Zach. Always up to something. And then Simon.

Quinn's mouth went dry as her eyes met his and stuck. Blue eyes like his mom's, eyes that could take her down with laughter and then turn around and do this. His dark hair fell loose over his forehead and he raked it back, making her gasp. *Shit.*

She licked her lips and looked down at her camera a moment under the pretense of getting it ready, but really she just needed to breathe. Eric was right back there, and she needed to stop losing her shit every time Simon looked at her like that.

Just stop looking at him.

There. That was a great idea.

"All right, y'all," she said. "Get ready. Miss Lou, I don't know what water you drank when you were pregnant with all these people, but my Lord, you could make a fortune selling it with these photos."

The room laughed as a whole, and the entire shoot became more relaxed as they got comfortable with themselves and had fun with it. Elijah picked up Hannah at one point and she struck a pose in his arms, grinning devilishly at a striking and slightly familiar-looking man just a few feet away. Quinn turned to surreptitiously snap a few shots of his face as he looked at her.

That's what Quinn loved about photography. That right there. The honesty. The rawness and the reality that could not be faked. She'd grown up in a world of pretense and polite falsehoods, and fell in love with the truth that a camera lens could find.

Nicole was looking over her shoulder at the images as they showed up on her screen.

"That's amazing," she said. "He's just standing there, but what you caught—"

"—is what he's thinking," Quinn whispered, smiling at her. She glanced over at the Chases, cutting up and pulling their mother into it. She had a few seconds to regroup. "You can't fool the camera," she said. "There's no faking it, no putting on airs or hiding behind a smile." She looked up at Nicole and grinned. "The lens knows. It will find you."

Nicole chuckled. "What you artists are able to capture always blows my mind. I can see it after the fact, running through tape, finding the gold, but y'all—you pull it from nothing and make it magical."

Quinn winked and turned back to the crazy group of people in front of her. "It can be."

Zooming up on each one of their faces as they laughed and talked and were completely unaware of her, she snapped away, falling into her zone. This was the moment she loved the most, when the photographer becomes invisible. When the subject loses the self-conscious worry of appearance and just falls into their natural self. Quinn's breathing slowed as she dropped into that rhythm, laughing when Hannah's eyes suddenly cut her way and she snapped the microsecond. Hannah knew. She knew what Quinn was doing, and was one of the few people who could remain at ease with that.

Still chuckling, she moved the lens along, snapping away at their expressions, and then she landed on Simon's face. And felt her heart slam against her ribs so hard, she nearly dropped the camera.

He was staring at her. Not hard-core or intense like before, not raw like he had from across the room earlier. Just watching her. Watching her do her thing, a small smile touching his lips and matching his eyes. Like someone who was proud of what he was looking at.

Slowly, she lowered her camera and maintained the eye contact, hearing her own breathing in her ears as everything else became background noise. She felt the hot telltale burn behind her eyes and pulled in a deep breath.

"You done?" Eric's voice said from behind her.

Quinn whirled around, blinking quickly, breathing like she'd just jogged around the house a couple of times.

"Yes," she said. "I think so. For now."

"Want something to drink?" he asked.

"Guess what?" she said suddenly.

"What?"

"I have nothing on under this dress," she said.

God, that didn't go according to plan. Nothing was working right. Nothing about what she'd just said was remotely sexy. It sounded like she'd announced she was going to the grocery store.

Eric's eyebrows lifted way up, however, and he took a tiny step back to look at her. Kind of like he might be assessing her sanity, but still—he looked interested.

"Come again?"

Hannah walked by then with a freshly mixed drink of some sort and Quinn snatched it from her hand. "Thanks," she whispered.

Hannah's eyes widened, too, as she stopped and found herself with an empty hand. "Okay then," she mumbled, walking back to the kitchen.

Quinn took three big gulps as Eric watched, licking the sour sweetness from her lips.

"Hey, take it easy, babe," he said. "You don't drink like that."

"Living on the wild side tonight," she said. "So. You heard me," she said, letting the liquid heat sizzle into her body. "Commando."

A small smile tugged at his lips. "Because?"

"Because I thought it might be fun to walk around tonight with a secret that only you know about," she said, patting his chest. "And for you to watch me do it."

His eyes darkened with desire. "Really, now," he said. "And what do you plan to do with that later tonight?"

"Nothing," she said, taking another large swallow. "I say we tease each other for the next month and give nothing so the wedding night will be extra hot."

The desire morphed into something more along the lines of *Are you crazy?* Quinn just smiled and chuckled at his expression.

"You're serious?" Eric asked.

Quinn pressed herself against him suggestively. "Could be fun to make it a game," she said. "See if we can hold out."

Eric raised his hand like he was in school. "I can't. You win. Game over?"

She laughed. "Come on."

"Hey."

Quinn started at Simon's voice suddenly at her left. She looked up to see him grinning—not quite like normal. Like he was nervous. Like he had a hot woman on his arm and didn't know what to do with that.

Like *he* was nervous?

"H-hey," Quinn attempted, clearing her throat. Talking about being half naked while Simon walked up made her skin go hot—again—so she knocked back the rest of Hannah's drink. Liquor wasn't that bad, after all, she thought. She felt much more at ease, much faster, without the heartburn beer and wine coolers always gave her. "What's up?"

"Simon," Eric said.

"Eric," Simon said in the same disinterested tone.

"How's the weather business?" Eric asked, a practiced smile warming his features.

Simon grinned back and gave a little shrug. "It's like breathing, Eric, it's always there." He turned back to Quinn. "I wanted y'all to meet Stacey," Simon said, his hand at the small of the woman's back. An intimate gesture.

They're more than friends.

"Stacey runs the Trinity Outreach Center," Simon continued.

"Hi," Quinn said, reaching for her hand. "I'm Quinn Parker, so nice to meet you. This is Eric—"

"Eric St. James," he said, cutting her off. "Very nice to meet you. You run the center?"

Stacey chuckled, glancing up at Simon and then back to Eric. "I do. You know it?"

"I know of it," Eric said. "We are always looking for charitable organizations—especially local ones—to link up with for our marketing campaigns. I'd love to talk to you about it."

Of course, Quinn thought. He was making it about business.

Stacey blinked and appeared to process what he said. "We—meaning who?"

Eric smiled and put a hand to his chest ingratiatingly. "I'm sorry. My company—my family's company. SJ Enterprises."

"SJ Enterprises is your family?" she asked.

"It is," Eric said. "My father's baby."

"And when you say link up with, what does that mean exactly?" she asked, glancing up at Simon.

"We have it in our budget this year to hit the donation trail," he said, nodding as if this should earn him a gold star. "We are lining up charitable organizations like yours to set up regular contributions, run television ads, and so on."

Quinn wanted him to stop. She'd only shared air with this woman for thirty seconds and she could already tell that she wasn't in her job for the pat on the back. She took the topic seriously.

"Let's not talk business tonight," Quinn said. "I'm sure everyone has cards, right?"

Stacey smiled and pulled one from her tiny bag. "I agree. But I'm definitely interested in talking. We could use the help."

Eric's gaze landed on Quinn just long enough for her to see that he was a little ticked at being cut off, and then he smiled and dug a card from his wallet. Oh well. He'd survive it. Not everything was a networking opportunity. Still, she knew she'd hear about it later. Eric never liked it when Quinn joined in a business conversation.

"So Simon mentioned that the two of you are about to get married as well," Stacey said, touching Simon's arm.

"Yes, ma'am," Eric said, perfect smile back in place. "Just under a month away."

"Wow, how exciting," she said, smiling at Quinn. "Are you having a small wedding like this, or a big event?"

"Oh, I'm sure it'll be monstrous," Quinn said, instantly wishing she'd chosen a different word. "By that, I mean my mother is making sure it's an event of huge proportions."

"It will be beautiful," Eric said, almost defensively. "You know she's just trying to give you an amazing day."

"She's giving herself an amazing day," Quinn said softly, smiling up at him. "But that's okay," she added, facing the gorgeous couple that was Simon and Stacey. Their names even went together. "We have a honeymoon getaway planned that I can't wait to get to."

"Oh?" Stacey said, tilting her head in interest. Quinn had to give it to her, she was trying. "Where are you going?"

"Colorado," Quinn said, feeling warmer inside just thinking about it. It was so her kind of vacation, snuggling in a mountain cabin, hiking in the woods, reading by a bubbling stream. That made the hideous event that her wedding was going to be all worthwhile. "Eric found a mountain-cabin getaway that's part of a resort, but there are individual cabins so you feel like you're alone."

"Oh, that sounds amazing," Stacey said.

"There was another plan, but it got vetoed," Eric said, his tone taking on an unmistakable flatness. "A VIP cruise with spas, first-class excursions at all the stops. Top-of-the-line food. We'd have a suite instead of a regular cabin."

"On a boat," Quinn quipped.

Eric shrugged and laid a hand on the small of her back. "She doesn't like boats."

"Nah, the boats are fine," Quinn said, forcing a grin up at him in spite of his patronizing. "It's just the water they're floating on."

"You don't like water?" Stacey asked.

Quinn's eyes flew to Stacey's, ready to go on the defense, but there wasn't anything antagonizing there. She shook her head and swung the strap of her camera over her head, letting it hang.

"I only ask because I have a cousin with that same phobia," Stacey said. "She can't get around water of any kind."

"It's not—" Quinn began. "Not really like that. I just had a bad experience when I was a kid."

More than anything in the world, Quinn wished for all the awkwardness of the past hour to return, because that was a million times better than having this conversation. Her own family barely talked about that day, so chatting about it randomly with others was basically a no-go.

Stacey held up a hand. "Say no more, I understand," she said.

Really? That was probably a first.

"And now we can never go near an ocean, lake, pond, or a boat again," Eric said.

Quinn glanced up at him questioningly. *Simon's date* got the point in three seconds, and he was still fighting it after three years. "Um, so, what can I say? You and my mother get the wedding of your dreams, and I get the honeymoon of mine."

Stacey laughed, and so Eric did as well, playing the humbled fiancé. Quinn just smiled and noted that Simon did, too, watching her. Checking to see if she was okay again. The sound of a camera clicked behind her, and she turned to see Hannah let her camera hang as she picked up two drinks and handed her one.

"Had a hunch," she said with a wink before walking back to the foyer toward the same man Quinn had noticed watching Hannah before.

He looked less pleased than he had just moments earlier. And still familiar. Quinn's tipsy brain tried to link the reasons, and then she snapped on the resemblance.

"Holy hell, is that Maddi's brother? He grew up well," Quinn said, making Simon look at her in amusement. She snickered and took a sip of her new drink, which was slightly stronger than the last. "Sorry, was that out loud?"

Simon turned to look. "Yeah," he said. "Heard Eli talking about him being back in Dallas."

And it made sense now that he had zeroed in on Hannah. She remembered Hannah telling her about running into him at Deke's a few months back. And that he was intense. And hot. And yeah—he was definitely both of those.

"He doesn't look happy," Quinn said, narrowing her eyes.

"Do ex-marines ever look happy?" Simon asked.

"True, but Hannah doesn't look happy, either," Quinn said. "Maybe I need to go—"

"Hannah's a big girl," Eric said, running his fingers up under her hair on the back of her neck possessively.

Quinn darted a glance to Simon at the move, and meeting his eyes at that second made her do the next spontaneous thing. Gulp down two more swallows. What the hell? Why did she look at him? Why did she—

"Okay, so let me get this all straight," Stacey said, thankfully circling the conversation back around. "Your brother Zach is marrying the producer of your reality show."

"Sort of," Simon said. "Maddi is the assistant producer's assistant."

"Who hopefully will get a promotion after getting *The Chase* on the network's lineup," Quinn said.

"And they met that way?" Stacey asked.

"Oh, no," Simon said, laughing. "That's a whole other fairy tale there."

"There was another wedding day years ago, but she got buried in the rubble in a tornado they were chasing—" Quinn began.

"You weren't with us?" Simon interjected.

"Not yet," Quinn said. "Hannah and I had just graduated from North Texas, but I wasn't part of the team yet."

"Ah."

"So she left and they just hooked up again when this show came about," Quinn finished. "CliffsNotes version."

"Wow," Stacey said, looking back and forth between Quinn and Simon. "That's quite a story."

"With a happy ending, though," Quinn said, swirling her drink.

"And what do you do on the team?" Stacey asked.

"I'm whatever photography they need," Quinn said, laughing. "See, sometimes we go out in two vehicles, with Hannah in the lead and Eli and me in the secondary. I used to shoot video while Hannah did the still shots. Or vice versa. Now that we have a film crew following us around, it really depends on the severity of the storm."

"Sometimes it's just one vehicle," Simon said. "So we don't need the whole team every time if we have the network filming in another van. Other times, in really big events, it takes all of us."

"I like it better when it's all of us," Quinn said, inhaling deeply. She could almost feel the rush of it. "Something about when we're all there yelling and everything goes crazy—"

"—and Zach loses his mind," Simon added.

Quinn laughed. "Which is most of the time."

"Sounds a little dangerous," Stacey said. "But in a fun way."

"And I for one will be glad when all that's over," Eric added, making Quinn blink up at him to try to understand.

"When the season's over?" she asked. "I told you we signed on for a total of ten. It's gonna be a while."

"No, I mean—yes, when the season is over, when the show's over," Eric said. "But I'm talking about after that, when you're out of all of it. All this crazy mess."

Quinn's tongue felt tingly, and she lifted the glass to her lips automatically. "Crazy mess?" she asked over the rim. "You mean my job?"

"For now," Eric whispered, as though it were a secret. Clearly it was, because she didn't know about it.

"What do you mean?" she whispered back, laughing.

"Lovebug, you won't be running around chasing tornadoes forever," he said.

Something tickled along her spine. Something that made her want to scratch it.

"Never know," she said with a chuckle that felt staged and off balance. "I might still be out there hanging out the window when

I'm Simon's grandmother's age," she said, gesturing with a nod toward the old matriarch across the room.

Eric's amused laugh did nothing to ease that itch—it just turned into a burn that felt attached to his hand on the back of her neck.

"Come on, Quinn," he said. "That's all in good fun, but—"

"You think it's for fun?" she said.

Eric's eyes did a nervous scan among the group. "I'm just saying there are more responsible things you can do once we settle in."

"Once I'm a mom," Quinn offered.

Eric's eyes widened a little, and he nodded as if that were a fabulous idea and he had never thought of it.

"Among other things, but yeah," he said. "My uncle just mentioned something the other day about a web designer position in his department. You could apply for that and have an office job when the show's over." He chuckled and squeezed her in a little hug with the hand on her neck. "Wear heels to work instead of sneakers."

Quinn took another swallow, even sucking an ice cube into her mouth to crunch. The air in the room suddenly felt heavy. He didn't—he *didn't* just say that.

"Web design," she said around the ice. "Photoshopping pictures and uploading to websites."

"I—don't claim to know the ins and outs of that," Eric said. "But it would be in your field."

"My—my field?" she said. "Because there are photographs involved?" Quinn held up her phone. "I have pictures on my phone, too—should I go apply at a cell phone kiosk?"

"Quinn," Eric said, smiling in that way of his that meant he didn't want to make a scene. Oh, he'd brought the scene. But she wasn't brought up that way, either.

"I wear boots, by the way," she said. "Work boots. I'm gonna go check on Hannah and Maddi now. The big girls," she said. "See if they need any help." She smiled at Stacey and Simon with all her still-a-Clayton-girl social upbringing. "Excuse me. Really nice to meet you, Stacey."

Two more gulps finished off that glass and she set it on the table on her way across the room. *Don't follow me*, she thought. *Don't you dare follow me.*

Chapter Seven

That wasn't good. Simon had seen Quinn upset before, even irritated, but he had to admit he'd never seen her truly angry. Till now. The woman who'd just polited herself out of the conversation and walked away knocking back alcohol like a professional drinker was not a Quinn he'd seen before.

"So is there a ladies' room I can borrow?" Stacey asked.

"Right down that hall," Simon said. "Want a drink?"

"Sure," she said, gesturing with a tilt of her head. "I'll have what she's having."

Simon had to grin as she sauntered away. Cute. That was cute.

"Excuse me," Eric said. "I think I need a drink, too."

"I'll bet you do," Simon said under his breath as he headed toward where Hannah and Monroe were talking to Levi. He clapped his brother on the shoulder. "Catching up, little brother?"

"More or less," he said, giving him a look that said, *Don't say anything.*

Okay, then.

"Maddi's parents aren't coming," Hannah said, shaking her head.

"What?" Simon said, looking at Monroe. "Why?"

He closed his eyes in a version of a facial shrug. "Because they're them," he said, the irritation clear in his tone. "They just texted us. They couldn't get a flight out of Colorado."

Simon frowned. "Couldn't get a flight?"

Monroe held up a hand. "My father didn't want to travel, so my mother placated him," he said. "That's how it goes with my parents. Maddi knows that."

"How is she?" Simon asked.

"She's okay," Hannah said. "Quinn's helping her with her old-new-borrowed stuff, and she'll be set in a few."

"No, I mean about her parents," Simon said.

"She's *okay*," Hannah repeated.

"It's not her first rodeo with them," Monroe said quietly. "She gets it."

"Doesn't make it right," Simon said.

"We have each other," Monroe said, his solemn eyes crinkling a little in a small smile. "We've always had each other."

"You walking her down the aisle?" Hannah asked. "Or the patio, such as it is?"

"I'll walk her wherever she needs walking," he said, chuckling as Zach came up, pulling at his collar. "Gaining quite a crowd, Zach," he added.

Zach grinned. "That it is, *brother-in-law*."

Monroe chuckled and shook his head. "Not yet, man."

Simon laughed at the old animosity between the protective brother and the man that loved his sister. Zach and Maddi did have quite the story. And they were getting their happy ending. Not everyone got one of those. Simon looked around, waving at Stacey as she came out, eyes scanning the room for him.

"Harlan's here," Hannah said, pointing to where the old man stood in probably the same suit he'd owned for thirty years, talking to their mom.

"Jonah's not," Simon said, purposely not looking at Hannah.

"Harlan and Zach are friends," she said tightly.

Simon glanced back at his sister, working to keep the smile away. "So they are."

"Be nice," Zach said. "He's still friends with Mom, too. He's not hurting anything."

"Everyone, we're about to start," his mother called out, drawing silence from the room. "If you'll make your way outside and find a seat, we'll get these two married."

"Let's do it!" Zach exclaimed, clapping his hands together, bringing warm laughter around the room.

Quinn came down the hall, her green eyes brighter and shinier than usual. She smiled at Simon before dropping her expression to a more generic version for Eric as she plucked a zoom lens from a side table and took his arm.

"This could be interesting," Simon said, not realizing he spoke aloud.

"What?" Stacey said, taking Simon's arm as they fell into a line of sorts heading out the back door.

"Quinn," he admitted. "She's pissed. And she's drunk."

Stacey looked up at him, amused. "And you've got it bad."

Simon's feet faltered under him. "What?"

She laughed. "Come on, Simon. I've pretty much seen everything there is to see with you. All your looks. All your body language."

He sighed and focused on walking forward. "Please don't do this," he said under his breath.

"You and her?" she continued, squeezing his arm with a little grin. "That cute witty little banter the two of you have? The way you look at her?"

"Stop."

"Is our Simon *in love*?" she said.

He stared down at Stacey, the words screaming as they pinged around his head like they were in a pinball machine. "Have you lost your mind?"

Stacey laughed. "It's okay, *dear*, we aren't a couple, remember?"

"Doesn't matter, *dear*," he threw back. "It's not like that. We're friends. We work together. She's engaged to that jackass, if you noticed."

Stacey snickered. "Such vitriol. And such denial."

"Such bullshit," he said with a smile.

"It's mutual, by the way," she said.

That time his feet really did stop, causing Eli and Nicole to run right into them.

"What?" Simon said, looking straight into Stacey's eyes.

"Can you go?" Eli said. "Second time tonight you've held up traffic."

"You don't know that," Simon said, his voice just above a whisper.

"Call it intuition," Stacey said, pulling him forward again. "I know the look."

"She's getting married," Simon said, his head spinning.

She leaned in, tilting her chin up against his shoulder. "Or waiting for someone to stop her."

"I now pronounce you husband and wife," the preacher said, although the hoots and squeals pretty much drowned out everything after *husband*.

Every woman there was crying, Hannah and Quinn were clutching each other's hands and looked ready to dissolve as Maddi and Zach said their vows. Even Simon had to take a deep breath when

Zach got choked up. It was an emotional moment, the two of them finally making it to that point.

"You may kiss y—"

The preacher's words were cut off by another round of hollering by both genders as Zach grabbed Maddi and laid a kiss on her to stop time. Laughing, Maddi wrapped her arms around her new groom and looked as if she'd be good kissing him for days, regardless of how many people stood around and watched.

Simon laughed and clapped with everyone else, but his eyes kept landing back on the blonde sniffling between his sister and Eric.

It's mutual, by the way.

No sentence had ever messed him up more.

Until today, he would have argued that point to the moon and back. Quinn was engaged to someone else and had never given any indication that she felt otherwise. Until today, she always treated him just like the rest of his family. Didn't she? Until today.

Didn't she?

Shit, he had no idea.

Simon rubbed at his eyes, suddenly wanting to scrub his whole brain. The way she'd looked at him—the way she'd acted around him—he thought he was just imagining things, but then Stacey said—

Fuck. And then that *waiting for someone to stop her* comment. He was done. He was useless.

Simon had spent the last two years she'd sported that ring telling himself it was all for the best. That Quinn was meant for better things, a better life—a better man. That what he felt for her was just physical attraction, just like every other woman in his life. He didn't allow anything else to play around with his logic, there was no point. She was in love with Eric St. James. She was taken. She was—*she wasn't his*. Period.

And then today happened. What the hell made today happen? Made her look at him that way, created that damn vortex that sucked them in? Suddenly, all that had been concrete and solid was now made of fucking Jello.

Quinn was getting married in a month. *Or waiting for someone to stop her.*

"I can't do that," Simon whispered, his throat feeling tight.

"Can't do what?" Stacey asked.

Her voice yanked him back to the present, as he focused on the woman at his side dabbing her eyes.

"You okay?" he asked.

"Yes!" Stacey said, clearly embarrassed as she chuckled to cover. "That was just the sweetest ceremony I've ever seen." She gave his steady gaze a double take. "What? I'm a sap when it comes to romance."

"Really?" Simon asked. "Then why don't you date for real?"

"Because it's only good on other people," she said, elbowing him. "You, for instance."

Simon shook his head. "It's not good on me, either," he said.

"Oh, yeah? When's the last time you took it for a spin?" Stacey asked, cocking an eyebrow in a teasing smile.

Simon matched her grin. "You want me to toss all these party favors right back your way?" he asked. "Because we can go there."

"No, no, no," she said, patting his leg as she recrossed hers, showing a generous dose of sleek thigh. "I came here to dress up, feel like a woman for a change, and have some good hot fun," she added on a whisper close to his ear.

A laugh bubbled out from his chest. "Oh, I remember."

"Which is still on, by the way," she said softly, tossing her hair over one shoulder. "Someone else might be stealing your heart, but I have an uncovered Brazilian wax that says you're mine tonight."

Simon closed his eyes and blew out a breath, passing a hand over his jaw. No one was stealing his damn heart. No one was doing anything. Nothing changed. And the sexy woman melting the chair next to him was ready to be liquid in his hands.

"You are a wicked woman." He slung an arm along her chair.

"And you like that," she said.

He met her eyes and smirked. "You know I do."

"So," she said, her expression going curious. "SJ Enterprises, huh? Eric St. James. Interesting tactic," she said. "I wouldn't have thought about corporate sponsorship."

She thought *that* was the introduction he'd promised. Even better. If St. James actually followed through, he wouldn't have to involve Gran. Or he still could, and double up the income. Regardless, Stacey didn't have to know that.

"Might work out really well," Simon said.

She held up a hand. "Hey, if it keeps my doors open, I'm all for it." She rested the hand on his thigh. "Thank you."

The feel of her fingers on his thigh and the look in her dark eyes that said she wanted to thank him in all kinds of dirty ways—ways he already knew from experience were mind-blowing—got his blood moving in all the right directions. Good. That's what he needed. A hot night with a woman who wanted him just for the pleasure they could give each other.

"So how long do we have to hang out for?" she asked, glancing around as people began to mill, congratulating the happy couple.

Simon's gaze landed on Quinn, laughing now, talking with Hannah and Levi and Monroe, and, from the looks of things, doing her damn well best to ignore Eric. He stood to the side, playing the proud fiancé, letting her be pissed off. Good for him.

Nothing changed. They'd weather it.

"Not long," Simon said. "Just enough to make the rounds—come on," he added.

He wanted out of there, too. More and more as the seconds passed.

They made it to Maddi and Zach first, then his mom and Harlan, a quick chat with Monroe and Hannah, nods to the crew members that were there, Eli with Levi and Kinley, and then walked up to Quinn and Eric as Nicole Brian brought them all fresh drinks.

Quinn grabbed hers a little too quickly, he thought.

"Hey, Simon," Nicole said. "Can I make two more drinks for you?"

She made to head for the kitchen, but Simon held up a hand. "That's okay, we're about to head out."

"Beautiful wedding," Quinn said, pulling his eyes to her. Her mouth smiled, but her eyes did anything but. He narrowed his gaze, trying to read her. Normally, he would have been able to. Normally he'd dig around and make sure she was okay. Now he was afraid of what he might find.

"We were just talking about her plans," Nicole said, taking a sip from her glass. "And I'm finally getting to meet the mysterious groom."

"Not so mysterious," Eric said, grinning with all the charm he had. "Just busy. Quinn here has been pretty tied up herself, what with two jobs and planning a wedding."

"Just two jobs," she said, making a big circle in the air with her hand. "My mom has the rest."

"Well, how does it feel to have a celebrity wife? Or almost-wife," Nicole amended, laughing and holding up her drink. "Ooh, that's a good interview question," she said—to herself. "I need to talk to Charlie about that."

"Who's Charlie?" Quinn asked.

"Maddi's assistant," Nicole said.

"Maddi has an assistant?" Simon blurted.

"Maddi's getting promoted?" Quinn asked at the same time.

"No," Nicole said. "Just filling in where she isn't. Taking her place here while she's gone."

"Taking her place?" Quinn asked. "She said she was fine. She didn't need help."

"Just temporarily," Nicole said, holding up her glass in one direction and her palm in the other. "Everybody breathe. Filming must go on, and Maddi's taking off for a week. Maybe more while she and Zach settle in."

"So you miss a storm or two," Simon said, frowning. "Or maybe nothing. There aren't storms every week. Why the big crunch?"

"Not storm footage," Nicole said. "It's time for some meat and potatoes in this thing."

Quinn's right eyebrow lifted. "You want dirt."

"I want life," Nicole said. "The one-on-ones, the talking around the house, the relationships, the drama."

"You want dirt," Quinn repeated. "And Maddi doesn't go there. So you're grabbing your window."

Nicole flushed a little, her red hair making it glow even more.

Simon sighed and shook his head. "Eli is going to balk at it," he said. "You finally got him on your side with this show and you have to throw a nail under the tire?"

"He'll come around," Nicole said with a wink. "You just let me worry about Eli."

"She makes that sound easy," Simon said to Stacey, but Quinn laughed.

"Well, we never thought he'd come this far," Quinn said. "Maybe we'll be surprised."

"I'm very proud of Quinn," Eric said, causing a pause as everyone looked at him blankly. "In answer to your earlier question," he added.

"Oh!" Nicole said, laughing. "Sorry, I got a little off topic there, didn't I? Hazard of the job, I'm afraid."

Eric smiled down at Quinn, one hand resting under her hair. Again. This time she twitched and moved so that his hand had to slide down over her back. "She's accomplished something most people never do," he said. "Being on a television show. How many people can tell their kids they were once on a reality show?"

Simon's gaze flew to Quinn as hers turned sharply toward Eric. She'd evidently heard the same thing he had. *Once.* It was subtle, but not subtle enough.

"Well, hopefully it will be successful enough that they can see it for themselves," Nicole said, blatantly throwing it out there. *Go, Nicole.* Nothing subtle about that woman.

Eric's condescending eyebrow-raise as he averted his eyes spoke as loudly as if he'd fallen on the floor in a fit of laughter. And from her expression, Quinn caught every nuance. Stacey's discreet squeeze of Simon's arm both reminded him of the task at hand and made him regret missing the train wreck that was clearly looming.

"So anyway, we're gonna head—" Simon began, cut off by the sound of a xylophone.

Stacey's hand darted to her bag to pull out her phone. "Crap, it's the hospital, I have to take this. Be right back," she whispered in an add-on to Simon, already walking away.

"Who's at the hospital?" Quinn asked.

Simon shook his head. "No, it's her job."

"I thought she ran the shelter," Quinn said, the little lines above her nose furrowing.

"That's on her off time," Simon said. "She's also an ER nurse at Trinity Medical."

Quinn's gaze dropped as she nodded, and she took another swallow of her drink, her tongue darting out to catch a stray drop on her lips.

Simon looked away. He needed a drink. "Excuse me a second," he said.

He headed to the kitchen where his mom had left out a miniature liquor treasure trove. Pouring himself a whiskey neat, he knocked it back, closing his eyes as the fire burned down to his belly.

"Tick, tock," said a voice to his right.

Nicole Brian morphed at his side and gave him a look.

"What?" he said, confused.

"Running out of time on that, aren't you?" she asked, nodding out toward where Quinn and Eric were talking.

Simon followed her gaze and smiled politely. "I don't know what you're talking about."

Nicole chucked and crossed her arms over her chest. "Okay," she said with a shrug. "But the screen doesn't lie. She herself told me that the lens finds the truth, and the chemistry between you two is palpable. You really gonna let pretty boy over there swoop down and turn Barbie into Mrs. Ken?"

Simon opened his mouth and then closed it again. "Quinn's life is hers, Miss Brian. She's happy."

"Seems to be," Nicole said, just as they both watched Quinn saying something with very tight lips and Eric looking at her like she was a talking monkey. "Then again," Nicole said as Eric shot his hands up in a clear *this-conversation-is-done* gesture and stormed away.

"That didn't look good," Simon said under his breath, zeroing in on Quinn's body language.

She looked like a bird ready to take flight, and he found himself walking toward her before he'd even put thought to the action.

"Hey," he said when he was close enough.

Quinn's eyes rose to his and down again in the same second, but it was enough for Simon to see a shitload of pissed off. And a little bit of hurt in there for good measure.

"You okay?" he asked, leaning over to try to make her look at him.

"I'm grand," she said, holding up a half-empty glass of dark liquid. Her eyes were slightly reddened and wet, and her neck was flushed.

"I can see that," Simon said. He gently took her glass from her hand and smelled it. "Not your normal poison, is it?" he asked, setting it down just outside her reach.

"What difference does it make?" she said. "Or is someone going to decide that for me, too? No bourbon. No daisies. No gazebo. No picante dip—" Her whole expression changed then. "Oh, I want some picante dip," she said, moving toward the kitchen.

"Quinn," he said, holding her arm. "What happened with Eric?"

Suddenly, Simon didn't want to leave. He didn't like the idea of leaving her there, three sheets to the wind and upset.

"Eric?" she said, laughing bitterly as she ran a finger under her right eye. "No cobbler. No brownstone. No job. That's what happened with Eric."

Simon stared at her, trying to piece together her babbling.

"Simon?" Stacey said, appearing at his side. She sighed heavily. "I have to go."

He frowned. "What?"

"Four-car accident on the highway," she said, her expression already falling into work mode. "I have to get there now." She tilted her head with truly disappointed eyes. "I'm sorry. Tomorrow night?"

Simon touched her cheek. "I'm back at the station tomorrow night," he said, smiling at her. "But it's okay, Stace."

"God, our timing sucks," Stacey said, shoving her phone back into her bag and trading it for her keys. She glanced at Quinn and then back at Simon, giving him a knowing look. "Then again."

"I'll walk you out," he said quickly.

"I'm good, Simon," she said on a chuckle, reaching up to kiss his cheek in a very sexy, seductive way. "Ten bucks says this makes her crazy jealous," she whispered in his ear.

Simon poked her gently in the ribs to make her jump and then rocked her in a hug as she laughed. "You're bad," he said against her ear.

"Gotta go," she whispered back.

"Be careful," he said, squeezing her hand as she walked away. "And hey," he said.

"Yeah?"

"Thank you."

She smiled and winked before disappearing around the corner.

Turning back to Quinn, or where he thought Quinn was, he was met with open space. Scanning the room of people as they laughed and drank and ate, he finally spotted her in the kitchen perusing the food choices. That was good. She needed to eat. So she hadn't seen Stacey's little show. That was well enough. Her theory was probably bunk anyway.

Hannah walked up and linked her arm through her brother's. "You look deep in thought," she said. "Where's your date?"

"She had a work emergency," Simon said. "Had to go. Where'd Eric storm off to?"

"Asshole-land," Hannah said. "He left. So help me make sure Quinn doesn't get drunk and strip or something just to spite him. She has nothing on under that dress and she might forget that with all the bourbon she's sucking down."

"She—what?" Simon asked, looking at his sister.

Hannah rolled her eyes. "Be a big boy, Simon," she said, sauntering away to talk to the happy bride and groom.

Simon turned his gaze back to Quinn, and—Jesus, that image about did him in. "What the living hell are the women in my life trying to do to me tonight?"

The women in his life.

No, Simon.

No.

Chapter Eight

Quinn stared unseeing at the smorgasbord of food swimming in front of her.

Why? Why was the image of Stacey kissing Simon kicking her in the gut repeatedly? She just kissed him on the damn cheek! God help her if he'd actually kissed his date good-bye for real. *His date*. And the way they'd hugged playfully and laughed together—Miss I Save the World and Feed the Homeless. She really was Wonder Woman.

And Eric—Quinn shook her head and then had to grab the counter from the spin that caused. Eric, that asshole.

"Asshole," she said, echoing the word.

"Too bad he can't hear you," Hannah said, suddenly appearing at her right. "Why don't we get some gumbo and go sit outside and eat?"

"I'm not hungry," Quinn lied. She was starving. But the food kept moving and the fact that a wrecking ball kept slamming into her chest didn't help.

"Well, I'm hungry," Hannah said. "So load up a plate of finger food and you can sit and watch *me* eat."

"Three years," Quinn said, looking up and blinking to bring Hannah into focus. "Three years, two of them with this!" she said, waving her left hand around to show the offending bling. "And he's never said any of these things. He's never been my mother before. She—she voodooed him."

"Your mother knows voodoo?" Hannah asked, popping a tiny bacon-wrapped pepper into her mouth.

"I wouldn't put it past her," Quinn said.

"She is kind of scary."

"Maybe he didn't mean it," Quinn said. "Maybe—I mean, surely, right?" She walked away from the food and toward the assortment of bottles and soda.

"Hey, let's dial back the happy juice and eat first," Hannah said.

"Getting some Coke," Quinn said, pouring her glass half full. "And some flavor," she added, picking up a bottle of Jim Beam.

"Quinn—"

"I'll eat," Quinn said, holding the bottle out of Hannah's reach. "I just—I just need to be a little drunk," she said.

Hannah laughed. "A little?"

"I never get drunk," Quinn said, pointing the bottle at her.

"I know."

"So I'm due," Quinn said.

"Maybe," Hannah said. "But there are a lot of people here," she said. "Try to keep yourself together."

"Some people left," Quinn said, pouring the dark liquid into her glass. "Eric left."

"Yes he did."

"Asshole."

"Yes he is," Hannah quipped.

"Wonder Woman left—did you meet her?" Quinn asked.

"Wonder Woman?"

"Simon's *date*," Quinn emphasized. "She can leap tall buildings in a single dress."

Hannah laughed and Quinn turned questioningly, smiling, too. She'd said something funny.

"Yes, I heard she had to go," Hannah said. "I thought she was nice. You didn't like her?"

"No, no, no, she was nice," Quinn said. "Simon did good."

The flash of his hand on the small of Stacey's back and the cheek-kiss and the ear-whisper with her hand on his face—all took her breath away at the same time.

"Shit," she muttered, setting down her newly filled glass so hard that liquid sloshed over the edges.

"What?" Hannah asked.

"Nothing."

"Come on," Hannah said, tugging at her arm. "Get you some food. It's awesome."

"I don't get awesome food," Quinn said, nearly at a whine, because damn it, that was the point, wasn't it?

"Sure you do," Hannah said, making a sweeping gesture around the kitchen. "It's all right here." She waved a hand at Quinn and grabbed a plastic bowl. "You know what? Suit yourself. I'm eating."

Quinn picked up one of the bacon-wrapped peppers. "See? This would be perfect." She popped it into her mouth and closed her eyes. "Moft dffnnmmm-mmmm."

"Yeah, try out about twenty more of those," Hannah mumbled, ladling gumbo over rice.

"Amazing," Quinn added after she swallowed. "I should bring one to my mom," she said, grabbing another.

"You might want to"—Hannah watched as Quinn opened her bag and dropped the little dynamo in—"wrap it in something," Hannah finished, holding up her spoon. "Never mind."

Quinn picked up her glass and watched the sweet dark liquid

swirl. It looked calming. She needed calm. She needed away from the turmoil in her head. The chaotic mess that was about assholes and brunettes and food and jobs and red dresses.

"I'm gonna go walk around outside or something," she said. "Get some airs."

"You mean air," Hannah said.

"No, I want them all," Quinn said, stepping over a dish towel that had landed on the floor.

"Okay, just one thing," Hannah said, approaching her with a snarky grin and setting her bowl down. She lifted the tiny flap on Quinn's purse and cringed before pulling out her keys with a finger and a thumb. "I'll take these," she said, adding under her breath, "and wash them."

"Knock yourself out," Quinn said, patting her arm.

Outside wasn't different, she noticed when she closed the back patio door behind her, just warmer. And magic, evidently, because she didn't remember walking there. Kinley was scarfing down a bowl of gumbo like she'd never had it before. Quinn tapped her shoulder.

"Did you see me walk out here?" Quinn whispered. Kinley raised her eyebrows in a question. "It's okay if you say no. I believe in that stuff."

Kinley pointed. "No, you just came out that door."

Quinn tilted her head and kept walking. "Hmm."

"Quinn, honey? You okay?" Miss Lou asked, rising from a chair.

"I'm perfect," Quinn said, hoping she'd pulled the facial expression to show that. She chuckled to further the proof. "Just thought I'd come get some fresh air for a bit."

"Okay," Miss Lou said, narrowing her eyes. "Can I get you something? Some chips and dip? Gumbo?"

Everybody sure wanted to feed her tonight.

"I'm good right now," Quinn said. "But thank you."

She wandered among the chairs, where a few guests sat talking and eating, balancing bowls and plastic plates laden with various goodies that weren't matched up or tied with monogrammed ribbons or planned for their complementary colors. They were there just because Maddi chose them. As beautifully simple as that. Just because—

"What the hell?" Quinn muttered, her thoughts interrupted as her bare feet landed on grass. She turned back, and yep, there were her shoes, heels impaled into the soft earth like they'd been planted there. She'd walked right out of them. "Good place for you," she said, flicking her fingers at them.

The old bench nestled between two trees at the edge of the property called to her to come sit. Which was a hell of a thing, seeing as it also sat at the edge of a creek. Nothing at the edge of any body of water ever called to her in any fashion—in fact, she avoided anything deeper than a hot tub as a general rule.

But Quinn's back suddenly ached, her feet were getting soggy, and something about the sereneness of the scene made her want peace in the worst way. Maybe sitting there watching the dusk fall over the water would calm her troubled mind. Stranger things had happened. She scooted tightly against the bench just in case her unstable feet decided to throw her in the creek, and then sat down.

"Okay, mind," she whispered, taking a large swallow of what was left of her drink. "Dial it back, will you?"

Simon didn't know how long Quinn sat there staring out at the quickly disappearing water, but he knew as darkness fell that he couldn't continue to just watch her shadow from the window. He'd known she never learned to swim, but until tonight that was just random information. He never knew there was a bad experience tied to it, and as inebriated as she was, she had no business being that close to the creek.

Zach and Maddi had snuck out, not wanting a big fanfare, and most of the guests had trickled out afterward. Hannah had left with Monroe—not that Simon wanted to know what that was about— but she had checked on Quinn once before she left and reported back that she had enlisted one of the junior crew members to keep bringing her drinks.

Great.

Hot, half naked, and wasted.

Simon had had his fair share of alcohol as well, but not nearly enough to handle that combination gracefully. He ran his fingers through his hair and blew out a breath. Before tonight, he could talk to Quinn about anything. Well, mostly anything. But he'd certainly never been knocked around by the thought of talking to her alone. They were friends—close friends. Outside of Zach, she was his best friend.

Tonight there had been a lightning strike of epic proportions, at least from his perspective. Something had gone incredibly weird, and he had no way to explain it.

It's mutual.

Fuck.

Opening the back door, two young crew guys nodded at him, kicked back in a couple of chairs, enjoying a smoke.

"We cut her off a half hour ago," one of them said in a hushed tone.

"Been keeping an eye on her, though," the other guy said—a junior cameraman named Casey. "She doesn't want to come in, and doesn't want to talk."

"Thanks, guys," Simon said. "I'll take it from here."

They ground out their cigarettes and got up, and Casey slapped Simon's shoulder as he passed. Simon's shoes sunk into the soft sod as he crossed the yard, and he nearly stepped on a pair of women's heels stuck in the ground. Pulling them from the ground, he let them dangle from his fingers as he rounded the bench.

"You seem to have trouble keeping up with shoes lately," Simon said, glancing up at the trees. "Or we have a tree troll that's gonna be missing these."

"I'm the tree troll," Quinn said, lifting her feet and wiggling her toes.

Simon set the shoes on the end of the bench and sat down next to her. Not close enough to touch, but he could feel her just the same. Smell the vanilla and berries still clinging to her.

"Yeah, I don't think you quite qualify for troll status," he said.

"I don't know," she said, running a finger under each eye and under her nose. "Others might disagree."

She'd been crying. Alone. *Damn it.* He wanted to touch her, hold her, be a friend, but—but what? Hell if he knew.

"Others like—Eric?"

"We're not talking about him," she said, her words falling out fast and a little slurred.

"Okay," Simon said.

"His name is he-who-shall-not-be-named," she said.

Simon bit back a chuckle. "Got it."

"So how long have you and Stacey been together?" she asked, staring forward.

"We're not together," he said.

Quinn cut him a look that even the pretwilight darkness couldn't hide.

"Please, you were so together," she said. "And that's okay!"

"No, seriously—"

"Seriously, you deserve a smart, independent woman like that," she said. "Someone with no strings."

Okay, now he was officially confused.

"Strings?" he asked.

"Puppet strings," she said slowly, lifting up her arms as if an invisible puppeteer were moving her. "You're a lucky guy."

He studied her profile in the dark. Eric was the lucky one. He was about to get *her*. Hell, he already had her.

"You think people are pulling your strings?" Simon said.

Quinn threw back her head and laughed. "You know, I never knew I had them until tonight?" She held up her hands. "I mean, I saw the little marks," she said, pointing at tiny freckles on her arms. "I kind of suspected, but I never saw them come out of their hiding places till today."

"Quinn, you aren't a puppet," Simon said, nudging her. "I think you need to stand up to your mother more, that's true, but nobody yanks you around."

"You don't," she said, looking his way. All he could see was the shine of her eyes. "You never tell me what to do, or how to do it, or tell me I can't cut my hair—"

"You want to cut your hair?"

"I just told you that earlier," she said.

"Sorry, I was distracted," he said. It wasn't a lie.

"Okay, so maybe you don't have the best attention span," she said, waving her hands around for some reason. "But you don't put down my choices, or make fun of me—"

He didn't know where she was going with this, but before he could ask, she got up, teetering far to the left.

"Whoa," he said, reaching out to steady her.

"See?" she said, laughing as she pointed. "You always take care of me. You always look out for me."

"I always will," he said before he could think, looking up at her. *Don't go there. Say something else.* "But Eric will, too."

"Gah!" she said, backing up and holding out a palm. "I said *not-be-named.*"

Simon chuckled. "Sorry."

"You know, I used to have a bucket list," Quinn said, changing the subject so fast Simon had to blink twice to keep up with her. She turned and twirled in place at the edge of the drop-off, and he leapt up just in time to grab her by the waist and yank her to him.

"Quinn!"

"Oh!" she gasped as her body crushed against his.

Fuck if he didn't damn near have a heart attack and a raging boner at the same time.

"Shit, Quinn, you nearly stepped off the damn bank," he said, pointing as he backed up with her still in his arms.

She looked down behind her at the two-foot drop and the dark water below. Not life-threatening, but could definitely break an ankle and freak the hell out of someone afraid of water.

"See?" she said again, her voice going a little breathless.

She was too close. Her body felt too fucking good against his, especially knowing how little she had on. He could feel her breathing, and her face was right there, and—

"I might be a little drunk," she whispered.

"You think?" Simon said through his teeth. "Come sit back down."

He was her friend and he wasn't about to take advantage of the situation, but he wasn't a damn saint, either. With everything he had in him, he released her and tugged at her hand. She pulled free and lowered to the grass by the bench instead, tucking her legs to the side. Sighing, Simon sank to the ground next to her, using the bench as a backrest.

"So tell me about this bucket list," he said, trying to discreetly move his dick away from his zipper. Wasn't working.

He watched her close her eyes in the darkness. "Hannah and I both made one," she said. "We wrote them down years ago and never showed them to each other. Said we'd only show when we'd checked off everything."

"And what's on yours?" Simon asked.

She chuckled. "Oh, travel, adventure," she said. "The normal stuff. Zip-lining. Riding an elephant."

"An elephant?" Simon said. "Really?"

"Of course," she said. "And skydiving."

"Checked any of that off yet?"

Quinn scoffed. "He doesn't even want me chasing rain in a car," she said, her tone acidic. "You think he'll be on board for skydiving?"

"Is this he-who-shall-not-be-named?" Simon asked.

"Or ass hat," she said, flipping a hand in the air.

Simon laughed. "What?"

"It's shorter."

He laughed harder, amazed that this woman could still surprise him after so many years.

"I can't have daisies," she said then.

Simon leaned his head back against the bench and shook it. "Help me here."

"At my wedding," she clarified. "No daisies. No cobbler."

"And you want cobbler?"

"So much. And daisies," she said, nodding.

"Well, yeah, that goes without saying."

A giggle escaped her lips after a pause, and then it died as quickly as it came.

"Strings," she said softly, lifting an arm. "You see them now?"

Was he that far gone that she was starting to make sense?

"You have to start somewhere, Little Bit," he said. "Pick a small battle and stay on your feet till you win."

She blinked. "A small battle."

"Even one just for you," he said. "Something you don't have to fight them over. Something they can't take away."

"My bucket list," she whispered.

"Your bucket list?"

"There's one thing on there they could never take away," she said so softly he almost couldn't hear her.

"What's that?" he asked.

"Kissing Simon Chase."

Chapter Nine

Her head was spinning madly, and she couldn't focus on any one thing. She closed one eye to stop the separations, but they split anyway. Damn it, there were still two of him, and both of them looked delicious in the dark.

"What did you say?" Simon said, his voice sounding odd.

"You are always there for me, Simon," she said, her words on a delay. Like when you watch a movie and the sound doesn't match the lips. That's what it was. She was on a movie reel and her words would come out later. She reached for his face so she could see him. "Always there. You catch me if I fall. You zip up my dress. You would never make me quit my job or give up my coffee mugs."

Simon was looking at her funny as she touched his face. Even in the dark she could see the look—*that* look. That one from earlier that he wasn't giving to Wonder Woman. The one that at this proximity felt like it had supermagnets in it, pulling her in. The stubble that was growing back on his jaw felt rough against her fingers.

"Coffee mugs are important," he said, his voice low.

"Exactly!" she said, her eyelids having trouble coming back up from a blink. When they did, her stomach did a body slam against all the other organs. Simon's blue eyes were very dark in the low light from the back patio, in a face that was very close. And her fingers were exploring it. "Bucket list," she whispered.

"That again?"

She smiled. He was being funny. Simon Chase was funny. "Kissing Simon Chase was number four," she said, the words little more than puffs of air as she threaded her fingers into his hair. "I wanted to do this."

She pulled his face the remaining few inches until his lips met hers, and then everything dizzy spiraled into that one union. His lips were hot and soft and sweet and salty at the same time. They moved on hers tenderly, tasting, testing, and when his tongue touched hers it was better than she could have imagined. She sighed into his mouth, feeling his hands in her hair, feeling his mouth claim hers, feeling her body let go.

She was kissing Simon Chase. *She was kissing Simon Chase.*

Wait . . .

She couldn't just let go. There was a reason she—but oh, God, he dove deeper, cradling her head in his arms as he explored her mouth like a man starved. She was starving, too, and she wanted—oh, God she wanted—

And she wasn't pulling away.

She was talking and then she was touching him and then before he could process what was happening, her mouth was on his. That incredible mouth was on his and she was pulling him in for more. Everything in his being said to push her away but this was Quinn, damn it. This was Quinn. And he wasn't just kissing her. She was giving it back. Going full steam and then running her tongue along his lips to taste him before twisting her fingers in his hair like a lover and kissing him like they were about to be.

Fuck, he was only human.

Holding the back of her head and feeling the silky strands of her hair caress his hand, he cradled her face with the other and dove deeper into her mouth. Tasting her, needing her, feeling her sigh into his kiss and sending his dick so painfully into his zipper, he was pretty sure there would be marks.

She tasted like vanilla and bourbon, and something sweet and uniquely Quinn that he knew he could never have enough of. And then the bourbon popped back into his own alcohol-tinged thoughts, and little bells rang. Annoying bells that reminded him he wasn't that guy.

Just as she pulled back and tried to look at him.

"Quinn," he said, breathless against her lips.

"Mmm, you taste so good," she sighed against his.

God, he wasn't that strong. He tugged her closer, letting his fingers tangle in her hair as she wrapped both arms around his head and kissed him with—fuck, with her whole body. It was unlike anything he could have ever imagined with her. But something poked at him. Something that wasn't delicious and warm and wanting him. He had to—he had to stop. With great difficulty he pulled back from her and let her go, unable to trust himself that close.

"Little Bit," he said softly, running a finger over her bottom lip in lieu of kissing it again. "Hey. Look at me."

Her eyes started the struggle up to his, telling him all he needed to know. She didn't know what she was doing. She didn't even know who she was kissing. What the hell was he thinking?

"Hey," she said, a sleepy smile pulling at her lips.

"What are we doing?" he asked.

"*I'm* kissing," she said slowly, a laugh bubbling up. "What are you doing?"

"Uh-huh," he said, running a hand over his face. *Get it together.* "Who are you kissing?"

She chuckled. "Weren't you there?"

He had to grin. She was so damn adorable. So fucking sexy with her lips all puffy from his kisses.

"Who were you kissing, Quinn?" he repeated.

"Simon Chase," she said, then one eyebrow dipped down. "I kissed Simon Chase. Oh . . ." she added, the word fading off.

"What?" he asked.

"I probably wasn't supposed to do that," she said, touching her own lips. Her eyes fluttered closed, and she leaned her head in against his chest. "Damn it, I did something crazy, didn't I?"

That's what it was about. She was mad at Eric.

"Maybe," he said, resting his chin on the top of her head. "But it's okay."

"I get to check something off my list," she said on a sigh.

Simon shook his head. "That, you do."

"I was so stupid tonight," she said, her words tumbling together against his shirt. "Trying to be different, kicky, naked—"

Don't go there.

"No underwear," she said, flitting a hand as if it were nothing. "Tried to be sexy but it didn't work."

"Oh, it worked," Simon muttered, thinking of the operation he was going to need to straighten his dick back out. He looked down at her falling asleep on his chest, her hair falling across her face. She looked like an angel. But she wasn't his angel.

She hadn't ditched the undies for him—she'd done that for Eric, and then they'd had a fight. And then she drank too much. And then some part of her from the past that put him on a bucket list once started flirting with him, and he jumped on it like a starving man and they fell headfirst into a pond they had no business swimming in.

No pun intended.

"Hey, let's get you to bed," he said, moving her hair out of her eyes. "Alone," he added quickly.

"Mmm," she grunted, not moving.

"Yeah," he whispered.

Adjusting her weight so that he could leverage his, he pushed to his knees, then to his feet, praying his own buzz didn't take them both down. After one questionable step to gain his balance after looping her shoes on his fingers, he shifted her in his arms and walked slowly back to the house.

Thankfully his mother was walking out just about the time he was wondering how he was going to open the door.

"Oh!" she cried, startled. "Jesus, Simon, you scared—what the hell?"

"She passed out," Simon said.

"I thought you all were gone!" Miss Lou said, lowering her voice to a whisper.

"Not quite," he said. "Can you hold open the door? I'm gonna put her in Hannah's bed."

"Good idea," Miss Lou said. "I'll get some aspirin, too. She's gonna need it when she wakes up."

"Get some for me, too, please," Simon said. "I'm gonna need it now."

As the blood decided it wasn't needed elsewhere, it was all rushing back to his head with a vengeance.

His mom gave him a look he didn't have the brainpower to deal with, and he hoped she didn't feel the need to voice that particular opinion. He wasn't up for it. Not tonight. Not now.

Simon made it to Hannah's old room and laid Quinn in the bed, setting her shoes by the nightstand. The dress had to be uncomfortable to sleep in, but he wasn't going there. Especially knowing there was nothing underneath it. He found a light blanket and covered her, pushing her hair from her eyes again as his mother set a glass of water and two pills on the nightstand.

"She'll be fine," she said, handing him two pills as well. "What about you?"

He palmed the pills and tossed them to the back of his throat, picking up the water and stealing a swallow.

"I'm good," he said. "I'll just walk down to Zach's, I have a key. My stuff is there."

"You're not driving home—"

"No, Mom," he said, hugging her neck. "I'll crash over there tonight."

"There's still a bed in your and Eli's old room," she said. "Or the couch."

They left Hannah's room and shut the door, and Simon laid a hand on the door jamb, letting out a breath.

"I need to not be here, Mom," he said, shaking his head. "Not right now."

When he looked back at her, she was looking straight through to his thoughts, and he started walking. He didn't want to hear it.

"Be careful, son," she said.

He turned and winked at her, grabbing his jacket off the back of a chair. "It's a two-minute walk, I'll be good," he said with a grin.

"I'm not talking about the walk, baby."

He backed up a couple of steps and turned for the door.

"I know."

She was slamming her head against a door, over and over. Quinn kept yelling at herself to stop, but she couldn't. And then she realized that something else had control and was standing behind her with a fire bell, clanging it every time it pushed her into the door. She flailed around behind her for whatever it was, trying to make it stop, but her hand slammed into something hard and on the way back, something moved and sprayed her in the face with water.

Quinn sucked in a breath—the clanging, still the clanging—

"What the hell?" she yelled, her voice hoarse, bolting upright in bed. "Oh, son of a—" she moaned, curling back into a fetal position with the pillow over her head to block the screaming sunlight.

Tiny trolls were ripping holes in her brain with grenade launchers. And she was wet—her head was soaked and so was the pillow. And the side of the bed where she felt blindly with one hand.

Peeking out from her cave with squinty eyes, she spied an empty water glass laying on its side. Water dripped down the side of the nightstand.

"Great," Quinn whispered, pushing the pillow back down.

Bells from hell exploded behind her, resuming the clanging from her dream and sending her tumbling out of the bed.

"Gah!" she sputtered, tears springing to her eyes with the pain in her head from the sudden movement. Her phone was ringing from somewhere in the bed. "Make it stop," she cried, yanking all the covers onto the floor with her till her phone came bouncing down, too.

Picking it up with shaky hands, she turned it over clumsily, desperate to end the infernal noise. Phoebe's name was sprawled across the screen.

"Shit," Quinn muttered, blowing out a breath and then recoiling from it. She touched the answer button. "Hello?" she whispered.

"Quinn?" came her sister's voice screeching over the line.

"Down," Quinn croaked in a grimace.

"Down?" Phoebe echoed.

"Voice," Quinn responded, holding the phone away from her head. "Down, please."

"Ooookay," she responded, talking just above a whisper. "Why am I whispering?"

"Because I'm dead," Quinn said.

"Well, hell, that sucks," Phoebe said.

Quinn curled in the wadded up bedding. "You have no idea."

"I take it the wedding was quite the party?" Phoebe asked.

"Evidently," Quinn said. "I'm not at home."

"Where are you?"

Quinn blinked slowly, grabbing the naked bed next to her for grounding as the room moved with her.

"I—I think—Hannah's old room at the Chases'," Quinn said. "But then again, it could be hell." Her gaze froze on the image across the room. It was her. Looking back at herself in a full-length mirror, still in last night's dress, looking like a deranged mental patient.

Her eye makeup was smeared all down her cheeks, her hair matted and wet on one side and doing some sort of giant salute on the other.

"I think something took a shit in my mouth," she said, holding the phone away again as Phoebe laughed in her ear.

"Weren't you just the party girl?" she said.

"No," Quinn said, trying to pull her hair down from the sky. She saw two pills on the floor next to the bed, glanced up at the overturned glass, and a few logical dots connected.

Bless you, Miss Lou.

"Eric and I got in a fight," Quinn said, scooping the pills from the floor and tossing them into her mouth. The taste couldn't get any worse in there.

"Uh-oh, what kind of fight?"

"He left the wedding reception alone, kind of fight," Quinn said.

Something else was swimming around up there with all the fermented liquor she'd absorbed. Something important.

"Oh, shit," Phoebe said.

"Yeah."

"Is it serious?"

Was it serious? Quinn couldn't remember all of it, but her gut told her it wasn't something to blow off. She remembered the job conversation. Her head hurt too much to find the rest.

"Probably not," Quinn said, trying to push to her feet. "I'm sure we're fine. Just prewedding crap. Probably we just—oh—"

The room went sideways as she raised up on shaky legs, and she went back down on her knees.

"I gotta go, Pheebs," she said on a whisper, feeling her whole body break out in a sickly sweat.

"Oh, Lord, pull your hair back and call me later," Phoebe said. "Don't forget dinner and shopping tonight—"

Dinner did it. Quinn dropped the phone, crawling on all fours to the bathroom as fast as she could. The lid almost didn't lift quickly enough before everything she'd ever eaten in her life came up with a vengeance. Her body took over, expelling toxic waste with one convulsion after another.

God, she was going to die. There was no air. It was like drowning. She knew a little bit about that. Her delirium swam through the memory of pressure on her lungs as the water tightened around her body. She choked out a cough and gulped in the foul-smelling air, her head pounding mercilessly with the exertion. The imagery cleared with the oxygen. As it should. There was no comparison. Back then had a purpose. This was just stupid.

She flushed and laid her head on her arm and took deep breaths until the next round of retching began. God, she was so stupid, so

130

foolhardy, so ridiculous for drinking so much. Not eating anything. Going outside—

The cold sweat that broke out anew had nothing to do with her hangover. Hot tears burned her eyes as she struggled to breathe normally.

"Oh, my God," Quinn croaked, shutting her eyes tight. She pushed away from the toilet and moved to sit against the opposite wall, letting the whiskey-soaked memory unravel slowly, second by microsecond. The things she said, the things she—the way he tasted. The way he kissed her back. "Oh, my God, what have I done?"

There were better questions to be asked, like *What the hell am I going to do now* and how she could possibly erase Simon's memory of that whole—

"Shit," she muttered, burying her face in her hands. How was she ever going to face him? Or Eric? Or herself, for that matter? There was a mirror up there over the sink and she was already plotting how to wash up without looking in it.

Quinn's stomach roiled for a third round, and she pulled herself back around the porcelain to ride out the wave. Someone would come for her eventually, and she needed to be past this.

Christ, who was she kidding? There would never be a *past this*.

Chapter Ten

Simon stared at the ceiling above Zach's couch, at the same three dots he'd been analyzing all night as he drifted in and out of a fitful horny nonsleep. He heard the coffee pot turn on, smelled the distinct aroma that meant he was supposed to be awake now, unlike the six other hours he'd already logged.

He'd fantasized about Quinn in probably every possible way over the years, including some things he probably wouldn't tell her even if they were married for fifty years. But nothing compared to touching her for real. To feeling her under his hands, to tasting her with total abandon, to the feel of her fingers clawing into his hair as she sighed with desire—God, every time he got to that part and thought about her with nothing on under that dress and how easy it would have been to slide a hand up her thigh and—

Needless to say, it had been a long night.

Not just because of the sexual frustration, because he could have taken care of that. He didn't want to. Fuck, he didn't want to.

Because that whole little scenario that had probably topped out at fifteen—twenty minutes, tops—had changed everything. Not for her. Hell, no, nothing would change for her. But for Simon, everything that had always just felt like a fantasy, a thought, a wish, a dream that was outside his reach and nothing that could ever be real, was suddenly live and in color. He had touched real. He'd kissed real, and she had kissed him back. Kissed him *first*.

He had wanted it before but accepted that it wouldn't happen. That acceptance was gone now. And that was bad. Because now he didn't want to just fantasize about it. He wanted the real thing, the real girl, the whole package, and she was still going to walk down the aisle and put another man's ring on her finger.

Now it was going to hurt.

His phone rang from the end table, and he grunted himself into a sitting position, grimacing as his head pounded out a good-morning rhythm. A little too much imbibing, maybe, but nothing compared to what Quinn must be feeling.

"Hello," he said, not even looking.

"Hey," Hannah said. "Did they call you?"

"They—they who?" Simon asked, rubbing at his dry eyes.

"Well, Mom called me," she said. "Nicole called her and asked if it was okay if the new Maddi showed up at the house this morning with the crew."

Simon's thoughts swirled with her words. Maybe he was more hungover than he thought.

"The new who?"

"New Maddi," Hannah said. "Her assistant. Some guy named Charlie. You didn't hear?"

"Well, Nicole was spouting something about how the show must go on," he said, swinging his legs down and scrubbing his fingers through his hair. "But I thought we were taking a few days off."

"So did I," Hannah said. "I have to go do a photo shoot in a couple of hours, but I'm swinging by Mom's first because this guy's wanting a meeting of some sort. So I'm giving you a heads-up."

Great. "Okay."

"Hey, and Quinn never came home last night and didn't answer her phone just now," Hannah said, sending a virtual fist to Simon's gut. "Did she stay, or go to Eric's? Do you know?"

Well, he did physically lay her in the bed. *Put* her. He put her in the bed.

"She stayed at Mom's," Simon said, his voice sounding like someone else was talking. "I—Mom set her up in your old room."

"Good," Hannah said. "So she's probably still there. I'll bring her some clothes."

"Yeah," Simon said, suddenly wanting out of his own skin. "Okay, see you there."

He hung up and tossed the phone on the couch next to him, leaning over on his knees. No more time to dwell. But shit.

Thank God for Maddi's influence and the presence of a coffeemaker. He got up and poured himself a cup and walked to the shower, glad he'd brought a gym bag with a change of clothes just in case he'd need to crash. Stepping into the shower, he hesitated for the briefest of seconds. He was about to wash all traces of her off him.

"Quit being a woman," he muttered, stepping under the stream.

If it was done, it was done. No matter how much he wanted otherwise, he probably would never get another chance. He hadn't even really got the first one. She was just drunk. He needed to let it go.

The water pelted him, steaming everything away. Melting everything away. He hung his head under the shower and watched the water swirl all his demons down the drain.

It wasn't working.

The knock on the door nearly sent Quinn running for the toilet again.

"Quinn, honey?"

It was just Miss Lou. *Just* Miss Lou?

Simon's mother. Oh, dear God, what if she saw?

"Are you awake?" she called through the door with another light rap of her knuckles.

Quinn broke out in a fresh sweat walking to the door. Her hands were still shaking, but at least she'd washed her face and found some mouth wash under the sink. Reaching for the knob, she forced a smile.

"Yes, ma'am," she said as she opened the door. A fresh wave of too-much-movement swam through her body, and she gripped the knob a little tighter.

"Oh—" Miss Lou said, managing a sympathetic chuckle. "Oh, honey, you look like the walking dead."

Well, that was encouraging. She reached up with her other hand to push down on the crown of her head. It kept the pounding to a dull hammer.

"That's about the size of it," Quinn said softly.

Miss Lou laughed aloud, and Quinn's outermost nerve endings keeled over and went into a fetal position.

Miss Lou grimaced and clapped a hand over her mouth, lowering her voice to a whisper. "Sorry, baby. Did you find the aspirin I left for you?"

"Yes, thank you so much," Quinn said, touching the older woman's arm. "I am so sorry you even had to deal with me like that." She closed her eyes. "I am so embarrassed."

"I just snagged you a couple of pills," Miss Lou said, waving a hand. "Simon carried you to bed."

The room moved again as her knees went soft.

"He—carried—"

135

Miss Lou chuckled. "Sweetheart, you were out cold. He brought you in the house, put you to bed, and walked down to sleep at Zach's."

Just when she thought the morning couldn't get any worse. *Oh, my God.* Simon carried her in like a drunken rag doll. Yeah, nothing says sexy after making out like—passing out. Not that it mattered. It didn't matter.

"Jesus," Quinn muttered, rubbing her eyes.

"Don't sweat it honey," Miss Lou said, laying a hand on Quinn's back. "I heard you and Eric had an argument." *Oh, God.* "We've all been there." *That doesn't make it better. That doesn't make it okay.*

"Well, I'll be out of your hair in just a—"

"Actually, that's what I was coming to tell you," Miss Lou said. "Hannah's bringing you some clothes. Maddi's assistant is here with a small crew already this morning."

Quinn frowned. "What?"

"I know," Miss Lou said. "I wasn't expecting it, either. I had my cleaning lady coming today to clear out the mess."

"They're filming?" Quinn asked, incredulous.

"I don't think so," she answered. "I think it's just a meet and greet and—well, who knows?"

"Fabulous," Quinn said, covering her face with her hands.

"I have biscuits to—"

"Mmm—" Quinn moaned, turning one palm outward. "Please don't say—"

"Sorry," Miss Lou said, leaning in to hug her. "You finish up what you need to do and I'll send Hannah in with your clothes when she gets here."

"Thank you, Miss Lou," Quinn said, feeling like an errant teenager instead of a thirty-year-old woman. "I should probably call my sister back, too," she said, looking at her phone still lying on the floor. "And Eric."

"Well, I'll leave you to it," Miss Lou said, clicking the door shut behind her with a wink.

Eric.

Quinn felt hot tears burn the backs of her eyes.

Fight or not, what she did was wrong. She'd been out of her mind, but Eric would never forgive her. And Simon—that was the purest hell of it, more even than Eric. And maybe that in itself said something, but it was how she felt. Simon was her best friend. And she'd—crossed over. Way over. Because that was no innocent curiosity last night. That was real.

That was past real.

She called Phoebe back and confirmed that yes, she would survive, and yes, she would still go shopping with her but not till tomorrow because she had to work tonight. And no, there would be no dinner. Ever. She was swearing off food for the unforeseeable future.

Quinn was still staring at the dark screen of her phone when another knock sounded at her door, followed with its opening by someone who didn't care if she was ready or not.

Hannah stood there in dress Capris and a sleeveless V-neck sweater, looking like a million bucks, with a plastic grocery bag dangling from her fingers.

"Hey, sunshine," she said. Too loud.

"I'm not done puking," Quinn said, pressing her palms against her temples. "And judging from this morning's history, I can hit you with it from here."

"Yikes," Hannah said in a softer tone, tossing the bag on the bed. "That bad, huh?" She did a double take at the comforter wadded up on the floor.

"Remember when I had the flu last year?" Quinn asked, climbing back onto the bed and curling herself around the bag.

"Yeah."

Quinn gave a thumbs-up. "That was candy."

"Damn."

"Ugh," Quinn said, rubbing the back of her neck, damp again with sickly sweat. "Candy. Bad example."

"So you're looking . . ." Hannah let the words trail.

"Like I've been poisoned, stabbed, and hit by a truck?" Quinn finished.

"Well, I was gonna say dead, but we can go with yours," Hannah said. "I take it you didn't slow down after I left. Or eat anything."

"Don't say eat," Quinn muttered.

"Hear anything more from the dickwad?" Hannah asked.

"No."

"He'll call," Hannah said. "Just get your ducks in a row while you're waiting."

She thought Quinn was waiting on him to call and apologize. Oddly, that hadn't even crossed Quinn's mind. Maybe because his actions seemed so trivial now. Or no—they didn't. She was still pissed. He had still blindsided her with a perspective he'd never brought up before. Had he just been biding his time, waiting till they tied the knot to strip her of her identity and park her behind a web designer desk for eternity?

That was too much thought for not enough living brain cells.

"God, I smell bacon," Quinn said, burying her nose in the bare sheet.

"Mom's cooking some," Hannah said.

"No, I mean like—it's on me, strong and—"

"Where's your purse?" Hannah asked.

"What?" Quinn said, lifting her head.

"Purse?"

Quinn pointed to the floor, behind her shoes. Hannah picked it up, opened the flap, and jerked her face away.

"Yeah, that's what I thought," she said with a grimace, lifting a dilapidated bacon-wrapped pepper from its confines, barbecue sauce congealing on it.

Quinn clapped a hand over her mouth as her stomach convulsed, then stumbled to the bathroom, not even bothering to shut the door. Up came another round of not much, ending in dry heaves and tears as she laid her forehead on her arm.

Hannah handed her a towel and flushed.

"Come on," she said.

"I'm good," Quinn hiccuped. "Just let me die."

"Nobody's dying today," Hannah said, pulling Quinn to her feet. "But they are expecting us out there, so come on, clean yourself up again and change your clothes."

"Thank you for the clothes," Quinn whispered.

"You're welcome," Hannah whispered back, sounding suspiciously amused. "I put a toothbrush in there, too. And some body spray."

Quinn paused at the sink and met Hannah's gaze in the mirror. "I love you."

Hannah laughed. "I know."

Quinn blew out a breath and looked into the sink before coming back up to meet her own eyes. She didn't want to, blinking away and looking at Hannah again.

"Why do you look so cute?" she muttered, pulling her hair up in a messy bun.

"I have a photo shoot to do after this," Hannah said. "Whatever *this* is."

"What kind of shoot?"

"Engagement."

"I have to do payroll tonight," Quinn said, shoving a bobby pin into her head extra hard in case it might poke a hole and let the pain leak out. "The way I feel right now, nobody's getting paid."

"Well, get dressed," Hannah said. "They're starting to circle out there."

"Who's starting to circle?" Quinn asked, trying to keep the paranoia out of her tone.

"Everyone," Hannah said.

Everyone.

"So where'd you go last night?" Quinn asked, trying to concentrate on deep breaths that didn't make her want to vomit.

"You noticed I left?" Hannah asked, one hand on a cocked hip.

Quinn glanced at her in the mirror. "No. You said *after I left* a few minutes ago."

"Ah," Hannah said, going back in the room and rummaging in the bag she brought. She came back in and handed Quinn's toothbrush to her. "Left with Monroe."

"Thanks," Quinn said, turning on the water. "So, you and Maddi's brother, huh?"

Hannah got a confused look on her face. "Well—I thought so. Maybe."

"Meaning?"

"I don't know," Hannah said. "It was odd. He brought me to this remote place to sit outside and look at the stars."

"Mm-hmm," Quinn mumbled around the toothbrush.

"I mean, he could have had me on the hood of his truck if he'd asked," Hannah said. "My God, the man is smoking hot." She shook her head.

Quinn spit and wiped her mouth, praying for the spins to stop. "I'm guessing he didn't?"

"Nope."

"Anything?"

"He kissed my hand."

Quinn frowned and turned—slowly. "Your hand?"

Hannah shrugged. "I know."

Quinn blinked in the pause. "Hmm."

"So a make-out spot for the record books," Hannah said, "and nothing. And then he brings me home and kisses my hand. So am I just too tainted to recognize romantic gestures, or was that a blow-off?"

"I guess you'll know if he calls," Quinn said.

"He didn't ask for my number."

"Seriously?"

"So it was a blow-off, right?" Hannah said. "Because I am totally perplexed on this one."

"Well, he is best friends with Eli, and now a brother-in-law to Zach," Quinn said.

"I don't see him asking Eli or Zach for their sister's number," Hannah said, crinkling her nose. "He might have better luck with Simon." She frowned. "Okay, you just went gray again."

The sound of Simon's name in the air made her heart slam against her ribs.

"Baby steps," Quinn said softly.

"Well, I'm going out there. You okay?"

Quinn nodded. "I think so. I'll change and slither my way out."

"All right. See you in a few," Hannah said as she closed the door behind her.

The quiet rang in Quinn's ears.

There was Eric to think about, but right now there was Simon. Right down that hall. Was he thinking about all this, too? Of how the dynamics had changed? Or did guys think like that? He had to remember—if she remembered, he had to. And she remembered every nuance of kissing Simon Chase. The feel of his skin under her fingers, the stubble on his jaw, the softness of his hair, the heat, the smell of him, the way his breathing caught and got faster like hers did, his hands in her hair and on her face. The way she'd wanted him to pull her closer. She remembered that, too.

And his mouth. Oh, dear God, her headache pounded harder as she realized she was holding her breath through the recollection. But Jesus, his mouth. The way he tasted her and took her lips, almost without mercy. It had been better than she'd ever fantasized. And she had fantasized plenty.

He had gotten into it, too. And then he'd stopped them.

Quinn closed her eyes and then popped them back open again as the floor moved under her feet. No eye-closing.

But that thought was just as sickening as the toxicity running through her veins: Simon had stopped them. He had said her name against her lips and stopped her. Asked her what she was doing.

Damn, shit, hell, and so many things. Quinn sank onto the nearly naked bed, pulling jeans and her favorite soft T-shirt—the faded-green one with the cat eyes—out of the plastic bag. Oh, and a pair of panties and a bra. *God bless you, Hannah.* She'd gone commando long enough.

"Oh, shit, I kissed him with no underwear on," she whispered, shaking her head. Not that that made it better or worse, but somehow it just seemed more *something*.

Simon had kissed her back—there was no doubt about that. But he'd been the one to remember reason. To remind her she shouldn't be kissing him.

"God, how mortifying," she cried, burying her face in her T-shirt.

Breathing deeply the scent of her laundry soap, Quinn swallowed back the embarrassment, the fear, the oh-shit of it all. It was done. She couldn't take it back. There was only forward.

She could go out there and see what his reaction was and take her cue from that, or just go out there laughing it off as a drunken night of really bad decisions. Or just apologize. And hopefully manage to redeem their friendship.

Or pretend nothing happened. That she didn't remember.

"That's mature," she said, the words barely making sound and yet still painful to the rocks bouncing around her skull.

Hearing voices down the hall then spurred her into motion, and she made her decision.

Chapter Eleven

Simon ladled a generous portion of gravy over his biscuits and snagged two pieces of bacon off a platter without really seeing any of it. As soon as he'd entered the house, he felt the energy go south. The tide had shifted between them. He knew it before he even laid eyes on her.

Damn it, he knew she was drunk last night. And he'd certainly been around the block enough to recognize when a move was about to be made, alcohol-induced or otherwise. He should have stopped it before it became—fuck, before it became so all-consuming that he had to put the brakes on before there were no brakes.

But damn if he didn't forget his own name when she said that bit about kissing him being on her bucket list. And then she—fuck. And now his whole body wanted more of that.

"Hey, leave some gravy for the rest of us, hog," Levi said, nudging him with an elbow.

Simon glanced up to his right at his *little* brother, dressed in nice jeans and a button-down shirt, dwarfing him by about three inches.

"What are you all dres—oh, that's right," Simon said, lowering his voice.

"Later," Levi said under his breath as his daughter wandered into the kitchen, still in an oversized T-shirt and shorts.

"Oh, my gosh, this is like real breakfast," Kinley said, rubbing at her eyes.

"Hey," Levi said, turning halfway toward her. "You get real breakfast."

"You have cereal and packaged muffins at your house," she said.

"Our house," Levi corrected, turning to snatch a piece of bacon with a twitch to his jaw. "And I've made you bacon."

"At Mom's house, everything is organic," Kinley said with a lip curl. "Disgusting."

"I'm with you there," Simon said. "Did you know Vienna sausages never go bad?"

"I *love* Vienna sausages," Kinley said with dramatic eyes.

"And they last forever," Simon said with a shrug and a look at Levi.

"Let's not get crazy," Levi said.

"What are you dressed for?" Kinley asked, her breath catching. "I heard someone say the film people are coming, are we in it? Do I need to go change?" She dropped the napkin she was holding and made to bolt.

"No," Levi said, grabbing her hand. "And keep your voice down." He pointed to the big table where some of the crew weren't outside on the back patio had already gathered. "They are already here."

"Come on," she said, tilting her head with a whine.

"I have to go see a couple of people while I'm here," Levi said. "Do you want to go see your MawMaw Walters while I'm out? Or hang out here at the house—*out* of the way of their business," he added quickly.

She sighed like the weight of the world was on her, and Simon had to turn and chuckle. The girl had the Chase flair for dramatics, that was for sure.

"I'll stay here," she said, picking at a biscuit.

"Get a plate," Levi said, pulling her fingers away.

"Listen to you," their mom said, breezing into the kitchen with a wink, tucking stray hairs back in a barrette. "All mannered up and saying *get a plate*," she said, deepening her voice. "I remember you eating straight out of the pot."

"Thanks for that," Levi said, kissing the top of her head as he passed. "Hey, Quinn."

Simon nearly bit his tongue off biting into a piece of bacon as Levi said her name.

"Damn it," he muttered, opening the freezer for an ice cube.

He turned back around just as she walked through the doorway in worn jeans and a T-shirt, looking like the sweet fresh-faced girl she always did instead of the fuck-me fantasy she had going on last night. She was wearing that cat-eye shirt she loved so much that matched the green of her eyes and always made it look like her tits were watching him.

But it wasn't her shirt that he was paying attention to this time. It was her eyes. And how they widened and then darted away as fast as they landed on him.

"Morning, y'all," she said, tentatively smiling and then patting at her face as she saw the food. "Um," she said, resting her other hand over her belly, "I'm just gonna get a little coffee."

"Good idea, honey," his mom said, chuckling. "Drink lots of water today, too."

Quinn nodded as she left. Left them alone in the kitchen, where Simon had the distinct feeling Quinn didn't want to be.

"You all right?" he asked, noting her shaking hand. "Hey," he said, taking the mug from her when she nearly dropped it. "Let me do this, and then you two-fist it."

"I—I've got it," Quinn said, her tone going irritable.

"I can see that," Simon said, chuckling, trying to find the normal between them. Damn it, if he could just go back and undo—

"I'm just—it's good," Quinn said, reaching for a nearby kitchen towel to mop up the places she'd spilled. "Just not my best this morning."

Her skin was pale, free of makeup; she had dark circles under her eyes and an expression of intense discomfort on her face. Not being at her best was an understatement. And it was everything Simon could do not to pull her into his arms and comfort her. He needed to walk away.

"Everybody has had hangovers, Quinn," he said, resting a hand on her shoulder. Her sharp inhale at his touch made him recoil. "Sorry."

"No—" she said, turning quickly and sloshing hot coffee over the edge again and on her hand. "Ow—shit."

Simon took the mug from her and set it on the counter, grabbing the towel and wiping the floor and the cabinets where it had splashed. Quinn never moved, standing there with her hand out as if it were still holding the mug. From his kneeling position in front of her, he looked up, intending to say something funny or witty or something to make her laugh. The look on her face, however, whisked all thoughts from his head.

Tears brimmed in her troubled eyes as she looked down at him with an intensity that sent his heart slamming against his ribs.

Fuck.

"Hey," he said, rising slowly, holding those eyes with his all the way up.

She blinked and two big tears fell free, and before he could think what he was doing, he reached out and wiped them away, pausing as his fingers felt her skin.

Again.

He shouldn't have paused. Because in that second, they weren't the Simon and Quinn of norm, they were the couple from last night, making out on the grass by the creek.

It was different now.

He dropped his hand and both of hers shot up to swipe at her face.

"I'm being ridiculous," Quinn said. "I just need to go home and sleep this off before work tonight."

"Hangovers do take longer to recover from, the older that we get," Simon said.

"Well, thanks for telling me I'm old," she said, attempting a weak smile. "I feel much better now."

"What I'm here for," Simon said with a smirk.

She smiled for real and shook her head, then reached for her coffee. This was better. This was less awkward, and Simon would do just about anything for that.

"I'm gonna go sit somewhere far away from everyone else, in case I trip over my own feet," she said, giving another small grin that didn't reach her eyes that time.

"Want something to soak it up?" Simon asked.

Quinn held out a hand, her face going gray at his words.

"Not even a little," she said. "Let's just go get this over with."

Simon followed her out, noting her choice to go sit on an ottoman alone, away from the others. Away from Hannah, even, who was curled up on the couch next to Kinley and the dog. It was clear that Quinn felt like hell, but the trouble showing in her eyes wasn't about that. She looked down at the ring on her left hand, then leaned over onto her elbows as if that zapped her.

And shit if he didn't feel like a world-class dick.

Quinn hadn't been back there worrying about seeing *him* this morning. She'd been thinking about the fact that she'd betrayed Eric.

Kissing Simon may or may not have been on a bucket list from years ago, but marrying Eric was on her life list.

Simon sat down at the table with his plate, staring down at it.

No. He would not be that guy.

It didn't matter that everything had flipped inside him now. It didn't matter that all the possibilities he'd closed off were opened up in his mind now that he'd had a taste of what he really wanted.

Because they hadn't opened up in hers.

She was still marrying Eric St. James.

And Simon was not going to continue to be the pathetic one left behind, pining for a woman who was in love with someone else. He'd had enough of that. And her reaction this morning told him all he needed to know.

"Where's the new guy?" Eli asked, bringing Simon out of his misery. Simon glanced at his brother leaning over his plate, gnawing on a piece of bacon slowly as if he might be a little green, too. "I thought he was supposed to be here."

"I don't know," Simon said. "All I see is crew. You hurting, too?"

Eli shrugged. "I might have toned down the celebrating if I'd known we had to pony up today. New guy has a point to make, I guess?"

"It's not a guy," Casey said, the camera tech sitting on the other side of Eli. "Charlie's a—"

"Hey, everyone," said a female voice that turned everyone's attention to the front of the room where a slim woman with light-brown hair had emerged from the hallway. "Listen, I know it's early and unexpected," she said. "And I understand there was a big party here last night, but we have a schedule to keep and I want to get up to speed."

Simon looked at Eli questioningly, but he was busy frowning at the woman, eyes narrowed and suspicious.

"My name is Charlie Bell," she said. "I'm kind of Miss Hayes's assistant," she said on a nervous laugh. She stopped, clasped her hands together, and gave an apologetic smile. "Actually that would be Mrs. Chase now, wouldn't it?"

"My Uncle Zach married Maddi," Kinley piped in, nodding seriously as Levi shushed her with a finger.

Chuckles went around the room, including Charlie.

"Yes, he did," Charlie said. "And I've talked to Miss Brian and I've been briefed on everything in Maddi's absence."

"Her absence is only a week," Eli said, his voice booming through the room. "They'll be back in seven days. What kind of plan can't wait seven days?"

Charlie's expression morphed into one of studied amusement, and she crossed her arms over her chest, lifting one finger.

"Elijah, I'm betting," she said.

"Feel good about that bet?" he said softly, turning Simon's head back to him on a swivel.

Whoa, Simon thought. Eli was in rare form. Maybe he got laid last night. Nicole had been sniffing around him for a while now. Maybe she'd come out with no underwear, too, and hit him up. Maybe *all* the damn women went commando last night.

Simon ran a hand back through his still-damp hair and then stabbed at a piece of biscuit. There was a chance he needed more coffee.

Charlie's mouth pulled into a grin on one side, clearly more entertained than put off by the challenge in Eli's tone.

"I think I do, yeah," she said. "And to answer your question, Elijah—or *Eli*, is it?" she added, light-blue eyes widening in something that was supposed to mimic innocence. "The production schedule is the plan that can't wait seven days."

"The deal for this little shindig"—Eli folded his hands in front of him, looking every bit the calm but ready-to-pounce alpha dog—"was for the show to follow us, not the other way around."

"Miss Brian—" Charlie began.

"Miss Brian is aware of the terms," Eli said. "She sat at this very table when we made them."

"Miss Brian," Charlie repeated with a smile, "sent me to push things along this week."

Eli's expression transformed into something between pissed off and wanting to laugh.

"Well, Miss—*Bell*, is it?" he said, making Simon lock eyes with Hannah across the room. Her holy-shit-big-brother's-on-a-tear look confirmed his thoughts. "We can't just pull a storm out of our asses to meet your schedule, which your boss knows fully well."

"We're not worried about the chasing," Charlie said breezily.

"That's kind of what we do," Hannah said around a mouthful of biscuit, raising her hand.

Charlie pointed at her. "Hannah."

Hannah smiled and shrugged. "Guilty."

"What we're looking to do this week is find the human element," Charlie said. "And you and Quinn—where's Quinn?"

Simon's gaze went automatically to where Quinn sat looking like she'd rather be watching water boil. On low. At the sound of her name, she looked up and waved a hand, meeting Simon's eyes. He looked away that time, before she could.

"There you are," Charlie said. "The two of you can be instrumental in this part of the program."

Hannah leaned forward, setting her plate on the coffee table. "How's that?"

"We have our camera techs, yes, but I want you two to contribute," Charlie said.

"Contribute what?" Hannah asked.

"Footage," Charlie quipped. "Film, still shots, whatever you see." She stepped closer and sat on the arm of the couch. Simon looked around for his mother to swoop in, but she'd gone back to the kitchen. "What you capture is gold. I've seen it. You make the viewers feel like the rain is hitting their faces, like the wind is taking their breath away. And we want you to do that every chance you get. If it sprinkles, if it's windy and a tree branch is swaying—get it on film. We can splice that in anywhere. In addition to that, this week is going to be"—she turned her head to look at Eli straight on—"the stuff you hate."

"Do tell," Eli said, his jaw muscles twitching.

"Interviews, talking, random conversations, asking questions about each other, working together, not working together, being a family," Charlie said, ticking the topics off on her fingers. "On being a part of this from *outside* the family," she directed at Quinn. "The personal stuff."

"Wouldn't some of that *personal stuff* involve Zach and Maddi?" Levi piped in, getting up from the table. "I mean, Zach is a major player, Maddi runs it, and they have that whole little marriage thing going on now."

"And we'll get them when they get back," she said.

"Or this was a really convenient time to blindside her," Levi countered.

Charlie grinned again. "You must be Levi."

He chuckled. "I must be. But you knew that before you ever came in here. You've seen the show, you didn't have to play that little point-and-guess game."

Charlie smiled and held up her hands as he passed on his way to the kitchen. "You got me," she said. "Anything else?"

Levi paused and shrugged. "Not my business."

Charlie turned back to Hannah as Levi disappeared in the kitchen.

"So what was I saying?"

"Personal," Hannah said.

"We've already done some of that," Quinn said quietly.

"Barely," Charlie said. "Some very minimal footage in the beginning."

"So there's going to be whole episodes of us just talking?" Simon asked. "How boring is that?"

Charlie turned to him. "Simon." She tilted her head with a small smile, probably stopping herself from pretending to guess. "No, this is filler. This is stuff we plug in all season long, where it will fit the best. And if the weather doesn't cooperate with us, we'll have entertainment value to keep viewers watching."

"So we're doing this today?" Hannah asked, gesturing toward the crew.

"This afternoon."

Everyone started talking at once.

"I have to work," Quinn said.

"So do I," Simon said, raising a hand. It wasn't actually until after seven, but he didn't want to stick around. More than anything, he wanted to get out of there and go home. Or go to the shelter. Something to keep busy and not be reminded of last night.

"I have to work in a little while," Hannah said. "But I can come back."

Charlie held up a hand and nodded. "It's all good—we'll start with those who can be here today and get the rest of you during the week. Plus we have a road trip on Monday."

That stopped the side talking.

"A what?" Eli asked.

"We're heading up to Lake Texoma," she said. "Or close to it, anyway."

"Monday?" Simon said. "That's the day after tomorrow."

Charlie nodded again. "Yes, our weather guy told us about a big storm cell hitting there then—"

"Excuse me?" Simon said, feeling his blood fuel his headache.

He pushed back from the table. "That's *my* job. And that cell is just a band of rain. There's nothing to chase."

"Relax," Charlie said. "I told you I wasn't worried about chasing. It's just good background—props, if you will—for the talking we want to get on camera."

Eli sighed, although there were definite growl properties in there. "A little overkill to drive all the way up there just to chitchat in the rain."

"We already have hotel rooms blocked," Charlie said.

"Overnight?" Quinn said, the word lilting up at the end. She started licking her lips like the Sahara had just landed there. "I might have to work then, too. I don't know yet."

"I'm on schedule, too," Simon said. "I can't just—"

"Look," Charlie said. "I know you all have other lives. So do I." She gestured with her arms held out wide. "But this is how a show works."

There was quiet as everyone rolled through their own thoughts.

"Quinn, can you see about getting off for a couple of days?" Charlie asked.

Quinn just nodded and pulled out her phone.

"Simon?" Charlie asked.

He blew out a breath, knowing Barry was going to shred him alive. Raymond Nance was going to make noise about contracts and additional days off and bend Barry's ear even more than usual. "I don't know, honestly. I'll see what I can do."

"Thank you," Charlie said. "Anyone else have issues? Okay, those of you filming this afternoon, get with me. The rest of you I'll see bright and early on Monday. Bring a swimsuit."

Quinn's eyes got huge.

"A swimsuit?" Eli said. "What the hell?"

Chapter Twelve

Quinn didn't even remember getting in her car. There was talk talk talk, blah blah, Monday hotel—she remembered that—and Hannah handing her keys to go with her plastic bag. The bag holding the vomitus-tainted never-to-be-worn-again dress and purse.

She didn't say good-bye to anyone, really. She didn't say good-bye to Simon. The man she'd come close to humping in the backyard last night. Okay, maybe it wasn't that intense, but fuck, who was she kidding? Even brain-addled with copious amounts of whiskey, she remembered it being that intense. And it was just a kiss.

And then the kitchen.

She might have been okay if it weren't for the kitchen.

Quinn hit the button on her steering wheel for the phone and asked to call Phoebe.

I do not understand that command.

"Call. Phoebe," Quinn repeated.

I do not understand that command.

"Call," Quinn yelled.

Who would you like to call?

"Feeeeee. Beeeeee."

Calling Phoebe. Please say yes to continue, or no to cancel.

"Jesus."

I do not understand that command.

"Yes!" Quinn yelled, blinking back tears that pissed her off for even being there.

Connecting . . .

Two rings were almost more than she could bear, before—

"Hello?"

"Pheebs," Quinn breathed, relieved.

"Quinn? What's up?"

"Are you home?"

"Pulling up in the driveway right now," Phoebe said. "The Super Mart had a sale on peanut butter, so I had to go load up."

Quinn swallowed hard against the bile that rose in her throat. "Having a peanut butter craving?"

"Oh, man, peanut butter on apple slices is amazing," she said. Quinn could hear the rattle of a plastic bag and the closing of a car door. "And my metabolism is so out of whack right now, I have to eat something every two hours or I turn into monster mommy. It's not pretty."

"So is Doug home, too?" Quinn asked, exiting off the interstate for Clayton.

"Um, no." Phoebe said. "Just me. He's at work. What's going on? You feeling better?"

"Mind if I come over?" Quinn said, hearing the wiggle in her voice.

"No, of course not," Phoebe said. "I thought you had to work, though."

"Not till tonight," Quinn said. "I'll be there in a few minutes."

She pulled up to the two-story dark-red brick structure with the flower beds full of peonies, and parked behind her sister's SUV. Before Phoebe got pregnant, she was driving a convertible Mustang.

Now she had a responsible mom car. Quinn would be willing to bet she already had the baby car seat installed.

She peeked in the backseat as she walked past and smiled in spite of the turmoil inside her.

The big wooden door opened before she even reached it, Phoebe standing there with one hand on her hip, the other on her belly.

"What's wrong?" Phoebe said.

Quinn walked right into her and wrapped her arms around her neck.

"Oh, shit," Phoebe said, hugging her back. "Do we need ice cream?"

"Don't make me throw up on you," Quinn mumbled into her hair.

"Okay, Sprite it is," Phoebe said.

They settled into the couch in the back sunroom, warmth emanating from the windows while ceiling fans cooled them off. Phoebe Parker Blackwell had never known roughing it. Never known the stress of paying a bill or having to sweat a little to keep the utilities down. She went from the comfort of their childhood home to the comfort Doug carved out for her. And Quinn loved that about her. She was made for it.

Quinn, on the other hand, wasted no time getting out of that life and had serious twitches about returning to it. But Eric was worth it. Right?

"Okay, spill," Phoebe said. "Pulled a big drunk at the wedding last night, I got that."

"Yeah," Quinn said, running a hand over her face.

"And y'all had a fight."

Quinn nodded.

"And Eric left," Phoebe continued, prompting.

"Yeah," Quinn whispered.

"So what aren't you telling me?" Phoebe asked.

A laugh that turned into tears escaped Quinn's throat, and she pressed her fingers to her lips in case the words fell out, too. Phoebe was always to the point. She didn't dance around. She also wasn't easily shocked, even when it came to her big sister's antics, but she would be this time.

Quinn was out of her element. She'd always been the caregiver, the one to make sure Phoebe was okay, to ensure she had her homework done and didn't lose her lunch money. To vet the guys that circled around her like hawks when she sprouted boobs and got her braces off. Ever since that day when they were very small, in the backyard, she'd made the commitment to take care of her little sister.

She wasn't accustomed to flipping that role. But there was no one else she could tell. No one else she could admit this to. Not even her very best friend, Hannah, because—because Hannah would lose her shit over this.

"Quinn!" Phoebe pressed. "Something is eating you up. What happened with Eric last night?"

Quinn shook her head.

"I kissed Simon."

The words were whispered, but they couldn't have been louder if they were screamed through a microphone.

"You *what?*"

Yeah, Phoebe's were maybe a little louder.

"I kissed Simon Chase," Quinn repeated, covering her face with her hands. "Oh, my God, it sounds weirder out loud."

"You—you—"

"I know."

"Eric saw?" she blustered.

Quinn shook her head, still hidden behind her hands. "After."

"You kissed Simon after he left?" Phoebe asked.

Quinn nodded.

"Holy shit, Quinn, quit with the miming! I need the story!" Phoebe burst out.

"Job, house, fight," Quinn said between her fingers. "Wedding, whiskey, Stacey."

"Wait, who's Stacey?" Phoebe said.

"Simon's date."

"Jesus, Quinn, I need a drink," Phoebe said. "Go ahead, I'll imagine one."

Quinn dropped her hands as Phoebe sat back deeper into the couch. She relayed the details of the arguments with Eric, the job he'd lined up for her, the snooty remarks, the fight, the leaving, the alcohol, and—the perfect woman on Simon's arm.

"She got called to work around the same time Eric left," Quinn said, tracing a floral pattern on a throw pillow. "She's a friggin' nurse. Of course she is."

"And you care because?" Phoebe asked.

"Because evidently I'm a whore," Quinn said.

Phoebe giggled at that. "Not quite, Lady Godiva, but—okay, how did you get from there to jumping into Simon's mouth?"

"I don't know," Quinn said, leaning over to bury her face in the couch. "I drank a lot. I went outside and sat on a bench by the water."

"The water?" Phoebe asked, surprised.

Quinn raised her eyebrows in agreement. "Like I said, lots of whiskey."

"Gotcha."

"And the next thing I remember was sitting in the grass with—wait," Quinn stopped, narrowing her eyes in concentration. "No, first he caught me."

"Caught you?"

"Yeah—like on the edge of the creek I guess. Had to be," Quinn said. "God, he's always doing things like that. Saving me from myself."

"Oh yeah, he's a real prince, kissing an engaged woman," Phoebe said.

"I kissed *him*," Quinn said.

"And he ran for the hills?" she asked.

"No."

Phoebe gave her a look. "Like I said."

"But he stopped us," Quinn said softly. "*He* stopped us. Not me. Phoebe, we were—I mean it was—"

"Intense?"

Quinn closed her eyes and let a breath go. "That doesn't even come close." She swallowed hard and clenched her eyes closed tighter. "It was—oh, my God—if he hadn't put the kibosh on it, Pheebs, I don't know where we'd have ended up."

Phoebe blew out a breath. "Crap."

"Yeah."

"So how do you feel about it today?" she asked.

"How do I feel about it?" Quinn asked, taking a deep breath and letting it go very slowly. "I drove straight here from the Chase house, smelling of puke and in desperate need of a shower, to tell *you* first. What does that tell you?"

"Annnnddd today?" Phoebe prodded.

"Today he—" Quinn stopped and swallowed hard, remembering him down on one knee then looking up at her. *Looking up at her.* Everything in her world had turned upside down in that moment. Everything she'd ever felt and denied, everything she'd ever wanted to see from him and hadn't realized. All of it was right there in those seconds as he rose to his feet and took her eyes with him. And then he wiped her tears—*tears!* She didn't even know she was crying, standing there staring at the most amazing man she'd ever known. "I have a problem, Pheebs."

Phoebe was looking at her with a worried look. Something Phoebe rarely did. Usually she was the sunshine girl, infusing all those around her with her carefree rainbow.

"Seems that way," Phoebe said under her breath. "What about Eric?"

Quinn's breath caught in her chest. "Shit, I need to—I don't know what I need to do. I need to call him. Look at him. Have crazy sex with him or something—"

"Maybe it's just a—thing," Phoebe said, nodding. Not very convincingly.

"Yeah," Quinn said, swiping under her eyes.

"Like cold feet."

"Or—yeah," Quinn said, fanning herself with a pillow. "We'll go with that."

"Did Simon say anything today?"

Quinn's stomach did another twist on the sound of his name, but at least it wasn't a run-for-the-toilet kind of twist.

"No," she said. "Or, not really. Just told me to relax, I think. Or something. Then he—he kind of wouldn't look at me later. Like after the kitchen."

"The kitchen," Phoebe echoed.

"I can't explain the kitchen," Quinn said, closing her eyes. "My heart stopped at the time so it's all kind of whirly—shit!"

The doorbell ringing made her jump, clutching the pillow to her chest.

"Oh, damn it!" Phoebe hissed, pushing up from the couch awkwardly.

"What?"

"Mom."

"What?!" Quinn leapt to her feet, then grabbed her head as the quick motion slammed hammers against her skull.

"I forgot she was coming over," Phoebe said.

"Crap," Quinn muttered, wiping at her face like bugs were attacking it. "I need to go! I can't—oh, but she's seen my car."

"Yes, and she's not the relationship secret spy," Phoebe said, pushing her back down at the shoulder. "Sit. You came to visit. That's not illegal. She won't know anything."

"She comes over here?" Quinn asked, her voice a whisper.

"Way too often," Phoebe said with wide eyes, stepping around her. "Doesn't she come to your place?"

"Never," Quinn said.

"Oh," Phoebe said, looking uncomfortable.

"No, really, it's okay," Quinn said. "I think she's afraid that the old lady always selling candy downstairs will mug her."

"Aw, I love Miss Molly!" Phoebe said, tilting her head and rubbing her watermelon child. The rainbow was back.

"I know, she's sweet," Quinn said.

"Okay, I'm gonna go let Mom in," Phoebe said. "You good?"

Quinn breathed in deeply through her nose and blew out through her mouth.

"There you go," Phoebe said. "Keep doing that."

Quinn sat back down, kicked off the slip-on shoes Hannah had brought her, and curled her legs under her, pulling the pillow into her lap for security. Like the twelve square inches of fabric and stuffing would shield her from whatever zingers her mother had to dish out.

"Quinn?" her mom said, walking into the living room. "I thought that was your car out there. Same dent in the passenger door."

Zing!

"Yep," Quinn said. "Same one."

162

"What are you doing here?" she asked, lowering gracefully into a chair in a manner Quinn never did learn to master.

"Visiting," she said. "You?"

"Oh, just checking on my future grandchild," she said, caressing Phoebe's stomach as she waddled between them to get back to her seat on the other end of the couch.

That had to get old, Quinn thought. Everybody thinking that it was fair game to molest a pregnant woman, like protruding an extra foot made it a free-for-all. She was just as guilty, putting her hands on her sister's belly every time she saw her, but now as she watched Phoebe endure it like it was the eightieth time that day, she made a mental note to quit. That would drive her crazy. One day. If she ever got pregnant.

"Little Wellie is doing just fine," Phoebe said, doing a half squat to position herself back in her corner of the couch. "We just had our last regular checkup yesterday afternoon, and all is good."

"I wish you'd quit calling it that," Adelaide said.

"Oh, it works," Phoebe said, waving a hand at her in a way that Quinn could never quite master. "Doug's buddies have been calling him 'Wellie,' short for Blackwell, for years now, and with not knowing the baby's sex—"

"Which I think is insane in this day and age," Adelaide interjected. "I mean, we didn't have the choice to know. We had to wait it out and guess, and deal with what came. Nowadays you could totally be prepared, have the clothes, decorate the nursery."

"We have plenty of clothes," Phoebe said. "They don't wear anything but onesies at first anyway. And I think the nursery is beautiful."

"So do I," Quinn said. "I love all the bright primary colors. It's like a bag of Skittles in there."

"Exactly!" Phoebe said. "That's what I wanted. And I want to be surprised when the baby comes. That just seems like part of the fun."

Adelaide laughed. "Phoebe, only you would look at childbirth as fun."

"Well, but finding out beforehand is like someone handing you a present and then telling you what it is before you unwrap it," Phoebe said. "Kind of steals the thunder."

"I guess," she said. "Oh, speaking of babies, Quinn."

Quinn lifted her eyebrows. "I don't think so."

Her mother sighed as if Quinn just wore her out. Quinn knew the feeling. "I had lunch with Bitty St. James yesterday. Eric's mother?" she continued when Quinn didn't respond.

Quinn nodded. "I know who she is." Snot. Backstabber. Made a mean vodka martini, though. *Ugh . . . bad thought.*

"I was telling her my plans to come see Phoebe today, and we got to talking about grandbabies and all," she said.

Quinn continued to nod. "And?"

"And—" her mom said. "She said there's an extra bedroom at Eric's house she's already eyeballing for nursery potential." She laughed. "I think she said the guest bedroom on the south side? Has its own bathroom? That'll be handy."

Quinn wasn't sure if she'd stopped breathing or if the banging in her head had just gotten louder.

"Because—an infant needs that?" she managed.

"Oh, you know what I mean," her mother said, shaking her head at Phoebe as if they were now both in on the cosmic mother-hood knowledge.

"*Bitty* has a room picked out?" Quinn said. "In my future home?"

Her mother looked at her funny. "Well, of course you can change it."

She could change it. "You think?"

"Oh!" she exclaimed, her mind already moving on. "Quinn, before I forget, you have a photography appointment for your portrait for the reception."

Breathe in, breathe out.

"Okay," Quinn said, smiling politely. "When is that?"

"Monday," she said. "The dress will be ready that morning from the seamstress, and your appointment is at two that afternoon. What?" she added as Quinn shook her head.

"I can't do Monday," Quinn said.

Her mother looked at her as if she'd grown horns. "What do you mean, you can't do Monday? That's when the appointment is."

"Well, I didn't make that appointment, now did I?" Quinn responded, feeling the defensive armor work its way up. "I'm sorry, I won't even be in town."

"Where on earth will you be?" she asked.

"Lake Texoma," Quinn said.

"For what?"

"Filming," Quinn said, wishing she could give it some kind of important attachment. Truth was, she felt like the rest of the Chase family about the outing. That it was a silly and gas-guzzling waste of time. Not to mention the hotel cost. At a hotel. With Simon.

Jesus, fool, you won't be in the same room.

"Oh, for pete's sake, Quinn, this is important!" her mom said, sitting forward in her chair. "Get out of it."

"I can't," she said. "We're already down Zach, and they want both Hannah and me there to get footage. I have to take off from work, too, because we're staying overnight. We'll have to reschedule the portrait."

"I made this appointment three months ago," she said, indignant. "I can't just reschedule for the next day."

Quinn's headache drummed a little harder. "You made it three months ago and you're just now telling me?"

Her eyebrows shot up. "I tell you as you need to know, honey. You aren't famous for writing things down. If I'd told you then, you would have already forgotten."

"Really?" Quinn said. "No, not really. Because there wouldn't have been an appointment to forget. I would have cancelled it and gotten Hannah to do it. In fact, I'll still do that."

Her mother sighed heavily. "I told you how I feel about that," she said.

Phoebe smiled. "Anyone need something to drink?" she asked. Quinn knew her sister was trying to diffuse the upcoming fireworks, but it wasn't the day to push her.

"I've got Sprite," Quinn said with a grin, holding the cup by her face in a pose.

"I'm good, honey," their mom said. "Quinn," she began again, focusing back on her.

"I don't care, Mom," Quinn said.

Her mother gave a startled head jerk. "What?"

"They are already doing the wedding photos and the video, and the reception," Quinn said. "So what if someone else does the portrait? Will the photo nazis come swarming in and arrest us?"

The etiquette daggers started forming in her mother's eyes. "That's not how it's done, Quinn."

Pick a small battle and stay on your feet, Little Bit, she heard in her mind, repeating from last night. God, now she was hearing his voice. But he was right. And cold sweat was breaking out again, so she had little concern at the moment for *how it's done.*

"I don't care," Quinn repeated. "It's my wedding, I'm getting nothing else I want, so either Hannah does the portrait shot or there isn't one. I'm—really good either way."

Her mother and Phoebe wore identical shocked looks, and honestly Quinn would have probably joined them if it hadn't come out of her own mouth. She needed to be hungover more often.

No. Scratch that.

"Have you lost your mind?" her mother asked, the words enunciated slowly for maximum effect.

"It's entirely possible, today," Quinn said, getting up and grabbing the arm of the couch as a wave of nausea hit her.

"You okay?" Phoebe asked.

"What's wrong with you?" her mother asked at the same time.

Quinn shook her head, smiling the smile of the about-to-hurl. "Just a little under the weather," she said. "I'm gonna head out, Pheebs," she added, giving her a look and then holding out a hand. "Don't get up. I'm good."

Phoebe nodded. "Call me later."

"Will do," Quinn said, already halfway to the door. "Bye. Mom, are you parked behind me?"

"No, I'm—"

That was all she needed to know as she made a full-out dizzy sprint for her car and made it as far as the third set of peonies. Hitting her knees, she spewed the coffee she'd drank, which wasn't nearly as pleasant coming back as it was going in.

"Sorry, Pheebs," she whispered, breathing hard, wiping her mouth as she pushed to her feet. The next-door neighbor guy was watering his rosebushes and looked away quickly when she glanced his direction.

"Yeah, don't look, it might taint you," she whispered, getting in her car.

It would get better. It would get better. She'd just keep telling herself that. The day had to improve—it had pretty much kicked off at rock bottom.

Quinn made it to her brownstone, feeling the familiar sense of comfort as she pulled into her spot and looked at the happy plants Mrs. Bernstein had on her balcony. She got out and trudged into the building and up her stairs, toting her plastic bag of shame on one finger. A shower and some more aspirin and some crackers and Coke and she'd be right as rain.

The other ache she was feeling—that was something she couldn't deal with right now. Not yet. It was too confusing. And she was too splintered and scattered at the moment. And empty. And—

"Eric."

He was sitting on the floor in front of her door in jeans and a gray T-shirt, and she stopped short and gasped as if talking to him would somehow incriminate her.

He got up, never looking away from her face. "No one answered," he said. "I guess Hannah's not home, either."

"She—she had a photo shoot," Quinn managed, her voice sounding weak and odd.

Eric looked haggard, dark-blond stubble showing on his jaw, his eyes looking tired and red. He hadn't slept. She was a horrible person. A horrible, horrible person.

He glanced down at the plastic bag. "You didn't come home?"

"I spent the night there in Hannah's old room," she said. "Had a little too much to drink."

He nodded, letting his eyes study hers one at a time. He reached for her free hand. "So, can we talk?"

Chapter Thirteen

Simon headed to his mom's house Monday morning in a funk. It was drizzly rain, would be the whole way to Texoma, which was a lake about two hours north on the border of Texas and Oklahoma.

It was a silly, useless trip. For the first time, Simon agreed whole-heartedly with Eli. The show's producers wanted fake conversations so that the viewers would find them more real? What kind of crazy shit was that?

The whole thing was ridiculous. They were more likely to encounter storm cells at home than following the weather band north, but it wasn't about the chasing. It was about the personal talky-talk stuff that Miss Charlie decided they needed. Eli had even called Nicole about it, but evidently it was all on the up-and-up. She wanted it done.

And Simon's boss—that was another fresh new hell. Barry had barely given him the night off for Zach's wedding, and then having to ask for another one—for this? He was going to be sacked.

They hadn't even gotten to have a proper good-bye with Levi, as he had to leave Sunday to get back before work and school on Monday. Simon had wanted to take him out to dinner or something. Find out how the job interview went. But Levi wasn't really chatty about it and they never got the chance. Simon and the others had to film conversational interviews instead. Over and over. Talking about what they did in their spare time. What they did with each other. And there were entirely too many questions regarding him and Quinn.

What the living hell was with that?

And what was with her?

She was totally checked out. Zoned off into a whole other place. Was Quinn that eaten up over what they'd done? All through the interviews, all through the questions, Simon stumbled through all the pokes and prods about the two of them and their on-screen chemistry while Quinn answered almost robotically. Without a hint of their normal banter. Hell, she wouldn't even rise to a playful jab.

Not only was Quinn not interested in what had happened between them, it was like she was pissed off at him for it. At him! When she kissed *him*! And now everything was awkward and distant and tense, and Simon just wanted normal back. As amazing as that moment was, he'd dial it all back just to get the old Quinn in front of him again. The one not obsessed with her engagement ring and dropping the word *fiancé* five hundred and fifty times, and not snipping at everything he said.

Hannah's car was there when he pulled in, meaning Quinn was there, too. He stopped and blew out a breath. This was going to be a long two days if he didn't pull it together. It was work. Keep it work. If she wanted to be a little jerk while she got over her own issues, then whatever. Be a jerk.

His phone rang over the speaker, and Simon groaned when he saw the name. *No. No. Shit.*

"Hello?" he said, pounding the button.

"Simon."

It wasn't a question. It was pissed off.

"Barry."

170

"Are you still headed out of town with your show people?" Barry asked, his tone acidic.

"Yes, Barry, I told you that," Simon said. His *show people*. Sounded like he was running off with the damn circus. "I'll be back tomorrow night, and I won't need to ask for anything else for a long time."

That was a blind promise, but it sounded good for the moment.

"You know, this wasn't supposed to be a conflict of anything," Barry said. "And it's turning more and more into a conflict of *everything*."

Simon blew out a breath. "I know. I know this sucks, and I know it puts Raymond in a tight spot. It came up unexpectedly, and—"

"Just know we need to sit down and have a conversation when you get back," Barry said. "You may be one of our best, but *best* doesn't do me a damn bit of good if you're never here. We need to draw some new boundaries."

Simon rubbed at his eyes. He should have said no to this trip. He should have bailed on it. His job was supposed to come before the show. It was always supposed to come first.

"I hear you, Barry."

"And keep your eye on the radar," Barry said. "Something's brewing up north."

"I'm headed north."

"So it'll be easy to watch, then."

The dial tone filled Simon's speakers. Good times. He got out and swung his computer and duffle bags over one shoulder. He almost welcomed the thick, drizzly air that blanketed him. Maybe it would wash all the toxicity down into the earth and bring normal back.

As soon as he reached the big wraparound porch, however, the front door swung open and Quinn, pulling the hood of her hoodie jacket up over her hair, came out hauling a purple backpack and her black camera bag.

"Oh—" she said on a gasp, stopping short in front of him and backing up one step. Her eyes took off, looking for anywhere to land but on him.

"Sorry," he said, for lack of another response.

"Nah, just"—she pointed at the black SUV they used for chases and trips as if it would do the explaining for her—"throwing my stuff in the back."

Simon stepped to the side and gestured with a hand. "Don't let me stop you."

Those eyes that had been avoiding him flew up to meet his long enough for him to see the turmoil churning there. There was surprise over his shortness, mixed with disappointment and a clear *oh yeah, I'm not supposed to talk to you* in there before she quickly moved past him.

He watched as she lifted the back hatch on the SUV, the gray hoodie covering her head and face. Any other time, he would have been over there opening it for her, watching her roll her eyes and letting her gently chide him for being chivalrous. Now he was just rooted to the porch, watching without words, unable to even go inside and ignore her. This whole thing was wrong.

Her footsteps faltered when she turned back around and found him still there.

He was busted. And didn't give a shit.

"What?" she asked.

Her body language was defensive, her arms crossed, pulling the jacket tighter around her in warm, sticky temperatures.

"I'm asking *you* that," he said quietly.

She shook her head and kept walking.

"I don't know what you're talking about."

"Quinn," he said emphatically as she passed.

"Simon," she said in a huff, blowing out a breath as she stopped and looked at him wide-eyed. She looked at him. But not really.

"This is where we are now?" he said after a pause.

"We aren't anywhere," she said, blinking away. "Or anything. I'm engaged."

"We *aren't anywhere?*" Simon repeated. "Since when? Last I checked, you were one of my best friends."

"Of course we're still friends," she said, staring at the door.

"I see," Simon said. "Just the nontalking kind."

Quinn's eyes fluttered closed for a moment.

"Simon—"

"All because a crazy drunk moment that didn't mean anything has you flipping out," he said.

It was the baldest boldfaced lie he'd ever told. *Didn't mean anything?* It had meant everything. But that *we aren't anywhere* comment was like cold water in his face.

His words caught her attention, because for the first time in two days, she was staring right at him. Green fire flashed as she pushed her hoodie back off her head.

"You're right," she said. "There's nothing to flip out over."

"Exactly," he said, not feeling exact at all. Everything had flipped.

"Exactly," she echoed. "So come on. Everyone needs to get wired up so we can go."

"Casey, you're going to ride in the vehicle with the family," Charlie said, reading from a clipboard.

"We—um—why?" Simon asked.

"Yeah, I thought taping started when we got there?" Hannah asked.

"And you asked *us* to get the footage," Quinn added.

"But you can't film yourself," Charlie said distractedly, running a finger down the board. "The van will be following you, but Casey will have a minicam to catch anything good inside the car."

Eli looked ready to split his own head open. "Are we ready?" he growled.

Charlie looked up and smiled. "Ready when you are."

"I have to make a couple of stops," Simon said as they loaded into the vehicle.

"The network van is following us," Hannah said, turning to give the eye to Casey, the cameraman sitting between her and Quinn.

"Hey, I just do as I'm told," Casey said.

"And they can follow us all over town if they choose," Simon said. "Or they can go directly to the hotel *they* reserved and wait."

"Okay, then," Hannah said, sitting back. "Who pissed in your cereal this morning?"

I did, Quinn thought.

She had been a total bitch. Ever since she found Eric looking like a little lost puppy on her doorstep, and he'd held her and made her his special hangover recipe and they'd talked for hours—she'd been a raving lunatic.

Eric was trying. He said he was willing to stop pushing the job thing and let her follow her dreams the way he'd followed his. He would quit trying to control her every move and he'd do whatever it took to make her happy. That night had scared him. He saw a glimpse of life without her, and he wanted no part of it. So he was trying.

And so Quinn was going to as well. If he could go the extra mile to be a good husband, then she could certainly quit obsessing over another man.

Jesus, that was messed up.

So she did the only thing she could do. Went the ass-opposite direction. Shut it all off and wouldn't even look in Simon's direction—which was rotting a little bit of her soul. So she was almost relieved when he'd called her on it. Until he'd said *that*.

"The hospital in Trinity, and then an old warehouse just a few blocks over."

"What's at the hospital?" Eli asked from the driver's seat.

"Stacey," Simon said. "You met her the other night."

Quinn's throat felt like it would close up. And she wasn't sure which reference threw her the most, Stacey or mention of that night. The combination sent her hands up to pull her hair down from its clip and twist it right back up again.

"Because?" Eli prompted.

"She has a pan of food to drop off for another friend of mine," Simon said. "And she has to work a double, so she won't get the chance." He threw a second glance at his brother, who was giving him an irritated look. "What? It'll go bad. It's a dessert from the shelter."

"And it's your business why?" Eli said. "Making points with your woman?"

Down came the hair again, and this time Quinn threw the clip behind her in the trunk. Her fingers took to braiding it like her life depended on it.

"Whatever," Simon muttered. "Just doing a nice thing. I help out there whenever she's in a bind. And *she's in a bind*. Won't take but a minute."

So Stacey the wonder-woman nurse and feeder of the poor really *was* his woman. Not that Quinn cared. At all. She was engaged.

"Eric worked in a soup kitchen when he was in college for liberal art credit," she said. "I think we might start doing that together for holidays after we get married."

Hannah raised an eyebrow.

"Aw, man, I did that, too," Casey said. Hannah and Quinn both looked at him. "Right after high school," he said, nodding. "You know. Give back and all that."

"Yeah," Hannah said under her breath.

They pulled into the hospital parking lot and Simon pulled out his phone to text someone. Quinn presumed it was Stacey. *Gah! Think of something else!* Orchids. She could get behind orchids. Right? They were pretty. All the pinks and purples and reds, and—

"Be right back," he said, getting out.

"So he's Florence Nightingale now?" Hannah asked. Within minutes, Stacey met him at the outer doors with two aluminum-covered pans. "Or Wolfgang Puck?"

Quinn didn't care—didn't even want to look. She wasn't supposed to look. But there she was, looking. Watching Wonder Woman stand there looking just as hot in purple scrubs. What kind of fair was there in that? Then he hugged her, laughed about something as he shook his head, and kissed her cheek.

All while Quinn's neck and head lit on fire.

"By the way, you're doing my portrait photo," she blurted out, bringing Hannah's gaze to her.

"Oh?"

"Yep."

Hannah chuckled. "How'd you pull that off?"

"Just told Mom it was happening," Quinn said. "Ascot is doing everything else, I get to have you do my portrait photo."

"It's not going to flow with the theme of everything else," Hannah said, an amused expression on her face.

"I don't care," Quinn said. "I want it."

Hannah gave a thumbs-up. "I'm on it, then. Let me know when you get your dress back."

"Hey, you know that field just north of here with the daisies?" Quinn said, sitting up straighter. "On the way to Dallas?"

Hannah's eyes narrowed. "Yeah," she said, drawing out the word. "Why?"

"Can we see if I can take the photo there?" she asked. "I'll drive up there when we get back, actually. There's a little house on the property. I'll knock on the door."

"I think that's a fantastic idea," Hannah said, grinning.

"Oh, this is good," Casey said, hitting a tiny button on a tiny camera.

"You were filming that?" Hannah said, twisting in her seat.

"It is what I'm here for," Casey said.

"Well, quit," Hannah huffed. "That was personal."

"Which is—"

"—what she wants," Quinn said with a sigh. "We know."

Simon walked back all carefree with his *meant nothing* self, wearing his Rangers baseball cap and a pullover shirt hanging loosely over jeans that fit him like they were lovingly sewn on. Carrying pans of something, with a stupid grin on his face.

And opening her door.

"Can you hold this?" he asked, depositing both large pans in her lap before she could answer.

"Um, what?"

"Just for a few blocks," he said, shutting the door again without ceremony.

Quinn sat there openmouthed as he opened his own door and got in.

"Okay, go up to the next stoplight and turn left," he told Eli. "Van still with us?" he asked, turning around. His gaze fell on Quinn after checking out the back, and he winked at her with a click of his tongue. "Hold on tight to that," he said. "That's Harry's dinner and dessert."

Quinn could hardly form words. Who the hell was this prick pretending to be Simon?

"Dessert," she managed.

"Harry?" Hannah asked, looking just as perplexed.

Simon twisted in his seat again with a grin. "Yeah, cobbler," he said to Quinn. "Old friend of Dad's," he said to Hannah. Then he turned his gaze back to Quinn. "Blackberry. The best."

The burn from her neck up to her face before had nothing on this one. He was using her own words. From that night. Dirty pool.

"Good for Harry," she said, refusing to even blink. His grin lingered a second longer before he turned back around in his seat and Quinn could take a full breath.

Hannah frowned, looking between the two of them. "What on earth did I miss?"

"What?" Quinn asked.

"You two are usually all sweet and disgusting," she said.

"Nah, we aren't anything," Simon said softly. "Or was it *anywhere*?" He shrugged. "Same difference." Quinn felt the blow as if he'd punched her right in the chest. Much like the one he'd delivered earlier.

"Eli and I are the cynics in this family," Hannah said. "And right now the ratio in the car is way off balance."

"I hear that," Eli said. "I'm used to rainbows and butterflies with you, Quinn."

Rainbows. That was how she usually described Phoebe.

"Sorry," Quinn said, gazing out the window. "Guess my butterflies took the day off."

"How many days till the wedding?" Eli asked.

Inwardly, Quinn groaned. She knew he was just making conversation to lighten her mood, but nothing on that topic was going to improve her frame of mind.

"Twenty-three days," Hannah said.

Oh, sweet hell, that certainly didn't help.

"That soon, huh?" Quinn said weakly, pulling the braid apart and just twisting her hair up into a messy bun with the hairband on her wrist.

"I'd think you'd know it down to the hour and minute, as much as you stare at that ring," Simon said.

Her blood ran hot in her face. "Well, maybe I don't want to saturate everyone with wedding stuff three days after your brother's wedding," Quinn said. "Think about that?"

"Hey, saturate away," Simon said. "Never get in the way of a bride and her wedding plans, right?"

Quinn's heart was about to explode out of her chest. Even Eli looked at Simon funny.

"Why are you being a dick, man?" Eli muttered under his breath.

"No, hey, it's cool," Quinn said, suddenly hyperaware of Casey next to her with that damn camera. "What would you like to hear about? The music? The food? The honeymoon?"

"What kind of music?" Simon asked.

"No idea," Quinn said. "Next?"

He laughed, but she had the distinct impression it wasn't joyous.

"Well, I already know about the food, and I think I'll pass on the honeymoon," Simon said, pointing for Eli to turn left, then right. "That's private between a husband and a wife."

"Good point," Quinn said sharply. "That's the stuff that *means something*."

Everything went very silent, very still, and Simon looked out the window. "Right here," he said quietly, pointing to the right.

Eli pulled into what used to be a parking lot for what used to be a building. Now it just looked like a bunch of crumbling stone and metal and wood, with no glass in the windows that were still intact. One center section towered above the rest.

"What are we doing?" Hannah asked.

"Making a house call," Simon said, opening his door. "Y'all stay here."

Quinn's door opened, and he reached in for the pans, their fingers brushing in the process. His eyes met hers in that second, and there it was again. Magnets, lightning, everything bad. And then he was gone, not even bothering to close her door.

She tugged it closed and watched him walk away, taking a deep breath to slow her heart. Looking at Hannah didn't help that.

The look on her face said she knew.

Chapter Fourteen

Simon pushed Quinn and her voice and her smart-ass little comments from his brain as he approached the large metal door. It wasn't worth letting it get under his skin. Letting *her* get under his skin. More than she already was.

He had *real* things to do. To worry about. To deal with. His boss. The shelter. Harry. Real-life things. Tangible, physical things that mattered and were somewhat halfway within his control.

Quinn was not. She would never be. Regardless of how mutual things were—and that was something he should have never bought into. *Mutual* only applied to that night. Anything after that was all in his own head.

"Harry!" he yelled as he got closer. "Harry? It's Simon! I'm gonna knock, so don't blow me up or anything."

He was only partially joking. Part of the shit he gave Harry was to give the old man something, but after the pencil incident, Simon was never completely off his guard.

"Shit," he muttered as the bottom pan's lid came loose. "Harry, hurry up, I'm dropping this!" He balanced on his left foot while he held the bottom pan up with his right knee.

He heard the quickened steps behind him before he could turn around.

"I've got it," Quinn said, grabbing the bottom pan from its precarious position.

"What are you doing out of the car?" Simon hissed.

Quinn jerked her head up, fastening the lid back with her thumbs as she narrowed her eyes. "Helping you, it seems. You're welcome."

"You can't be out here," he said.

"And you don't need to tell me what to do," Quinn said, her words clipped.

If Simon could have thrown his fucking pans at the wall and left, he would have. But then Harry would have had a damn fit, called it a conspiracy, waste of food, etc., and he wasn't up for it.

"Harry!" he yelled again, this time through his teeth, banging the side of his fist on the door.

"What?" came the grizzled voice on the other side. "What do you want?"

"Just put that pan down and leave," Simon whispered.

"No," Quinn said. "I'm not a child."

"Fuck," Simon muttered.

"Who is that?" Harry yelled, his tone hitting that paranoid place.

"Just a friend of mine, Harry," Simon said, shutting his eyes. "She's helping me with the pans."

"I don't need anything," Harry said. "Go away."

"Come on, Harry," Simon said. "You'll like this."

"Who are all those other people with you?" Harry said. "Whose car?"

So Harry did know when he was there. He had a secret spidey hole.

"It's my family and some friends," Simon lied. If Harry knew that was a TV network van with him, he'd probably never let Simon in again. "We're on our way to Texoma and I stopped and picked this up from Stacey to bring to you."

Quinn's gaze met his and then darted away. "Hi, Harry, I'm Quinn."

"Shut. Up," Simon said under his breath. "You don't know what you're doing."

She met his eyes again, green fire shooting out at him. "What do you care?"

There was a scraping noise and then a pause, and Simon shifted on his feet. *Come on, Harry. Don't be proud.*

"I don't like all these new people knowing where I am," Harry said finally.

"I promise they weren't paying attention," Simon said. "They don't even know what I'm doing. They were talking and I just told my brother to stop." He turned a hard look to Quinn. "Quinn's just hardheaded. Like you."

Another pause from inside while she gave him a sarcastic smirk.

"What do you have?" Harry said finally.

"Open the door and smell for yourself," Simon said.

"Just leave it," Harry said. "I'll get it if I want to after you're gone."

"All right," Simon said. "But don't wait for the bugs to find it first."

"Bye," Harry said.

Simon laid a palm against the hot metal door. "There's a little rain coming, Harry," he said. "Make sure your holes are covered up. You hear me?"

"Affirmative," Harry said.

It was all he was going to get, so Simon set his pan on the concrete and Quinn did the same.

"Let's go," he said harshly.

"Affirmative," she snipped, walking ahead of him back to the car. He stopped and watched her get in and slam her door. *They weren't anywhere.*

He held her gaze all the way till he got to his door, then he got in and stared straight ahead. "Okay. I'm done," Simon said. "We're good to go."

Quinn flopped across the double bed, her wet backpack dropping to the floor.

"So much for light drizzle," she said. It had taken a full-out run from the car to the door of her hotel room to keep from getting drenched.

"No kidding," Hannah said, perusing the hotel binder under the phone. "I think Miss Bell was feeling a little optimistic about the *swimsuit* plan. Oh—then again."

Quinn raised her head, pushing a wet lock of hair off her face. "What?"

"They have an indoor pool and hot tub here," Hannah said with a wry grin.

Quinn dropped her head again. "Of course they do."

"It's cheap sensationalism, what she's doing," Hannah said.

"You're one of the prettiest families I've ever seen," Quinn said, eyes closed. "It's actually smart, from a marketing standpoint. The viewers will find someone to lust after."

"You realize you're in there, too, right?"

God, did she. The thought of parading around with Simon in that much state of undress had her insides twitching.

"Did you tell Eric what to expect?" Hannah asked.

"No," Quinn said. "I'll tell him before it airs, though. If any of it even makes the final cut."

"How much you want to bet Eli comes out in jeans?" Hannah said.

Quinn laughed. "Just to spite."

"I don't think he likes Charlie much," Hannah said.

"I don't think he likes change much," Quinn added.

"True," Hannah said, turning pages. "Ooh, they have a pancake breakfast. And a coffee shop."

"Are they still open?"

Hannah's shoulders sagged. "No. We just missed it."

"We'll hit that tomorrow," Quinn said. "Damn, we should have brought snacks."

"Done!" Hannah said, picking up her bag.

She pulled out a bag of chips, two bags of flavored popcorn, and a box of Twinkies.

"Oh, my God, you cleaned out the snack cabinet!" Quinn said, laughing. "You're the bomb!"

"Only you can eat like this three weeks before you have to put on a wedding dress," Hannah said.

Quinn nearly dropped the package of Twinkies she was opening. "If it doesn't fit me, I'll pull out the little white dress I wore to your birthday bash last year."

Hannah coughed on a piece of popcorn. "Your mother would kill you."

"The dress is for me, not the other way around," Quinn said with a shrug. "And it's not three weeks."

Hannah gave her a look. "Three weeks and two days."

Quinn raised an eyebrow. "Like I said." Shoving the spongy goodness into her mouth, she moaned. "Mmm."

"So what gives with you and Simon?" Hannah asked, eyes going as shrewd and all-seeing as Granabelle's.

Quinn pointed to her full mouth as she chewed, knowing that her best friend wasn't stupid and needed to be told, but at the same time not wanting to admit her craziness to another person. Especially not his sister.

"Yes, like that's stopped you before," Hannah said dryly.

"Hmm—mm—mff," Quinn said holding up a finger.

Just then both their cell phones went off. Quinn picked hers up to see a text message from Charlie.

Rec room in ten mins. Swimsuits.

"Seriously?" Hannah said, tossing her phone onto her bed. "It's ten thirty in the morning."

"Let's go get this over with," Quinn said.

"Hmm, amazing speech recovery," Hannah said with a knowing look before she unzipped another portion of her bag. One not filled with food.

Quinn turned and retrieved her backpack from the floor. A momentary reprieve, but she wasn't sure which was the worse option—a skin show with Simon or true confessions with Hannah.

She dug through her backpack just as her phone sang from the bed.

"Oh, hell," she muttered.

Hannah glanced over. "Better answer or she'll burn your phone up."

"Pray for me," Quinn said, hitting the button. "Hello?

"Quinn?"

"Yes?"

"Are you working an early shift today?" her mother asked.

Quinn sighed. It wasn't her mother's job to keep up with where she said she was going to be, but still—one would think sometimes it might stick just by accident.

"No, Mom, I'm on a shoot." God, that was about the lamest thing to call this little expedition, but the truth would bring on a much longer conversation. Time she didn't have, since she was needed in a swimsuit in about eight minutes.

"Well, when do you get done, honey?" she asked. "I brought your dress over, but you weren't home. You have the portrait appointment this afternoon."

Quinn had been severely, painfully hungover when they'd had the conversation, but she still very much remembered telling her mother that was off. That Hannah was in. The whole *that's not how it's done* and all that was still dancing around in her brain somewhere.

"No. I don't," Quinn said, pulling her bikini from the depths of the backpack with one hand. The only one she owned. Not much need for one in her life, but she had it just in case. Pool parties and such, where she could sit on the side and pretend. "I told you I was out of town today."

"I thought you would reschedule!" her mother exclaimed, the tone making Quinn hold the phone away from her ear.

"Why would you think that?" Quinn said. "Out of all the words we said, where did you get that impression?"

"Because you don't just get an appointment at Ascot, Quinn," her mother said, spewing disappointment with every syllable. "And when you do, you schedule everything else around it!"

"Well—the producer of the show didn't much care for Ascot's need to be petted, Mom," Quinn lied. "They have their own priorities and schedule, and my wedding photos didn't make the cut."

"But—"

"*And* I told you at the time that I had a prior commitment and couldn't come," Quinn said, widening her eyes at Hannah. "And that I was using Hannah to do the portrait."

"Quinn, you can't be serious," her mother said.

"So serious," she quipped.

There was a deep and ominous sigh on the other end that Quinn could totally picture. "That's not how—"

"—it's done," Quinn finished with her. "Yes, I know. That's okay. It's how it's done now. I'll start a trend." She tried digging flip-flops out but could only find one. "Mom, I gotta go. They're waiting—"

"Do you know what kind of spot you're putting me in?" her mother said.

"Well, then you shouldn't have made the appointment without asking me first," Quinn said, slinging the flip-flop onto the floor and unzipping her shorts. "Or at least canceled it two days ago when I told you. Or even better yet, you could have just let me do it myself. Then your spots would be all shiny."

"I'm letting you go," her mother spat.

"Love ya, bye!" Quinn sang, throwing her phone back on the bed as she hopped out of her shorts.

"Your mom loves me so much," Hannah said with a grin.

"She does love you," Quinn said, stripping naked. "Probably more than me. She just doesn't think anyone is worth paying if they don't charge out the ass."

"I can totally triple the charges and make her feel better," Hannah said, already suited up with a long tank top coverup hanging low over her shoulders.

"Please do," Quinn said. "That would be awesome."

Ten minutes later—clad in a bikini, an oversized ratty red-and-white Coca-Cola T-shirt, and no flip-flops—Quinn followed Hannah down the sidewalk to the rec room, trying to dial back her nerves. Hannah was striding along cool as a cucumber, but going to hang out with your brothers wasn't a big stressor.

The rain had let up a little, but even so, Simon's computer was out on a table when they walked in, analytics already running. He wasn't anywhere to be seen. Charlie and Casey were setting up the lights on one side of the room while three others were busy fiddling with mike packs by the hot tub and the kitchen area.

Eli was on the phone, pacing the room and looking ready to pull someone apart with his teeth. To his credit, he did have on swim trunks with a gray T-shirt.

"Let's commandeer a table," Hannah said. "So in case this goes crazy-awry, we have a place to grab our stuff and bolt."

"Thinking positive?"

"Thinking Eli."

Quinn smirked, dropping a towel and her phone on the table next to the hot tub.

"Is everyone here?" Charlie asked.

"Simon," Quinn said, oddly disappointed that her stress factor was missing.

"He's here, he had a phone call," Casey said.

"Everyone still wired?" Charlie said.

"Yeah," Hannah said, lifting her shirt with a twirl. "So how's that gonna work?"

"We're about to take all that back off," Charlie said. "Casey and the others are wiring the room now in lieu of body mikes."

Eli walked up. "Nicole's not answering," he said through his teeth. "I'm so damn tempted to go back to the room till we leave tomorrow."

"It won't be that bad," Hannah said. "Just—just roll with it."

"It's damn ridiculous," he said. "Driving two hours to sit in a hot tub and talk while it rains outside."

"Eli, we're just trying to keep the show balanced," Charlie said, tucking her hair behind her ears.

"And how does this little stunt do that, exactly?" Eli asked.

"Reality shows are about ratings," she said.

"I know."

"And the storm action is hot," she added. "But we need filler. We need stuff to plug in when there aren't killer tornadoes on the loose. Plus the viewers need to get to know you. They need to feel like they do."

"And so we have to do something we would never really do—hang out in a giant hot tub together—to make viewers feel like they know us?"

"Come on, Eli," Charlie said with a tilt of her head. "You're a smart guy. You know what you look like. What all of you look like."

He gave her a slow smile. "And if I don't want to be part of the peep show?"

"Peep show?" Charlie laughed, touching his arm. "Elijah, I'm not asking you to strip."

"Oh, but she wants him to," Hannah whispered behind her hand to Quinn, who had to press her knuckles against her mouth to keep from laughing.

Eli glanced down at her hand. "Just the same, I think I'll sit at that table *by* the hot tub. *With* my shirt on."

Charlie sighed. "Viewers will be disappointed."

"They'll survive," he said. "I'll be the man of mystery."

Hannah snorted out loud as Charlie gave him an exasperated yet endearing look and walked away.

"Was that flirting, big brother?" Hannah said.

Eli cut his eyes her way. "Hardly."

"No, you smiled," Quinn said. "I distinctly saw you smile at her."

"I smile all the time," Eli said.

"Actually, you just grimace," Hannah said. "Although it does use similar muscles, so I can see—"

"I wasn't flirting," Eli said in a dramatic whisper.

"Wouldn't be bad if you were," Quinn said. "She's kind of cute."

"She's kind of crazy, too," Eli said.

Quinn's laugh choked in her throat halfway out as her phone rang again. Eric. She could let it go to voicemail, but that trying thing pushed its way to the surface and made her hit the button.

"Hey, lovebug."

"Hey . . . What's up?" Quinn asked, glancing around at the techs buzzing through the room.

"Just had a phone call," he said.

"Oh, you've got to be kidding," she said under her breath.

"She's pretty upset, Quinn," Eric said. "She wants everything to be perfect for you."

"Which, if she'd just leave things the hell alone, they would be," Quinn said. "She worries about the stupidest things!" Quinn blew out a breath slowly and walked a few steps away. "Who cares if two different photographers get in on it," she said. "Hannah's done it. I wouldn't have a problem with it."

"But she said they won't match," he said. "And something about table cards."

Oh, sweet God, the cursed table cards. "I don't care about table cards," Quinn said under her breath. "They are place cards that match the portrait in the main hall of a reception, in everyone's seat. And it's ridiculous and overkill and something everyone just throws away."

"Baby, I know, but is there any way you can do this for her?" Eric asked. "She's—"

"Eric!" Quinn exclaimed, pulling the phone away to stare at it as if it were tricking her. "You know I'm two hours away."

The second heavy dramatic sigh within the same twenty minutes filled her ears.

"Which is insane. You need to start showing some interest in this," he said.

He's trying. I'm trying. What the living hell.

"Some—some interest? In what?" Quinn's whole body went hot as she stood with her back to everyone in the room and listened to the ludicrous words coming out of what she thought was an intelligent mouth. "In getting married?"

"In the *wedding*," he emphasized. "It's like you couldn't give a shit about any of it."

"I *couldn't* give a shit about any of it!" Quinn yelled, pulling in a breath to take her tone down. "It's not my wedding, Eric, I told you the other night. It's hers. I hate it. I'm showing up only to marry *you*. That's it. Now, can you start backing *me* up on a thing or two, or is it always going to be you and my mom in the same corner?"

"I'm letting you go," he said, hanging up.

"Good!" she yelled, wheeling around just in time to see Simon push through the door like one of the Horsemen of the Apocalypse.

All sets of eyes went from her to Simon.

"Whoa, dude, what's the matter?" Hannah asked, darting a glance back to Quinn.

Simon raked his wet hair back with his fingers and took a deep breath. "Nothing a little cloning wouldn't solve."

"We ready to get started now that all the players are here?" Charlie said.

"Absolutely," Quinn said, pulling off her T-shirt and wadding it on top of the table as a pad for her phone. She didn't want it with her, near her, or within her hearing if she could help it. In fact, she turned it to vibrate. And then she just turned it off.

Simon blinked, licked his lips, and looked like he was a million miles away. Which was probably a good thing because Quinn was too angry to deal with more shit from him. Or even anything on the flip side. If he looked at her like he had the other night, her swimsuit might fall off on its own.

"So what are we doing?" Simon asked irritably.

"Take your mike pack off," Charlie said. "And you're getting in the tub.

Simon looked at the tub, bubbling and giving off steam. "Let's get this over with," he said, yanking his wet T-shirt off in one move.

Quinn made herself look away as hard muscle stood before her just feet away, clad in only a pair of swim trunks. She wouldn't look. She wouldn't think. God, how could Eric be such an ass? Why did Simon have to be so—infuriating? Why were they making it all so damn difficult?

"You okay?" Eli asked, pulling her from her reverie.

Quinn looked down at where he sat kicked back in a patio chair, looking up at her with concern. She glanced around to see everyone giving her questioning glances. Everyone except Simon, who mercifully missed the big show.

"I'm —yeah," she said. "Just—" She shook her head. "Just stuff."

"So we heard," Eli said.

Great.

Quinn started peeling tape from her skin. "It's all good," she said evenly. "Let's do this."

Chapter Fifteen

Simon yanked tape and wires from his body as two camera techs jumped to rescue the equipment he was tossing aside.

"You have somewhere to be?" Charlie asked.

"Yeah," Simon said under his breath. "Possibly looking for another job."

That wasn't all. The real shit of it was, that wasn't the worst of the two phone calls he'd had.

The second bitch-out from Barry was bad enough, telling him that bad weather was definitely impending and they needed him there. They needed him at the station to do the research and magic he always managed to provide. The veiled threats, all because of this. Filming a conversation in a fucking hot tub, two hours away. All of it was enough to give him a headache from hell. Then Stacey had beeped in.

"Simon, where are you? Are you still headed out of town?" she asked.

"No, actually, I'm at the hotel now," he said. "What's up?"

"How far?" she asked, panic sending her words up another octave at the end, prickling his skin with worry.

"Stace, what's wrong?"

"How far out of town?"

"Two hours," Simon said. "Talk to me."

"Shit," he heard her say, with a hint of maybe some tears coming into play. His whole body went cold. Stacey didn't cry. She didn't panic.

"Stace!"

"I just got a phone call from the county inspector's office," she said. "They got an anonymous tip that we're violating the health code."

"Fuck."

"Yeah."

"Are you?"

"Right now I am, yeah," she said. "Everything is breaking. I have full beds and only one working shower. Two working toilets. There's mold growing in the hole under where the air conditioner leaks, and all I can afford to do is spray bleach at it."

Simon heard a shaky breath and then a hand over the receiver as things went muffled. He could hear fast talking, Stacey barking orders at someone, and then she was back.

"I should have turned people away, Simon," she whispered, sounding so broken it hit him in the gut. "I should have, to stay up to code. But I couldn't. And now the inspector is coming and I can't leave work. Now everyone will be turned away."

"Don't say that. We don't know that," he said.

"Yes, we do."

"Shit, shit, shit," Simon muttered. "Of all times to have to film bullshit."

"It's okay, I know you're stuck too," she said. "I've tried Barney and Ava, but they aren't answering."

"Barney?"

"Daniels."

"Shit, I never knew his first name," Simon said. "What? To warn them?"

"Yeah," she said. "That. Clean up. Try something. I don't know."

"Maybe they won't come today," Simon said. "Maybe they won't, and I'll be back tomorrow afternoon and we'll have time to pool some resources."

"Simon," she said, her voice the opposite tone of what it had been just minutes earlier. She was calling it.

"No."

"Simon," she repeated. "I've let them all down. They're gonna close us."

He flashed on his dad holding him up, his fingers touching the sign.

"I don't accept that," he said, pacing the sidewalk, the rain pelting him.

"It is what it is," she said.

He'd been her last-ditch effort. She'd called him hoping he could pull out a miracle.

And where was he? Getting ready to sit in a hot tub with his siblings—and Quinn—and talk about bullshit for a camera. People he cared about were losing the only roof and hot meal they had, and he was—about to have a coronary if he didn't calm down.

Swiping Eli's water, he downed a third of it before pulling his wallet out of his pocket and sliding out a five.

"Here, buy another one," Simon said, tossing the bill and his wallet on the table.

"Okay, Simon," Charlie said. "Get on in. Hannah, then you, then Eli—you sit across from Hannah. Quinn, you sit facing Simon."

Simon got in, needing the burn, relishing the boil of the water against his skin. He needed something burning hotter than he was.

"I'm good right here," Eli said, holding up what was left of his water with the gesture of a toast. He kicked back in the patio chair with his legs crossed at the ankles, shirt on. "I'll even talk," he said with a grin. "How about that?"

Simon chuckled. The rebellion felt awesome. For once, he wanted to be Eli and feel that in living color.

Charlie looked like she wanted to string him up by those ankles, but she mumbled something to a camera tech instead, who hopped into action, changing the angle on both the tub-level camera and the wider-perspective one.

Hannah pulled off her tank top and draped it over her chair, pulling her curls up in a messy half ponytail with a band on her wrist while the tech unwired her.

It was Quinn that Simon was trying not to watch and failing. She wore a white bikini with boyshort bottoms that hugged the world's most perfect ass. The top outlined her tits so perfectly, Simon knew in seconds that he'd have to be the last one out of the hot tub. With his towel nearby. But it was her face that had his real attention. She looked like he felt.

Wadding the tangle of wires and tape in a ball, she set the whole mess next to her phone and walked to the edge of the hot tub, staring down at the water. And in that one moment, Simon felt his heart for the first time since they'd left the house. He'd vowed to shut it down after her little comment, but watching her stare with anxiety at something as innocent as a hot tub made him want to do something stupid like hold her hand or pick her up. God, he needed to not care. For one damn night, he needed to not give a shit. He'd kind of had enough.

Long legs stepped onto the first step, then the second, and she lowered herself to sit on the first instead of all the way down. His eyes dragged their way up her body to finally land on her face, and his dick twitched at the look he saw there.

Desire. Anger, and stubbornness, as she set her chin and met his gaze with a don't-fuck-with-me look, but desire just the same. He knew the look well. He'd seen it even in the dark just days ago.

It's mutual.

God help him, he didn't need this. He didn't need to see that. She didn't need to feel it. They didn't need to be thinking like this. They never should have let it happen. *He* shouldn't have let it happen.

Her eyes fluttered, and she looked away as she crossed her arms in front of her. Well, at least that was something. Watching the water bubble madly around her thighs and between them would be a hell of a lot easier without the added perfect outline of very hard nipples.

"Quinn, you can get all the way in," Charlie said.

"This is fine," she said with a tight smile.

"It would be better if—"

"This is as far as I go," Quinn said. "It's this or I sit up there with Eli."

Simon's eyebrows raised a notch. Tensions were certainly running high in there tonight. But he knew her dilemma. And as pissed off as he was, he would still fight for her right not to cross that line.

"Let her be," Simon said. "It'll look less staged, anyway."

What looked like a tiny flicker of gratitude showed in Quinn's eyes. A hint of the old comfort level circled around them for about two seconds.

"So just talk normally," Charlie said, breaking the moment. "Whatever you'd normally talk about right now. Like we aren't even here." She pointed at the wide-angle cameraman. "And—go."

All four of them looked at each other.

"So," Eli began. "Anybody else notice the pancake breakfast?"

"Totally on that," Hannah said, raising a hand.

"Amazing to drive two hours to get pancakes and talk while it sprinkles outside, isn't it?" he continued.

Simon smirked.

"Cut!" Charlie called, tilting her head at Eli. "Come on."

"You said to act like you weren't there," Eli said, holding up a hand. "I promise this is what we'd talk about."

Charlie blew out a slow breath and set her clipboard on the table next to Eli before sinking into the nearest chair.

"Please work with me," she said softly. "I drove two hours, too. And I'm just trying to do my job."

"Don't you mean Maddi's job?" Simon asked.

"No, I mean mine," Charlie said, meeting his gaze. "Maddi's not going anywhere. My job is special projects, and right now that involves you." She focused back on Eli. "This show is what I'm assigned to at the moment, but when she comes back, I could be doing something else entirely. So can you guys please help me out here?"

Eli rubbed his eyes, and Simon knew she'd won. *Pushover*. But she did seem nice. And the blue eyes were pretty to look at. Jesus, he'd gone soft.

"Fine," Eli conceded, waving a hand at the camera. "Let's roll merrily along."

"Thank you," Charlie said, touching Eli's hand as she stood and walked back behind the cameras. Eli's gaze dropped to his hand and then followed her.

Well, well. What would Nicole say?

Thunder rolled over them, a slow grumbling build that went on for a full ten seconds. Hannah raised an eyebrow at Simon.

"That sounded interesting."

"It is supposed to be picking up, according to my boss," Simon said, staring at the bubbles regenerating by the filter. Over and over and over, a never-ending supply.

"Even better," Charlie sang from the back. "Roll."

"Rain's supposed to be picking up, according to my boss," Simon repeated emphatically, making even quiet, sullen Quinn give in to a smirk, he noticed.

"And that thunder—did you hear it?" Hannah asked, wide-eyed.

"It sounded interesting," Simon finished.

"Y'all are freaks," Eli said.

"Man, we need Zach here," Hannah said. "Zach would liven things up."

"Hey," Simon said, pointing at his chest with pretend indignance.

"Sorry," Hannah replied. "But you're gripey, not lively."

"Did I tell you that I ran into Derrie Boudreau?" he fired back, watching the smart-assery drain right out of his sister.

Derrie was the wife of local rival storm chaser, Jonah Boudreau. Jonah was generally a pain and always a thorn in the Chases' collective side. He was also Hannah's first love. Possibly the only one. And the only person Simon had ever seen have the power to turn his sister inside out.

"Nope," she said, recovering. "You didn't."

"She thanked us profusely for letting her and Brax come to Zach's storm room last time," Simon said.

Hannah's smile was tight, but she nodded. "Good deal."

Simon felt another question coming to his lips regarding Jonah and Derrie's son, but he bit it back, realizing he was crossing too far. This was his sister. And the camera was rolling. What the hell was wrong with him? He rubbed at his face with a wet hand, letting the air chill the droplets on his skin. *Shit, dial it back.*

Unfortunately, he'd only started an unhealthy ball rolling. He saw it in Hannah's face.

"So Quinn, what was that phone call about?" she asked. "Mom or man?"

Quinn's gaze slid sideways to fix on her friend with an alarmed look.

"Hey!" she said.

"What? It's just a question."

"Nothing important," Quinn said, pasting on a smile that didn't reach her eyes.

"There was yelling," Eli said.

Quinn's head swiveled back in Eli's direction. "Really? Et tu?"

Eli shrugged with a small smile, in a bit of a rare playful form for him.

"We're supposed to talk," he whispered loudly.

"So talk about you!" Quinn said, chuckling.

"This is good. Keep rolling," Charlie whispered loudly to Casey. "I'll be right back."

"I missed the yelling," Simon said as Charlie exited the room. "What happened?"

Anger, frustration, and something much more primal were palpable in Quinn's eyes when they landed on him.

"That's my business," she said, ice lacing each word.

"Ah, that's right," Simon said softly, a smile tugging at his lips. "We aren't—"

"Oh, my God, enough with that," she fired back before he could finish. "What about *your* call? What got you all cranked?"

Simon felt his jaw twitch. "Quid pro quo."

Quinn laughed bitterly. "You're so full of it."

He shook his head, not blinking. "Your ball."

"No, thanks."

"Afraid?"

"Annoyed," she said, raising her voice. "What's your problem?"

"What *is* your problem?" Hannah echoed. "Jesus, Simon."

"Nothing," Simon said, shutting his eyes and leaning his head back. Shutting out the image of Quinn sitting in front of him, looking like dessert with whipped cream. "Just too much in my head right now."

"And you're the only one?" Quinn said.

Simon sighed and opened his eyes, staring at the tiles on the ceiling. "Clearly not."

"You don't have the market on problems," she said, gripping the back of the tub behind her.

"Hence the evil phone call?" he said, lifting his head to meet her gaze again.

"It was my *fiancé*," she said, enunciating the word so damn slowly it had like five syllables.

"Isn't it *always*?" Simon said just as slowly.

Quinn's upper lip twitched. "Calling to tell me I should appease my mother by miraculously not being where I am right now. And then that I need to care more about *her* wedding. Fifteen minutes after having the same conversation with her."

"Her wedding?"

"That's the gist of it," Quinn said flatly. "Your turn."

"Stacey," Simon said, a surge of satisfaction hitting his gut at the flash of irritability that crossed her face when he mentioned Stacey's name. *Why was that satisfying? Walk away.* "Telling me the shelter's being shut down." Simon felt those words in his bones. "My father's shelter is being shut down."

Quinn's eyebrows drew together in a concerned frown, the pissed-off fading for a minute. "I'm sorry."

"It wasn't actually Dad's shelter, Simon," Hannah said. "I mean—"

"In every way that mattered," Simon said through his teeth, "that place was Dad." He stood up so fast the water sloshed over the sides and Quinn gasped. "Now I'm about to get sacked at work."

"What? Oh, shit," Quinn said.

"Yeah. Oh, shit," Simon echoed nastily, making Quinn jerk her head back as he stepped out of the hot tub and started walking for the door. God, even he could see he was being an obnoxious ass. He needed away. Now.

"Hey!" Quinn yelled. *Keep walking.* He heard the slap of wet footsteps behind him and inwardly groaned. "Hey!"

"What?" Simon yelled, turning on his heel. If he weren't so churned up, he would have been massively turned on. Storming after him, flushed and half naked and partially wet, breathing fast with anger, she was phenomenal.

"You don't need to be a dick to everyone just because you're mad at me," she seethed.

"I hate to break it to you, sweetheart, but I have more to worry about than you, Quinn," Simon said, stepping forward and feeling the challenge her lifted chin presented. "Just like you do."

"Don't flatter yourself," she spat back.

"I don't have to," he said. "You kissed *me.*"

Quinn sucked in a breath, and somewhere in the deep recesses of logic that weren't fueled by the fire boiling his blood, Simon knew he'd crossed that line again. In a big way.

She narrowed her eyes and her lips went white. "Well, I didn't see you throwing me in the creek over it. You sure as hell stayed there a while."

Because it was the best thing that had ever happened to him. *Say that, asshole.*

"It was a mistake."

Yeah, that was infinitely better.

Quinn scoffed, laughing bitterly as the tears welling up in her eyes fell free. "Wow, Simon. Now not only did it not mean anything, but it was a mistake, too?"

"Damn right it was," he said, advancing on her. "Three days ago, we were friends. You were my *best* friend. Now we're—what? Nothing, according to you."

His whole body felt like it was on fire. His head was pounding and his skin felt like it could light a match as he met her angry glare. Then his eyes dropped to her hands, nervously twisting her ring around and around her finger.

And then there was that.

"I'm going back to the room," he said under his breath.

"You're an ass," she hissed. "And you know what?"

"Astound me," he breathed.

"I feel sorry for Stacey now."

Confusion threw him for a detour. "Stacey?"

"To think I envied her," Quinn said almost to herself.

"You envied her?" he asked.

Quinn scoffed. "Not anymore."

"Good," Simon said. "You can move forward with your Barbie-doll life now. You and Ken should be very happy. Good luck with the Martha Stewart wedding and the web design job."

There you go, Simon. Jump off the damn cliff.

"How dare you," Quinn cried, new tears springing to her eyes as she swung the only thing she had. A damp towel.

Simon grabbed it and pulled her in with it. Quinn's hand on his chest stopped her from crashing into him but not from gasping at the very close heat between them.

"What do you want from me, Quinn?" Simon said, feeling the heat of her hand like a branding iron on his skin. Her face was right there. Her mouth was right there. Her eyes dropped to his mouth, the green going dark. *Fuck.* "You want me to even the field?"

She didn't answer, and it wouldn't have mattered if she had.

Simon dropped the towel and pulled her face to his, covering her mouth with his. It was wrong and bad timing and bells were going off in his head all over the place, but he couldn't stop. He couldn't be that close anymore and not touch her. Not taste her.

And the way she melted against him, skin to skin, kiss for kiss, fingers starting to splay over his chest as her breathing quickened, she was right there with him. And it was going to be the undoing of them both.

Simon tore his mouth away from hers as they each drew in a shaky breath. Her eyes were closed, as if that would make it not real. She wasn't drunk this time. It didn't get more real.

"There," he said on a whisper against her lips. "I'm the bad guy now."

He let go of her as she opened her eyes with a look that he knew mirrored his own. They were screwed. He backed up a step and ran both hands through his damp hair, clenching his jaw, kicking the towel at his feet.

"You're marrying another man, Quinn," he breathed. "Damn it, there were reasons why we stayed where we were." He stepped into her again, trying his hardest not to breathe her in. "This," he said, gesturing between them. "*This* is why. At least for me. Because I can't go backwards now."

"Stop filming!" Hannah cried from across the room, spinning Simon and Quinn both around and out of the bubble they'd made for themselves.

"Oh my God," Quinn whispered in horror.

Hannah leapt from the hot tub in a spray of water. "I said stop!" she yelled. "This is private!"

"This is gold," Casey said, still rolling. "This is reality, people."

"No, no, no," Quinn said, her feet propelling her forward.

Eli's chair scraped against the concrete floor as he pushed up and out, but Simon was there before anyone else. He grabbed Casey's arm and his shirt collar at the same time.

"You erase that," Simon said through his teeth.

"I can't—"

"The hell you can't," Simon said. "You're messing with someone's real life right now. Look at her." He jerked Casey to the side where Quinn was frantically pulling her T-shirt back on with shaking hands. "Look at her!"

"I'm looking!" Casey yelled.

"You want to destroy a good person?"

"No," Casey said miserably. "But—"

"But nothing," Simon said. "You lose it right now, or you and your camera are going in the water," he added, pulling Casey to him for leverage as Eli loomed, ready to help push. "I don't care what it costs me."

"This is a seven-thousand-dollar piece of equipment," Casey said.

"Bill me," Simon said.

"He said *now*," Eli growled, making Casey do a double tak.

"Okay!" Casey said as Simon gripped him tighter. "Shit, okay!"

"What's going on?" Charlie said, walking in.

"Delete," Simon muttered.

Casey fumbled with a button and then held his free hand up. "It's done."

"Guys?" Charlie said.

Simon let go of Casey, pulling in a deep breath and walking a few steps away. *Shit.* He rubbed at his face, the adrenaline still pumping through his blood at top speed. He could still taste her on his tongue, and he closed his eyes. What had he done? What the hell was he doing? Like his life wasn't messed up enough right now.

Eli rounded in front of him as the chatter droned on behind them. His look was as judgmental as usual, but his tone was soft.

"You all right?" he said.

Simon chuckled, suddenly exhausted from a day that had barely begun. "Do I look all right?"

"No, you look like you're about to self-combust," Eli said.

"Well, as long as I'm fooling everyone," Simon said, working the back of his neck with a hand.

"That was unexpected," Eli said.

"You have no idea," Simon said, not looking him in the eye. "And thanks—for back there. Helping me out."

"Always, little brother," Eli said. "I don't have to agree with you to have your back."

Simon met his gaze then. "I know."

"Nice bluff about the seven thousand, too," Eli said with a smirk.

"Shit," Simon breathed. "I would have had to take out a damn loan."

Eli laughed, slapping Simon on the shoulder as he walked away. "The things we do."

Simon turned to see Quinn sinking into a chair opposite Hannah, her eyes meeting his for a brief second before blinking away. It was enough.

"The things we do," he said under his breath.

Chapter Sixteen

Quinn had to look away from Simon. Had to look away from Hannah. Damn it, she just plain couldn't look at anyone. She was a horrible person. Simon had called her a good person during the camera drama, but she wasn't. And now everyone in the room knew it.

They were taking a break as the cameras were reset for another plan, and Quinn watched Simon grab his shirt and his computer and leave, taking half of her insides with him. The other half was sitting two hours away, probably having coffee with her mother and not having the foggiest idea what a fraud he was marrying.

She leaned her elbows on the table and buried her face in her hands, knowing full well that Hannah was staring her down. Waiting.

Quinn could still smell him on her hands. Taste him. She shut her eyes tight as her stomach shimmied over the memory of the oddest and hottest kiss of her life. Throwing insults and angry words back and forth until he just took what he wanted, adrenaline pumping and desire going ape-shit. Who the hell was she for that to turn her on? Because it had. He could have had her right there on the concrete floor between the swimming pool and a foosball table. Because as soon as he'd pulled her to him, she'd forgotten anyone else was even in the room. Forgotten about the camera. Forgotten about Eric.

Again.

What the hell did that say about her?

"Well, that was intense," Hannah said finally.

"Yeah," Quinn said into her hands.

"So I guess that answered my question from earlier."

Quinn nodded into her hands. "I'm sorry."

"I—don't think it's me you need to be sorry to," Hannah said.

Quinn dropped her hands. "I mean I'm sorry I didn't tell you. I didn't—I couldn't—"

"Don't sweat it," Hannah said. "I understand the weird." She leaned forward. "But now you need to spill."

Quinn's eyes filled with unbidden liquid fire. "That I'm a horrible troll?" she asked, her voice quivering.

"You're not a troll," Hannah said, tossing a towel her way.

"A horrible, secret-keeping, cheating troll," Quinn said, blinking hot tears down her cheeks and quickly wiping them away. "What is wrong with me?"

Hannah's eyes narrowed as her brows lifted. "Did something major happen?"

Quinn shook her head. "Just kissing."

"Since when?"

Quinn took a deep breath. "The night of the wedding."

"Ah," Hannah said. "The drunk fest. I wouldn't call it cheating, then."

"Uh, *I* would," Quinn said, lowering her voice. "If Eric was making out with another woman, I would call that cheating."

Hannah sighed. "You're talking to someone who's had an affair with a married man for basically a decade," she said.

It was one of the rare times that Hannah even acknowledged it. Most of the time, it was spoken about in code, and Quinn could tell when it was on or off.

"A kiss—ehh," Hannah continued with a shrug. "Call it wedding stress."

"It's not wedding stress," Quinn said, realizing with a start what she was admitting. "I mean, there's a lot of that, but Simon's not— he's—" She didn't know how to even articulate the effect Simon had on her. "It wasn't just a kiss, it was—" Her hand went to her chest as she blew out a steadying breath.

"Shit," Hannah whispered. She sat up and gave a polite smile to Charlie as she passed, then leaned in again. "So what are you saying?"

"God, I'm too old for this," Quinn said, rubbing her temples. "My little sister is married and about to be a mom, and what am I doing? Crushing like a schoolgirl."

The eyebrows shot up again. "On Simon?"

"You know how you said he'd always had a thing for me?"

"Yeah."

"Well—" Quinn said, holding out a hand toward the scene of the crime.

"Oh, Lord," Hannah muttered. "Why didn't you ever say anything?"

"Because!" Quinn said, feeling like an idiot teenager. "He's not just some guy, he's your brother, and we work together, and oh, God, I've totally screwed everything up."

I can't go backwards now.

Hannah fiddled with a corner of the towel she'd tossed on the table, studying it like it fascinated her. Quinn knew the tough stuff was coming.

"Say it, Hannah," Quinn said.

Hannah licked her lips and pulled a tiny frown. "Let's put Simon aside for a second. Because I know all about the thrill of something you aren't supposed to have. The forbidden fruit." She looked up, straight into Quinn's eyes. "It can sway you. Color things in shades that aren't really there. Make normal not look normal."

"Are you saying that you and Jonah—"

"I'm not saying diddly-shit about me and Jonah," she said. "I'm trying to tell you not to let Simon in your head when you're thinking about Eric."

Quinn's eyes fluttered closed.

"Have you seen Eric since?"

"Yeah," Quinn said. "And it was good and I was able to sort of—blame it on the alcohol in my own mind, but—"

"Yeah—but then today."

Quinn scoffed. "What do I blame today on?" she said. "The rain?"

"But if there was no Simon," Hannah said. "That's where you have to go with Eric. Assess it on its own merit without Simon in the equation."

"Assess it?" Quinn said. "I'm marrying him."

"Because?"

Quinn gave her a look. "Because what? Because I'm engaged to him."

"Engaged isn't married, Quinn," Hannah said. "It's not binding. You can still change your mind."

"Change my mind!" Quinn exclaimed, laughing. "Our families would disown us. My mother alone would stage an intervention to stop time. Why would I do that?"

Hannah sat back in her chair. "Because you just told me you're marrying Eric for your families and because you're engaged. Not once did you say because you love him."

Had she really not said that? "That goes without saying," Quinn said, feeling the room start to spin again.

"Not when you're kissing another man, it doesn't."

Quinn stared at the alarm clock between hers and Hannah's beds for the fortieth time in the last three hours. She'd passed out from exhaustion after the emotional roller coaster of the day and fifty different hikes up fifty different hills, talking about random things in the pouring rain, and getting promo shots of the show's cast pretending to do things. At Texoma. Where it was hilly and treed and beautiful and clearly not where they lived and worked.

While she and Simon avoided each other and barely spoke a word.

The whole experience was draining.

But at one in the morning, she was wide awake, listening to the rain. Staring at the bland ceiling above her and her new life ahead of her, seeing a disturbing resemblance.

At two, she'd opened a book on her phone and tried reading but couldn't concentrate. Eric's smiling face kept swimming before her, always followed by Simon looking at her with pride when she saw him through the camera that night of the wedding. Followed by the first time she kissed him, and how mind-blowingly intense that got. The feel of his hands on her . . . And then yesterday. His mouth . . . his eyes . . .

You're marrying another man, Quinn.

I can't go backwards now.

And then his face looking at her through the camera again . . . and it would start all over.

At four, she got up and made a cup of coffee in the little machine that sat in the bathroom, probably hardly ever used. The coffee was cheap and nasty, but it was hot, and with enough cheap creamer it was acceptable. The rain sounded more intense, and she decided to take her coffee outside to watch it.

Trying not to wake Hannah, she opened the door slowly, the sound of the rain on the metal awning that covered the sidewalk louder than anything else. Quickly, she slipped outside and clicked the door shut behind her, and nearly swallowed her tongue when she turned around.

"Shit, Simon!" she yelped, clapping a hand over her mouth.

He was sitting in one of the plastic chairs by the door, head leaned back against the brick building. In the low light from a parking-lot safety beam, she just saw a silhouette at first, then his shape and telltale ball cap came into focus.

"Sorry," he whispered.

"What are you doing?"

He rolled his head her way, and as her eyes adjusted to the dark, she could see his eyes. Damn, those eyes. Quinn felt the contraction in her gut and knew the smart thing would be to go back inside.

So she sat down in the chair beside him instead.

"Probably the same thing you're doing, I imagine," he said. "Wanting to look at something besides the ceiling."

"Pretty much."

The quiet that settled between them was both comfortable and suffocating. It was nice sitting next to him, watching the rain blow sideways through the parking lot, and any other time Quinn would have loved it. But now—now there was so much left unsaid. And too many reasons not to say any of it.

"So what's this doing?" Quinn asked, gesturing at the rain.

"No circulation to speak of," Simon said with a shrug. "But it could change."

"Think we should make a run?"

"We'll see at daylight," he said. "I don't want to get everyone up and out there in the dark for just a little rain."

"Zach would," Quinn said with a grin.

"Yeah, well, Zach's the tornado whisperer," Simon said on a chuckle. "He *feels* if there's something in there."

Quinn laughed. "True."

She felt his eyes on her and all she could do was close hers. She couldn't look at him. *She couldn't look at him.*

"Quinn," he said softly.

She shook her head, keeping her eyes closed. The burn was coming, damn it, and she should have never sat down, but it was nice. There for about ten seconds, it was like old times. Old times that were just last week. He wasn't calling her Little Bit anymore, she noticed. Things had changed. Everything had changed.

I can't go backwards.

Yeah, neither could she, apparently.

Then she felt the warmth of his hand on hers, resting in her lap, and her eyes shot open.

"Quinn, I'm sorry," he whispered. "For being an ass. For saying—"

"Don't," she said. "You don't have to be sorry."

"I said some shitty things to you yesterday," he said. "I escalated that whole thing. Got you all fired up."

"You gonna tell me it meant nothing to you again?" Quinn asked, steeling herself when his eyes landed on her hard in the dark. "Because I will sock you in the neck if you do."

She was already hyperaware that his hand was four inches from ground zero, so it took that level of sarcasm to balance out the curling of her toes.

"Did it feel like it didn't mean anything?" he asked after a pause.

No sarcasm. Damn it, the intensity was going to take her down.

Just the look on his face alone, in the dark, was stealing her brain cells.

"No," Quinn whispered, not sure if the word even made it out of her mouth.

"Well, there you go," he whispered back.

She couldn't breathe. His eyes held her captive and all she could feel were the magnets pulling her in. Finally, blinking hard and fast, she looked away, drawing a breath like she'd been underwater for twenty minutes.

"*I'm* sorry, Simon," she said, her voice husky as she focused on the rain pounding the pavement. "I started this. I messed everything up. We—we can't go forward. We can't go backward." She downed a swallow of lukewarm coffee. "I changed something. I changed *us*. All because—"

"Because what?"

Quinn inhaled slowly, wishing she could laugh it off. Wishing she could say anything but the mortifying truth. "Because I wanted to kiss you."

Simon chuckled and let go of her hand, reaching up to turn her face toward him with one finger. "Well, I don't recall throwing you in the creek over it. I did stay there awhile."

Quinn clamped her lips together to hold back the laugh. "Good point," she said, smirking.

Simon ran his thumb along her jawline, his eyes dropping to her lips, and that one stroke sent all her southernmost parts into a full-blown nuclear meltdown. Quinn bolted to her feet before the rest of her decided to join the party.

"Shit," Simon muttered. "Quinn, I didn't mean to—"

"No," Quinn said quickly, holding a palm faced out. "You're fine. It's me. I'm just—"

"—engaged to Eric," Simon said, swiping a hand over his face. "I know."

Actually she was thinking more along the lines of *I'm just really wanting you to keep going*, but his was probably the better path.

Shit, damn, hell.

Quinn backed up against a pole, feeling the misty spray of rain on her back and not caring as she slid down to a crouching position.

"God, I've made such a mess of things."

Simon leaned forward on his elbows. "You had help, Little Bit."

She laughed, as hearing his nickname for her soothed some of the trouble in her heart.

"Thank you for what you did with Casey," she said. "That could have been a nightmare."

Simon nodded silently, and Quinn cursed her own mouth.

"Not that being with you is a nightmare," she said quickly. "I mean, obviously. I mean, I can't seem to keep my hands—or my lips—and just being near—"

He reached and grasped one of her wildly gesturing hands, stopping her babble and making her gasp.

"Take a breath," he said.

Quinn shut her eyes and just absorbed the feel of her hand in his. When had this happened? When had everything gone on double-sensitivity alert?

"Yeah, I'm kind of not doing so hot at that, either." She took a deep breath and let it go as she looked at their hands, pushing out a chuckle, hoping it sounded real. "I don't know when this happened, Simon. This thing we're dancing around." Yes, she did. Ten years of crushing. Not the point. "But it's not real. Or it can't be. It's like a fantasy, something I've built up in my mind or something, but—but I can't keep acting on it. I have someone that wouldn't appreciate it very much. I know I wouldn't."

Quinn's chest ached with the dual wish of wanting things to go back to normal and wanting to cross that space between them and dive into his arms. Her stomach contracted back to her spine at the thought of that, and she chewed at her bottom lip to detract from the feeling. God, if she'd only just kept her damn lips to herself. She could have harbored her crush in secret for the next sixty years.

"We aren't going to," he said. "Because it has to be over."

Quinn almost bit a hole in her lip.

"What? I mean—yeah. But—" Dear God, she needed duct tape.

He squeezed her hand and let go, leaving a cold void where it had been.

"In the last three days, I've watched everything I care about slip away," he said, rubbing his eyes. Suddenly he looked exhausted. Even in the dark, she could see that. "The shelter, probably my job, and now you."

"Me? Simon, I'm not going anywhere," Quinn said, reaching to take his hand back, wanting that warmth again, but he sat back in his chair. Almost like he didn't trust himself to be that close any longer. She knew the feeling. "I never meant that we weren't anything when I said that. I didn't mean it like that."

"I know—"

"I'm getting married, not leaving the country."

"Quinn, look how far we fell just since Saturday," he said, leaning forward again. "From a kiss."

Sweet God, the way he said the word *kiss* just about had her checking to be sure her pants were still on.

"That was more than just some kiss," Quinn whispered.

"Yes, it was," Simon said under his breath, holding her eyes with his. "So imagine taking it further."

The ground felt like it moved underneath her feet as she imagined that. Her fingertips went numb.

"Dealing with that fallout, the guilt, the arguing, the fighting, *me* being the drunk obnoxious asshole at *your* wedding because I won't be able to watch you walk down the aisle to marry another man after I've—" Simon stopped and breathed in fast through his nose.

Quinn forced out the breath she was holding and wound her arms around her knees before she did something impulsive, like wind them around him.

"So I'm saying, look what one little moment did," he said. "Like you said, we can't keep acting on that. I'm not willing to lose more of you. Of us."

"Okay, so we start acting like grown-ups and make better choices," she said.

"That ship has sailed," he said, pushing to his feet and holding out a hand.

Quinn looked at it like it could be either her salvation or her doom, and then took it as he pulled her up. Pulled her up very close. Close enough to feel his body heat and not back away. Close enough for those damn magnets to kick into high gear as she looked up into his face and her fingers automatically curled into his shirt.

"We can't go back," he said softly. "*I* can't go back, I should say," he amended, shaking his head slowly. "Not now." His hands slid up her arms, lighting her skin with little fires as they traveled. Up to her neck, her face. Quinn's breath caught in her chest as everything in her screamed *yes* when it should have been slapping her silly with *no*.

Simon dropped his hands like they'd betrayed him and looked over her head, his jaw tightening. "And this right here is why," he said tightly, backing up a step and scrubbing his hands over his face as if to snap himself out of it. "We can't do the friend thing anymore, Quinn."

"What?" she said, feeling the panic in her gut. Losing Simon completely? No. "What about not wanting to lose any more of us? You're jumping straight to losing more—"

"We can't right now," he said through his teeth, reaching for her face, and then stopping himself just short of it. "*I* can't. Until you're married—what, twenty-three days, you said?"

Quinn blinked and licked her suddenly dry lips. He was right. He was the one thinking logically. Again. So then why did her heart hurt? "Twenty-two now," she said weakly.

"Twenty-two days," he said. "Three weeks, roughly. We can be friends again then."

She shook her head. "Seriously?"

He backed up slowly. "I need to go run some data," he said. "Check radar and do a call-in."

"Simon."

He shook his head and turned toward his and Eli's door. "See you in a little while." And then he was inside.

Quinn stared at the door as it closed, then down at the empty chair he'd vacated. Sinking into it, she watched the rain as the wind picked it up in gusts and twisted it into tiny circles around the cars.

She wished for a gust strong enough to pick her up and whisk her away, which only reminded her of the tornado that had picked Simon up and deposited him on the other side of the road a few months back. There, for about two sickening minutes, she'd had to face the very horrifying possibility of life with no Simon in it. This felt frighteningly similar. Twenty-two days till she could call Simon her friend again, and also start her new life with Eric St. James.

The order those things landed in her mind wasn't lost on her.

Chapter Seventeen

"A re you ready?" Simon asked. For the third time.

"What the hell are you so itchy about?" Eli said, digging work boots out from under his bag. "There's nothing real out there, and for once we don't have Zach."

"Damn, Eli, brotherly love, much?" Simon said, checking his watch. "Sure hate to see what you say about me."

"Probably that you have crap timing with women," Eli muttered.

"No shit there," Simon responded without hesitation.

He'd come back in after the morning interlude with Quinn, antsy and more frustrated than ever. Every time they crossed paths, it left him needing her more. Needing to touch her if she was near enough. It was like a damn portal had been yanked open.

Quinn's hands on his bare chest yesterday had nearly taken him past all reason, and just saying the words *imagine taking it further* to her earlier—*well, let's just say I came damn close to doing just that.* Right there on the sidewalk.

And the really frustrating part was that he wasn't entirely sure Quinn would have said no.

God, he was screwed.

"And I only meant that Zach's the gung-ho one usually cracking the whip to get going," Eli said, bringing Simon back to the real world. "It's nice to not be in a hurry for a change."

"That hurry is what makes it fun," Simon said, checking his watch again. "And what gets us there before it's over. There's a possibility of this being bigger than you think."

"All right," Eli conceded with a sigh. "I'll meet y'all outside in five."

Outside, in the early-morning light, the rain reduced to a mist, the crew was milling around, loading up. Two guys were catching a last-minute smoke, one of them being Casey, who turned and found something to busy himself with the moment he saw Simon. Charlie was writing on her ever-present clipboard. Hannah and Quinn weren't anywhere to be seen.

"The girls ready?" Simon asked Charlie, hoping it sounded generic and not like *Have you seen Quinn?*

"They went to grab breakfast," Charlie said, not looking up. "I think they've already checked out, though. You said there's more coming?" she asked, glancing up at him. "Seems like it's petering off to me."

"I thought you had your own meteorologist," Simon said.

"He's not here," she said with widened eyes. "He's at the office."

"Hmm," Simon said with a wink. "Guess you'll have to trust me, then."

"There's a scary thought," said Hannah behind him, and he turned to see Quinn just a foot away, arms folded over her chest, eyes averted. Puffy eyes. Was she crying?

Not his problem.

It begins.

"How were the pancakes?" he asked, swallowing down everything else. Every need. Every desire. Every urge to tuck that stray damp tendril of hair behind her ear and ask if she was okay.

"Dry," Hannah said.

"Small," Quinn said, blinking against the mist.

"About what you'd expect from a free breakfast in a hotel," Hannah added.

"All right," Eli said emerging finally from the room. "Everyone ready?"

"We've been waiting on you, as I understand it," Charlie said.

Amusement danced in Eli's eyes. "Well, I hope I'm worth the wait," he said. "Let's go."

Charlie's eyes narrowed in either disgust or confusion, Simon couldn't tell, but he gave his brother a look as Eli got behind the wheel of the vehicle.

"I'm sorry, did he just do that?" Hannah asked. "It's early, so I might be delusional."

"This could be an interesting day," Simon said under his breath.

"Hannah, why don't you ride in the van this time?" Charlie said.

"What?" Hannah said, her hand already on the door handle of the SUV.

"We need one of you in each," Charlie said. "And I'm riding along in your vehicle. I want to see this action for myself." She shrugged. "Or Casey can go with you instead," she added.

"No," Simon and Eli said simultaneously.

"Kind of what I thought," she said as Casey shook his head and ambled over to the van.

"I'll go in the van," Quinn offered quickly, following him. "Hannah can stay."

"No, I want you in here," Charlie said, stopping her.

So she can instigate more drama, Simon thought. Quinn turned back reluctantly and opened the back door, meeting Simon's eyes for the briefest of seconds.

Twenty-two days. Just twenty-two more days.

"I can ride up front," Charlie said. "You two can have the back."

"No," Simon said quickly. Maybe too quickly. "I'm the navigator. I'm shotgun. Always."

Charlie gave him a little salute.

"Yes, sir."

"Wait, are we not getting wired up?" Quinn asked.

"Not for this," Charlie said. "Since it's just really an in-vehicle event, we'll stick with the car microphones."

"Okay, navigator," Eli said, cranking the engine to life. "Where are we going?"

Simon shut the door and pulled out his computer, trying not to think about Quinn sitting behind him again. At least this time she wouldn't be stripping.

"West," he said, grabbing the paper map that sat in the console—because Eli still trusted paper over GPS. "This area right here," Simon said, drawing a circle with his finger. "I watched every band come through there this morning, and each one gets circular when it hits here."

"Why is that?" Charlie asked.

"Wind currents through the topography," Simon said. "It's rugged here. Lots of hills. The lake plays into it, too." He tossed the map on top of the dash and tapped a button on his phone to call Hannah. "It's about thirty minutes from here," he said after a pause. "And from the look of this"—he pointed at his screen for those in the car—"we should have a welcoming party."

Quinn's phone rang and she hit the button to send the call to voicemail, but not before Simon recognized the ringtone she had for Eric.

"Everything okay?" Eli asked her, looking in the rearview mirror.

Great, now Papa Eli was taking over worrying about her.

"Fabulous," she said.

The tinge of sad in her voice made Simon's jaw clench. He couldn't fix this. He couldn't joke it away or make her laugh. He didn't even know if the crying had been about him or about Eric. Or about the wedding. Or about anything. Sometimes women just got stressed out and cried.

Simon's phone dinged with a text then, and he cursed under his breath reading it.

"Are *you* okay?" Eli asked.

His hands curled into fists on either side of his computer. "Yeah."

Instead of answering it, he hit a button to reply to Hannah and texted her.

Who's videoing, you or Q?

Isn't she in the car with you? she texted back.

Simon bit down so hard, he was afraid his teeth might break.

Please, he texted back.

I have my camera. Q has the handheld.

Shit. Shit. Damn. Hell. Everything was hell-bent on being difficult. He had a plan, and it very much involved staying away from any interaction with Quinn Parker until she was Quinn St. James. Including conversation, or her filming him. *Looking at her. Touching her. Ever laughing again.*

"Quinn, I need you to do me a favor," he said, rubbing at his tired been-up-for-entirely-too-damn-long eyes.

There was a pause, as he knew there would be.

"Okay."

Simon turned in his seat, ignoring Charlie's curious look as he steeled himself to meet Quinn's eyes.

When he did, it rocked his heart against his ribs. She held her chin up defiantly, but she'd never been good at hiding emotion. At least around him. And hurt was all up in there.

Please be about that stupid idiot, not about me.

"I need your help with something later," he said, closing his eyes briefly. "I'm sorry. I wouldn't ask—"

"I know," she said. "What's going on?"

"My boss," Simon said. "He's asking me to film a sixty-second piece on what's going on up here."

"Odd," Charlie said. "Is that normal?"

"No," Simon said. "But he's pissed at me and this is retribution."

"Not a problem," Quinn said, her tone cool. "Just let me know when."

Simon nodded. "Thank you."

"Don't mention it," she said, looking down at her phone as if there were something of vital importance residing there.

The splatter on the windshield turned from liquid mist to small rain droplets within minutes, and Eli upped the wiper speed. The radar confirmed the heavier activity as they drove closer, the colors on Simon's screen turning a deep red where they hadn't gotten to yet.

"Here we go," Eli said.

"Not just yet," Simon said.

"So Quinn, tell me about your wedding plans," Charlie said.

Simon turned to look at Charlie, imagining the same what-the-hell look on Quinn's face since there wasn't an instant response.

Charlie was focused on Quinn, however, or at least making a point not to look at him.

"Um, well, there's not much to say," Quinn said, reaching for her bag. "And we're about to be really busy."

"Three weeks away and there's not much to say?" Charlie said, laughing. "Lord, I was a loon before my wedding. Seems like it was nonstop."

"You're married?" Simon asked, glancing back at her bare finger.

"How did you know it was three weeks?" Quinn asked at the same time.

"Did my homework," Charlie said. "And divorced," she added in Simon's direction. "So you having a big blowout?"

Simon pulled his cap off and raked fingers through his hair, feeling he might pluck it all out one by one if he had to hear the lowdown on Quinn's wedding one more time.

"Probably," she answered, which made him smirk in spite of it.

"Probably?"

"I—really don't know," Quinn said, and Simon knew she was likely wishing to be outside the car in the rain rather than endure this questioning. "I assume so. My mother is handling all of it."

"Wow, that must be nice," Charlie said after a pause.

"You'd think that, wouldn't you?"

"We're about to hit it," Simon said, looking at the screen. He didn't have to say that. They'd figure it out. But he felt like she needed a diversion, and he jumped on the savior train as usual. "Y'all get ready."

Quinn pulled out the waterproof-cased handheld camera and tucked her phone into the back of the seat pocket just as it dinged.

Don't be Eric.

It wasn't. It was a text from Phoebe.

Where are you?

She put it on vibrate and texted back. *China.*

Mom called me.

Of course she did, Quinn typed back. *She recruited Eric.*

I heard, Phoebe texted.

Great. *From?* Quinn texted.

Both.

"Jesus Christ," Quinn muttered. "It's a damn soap opera."

"Problem?" Charlie asked, pulling out her own recorder.

226

"Nope, everything's dandy," Quinn said quickly, tapping out another message to her sister.

How much do you love me? Quinn typed and waited.

I don't know. What will it cost me?

"Ha ha," Quinn said under her breath. *Can you get dress from Mom's so I can come get from you? If I go there, one of us might go down.*

Will do tonight. You owe me dessert though.

TY and hugs and I'll pick up brownies on the way, Quinn typed. *Thanks for talking me down the other day btw.*

No problem, Phoebe texted with hearts on either side.

A hard slam of rain against her window, like someone threw a bucket of water at it, caught her attention.

Speaking of, how goes with Simon? Phoebe texted.

Gotta go. About to get real.

Mmhmm. I bet.

Quinn tucked the phone back into the seat pocket, stuffed a small towel on top of it, and pulled her left leg under her for leverage.

"Did you bring a towel?" she asked, looking at Charlie.

"No," Charlie said. "Are we getting out?"

"Maybe," Quinn said. "But I was talking about in here." She pointed at the recorder Charlie held in her hand, then worked her hand into the rubber lanyard that was attached to her own. "You might want to protect that."

Simon set his laptop into a slot in the dashboard where most cars have a glove compartment and pulled a towel around the sides.

"One day I'm going to figure out something more high tech than this," he mumbled from the front seat.

"Why would it get so wet in here?" Charlie asked. "You roll down all the windows or something?"

"Not all," Quinn said. "But in a storm, one's enough." She pulled her very unsexy plastic safety goggles from the bag and put

227

them on as the tiny hail pellets pinged off the window. "And it's showtime," she said, going up on one knee and hitting the window button.

Water assaulted her face, making her gasp first thing. There was always that first microsecond of fear, that feeling of panic as sheets of water blew into her face and she couldn't breathe. Every single time was a déjà vu moment, and she wondered if it would ever go away. That feeling of helplessness, of flailing panic.

She'd learned not to flail over the years, and she'd gotten good at covering her body's reaction to water as she glazed over and got into her zone, but that first gasp was inevitable. It was her tell.

"We're in the red," Simon said, raising his voice over the volume of water and ice hitting glass.

Quinn got on her knees, grabbed the handle overhead, and pushed herself out the window as Eli slowed a little. She angled the camera to catch a wide pan of the side of the vehicle all the way up the road as far as she could see. Which wasn't far.

"Whiteout ahead," Eli said. "Damn, I hate those."

Rain and ice stung her skin, pelting her face, whipping her hair free of the ponytail and slapping it against her cheeks.

"Gusts measuring fifty," Simon called out.

Quinn didn't care. She loved this part. The rush. The adrenaline. The violence of nature, buffeting a multi-ton vehicle around and reminding them that they weren't in charge.

"Small rotation north," Simon yelled over the clamor. "Don't know if it'll be anything, but—"

"Go!" Quinn yelled, leaning out further.

"Find your next right!" Simon added.

"You're gonna fall out the window!" Charlie yelled, pulling at Quinn's belt loop.

Quinn shook her head. "I'll anchor. I'm good."

Shit.

A hundred million times she'd ridden just like this with Simon in the front passenger seat. Even when it was just her and Eli, she rode in the back most times because she liked anchoring a leg around that front seat as she hung out the window.

With Simon there, it was always a joke that her leg wrapped around him. A joke she always got a secret thrill over, especially when he'd stroke her calf and make suggestive comments. It was all in fun—she'd thought. Once, he'd accidentally brushed the inside of her leg with the stubble from his chin as he turned to ask her something, and she'd had to grip the window frame to keep from falling out.

It was all there, she could see now, but then it was harmless. Now—not so much. Nothing felt harmless.

"Simon?" she said.

"Yeah?"

She took a deep breath and let it out. "Leg."

There was the slightest of pauses as he glanced over his right shoulder.

"Come on," he said, hitting his shoulder.

Don't think about it.

Quinn put her weight on her left leg and thrust her right one between the door and Simon's seat, positioning her hip against the window frame.

When the angle caused her lower leg to curl in toward the left against his arm, Simon took a different tack than usual. He leaned forward and then back against her leg, pinning it between him and the seat and probably being much more efficient.

Which only proved there was always more going on before, because he never used this option. This safer, more appropriate option.

Appropriate.

"You good?" he asked.

Quinn nodded, licking the rain from her lips. "Good."

"Be careful," he said, going back to studying the computer screen and the additional radar he had up on his phone.

"Always," Quinn said, leveraging herself back out the window with a rush of excitement and trepidation.

"Shit, you're crazy," Charlie yelled, laughing. "But crazy works!"

Quinn laughed, letting the adrenaline take her where she needed to go.

"You haven't seen anything yet!" she yelled as the wind swallowed her words. "God, it's beautiful out here," she cried, gripping the camera handle tight with her left hand as she leaned way out to get the swirl of the wind whipping around a different direction, making the rain dance for her as they passed through it. "Wait till you see—"

"Tree!" Simon yelled.

"Shit!" Eli growled, swerving hard to the right.

All Quinn saw was the shadow of something ahead in the whiteout before she slammed into the side of the SUV, her face planting into Simon's window.

Chapter Eighteen

Charlie shrieked, leaping sideways to latch on to Quinn's free leg as the car lost traction and spun to a stop on the side of the road.

"Quinn!" Simon yelled hoarsely. He was out of the car before it was even at a complete stop, pulling her from the window where she still hung on to the handle above it in a limp daze, as if she didn't know how to let go of it. "Quinn!"

"I'm—I'm good," she said, looking confused, blinking against the rain. Her safety goggles were cracked and hanging down the left side of her face, her left cheek cut and already swelling from the meet-up with car and plastic goggles.

Simon's heart felt like it would crack his damn ribs, it was beating so hard. He dropped to his knees in the mud, holding her in his arms, one hand cradling her head.

"Talk to me," he croaked, fear choking his words. He gently pulled the useless goggles from her head and tossed them aside, pressing his lips to her forehead. "Please be okay, baby," he whispered against her skin, knowing she'd never hear it over the roar of the wind and rain pounding on them. "I need you."

Her hand came up to his face and then the back of his neck, and he backed up a fraction to look in her eyes.

"I'm okay," she whispered.

"You sure?"

"I think," she said, holding on to him anyway. He didn't care. She could hold on forever if she wanted to. "Sit me up."

Simon lifted her slowly, trying to hold up a hand over her face to protect her as Eli came running around from his side and Charlie scooted across the seat to lean through Quinn's window.

"Is she okay?" Eli yelled against the wind, nearly going down in the mud in his haste to get to her. "Shit, Quinn, I'm sorry," he said, dropping to his knees beside them. "There's half a tree in the road over there. We almost hit it."

"Feels a bit like we did," Quinn said, touching her cheek gingerly as she leaned against Simon. "It's all good, though."

The van slid in behind them and Hannah jumped out.

"Oh, my God," she yelled. "Quinn, are you okay?"

"Did you see?" Quinn asked with a grin and then a wince.

"Did I see?" Hannah looked at Simon questioningly. "Uh, yeah, you crazy loon," she said, squatting to pull her in for a hug. "Don't do that again!"

"Help me up," Quinn said, reaching out for something to grab on to.

"Not yet," Simon said. "Let me see your eyes."

She was already on her way up, however, pushing on his head and Hannah's shoulder for leverage.

"Quinn—shit," Simon muttered, slipping in the mud as he tried to help her.

"My camera," she said, stumbling a little on her feet.

Simon was on his in seconds and moved Hannah aside. "Let me look at her," he said, raising his voice. The wind kept whipping her wet hair into her face, and Simon grabbed a handful of it and held it away. "Let me see," he yelled over the din of a million raindrops.

"No," Quinn said with a frown, pulling away.

"Let me see," Simon repeated, backing her up to the car and nailing her there with his gaze as he touched her other cheek. He didn't care who saw. He needed to know she was okay. Just the fact that she was standing had him nearly back down on his knees to give thanks.

"I dropped my camera," she whispered. So low, he almost didn't hear it. "Somewhere—"

"I'll look for it," Hannah said, splashing away in her boots.

"Stay still," Simon said, running his fingers over both cheeks gently to feel for differences as the wind threw gallons of water at them, over and over.

"Ow," Quinn said, flinching.

"I'm sorry, baby," he said, meeting her eyes as the word fell out of his mouth. Again. "And I don't care about your camera right now," he added, moving his hands to cradle her face so he could look in her eyes. For dilation. That was it. It wasn't because his heart was about to explode.

Her breath caught as their noses touched. Even in the roar all around them, he could hear that.

"Simon," she mouthed.

He blinked himself straight and focused on her pupils. "Are you dizzy?"

"I am now."

A gale-force gust slammed into them, rocking the car and knocking all four of them into it. Automatically, Simon put his body over Quinn's, shielding her as he still held her face in his hands. And there for about five more seconds, with Eli and Hannah and Charlie looking on, he didn't care. All he felt was overwhelming relief that she was all right.

His face was pressed into her matted wet hair above her ear, breathing her in. Absorbing her fear, her need, her stubbornness, her strength, her weakness, and giving her all he had.

"You scared me, love," he whispered, unsure if she could even hear him. It didn't matter. He just needed to say it. To feel her.

Feeling her hands come up his sides as she leaned her forehead against his chest was even better, but it was short lived.

"Simon," she said, lifting her face.

I'm leaving Eric.

I'm in love with you.

I want to do you right here on the side of the road in the pouring rain.

Any of the above.

"Y'all, look!" Charlie yelled, pointing past them in the distance.

Simon looked to his left while Eli did an about-face. The whiteout was lightening up as something was pulling it together. Where there was once a wall of white now gave way to the view just on the other side of the trees, down the gorge. The lake, angry and churning. With a perfectly formed curled waterspout worming its way from lake to sky.

"Holy shit," Quinn said, pushing Simon back. "Where's my camera?"

"Here!" Hannah said, running up, holding Quinn's and her own camera, keeping her face turned sideways to avoid the flying twigs.

"Oh, thank God," Quinn said, running her fingers over it. The case was cracked, but Quinn reacted as if it were a gift on Christmas. Her eyes dragged back to the scene in front of them.

"That's fucking beautiful," Eli said, standing there transfixed, leaves and small debris bouncing off him as if he were a boulder in their way. "But it's too close—we need to get out of here."

"Get over there, Simon," Quinn said, shoving at him. "This is the shot for your boss! Go!"

She was worried about his footage? "You need to sit, Quinn—get in the car."

"Hurry!" she said.

"The hell with that," Charlie said, getting out of the car and holding a hand in front of her face. "This is the shot for the show! God, look at that!"

The spout was white and beautiful, snaking rhythmically in a slow pulse, as if set to a slow, deep-beating ballad. Water sprayed from its perimeter like an obscene monumental fountain, and the rain hitting Simon in the face now took on a musty aroma. Like silt and surprised fish.

"You do the show shot, then," Quinn said. "I have something more important to do."

Hannah was already snapping away on her digital camera, but she reached for the little handheld recorder currently getting drenched in Charlie's hand. "I've got it," she said.

Charlie gave it up, handing it to Hannah without a fight, but then stepped in front of Quinn. "You've got this a little back-assward, don't you think?"

"Move," Quinn said, pushing Charlie to the side and propelling a stunned Simon to stand a few yards away.

"I'm not miked!"

Quinn raised her eyebrows. "Yell!"

The rain was washing the blood from her cheek, but the purple was growing. And all she cared about was saving his job.

"Hurry up, Simon!" she yelled, fiddling with the buttons on the mangled recorder. "Start talking!"

He did. Twisting to look at the beauty happening at his back, he turned back to face the beauty in front of him. The one hurt and bleeding and going to bat for him. Being his friend even though they couldn't be friends.

He talked as loud as he could, just short of throwing his voice out. Rattling off a bunch of technical jargon, laughing about watching to make sure it didn't sneak up behind him, and even ducking a large piece of a bush as it narrowly missed his head.

"Simon Chase reporting for Channel Four News, at Lake Texoma," he finished, giving Quinn a "cut" sign.

"Perfect," she said.

"Are you getting anything?" he called out to Eli, who had jumped into the vehicle to hit levers and pull information.

He saw Eli nod, so he headed straight for Quinn. "Send that to me," he said. "I need to send that in and shoot a message to the NWS."

"Already done," she said, still working buttons.

"It's breaking up!" Eli yelled, and Simon whirled around to see the spout breaking, spewing water in all directions.

"Back in the car," he said, propelling her. She looked up, wincing at the sudden move and sudden light. "Yeah, that," he said. "We're bringing you to a hospital."

"What?" she said. "No!"

"No argument," he said, his hand on her face, unable to stop himself. "This thing can start looking for land any second now, and I will pick you up and put you in there myself if I have to."

Quinn blinked fast. "Fine."

"Go," he said, stepping closer.

"Going."

Please be okay, baby. I need you.

Those words kept playing on long loop in Quinn's aching head, playing to the beat of the windshield wipers. Alongside the feel of

Simon's hands on her, the sound of his voice, the look of absolute—there was no way that look was what it appeared to be.

Eric didn't even look at her like that. Or he did, sort of. Sometimes. Nothing like what Simon had been giving her lately, though. The unabashed pride when she was doing the photo shoot at the wedding. The raw need and longing on the hotel patio in the rain. And then when he pulled her from the window after her accident—the fear, the dropping of all the walls.

The . . . love.

I need you.

Sweet Jesus, she thought as she held another icy water bottle to her face, she must really have a concussion. A free bleeder. Nerve damage. Brain damage.

You scared me, love.

Shit, shit, shit. Her head was killing her, and maybe her cheekbone drove into something important, something that worked out logical thought. Because logic wasn't even in the wheelhouse right now.

Charlie hadn't spoken two words to her since their little face-off, and that was okay. What was she going to do, fire her from the show? Quinn winced at the thought, hoping that wasn't an actual possibility. *Quinn* had signed the contract; *Quinn* was part of the team long before there was a show to speak of.

"We're going to have to go with Trinity," Simon said from up front, breaking her train of thought.

"We're thirty minutes from home at this point," Quinn said. "Seriously, just give me some aspirin and an actual ice pack and I'll be fine."

"You're going to get checked out," Simon said. "There was nothing else along the way, and Stacey can help get you in quickly."

Stacey.

Fresh blood pumped to her head with a vengeance.

"Besides, Phoebe is already meeting us there," Simon said.

"What? Why?"

"Because I texted her," Simon said, not turning around.

"You—what?" Quinn exclaimed, grabbing her head as the sound of her own shriek pierced her brain. "How did you even— you have Phoebe's number?"

"I do now," Simon said, handing over her phone.

Quinn took it and stared at the device in her hand. "You took my phone?"

"When you fell asleep," he said.

She looked at him, then at Charlie. "I fell asleep?"

"For a second," she said. "Till I kicked you."

"You kicked me?"

"If you have a concussion," she said, "you need to stay awake."

"And randomly falling asleep—" Simon began.

"I get it," she said, unsure what disturbed her more—passing out after a head injury or Simon looking at her phone. Possibly looking at her last text from Phoebe.

How goes it with Simon?

She shut her eyes tight. Oh, well, it was becoming the worst-kept secret in the universe anyway. Even from him.

Charlie kicked her foot. "Wake up!"

"I'm not asleep, will you stop kicking me?" Quinn said. "I know I filmed Simon's work segment instead of chase footage, but it was important."

"Shots like that are pretty damn important to the show, too," Charlie said. "We weren't even expecting anything that good. It was a gift."

"And Hannah got it," Quinn said irritably.

"Hannah just got the spout, but nothing of you doing anything," Charlie said. "No action. No—"

"No sound," Simon interrupted. "We weren't miked up for that. You told us that the car mikes were fine."

"I know!" Charlie said, rubbing her face. "But I thought we'd have time to think on the fly."

"There's no time to think at all," Quinn said. "We were damn lucky that thing danced as long as it did and then didn't come after us. We don't plan these things, and it doesn't always work like we want them to."

"I realize that," Charlie said.

"And Simon keeping his job was more important right then," Quinn said. She redirected to Simon. "Why did you text my sister?"

"To be there for you," he said.

Quinn widened her eyes. "Are you making me jump out of the car as you roll by?"

Eli laughed at that. "That's what I asked."

Simon shook his head as if they were both idiots. "You need a voice of reason there with you if they make you stay."

"You kind of sound like *you* fit that bill right now," Eli said, glancing his way.

Quinn saw Simon's jaw tense but he didn't turn around. "I can't stay," he said.

"So you tell a pregnant woman that her sister is hurt?" Quinn asked.

Simon did turn around on that one. "I could have picked Eric," he said. "Or your mother."

Oh, God. "Or Hannah," Quinn retorted. "Who is already with us."

"With no means of transportation," Simon said, facing forward.

"Again with the rolling stop," Quinn said. "You know, home is like ten minutes from there. Pretty sure *one* of you could have come back for me. For us. For whoever."

"It's done," Simon said. "Besides, you'd talk Hannah out of it."

"My powers are that strong, are they?" Quinn asked.

Simon turned very slowly and locked eyes with her, his showing amusement at her question—and something else. That other thing. That breathtaking other thing that wasn't—couldn't—be real.

"All right, we're here," Eli said, turning off into the parking lot of Trinity Medical.

"Oh, my God," Quinn muttered under her breath. "I can't believe you're actually making me—"

"You basically got hit by a car, Quinn," Eli said. "My car. With me driving it. It doesn't matter that you were hanging off it like a monkey at the time. So indulge me if I want to make sure you're okay, will you?"

"I know," Quinn said, leaning forward to squeeze Eli's shoulder. It had to have been a sickening feeling for him, too. "And you're right. I just—oh, mother of hell!"

"What?" Eli and Simon both said, but then Simon looked back the direction Quinn was looking.

"Damn," he said on an exhale.

"You were saying earlier?"

"I only texted Phoebe, I swear," he said.

Standing by the entrance was Phoebe. And Eric. And her mother.

"I'll pay you to turn around and keep driving," she said.

"Can't do that, Quinn," Eli said. "Put on your best face." He winced as he caught her eye in the rearview mirror. "Sorry, no pun intended."

"Ugh," Quinn muttered.

Eric was at her door before she even had her seat belt off. In suit slacks with his tie loosened and hair tousled with mist clinging to it, he looked like he'd just had a nap at work or a romp with the secretary. She knew better. The secretary was pushing sixty and would have cut his dick off with a spoon if he'd tried anything.

"What the hell happened?" he demanded.

"I'm fine, thanks for asking," she said, swinging her legs out.

"You know what I'm saying," he said, looking exhausted. "We get a text—"

"*I* get a text," Phoebe corrected, waddling up beside him, their mother on her heels. "At Mom's house. Where *he* wouldn't leave. And then read it over my shoulder. Rude."

"Whatever," he said. "It says that Quinn is hurt and to meet at Trinity Med—what the hell, Quinn, your face!"

"Well, that sounds promising," Quinn said.

"Baby, what happened?"

Baby.

Eric's didn't sound as nice.

"I was filming," Quinn said, grabbing her camera bag. "And we had to swerve hard to miss a tree in the road, so . . ."

Let that ride. He didn't need to know she was hanging on the outside.

"This is what I'm talking about," he said, shaking his head, touching her wounded cheek.

Quinn flinched and jerked back. "Ow!" she cried, then pressed a palm to her temple as her personal jackhammer amped up its speed. "Stop it!"

Simon got out and opened the back hatch, giving them a sideways look. He pulled out Quinn's backpack and handed it to Eric.

Eric grabbed it and unceremoniously tossed it aside.

"Hey!" Quinn said, frowning.

"I blame you, Chase," Eric said, pointing at Simon.

Simon's eyes took on a challenge that made Quinn's stomach twist.

"Of course you do," Simon said.

"She'd follow you anywhere," Eric said. "And I allowed that because I trusted that you'd keep her safe."

Did he just say that?

"Excuse me?" Quinn said.

"I'm sorry," Simon said on a smirk. "You *allowed* that?"

The van pulled into the next parking spot and Hannah jumped out, giving Quinn a wide-eyed look.

Eric's jaw twitched. "Don't put words in my mouth."

"I didn't," Simon said. "Those were *your* words. And I've never seen anyone *allow* Quinn to do anything."

"I look out for what's best for her," Eric said, stepping closer, pointing back at Quinn as if she were five.

"Really?" Simon asked. "Have you *met* your wife-to-be?"

"This isn't happening," Quinn whispered, linking arms with Phoebe.

"That's uncalled for," Adelaide bellowed, laying a hand on Eric's shoulder. "Eric knows Quinn like no one else. *He* is her rock. *He* will provide for her. This"—she gestured with a hand at the circle of activity—"is a distraction."

Simon didn't blink. "Have *you* met your daughter?"

"I'm so sorry," Phoebe said, turning to Quinn and pulling their mother with her. "Are you okay?"

"I cannot believe—" Adelaide seethed.

"Are *you* okay, Quinn?" Phoebe repeated with emphasis.

Quinn was boiling. She was shaking, she was so angry. But she managed a tight smile as she picked her backpack up off the pavement.

"Can we just go in and get this over with?"

"Absolutely," Phoebe said, flanking one side of her. "The dick-swinging is getting a little overzealous out here anyway."

"Phoebe!" Adelaide exclaimed.

"I'm pregnant, Mom," she said. "I get to say the word *dick*."

"There's *getting to*, and there's *should*," she said under her breath, following them.

"Can't wait to be a mom so I can say things like that," Phoebe said, winking at Quinn.

Turning back, Quinn stopped and held out her backpack. "Can you take this home, Hannah?"

"Sure thing," she said. "Need me to come back?"

"Please?" Quinn whispered.

"We've got this," Eric said, walking away from Simon and putting a hand on the back of her neck as if to steer her. "We're family, y'all can go."

Quinn stared up at him, her feet taking root in the concrete. The Chases had been more family to her than he had ever been, but she couldn't say that right now. Not with her mother and God and a parking lot full of people looking on. She couldn't make a scene. While every nerve ending in her body twitched to act, her Clayton brainwashing overrode it.

Where had *this* man been all these years? This possessive controlling person. Had she just not seen it? Did the stress of late bring it out? Or was it Simon?

"Baby, let's go get you checked out," he said, softening his tone. "The whole left side of your face is swelling up."

She glanced back toward the vehicles as everyone was getting back in to leave. Everyone except Simon, who stood leaning against his door with arms crossed over his chest. Like a bulldog ready to charge in and rescue her.

A small smile tugged at her lips as she looked at him, and more than that, tugged at her heart. Certainly more than was appropriate as she then walked in the door of the hospital with her fiancé.

Just say the word and I'm back there, Hannah texted after they'd been in the waiting room an hour. An hour of snotty kids, a man in a homemade arm sling who kept talking to the chair next to him, and a young scared-looking pregnant girl who kept eyeing Phoebe like she might be the mother ship of knowledge.

Nah, one of us should be comfortable, Quinn texted back. *No reason to come listen to my mom bitch.*

How's Eric?

Quinn looked at him sitting next to her, jaw tight, eyes distant, typing e-mails madly into his phone.

Thrilled, Quinn typed. *How was Simon?*

Growly. Like channeling Eli.

Quinn chuckled, picturing that.

"Something funny in there?" her mom asked.

Quinn glanced up to where her mother and sister sat across from her and Eric. "What?"

"Look at the three of you," she said, sitting there all proper with her Capris and her sculpted French pedicure. "All up in your phones and ignoring the actual people in the room."

"I'm working," Eric said, raking his fingers through hair that looked like he'd done that a lot already today.

"I'm looking at my registries to see what I still need to buy," Phoebe said, holding up her phone to show her. "Still need the play-time station."

"I'm texting Hannah," Quinn said. "About our photo shoot this week." Why the hell not. "I'm thinking of ordering pizza delivery next—who's interested?"

"I'm glad you find this so funny," Eric said, scrolling through messages. "I'm missing two meetings while we sit here."

Quinn narrowed her eyes. "Please feel free to leave," she said, flitting a hand. "There's the door."

He sighed. "I didn't mean—"

"Yes, you did," Quinn said. "I never asked you to be here, I certainly didn't ask you to stay, and clearly that whole family bullshit out there was just for show."

He looked at her sideways, fingers paused midscroll. "What is with you?"

"Why were you at my mom's house?" Quinn asked. "Without me?"

"Quinn, you're just tense," her mother said. "You've had a trauma and let's just leave it at that. No reason to cause problems."

Quinn looked from her mom to Phoebe, who'd written the whole scene off and gone back to her shopping.

"Okay, I'll leave. How about that?" Quinn said, standing. "No more problems."

"Seriously, Quinn, quit being dramatic," her mother said. "Sit down before you fall over."

"*I'm* being dramatic?"

Phoebe looked up and held up her finger and thumb. "A wee bit."

"Your sister isn't complaining and she hasn't even had her midmorning snack," her mom said.

"And Wellie is pissed about it, too," Phoebe said, twisting to look around the room. "I'm gonna go look for a vending machine."

"I'm so over this," Quinn mumbled, looking for a restroom. In lieu of walking out the front door and hiking home, it was the quickest route to privacy.

"Quinn Parker?" said a voice from the check-in desk.

"Yes?" she said, raising her hand.

"Follow me, please," a short stocky lady said.

"Hallelujah," Quinn said, grabbing her phone and wallet.

"Want me to come with you?" Eric said, standing.

"No," Quinn said. "I've got this. I don't need anyone."

Halfway to the lady, she heard her own words and realized how harsh they sounded. She turned around to see him still standing, watching her, looking lost.

It wasn't true, what she'd said. But the person she did need wasn't there. The one who'd whispered *I need you* desperately against her skin when he thought she couldn't hear. Who'd stood up to Eric and her mother. Who'd stoically watched her walk away. He wasn't there.

And how that made her chest hurt more than anything else—that was the most terrifying thing of all.

Chapter Nineteen

It wasn't Thursday, the regular dinner night at his mom's—it wasn't even dinnertime. But somehow, Louella Chase always knew when her ducks needed to eat. Or maybe it was just because Gran was there, Simon figured. Gram dropping by unannounced would be reason enough for his mom to decide a big lunch with more people to hold down a conversation was just the ticket.

And it was. There was nothing like home-cooked food after an exciting run, sitting around the big table and everyone talking at once. The only thing missing was Zach and his way of sharing the adventure. And Quinn's face down at the end, since sometimes she'd stick around and stay and laugh at the stories and Zach's embellishments. And smile at Simon in a way that lit him up inside. God, that sounded like something a woman would say. But it was true. No one had ever made him feel like Quinn did. Not ever. And that scared the living shit out of him. He faced down monster tornadoes and flying trees. He'd had an EF4 pick him up and drag him down the road like he was a toothpick. And what he was feeling for Quinn was infinitely scarier. Because she wasn't his to feel it for. She belonged to another man.

"I enjoyed meeting Stacey the other night," Gran said, bringing his thoughts back to reality. "A smart young woman, that one."

"Yes, she is," Simon said, stabbing at his baked potato. "She enjoyed meeting you, too."

"How's that shelter of hers?" she asked.

This was the prime opportunity to solicit his grandmother's help. Eric St. James might be willing to churn up an advertising campaign, but that was later on. That would keep it going long term. Right now, it needed a life raft. This was the time. And all he could think about at the moment was whether or not Quinn was okay, if she had a concussion, if she was going to text him to let him know. Because he was pathetic.

"Not so good right now, actually," Simon said. "Looks like it'll be shut down."

"Oh, no!" his mom said. "The shelter? Your dad loved that place! He believed in it."

"I know," Simon said, losing what little appetite he had. He set his fork down and wiped his mouth. "But it's running low on funds and running down, period. There are so many things wrong with that building, I'd need an hour to list them. I do what repairs I can, but Band-Aids only last so long."

"You've been doing the maintenance yourself?" Gran asked.

"Sometimes," Simon said. "Money is running out. Stacey can't always afford to pay someone, so I do what I can, but I'm no expert. And now—well, now it's getting bad enough I guess that someone complained."

"A *homeless* person complained that the shelter taking them in wasn't good enough?" Hannah piped in.

"Not them, Hannah," Simon said. "Someone in the neighborhood. They complain all the time, but I guess they finally found someone to listen."

"So what's happening now?" Gran asked.

"I'm not totally sure," he said. "I was out on this shoot, but Stacey called to tell me that some inspectors were coming out. Maybe this week. Maybe today. I don't know."

"And that will be the kiss of death," his mom said.

He met her eyes. "Pretty much."

"I hate to see that," she said, folding her hands under her chin. "Josiah—"

"Loved it, supported it, was its ray of hope," Gran said, nodding. "Yes, I get it. My problem is this."

"You have a problem?" his mom asked, her tone suggesting she was clearly torqued by being cut off on the subject of her husband. For the five hundred and fiftieth time in her life.

"I do, because they want money from me," she said, folding gnarled hands in front of her.

Simon felt what little tidbit of hope he had go plummeting to the floor.

"Gran, I never—"

"No, you didn't," she said. "And I'm not sure if that was you being sneaky and manipulative or just polite. Being my grandson, I'd like to think it was a little of both."

"Essentially," Simon said, tossing his napkin into his plate. He was too exhausted to argue and too bent out of shape to think creatively.

"And you didn't want to be obligated to me," she added.

"Score again," he said with a nod.

"So, back to my problem—Louella," she said, focusing her gaze on his mom. "I don't throw good money after bad, and it seems to me that I've been informed a bit too late."

"So you can't help?" Hannah asked.

"If the place is not up to code, my input will not change that quickly enough," she said. "If they shut it down, I'm just supplying a bigger Band-Aid."

Simon let that sink in. It was done.

"I'm gonna go change clothes and head over there for a bit," he said. "See if—I don't know," he added, rubbing at his eyes, his face, his neck. He just felt itchy and grimy and like his skin wasn't sufficient. Like if he could crawl out of it and be somewhere else, he would.

"Heard anything from Quinn?" Eli asked, the ever-silent one at the table today.

"Not yet," Simon said. "Hannah is her roommate, you know," he said with a grin that was no joy and all snark. "She'll probably know before I will."

Eli looked up from his plate with his signature don't-fuck-with-me look.

"I don't think I wronged you today," he said quietly. "But I can certainly shed some light on why I asked you if you're wanting to be a jerk right now."

"It's all good," Hannah said. "Come on, guys. Kumbaya, already. It's been a long couple of days."

"Yeah, I'm gonna go," Simon said.

"Something I need to know?" his mom asked, studying him too closely.

"No," he said, smiling just for her. He gave her a hug as he came around the table. "Thanks for lunch, Mom," he said, kissing her cheek. "It was awesome, as usual."

"Be careful, baby."

"Always," he said.

"So tell me about the run," he heard her ask at the table, the voices muffling as he walked toward the door. "Did you get pictures of the waterspout?"

"It was good," Eli said. "No Boudreaus up our ass for once."

"Shut up," Hannah said. "And of course, Mom, oh, man, you should see—"

He got out the door and pulled his phone from his pocket. Still nothing. Nothing. He could text her. Or her sister. Or he could mind his own business and let her family and fiancé worry about her.

"Not your world, man," he said under his breath. "Not your anything."

"I hit an SUV," Quinn said, pointing. "With my face."

"You were in a car accident?" Stacey asked, frowning at Quinn's chart. "This says you ran into something with goggles on."

"I did," Quinn said. "We were going along, and there was suddenly a tree, and Eli swerved to miss it. And I was kind of hanging out the window filming at the time."

Of course she'd get Stacey. Not that that was a problem, but surely there were other nurses who could witness her awkward lopsided face who didn't know her personally. Or sleep with Simon.

"How far out the window?"

"Kind of probably more out than in," Quinn admitted.

"Ah," Stacey said, scribbling something in her chart. Probably something along the lines of *needs psych evaluation*. "Well, that's a new one," she said. "And I see quite a bit."

"I'll bet," Quinn said. "So have you left and come back already?" she asked. "Or are you just still here from yesterday?"

Stacey laughed. "Still here. Had a little break, but I'm grabbing all I can."

"Wow."

"Yeah, I do that a lot," she said. "I need the money." She took a deep breath. "Let's see what you've got here." She put down the chart and pressed gently around Quinn's eye socket, working her way in to the actual cheekbone area. "I'm sorry," she said when Quinn winced. "The bruising and swelling has set in now, so I know it's tender."

"Did I break anything?"

"I don't think so," she said. "There would be twice this much swelling. What about up here?" she asked, pressing around Quinn's temple.

She had a nice touch. Soft, and her fingers were smooth. Which was completely irrelevant to anything. Except in picturing her touching Simon's face. Holding his hand—

"Nothing major," Quinn said. "I mean, it's all a little sore from the impact, but mostly it's just where the safety goggles and I tried to merge."

"Yeah, that's gonna be a couple of stitches there," Stacey said.

Quinn met her eyes. Pretty eyes. Dark and soft. Quinn remembered how good she and Simon had looked together.

"Seriously?"

"Afraid so—oh, you're getting married soon, aren't you?" Stacey said, her eyes widening. "Is that still on?"

Quinn pulled her head back in surprise. "Yeah, it's still on. Why wouldn't it be?"

Stacey looked like she wanted to eat her stethoscope. "No reason, my bad. So how many days out are we?"

"Twenty-two."

"No problem," Stacey said with a wave of her hand. "They'll be out in fourteen. And I'll do them really small so the scar won't show. Makeup will cover what does." She flicked on a little penlight and peered into Quinn's eyes. "Had your pictures done yet?" she asked distractedly.

"Oh, hell, my mother is going to let loose on that," Quinn said, continuing when Stacey looked at her curiously. "I was supposed to go yesterday. Was out doing all *this* instead, and now I've probably ended the world as we know it."

Stacey laughed. "She sounds like a handful."

"Well, when you hear the wailing later, you'll know to go the other direction," Quinn said. "I'm not worried about pictures. That stuff can be photoshopped out."

Stacey gave a little gasp. "Did you see the one on Facebook where they photoshopped that scrawny guy and made him all buff?"

"Exactly how it's done," Quinn said.

"That's amazing," Stacey said. "Follow my finger."

Quinn followed Stacey's finger with her eyes.

"I want that to come get me ready every morning," Stacey said.

Yeah, because Stacey was a hideous toad. But she was nice. And funny. And Quinn could see why Simon liked her. *Damn it.*

"Any headaches? Nausea? Unconsciousness?"

"Um—headaches, yes. It's killing me. Nausea, no." Quinn hesitated. She could be out of here quicker if she lied. "They told me I fell asleep in the car," she admitted.

"Okay, I'm gonna let the chief know, see if we can get a quick scan of your head. It's been a slow day, so shouldn't take long."

She disappeared and returned with a doctor who blessed the radiation, then got her dandy little sewing kit ready as he left.

Quinn had had stitches before. In her foot. And in her finger. But those times, she could look away. Not too easy to get away from your own face.

"Worst part is the shot to numb it," Stacey said. "Just lay back here and close your eyes."

She did.

"I heard about your shelter," Quinn said. "That sucks."

There was a pause and Quinn opened her eyes to see Stacey pulling supplies from a drawer.

"Or maybe I shouldn't have reminded you of that right before you're sewing my cheek back together."

Stacey chuckled. "No, it's fine. I just forget for a second that you're from outside these walls. Not that many here even know about it." She sighed. "I feel like I'm letting so many people down. They depended on me, and now—"

"Don't do that to yourself," Quinn said. "From what I've heard, you put everything you had in there."

"Wasn't enough," Stacey said. She worked in silence for a moment, preparing the shot.

"Simon's pretty upset, too." Quinn said.

"Yeah, it was his only real connection to his dad," Stacey said. "And besides that, he's good there."

"What do you mean?"

"It's his niche," she said. "Close your eyes."

Quinn felt the burn of the needle pierce her abused skin and grabbed the edge of the bed.

"There," Stacey said with a smile. "Now you won't feel the rest." She got the sewing needle ready and Quinn closed her eyes again.

"Simon's good at working a room. Putting those people at ease," she said. "They respond to him."

Don't do it. Don't do it. She's sewing your face together.

"So, how long have you and he been—a thing?"

A thing? Really? She said that out loud?

Please don't stab me in the eye.

Stacey's laugh put her a little bit at ease. Unless it was maniacal. She didn't know Stacey well enough to tell the difference.

"Quinn, we are no *thing*," she said. "Simon and I are just friends."

Okay, she wasn't that dumb, and that thought braved her up to open her eyes and raise an eyebrow at the woman holding a giant needle and thread.

Stacey did a little microshrug. "Okay, *with benefits* once upon a time, but the friends part was stronger. Neither of us was wired for more. We don't do love and strings and all that," she said. "Until recently, anyway."

Quinn's eyes couldn't have shut if she'd wanted them to. "You hooked back up?"

Another laugh, and a tug on her face. Jesus, there was thread in her face at that very moment. That was really bizarre.

"No, I'm not talking about us," Stacey said. "I'm talking about the dance you two are doing around each other."

If there weren't something connecting her cheek to Stacey's hand right then, Quinn would have probably sat straight up. As it was, her tongue might as well have been strung up on that thread, too, because all she could do was gape at the little smirky smile Stacey was giving.

"You're—you—there's no dance," Quinn finally stuttered.

Stacey slid her perfect chocolate-brown eyes to Quinn's and tilted her head. "That what you're sticking with?" she asked before focusing back on her task.

"No dance," Quinn repeated, feeling her stomach start to flutter. Maybe she did have a concussion, because she sure as hell was feeling nauseous.

"Please," Stacey said softly. "I've been there. Not with Simon— I had my own version of this particular song, but I know the choreography."

"I'm getting married," Quinn said, more forcefully. "There is no choreography with Simon." She inhaled a shaky breath. Yes, there was, but no one needed to be able to see it. *No one could see it.* "Don't say that."

"Because that will make it not true?" Stacey asked, raising one eyebrow and shaking her head. "Sorry. I don't know about normally, but it was all over you the other night."

Quinn suddenly felt like Stacey was sewing her throat shut as well, which was going to suck when she threw up. If it was *all over her* that night, it could only be more obvious now.

"It can't be," she whispered, surprised that the thought manifested itself out loud.

Stacey laid a hand on Quinn's arm, making her blink back her thoughts.

"If it makes it any better, it's all over him, too."

Quinn's eyes filled with a burn that she didn't see coming. "It doesn't," she said, no real sound coming out as two tears leaked from the sides of her eyes into her hair. Great. Crying in front of Wonder Woman. The day was getting better and better.

Stacey patted her arm and went back to sewing, closing the wound and tying a knot like she was sewing on a button.

"It's complicated, I know. My advice?" Stacey said, looking Quinn in the eye. "What's your fiancé's name again?"

"Eric."

Stacey nodded. "Keep it simple. The heart knows what it wants. Say to yourself, *If there was no Eric, where would I be?* Then *if there was no Simon?*" She shrugged. "Which one hurts more?"

Hannah had said nearly the same thing.

"I'm not breaking a date to the prom," Quinn said. "It's my life."

"And theirs," Stacey said, meeting her eyes. She blinked away and soaked a sterile pad with saline. "Almost done."

Chapter Twenty

Simon sat in his car just staring at the building. People still came and went. It wasn't time for dinner yet, so the big rush was yet to come. And it was Tuesday, so Miss Ava would be making noodle stew. It was stick-to-your-ribs food, but not appealing enough to attract the less than hard-core. Those individuals would find another meal, at another place. It might make for a hell of a walk, but they'd be back for the bed. For the shower. For tomorrow's meal, because Wednesdays were spaghetti night with chocolate pudding.

If there was another night. Another meal. A bed and a shower and some peace of mind for one night.

Not that Simon wanted there to be homeless people needing those things. People so destitute and zapped of pride that they'd walk miles for a free meal and a place to lay their head. Or their children's heads, as they themselves made do with a rolled-up blanket beside them, one hand on their child's arm so they'd know if they moved.

In a perfect world, those scenarios wouldn't exist and places like the Trinity Outreach Center wouldn't be necessary. But they did. And it was. He'd seen things there that made him ride the fence between never bringing a child into such a jacked-up world, and wanting to feel that kind of love so bad it ached. He'd seen people do horrific things without batting an eye. But he'd also witnessed selfless acts of humanity happen there among people who literally had *nothing*. Acts that those more privileged would never think of doing.

Every time he looked into a child's face and saw their innocence fading from their eyes as they watched their parents struggle, he knew that places like this were necessary.

Simon got out and walked slowly to the door, purposely looking away from the sign. He couldn't look at it as he touched it, as if somehow he personally had failed it.

"Hey, Mr. Simon," said a small girl sitting cross legged on the floor, playing jacks with one of the donated sets of toys kept in a closet.

"Hi, Laura," Simon said. "What number are you up to now?"

"Fours!" she said with pride, her blue eyes lighting up. "I've been practicing."

"Wow," Simon said. "You'd probably slay me now."

"Probably will if you haven't practiced," she said seriously, shaking her head. "You know girls are better at this."

"Well, my sister was, I'll tell you that," Simon said. "But that sure sounds like a challenge to me. Ready to back that tough talk up?"

She smiled up at him. "Ready when you are," she said, glancing around for her mom, who waved from across the room where free counseling sessions were going on for half a day. Another priceless gift they'd lose.

"I'll be right back," Simon said, noticing the light on in Stacey's office.

He saw everything as he moved through the room. The broken tile. The sagging, stained asbestos ceiling. The wires hanging from a corner where a speaker had broken off. The unusable window-unit air conditioner that sat like a boulder with a giant oscillating fan in front of it. And that was just this room. It got much worse.

Simon rounded the door into the office and was surprised to

find not Stacey, but Miss Ava and Daniels in there instead. Talking in hushed tones. Miss Ava was wiping at her eyes.

Simon rapped his knuckles on the doorjamb. "Hey, guys, sorry. I saw the light, so . . ."

"Miss Stacey's not here, she's at work," Daniels said softly.

"Still?" Simon asked, though it wasn't a surprise. Stacey frequently grabbed additional shifts for extra money. Lately she'd been throwing as much as she could into the shelter's funds.

"She was off for a few hours and came over," Miss Ava said, shaking her head. "Just in time to find out they're shutting us down."

Simon's heart sank. Even knowing the likelihood, he'd held onto a sliver of hope.

"Damn it," he said under his breath, sitting on the desk.

"You don't seem surprised," Daniels said.

"She called me yesterday while I was out of town," Simon said. "Told me it was a possibility. I was hoping." He ran his fingers through his hair. "How long do we have?"

"Gotta vacate by Friday," Miss Ava said, her chin quivering. "Some of these folks—they got nowhere else to go."

"And no means to get there if they did," Daniels said, crossing his arms over his chest. It was officially the most words Simon had ever heard him utter.

Simon's mind raced, searching for a solution. "Then we need to get on the phone to any of the other facilities—I don't care if it's up around Dallas. Call them all, see if they have room. Then we make a sign-up list. Those who truly don't have anything tying them here and want to go, we'll bring them ourselves."

"And those who don't want to?" Miss Ava asked, dabbing under her eyes. "They have jobs or something, trying to make better but aren't there yet—"

"I get what you're saying," Simon said. "I promise. But we can only do what we can do."

"They'll be out on the streets," she said. "Kids. Babies. Where's the justice in that? All because of a few code violations?"

"I know," Simon said.

"Oh, what is it you think you know?" Daniels said, looking directly in Simon's eyes in a manner he'd never done before. "What do you know about poverty? About loss and hardship?"

Simon met the older man's gaze. "I'm blessed to say not much, personally, but I've seen plenty here. I've been here about as long as you have, I believe, and I've fed just as many mouths."

"You're a rich man who won't even dip into his own pockets to save this place," Daniels said. "You think because you've slummed through some food lines that you're one of us?"

"You think I'm rich?" Simon said, laughing. "That's grand. And that's not me."

"I heard that your grandmother—"

"Is richer than God?" He asked. "She is. *She* is. I live on a junior weatherman's salary, which isn't much and may be about to decrease exponentially." Simon got up off the desk. "Daniels, I love this place. I have added what I could financially to help out, but it's never been enough."

"We know you do, Simon," Miss Ava said, glaring at Daniels. "We're just gonna be sad to see it go."

"So am I," Simon said, looking at Daniels. "You think because you've *lived* hardship, that gives you some kind of market on caring about it?" He shook his head. "You aren't the only one with ties here. Now if y'all will excuse me, I have a jacks date with a six-year-old."

He walked out, taking a deep breath. He was on edge, operating on no sleep and plenty of adrenaline and annoyance, and it wasn't the day to mess with him. He glanced one more time at his phone. Quinn still hadn't made a peep.

"You're back!" Laura said as he approached, her eyes lighting up.

Simon sank to the floor, sitting cross legged in front of her, trying hard not to think about where she and her mom would have to go.

"No place I'd rather be."

The only person to see Quinn walk into the waiting room was the one person she'd hoped had gone home. No such luck. They probably all rode together. And the look on her mother's face mirrored the feeling of pure hell that was bouncing around her head.

"Oh, my God," her mom said, dropping the magazine she was thumbing through as she stood. Phoebe and Eric both looked up from their phones, first at Adelaide and then following her gaze to Quinn.

"Jesus, Quinn," Eric said, getting to his feet and crossing the space to touch her face. Again.

"Ow," she said, jerking her head back. "See the bruise?" she asked, holding a hand in front of her face.

"No missing it!" her mother said, coming toward her with a look of horror. "It's more pronounced now than when you went in! And you have *stitches*?"

"Well, it was that or the gaping hole, so I figured this was the better bargain," Quinn said.

"You're getting married in three weeks," Adelaide said.

Quinn ran her tongue along the inside of her numb cheek. "Damn good thing people keep reminding me of that, because surely I'd forget." She sighed. "Yes, Mom, and the stitches will be out before then."

"But—"

"And I'll have makeup."

"But—"

"Photoshop will take care of the pictures," Quinn finished.

"I think it gives you character," Phoebe said with a grin and a hug. "Like a pirate."

"There you go," Quinn said to her mom. "I'm a pirate."

"You're a lunatic," Adelaide said. "What were you thinking?"

"That I was doing my job," she said.

"Exactly my point," she said with a nod to Eric.

Quinn narrowed her eyes, glancing at everyone in turn. "Why do you have a *point* with my fiancé, Mother? And why are *you* at my mom's house listening to it, Eric? In the middle of the day on a Tuesday? With all your important meetings?"

He gave her an apologetic if not placating look, and pulled her to him.

"A surprise for you," he said. "And listening is the polite thing to do."

"In my family, it's the about-to-stab-you-in-the-back thing to do. I haven't seen anything good come out of it yet," she said under her breath.

"You still look beautiful, Mrs. Frankenstein," Eric said with a chuckle. "Let's go home."

"Mine, please," she said, not impressed by his joke. She was just being cranky, she knew that. Normally, she would have laughed and joined in on the funny, but today—and all the days preceding—were kicking her ass.

His smile faded a bit as his eyes met hers with something more than concern.

"Why don't you stay with me tonight so I can keep an eye on you?"

"Oh, that reminds me," she said, turning to her sister. "I don't have a concussion. They did an MRI. I'm just really banged up, but everything is where it's supposed to be."

"That's good," Phoebe said, giving her an odd look. A look that said, *Talk to your husband-to-be, not me.*

"Yeah," Quinn said, patting Eric's chest. "So I can stay at my place. I just really want to," she added quickly when he opened his mouth to protest. "I just want to curl up in a ball and sleep till I have to go to work tonight."

"I think you can call in," Eric said, masking his disappointment. "I would assume it's justified."

"I've called in enough," she said. "I need to show up."

"Maybe you'll get points when they see you and send you home," Phoebe said.

Quinn chuckled and held up crossed fingers. "Maybe."

The ride to Quinn's apartment was quiet after they dropped off Adelaide and Phoebe, who left the dress cloaked in its pearlescent-white dress bag in the backseat. Quinn felt it back there, taunting her. Pointing at her. Accusing her of all kinds of horrible things that were tainting its perfection. Telling her that the man sitting next to her was who she was supposed to be thinking of, because in three weeks—twenty-two days—she would be wearing it to say *I do* to him. Damn thing sure had a lot to say, for a dress.

"Gotten any packing done?" Eric asked, looking at her like that was a completely innocuous question.

"No, Mother, I haven't," she said, moving his collar aside as if looking for a hidden microphone. "I didn't send the save-the-date things, either."

"What are you doing?" he asked.

"Looking for a wire."

"Seriously?"

"You tell me," she said. "You and my mother sure are cozy these days. And I've seen her make lapdogs out of some pretty powerful people."

Eric smiled, though his eyes looked shadowed. Troubled. He shook his head and focused back on exiting at the Shelby turnoff.

"That's what you think of me?"

"No, I didn't," Quinn said. "Until you called me to rake me over the coals while I was out of town working." She shrugged.

"What do you expect me to do?" he said. "Your mom keeps trying to enlist me to *turn* you back to the fold. She's about to be my mother-in-law. What am I supposed to say?"

"You say no, Eric," Quinn said. "You set a precedent now for how it's going to be."

"It's not that simple."

"It's totally that simple," she said. "I do it all the time."

"And look at your standing with her," he said.

"So?" Quinn said, frowning. "I don't have to have a *standing* with her. She's my mom. She'll always be my mom and I love her for that, but we aren't friends. You know this, Eric. Why are you suddenly acting like we just met and you're meeting my family for the first time?"

He ran a hand through hair that was already standing on end. "Maybe because family is important."

Quinn nodded. "Uh-huh. And you go sit around your family's dinner table and shoot the shit with your dad when?"

"That's not the same thing—"

"It's totally the same thing, just me instead of you," she said. "You have to stop this. You have to tell her no now or she's going to keep using you as a tool for the rest of our lives. Tell her that you're uncomfortable not backing me." Quinn flashed on Simon dressing them both down.

Have you met your wife-to-be? Have you met your daughter?

"Be my hero, Eric," she said, touching his hair. "Have my back. I have yours."

Guilt, crazy and boiling hot, hit her square in the chest. Did she? If so, that was pretty messed up. He would throw her ass out of the car into the nearest ditch if he knew what she'd been doing. What she'd been thinking lately.

Eric pulled into her brownstone parking lot and looked for a spot. Her first reaction was to tell him to drop her at the door, that she only wanted a shower and her bed, but something more reasonable found its way through. She couldn't do that to him. He couldn't be her hero if she wouldn't even let him walk her in.

He could carry the mouthy dress.

"Well?" Hannah said, on her feet from the couch as soon as the door opened. "How did that cluster—oh, hey, Eric."

"How's it going, Hannah?" he said.

"Great," she said. "Just got home. Oooh, is that the dress? Aren't you not supposed to be holding it?"

"He just can't see it," Quinn said, winking. "I think holding the bag is legal enough."

"So what did the doctor say?" Hannah asked.

"No concussion. No broken anything. Just severely bruised." She pointed at her cheek. "Miss Stacey gave me stitches and told me I'll probably have a black eye tomorrow."

"Cool, war wounds!" Hannah said, laughing. "Does it hurt?"

"My head does," Quinn said. "Cheek is still numb, but they gave me a couple of pain pills for when it wakes up. Have you checked any of the footage yet?" Quinn asked. Hannah's eyes darted to where Eric was hanging the dress bag on a coat hook.

"It still needs editing," she said.

"I mean the raw."

"Yeah, still needs work," Hannah reiterated.

Quinn frowned but went with it. Hannah didn't want to show the shots for some reason.

"Okay."

"But look at this," Hannah said, grabbing her camera from the coffee table. She pushed a few buttons and handed it to Quinn. "Scroll through that."

Quinn looked at the digital screen as the waterspout burst to life. The series of quick takes made it look like it was moving as Quinn scrolled through the shots.

"Wow," Eric said over her shoulder.

"Right?" Quinn breathed. "It was amazing."

"I've never seen one on water like that," he said.

"It's rare," she said, scrolling more slowly. "And so beautiful."

"And deadly," he said. "You were that close?"

"It was on water. Those don't look for land," she lied.

"And debris flying around?" he said, pointing at the sticks and leaves and a piece of plastic awning at one point.

"Part of the job, babe," she said.

"Yeah," he said under his breath, heading to the kitchen. "Mind if I grab a water? It's been a long morning."

"Go ahead," Quinn said. "So—"

Her thoughts collided in her head as her fingers landed on a still shot of Simon starting his spiel. She could hear her own breathing as she looked at him. She scrolled to another, and one more, with

Simon saying something to Quinn as she looked up at him, probably telling him to yell at that point. The waterspout snaking on the water behind them.

"You were asking something?" Eric said, coming back with a bottle of water. His tie was looser than before. He looked adorably tousled and rumpled.

"Nothing. I don't remember," Quinn said, handing the camera back to Hannah. She went into his arms and wrapped herself around him, needing to feel herself wanting that. He was going to be her husband. His body was the one she'd be wrapped around forever.

She felt his arms go around her, one hand up at the back of her neck. His face on the top of her head.

"I love you, lovebug," he said softly into her hair.

"I love you, too," she said, her voice muffled into his chest. And she did. She'd loved him for years. So what was her problem?

"You go get some rest," he said. "I'm gonna head back to work."

"Okay."

She reached up to kiss him, and he dropped a sweet kiss on her lips.

"I'll call you later," he said.

"Sounds good."

Quinn collapsed on the couch as soon as the door shut behind him.

"You two are like watching water boil," Hannah said.

"What?"

"Boring."

"We aren't boring."

"He might not be boring," Hannah said. "You are most certainly not boring, Miss Jane of the Jungle."

Quinn snickered and pulled a nearby blanket over herself. "Why, thank you."

"But the two of you together are a snooze fest."

Hannah picked up the network camcorder that Charlie had given her and turned it on, hitting buttons to bring back the footage she wanted. "Unlike you and someone else."

The footage started from inside the car, with Quinn anchoring her leg behind Simon and the look on his face from Charlie's angle. And then Quinn hanging out the window, the swerve, the slam of her against the SUV, which made her cringe to watch.

It was what happened next. Charlie kept filming out of the backseat and window as Simon screamed Quinn's name and pulled her out, holding her in his arms on the ground in the mud, the rain blowing sideways around them. Quinn's eyes filled with hot tears as she watched him kiss her forehead and her hand go around his neck.

Please be okay, baby. I need you.

It couldn't be heard, but she remembered it plain as day. Then her getting up, and him checking her cheekbones. The gust of wind that blew debris at all of them and Simon covering her body with his own, holding her face as he held her against the vehicle. The screen zoomed in on the two of them as he then backed up a fraction and Quinn looked up at him, their faces touching.

Quinn held her breath as the moment was broken and the spout appeared, and Hannah hit *stop*.

"Now *that* wasn't boring," Hannah said.

Quinn blinked two tears free and winced as she made to wipe her cheek and hit the stiff threads sticking out of it.

"We have to delete that," she said, her voice cracking.

"Well, I think I can find the frame-by-frame and delete *certain* parts," Hannah said. "The rest is good."

"Charlie knows," Quinn said. "She knows what to look for now."

"So you need to be careful what you show," Hannah said.

"And why did they give *you* the camera?" Quinn asked.

"Because she may have instinct, but she doesn't know what she's doing," Hannah said. "I suggested letting me put everything together," Hannah said. "Instead of sending her my files, like what really should happen. And she went for it."

"She won't next time, if you delete stuff."

Hannah tilted her head. "Which is why I'm telling you to be squeaky-clean now."

Quinn blew out a breath. "Yeah."

"And speaking of clean, you're not," Hannah said. "Go take your mud-encrusted ass off my couch and get in the shower."

The shower helped. Quinn felt human again. She was still a troll, and seeing it all unfold on film made it even clearer. She was living dangerously, and it was showing on the screen. And the camera never lied.

She needed to pull herself together. Looking across the room at the dress bag hanging on the hook like a large forgotten fish, Quinn got up and walked over to it, lowering the zipper slowly. Revealing the opulent details inch by inch.

Chapter Twenty-One

Simon sat in his condo, staring at nothing. He tried watching TV for a bit, but that was just noise, and the newspaper just blurred a bunch of ink together under his tired eyes. He should have been sleeping. He was coming off a nearly sleepless night, had major stress, and was due to work another night shift at the station later on. His mind wouldn't shut down.

Playing jacks with Laura, watching her mom trying to better things, Miss Ava crying, even Daniels being a dick—he understood that. In the old man's shoes, he'd probably look at someone like him as an annoying useless rich man, too. Someone who couldn't possibly understand poverty and was only there to appease some sense of giving back.

And truthfully he would have probably been right if Simon's dad had raised him differently. But Josiah Chase had managed to instill a heart for the cause in Simon. Not because it was the right thing to do, or out of any social conscience or obligation, but because someone had to step up and do it. Someone had to care about the people there. Yes, there were always the freeloaders, the ones who tainted the system with manipulation and wanting something for nothing. But Simon learned early on that those people were the fluff, the crumbs that got swept away, the here-today-gone-tomorrow souls that would disappear after awhile anyway. Those people didn't want substance. They didn't want real help. They didn't want career counseling or literacy programs. So things like that pushed them out, leaving the cream behind. The ones who cried when given a job. Who lit up when they read a menu for the first time. Who thanked him with tears rolling down their faces when he fed their children and read them a book.

Simon leaned forward on his knees and rubbed at his eyes. How would they tell these people they had nowhere to go? How would some of them deal with being relocated? They had kids in school here—the thought parade went on and on.

And then there was work. Hopefully the waterspout footage softened his boss's vitriol.

And Quinn.

He'd had a plan, damn it. And then she was dangling dazed and semi-limp from a window, and all that *not friends till you're married* garbage went straight to hell. Just like him.

He was messing around with another man's woman. Not in the way that would truly deserve the fires, but messing with what wasn't his just the same. He should have walked away after Zach's wedding. Jesus, how many times had he told himself that now?

He needed to drive around and clear his head. A nap wasn't happening, and his walls just weren't interesting enough. Simon grabbed his keys and left.

Quinn purposely didn't look as Hannah zipped her into the dress. She'd already seen herself in it when she bought it and again during alterations.

The original plan had been not to wear it again until the big day, but she'd forgotten about pictures and stuff when she'd forged that idea, so it was all good. And she wanted to see what her mother had changed.

"I'll go check out that farmhouse tomorrow," Quinn said. "Hopefully they'll be okay with us doing a shoot there."

"Sounds good," Hannah said, fastening a tiny button. "Okay, I think you can look."

Taking a deep breath, Quinn looked up, and her chest filled with a burn she couldn't identify. A panic that twisted her stomach and clawed at her throat.

The dress was beautiful. It was phenomenal. It accentuated her body perfectly, and her mom had tiny sea pearls and rhinestones added, dangling like a million prisms all over the bodice. Where it was once sleeveless and simple and elegant, there were now rows of sea pearls over the shoulders with strings of rhinestones dangling at different lengths down the tops of her arms. It was still beautiful and elegant, but more in a military or formal-ball kind of way. The back had more strings hanging down and woven into the tulle of the train.

It was still beautiful. But it wasn't hers. It wasn't the dress she bought. It wasn't her standing there in it.

Quinn struggled to pull in a breath that wasn't hot or thick, but they all were.

"You okay?" Hannah asked.

"Yeah," Quinn breathed.

"Want the veil, too?"

"I'm not wearing a veil," Quinn said, swallowing hard.

Hannah pulled out a tiara-type headpiece with a rhinestone-encrusted medium-length veil. "You are now."

It was at that moment that Quinn recognized the panic, the lack of air, the feeling of a burn so intense it would consume her. The last time she felt it, she'd been six years old.

"Get me out," she choked. "Unzip it."

Hannah unbuttoned and unzipped as fast as she could as Quinn's whole body flushed bright red with heat and she broke out in a light sheen of sweat.

"Hurry," she said, tears joining the sweat on her face.

"I'm hurrying," Hannah said, her voice sounding worried. "Damn thing has so many fasteners."

Then it was free of her and dropping to the floor, and Quinn stepped out of it in her bra and panties and left it there in a puddle of white as she curled up in the big wicker chair.

The panic wouldn't let go. The knowledge that she had to put it all back on again—this foreign dress that most women would kill for, the dress of most people's dreams—made her want to hurl.

"It's okay," Hannah said, kneeling in front of her. "Just a panic attack after a long crazy day."

Quinn shook her head. "That wasn't my dress anymore."

"It was like—fit for a queen," Hannah said.

"Exactly. Not me."

"You'll be fine, though," Hannah said. "Eric will lose his mind when he sees you come down the aisle in that."

"Why," Quinn said, feeling it all about to break inside her. Feeling the pain in her heart. The pain in her cheek as the numbness subsided and her salty tears hit her wound. "Why can't I just have what I want?" she said, her voice hitching as the sobs bubbled up. "Why does she have to control this? To control everything?"

"Hey," Hannah said, rubbing her arm, trying to soothe her. "You've had a rough day today. And your wedding day? Girl, all this fuss is about one day that means nothing in the grand scheme of things. It's not about that day. It's about the marriage. It's about spending your life with your best friend."

Those words echoed in her head. Simon had said the same thing. Quinn nodded, pushing back the memory. "You're right."

"Hell, you can wear shorts if you want," Hannah said. "Flip-flops. It's just a ritual."

"How funny would it be to see my mother's face if I walked down the aisle in shorts and flip-flops?"

"How funny would it be to do the portrait that way, just adding the veil?" Hannah asked.

Quinn tilted her head. "I love you."

Hannah laughed out loud and swung her arms around Quinn's neck.

"I love you, too, my friend."

Quinn took a deep breath and dabbed at her sore face.

"I think I need to get out for a bit," she said. "Drive around. Get some air and some alone time."

"I'd suggest some clothes first," Hannah said.

"Yeah, that's an option."

Hannah smirked. "Well, be careful."

As she threw on a tank top, shorts, and flip-flops, she had no idea where she was going. When she got in her car and turned the ignition, however, it was crystal clear. Past crystal. And not at all smart.

Simon knew where he was driving as soon as he turned left out of his parking space.

Why? Why was he so damn determined to be an idiot? He was smarter than this. He was better than this.

But there was something primal driving him, as if one thing could fix all the others. And the real shit of it was, that one thing wouldn't even fix that one thing.

He had to talk to her. See if she was okay, for starters. And then . . . he didn't know. Because Hannah would be there, too, and—well, the whole idea just got progressively dumber as he drove, but the car kept moving.

It was sprinkling again, the sky completely gray, but there was something ominous building in the sky off to the northwest. He'd look later. He'd have plenty of time to check that out from work.

When he pulled into the brownstone parking lot, he knew almost immediately that she wasn't there. Which meant she'd made it home. And was driving. So that could only mean that she was okay and didn't have any other dangerous injuries. Hannah's car was there. He could just as easily ask her. Or call her. But none of that seemed like the right idea. Involving Hannah in his love life—or non–love life—with her roommate would not be a good thing.

Simon moved on. He could go to his mom's, but he'd just been there and going alone guaranteed a heavy Q&A. He couldn't go back to the shelter, it was too depressing. Zach wasn't home or he'd go vent to him, and he and Eli didn't have that kind of relationship. He needed to sleep, but that wasn't going to happen.

At the next exit, Simon took a right and turned around. He could go check on Harry, at least. Make sure he was dried in for the next rainstorm. He'd just been there yesterday, and Harry would get noisy about it, but oh, well.

He needed to tell him about the shelter anyway.

He needed to talk to another human to get out of his own head.

Quinn's heart was beating madly, drumming extra loud in her ears as she turned the corner leading to Simon's condo. What the hell was she going to say?

Hi, I just had a mental breakdown putting on my wedding dress to marry Eric. I think I'm in—

"No," she said aloud, feeling the shakes coming back. "No."

Pulling into Simon's parking lot, she saw his spot was empty. An infuriating mix of relief and disappointment swam around her heart, squeezing the breath from her chest.

It was fate. That's what it was. It was cosmic intervention telling her she had no business going there, and to get her little butt back home where it should be. Resting up before work. Fate was much smarter than she was.

Quinn was too wound up to go back home, though. Just the thought of that damn dress pooling on the floor made her not want to cross that threshold.

She drove through to Trinity—hitting the windshield wipers as it started sprinkling—looking at how run-down so much of it had become. She remembered a park her mother used to bring her and Phoebe to there in Trinity when they were little. The last time she saw it, it was grown over with weeds and litter and crawling with drug deals.

Quinn thought about looking for the shelter Simon talked about, but she wasn't sure where it was located. And Trinity wasn't really a drive-around-sightseeing kind of place.

Why would she go there, anyway? What—what was she looking for? Simon? He wasn't home, so her brain was fighting fate and sending her on a quest to find him? Good Lord.

Harry.

Simon's friend in the abandoned building. She remembered where that was. The big crumbling warehouse had been right off the second exit, bordering the creek. Right in the middle of druggie territory. What the hell. She was itchy and crawling out of her own skin and feeling rebellious. She couldn't go home. Why not cross over into reckless?

She turned onto the street, and there it was. A big stone building with holes for windows, and part of the upper floors collapsed in on one side. Like it once wanted to grow up and be a castle and didn't quite make it.

The gravel crunched under her tires, sounding like she was driving over bubble wrap. Simon wasn't there. Again with the disappointment, stabbing her in the heart. What was next? Driving down to Cody to see if he was at his mom's or Zach's? Really?

No. Not really. Quinn just needed space. Air. Something. She rolled down the window, breathing in the hot soggy air. As she stopped and got out, she was fascinated by the isolation. The quiet. Her eyes panned the massive structure, amazed that someone could live like this. Would want to. On purpose.

Slowly, she walked toward the big metal door, glancing around her as she lifted her hand to knock. Why? She didn't know this man, and he hadn't seemed particularly friendly the other day, but—ugh, Quinn didn't understand what was driving her. Big groves of trees flanked each side of the building, with thick undergrowth all around and within. Across the street was the same, and she was suddenly very aware of the questionable neighborhood and how many steps she was from her car.

There was a metallic noise from within, making her withdraw her hand at the same time logic came knocking at her thoughts. She was being irrational and stupid, out there like a fool all because a dress knocked her off her orbit.

She turned around to head to her car at the same time another one came speeding across the gravel.

A car she knew.

Shit.

It stopped just feet from hers, splashing mud and gray water in its wake. Quinn steeled herself and raised her chin as Simon stormed out of the car like he thought he was Eli or something.

"What the living hell are you doing?" he demanded.

She raised her eyebrows and crossed her arms over her chest as he advanced on her.

"Just coming to visit your friend," Quinn lied.

"Why?" he asked with crazy eyes.

"Why not?"

"Because he's not your friend," he said. "Sorry, Harry!" he yelled at the building. "We're leaving now."

"What's your problem?" Quinn asked, trying not to soak him in. Trying not to remember his words against her skin. Trying to only see the pissed-off male in front of her.

"My problem is you trying to get yourself killed," Simon said, stopping a foot away from her. A foot that felt like an inch.

"Killed? Really?"

"Yes, really," Simon said, raking fingers through his hair. "This area is nothing but gangbangers and—" He stopped and lowered his voice. "And Harry isn't all there," he said under his breath. "He's a war vet. And sometimes he doesn't know where he is."

"You come here."

"I know *how* to come here," Simon said. "I know what to do and still he only meets me at the door. I went in unannounced once and damn near opened my jugular. Why are you here, again?"

Quinn didn't have an answer, and she felt her mouth trying to find words.

"I don't know," she said. "I just—too much of a day, I guess. I was antsy."

Simon took a deep breath and let it go as his eyes continued to pan the area around them. "I see you got stitched up and everything. All of that go okay?"

"Yeah. No concussion. I'll live."

"That's good."

The silence stretched. "Yeah."

"So—"

The air suddenly got thicker, if that was possible. Quinn felt every one of her nerve endings zinging as if a mother ship were calling to her from somewhere. And those magnets—damn it, those magnets were tugging at her. His eyes—

"Simon," she breathed, the word having no sound, and barely enunciation.

"I went to your place," Simon said, just as low. His eyes were crazy dark.

She licked her lips and watched those eyes drop to catch it, sending every ounce of feeling to one central place. She could hear her breathing in her ears, and it sounded like she'd just run around the building. Through sand.

Wait—*he came looking for her?*

"Why?"

The tiniest movement of his head signified a shake, but his eyes burned into hers.

"I don't know."

She did. It was the same reason she needed to walk away that very second.

Walk away.

"I guess I'll go, then," Quinn said, not moving.

Simon's jaw twitched madly.

"Please don't," he said finally. So softly she almost didn't hear it.

Except she did.

Her feet moved on their own, crossing the space between them, pulling his head down at the same time he reached for her. Her mouth met his the moment her feet left the ground.

Lightning rocketed through her body as Quinn found herself weightless, pressed tightly against Simon, their mouths hungry and searching, needing everything they couldn't reach.

He adjusted her higher so that their heads were at the same level, and on instinct her legs went around his waist, her arms pulling his head in to kiss him deeper. It was—oh, God, it was something that someone somewhere was yelling at her not to do, but that voice was so distant. So distant. And then he made this little growling noise in her mouth and turned them, pinning her back to the stone wall behind them.

"Oh!" Quinn cried out, locking her ankles behind him and gasping as he pushed hard between her legs, his hands sliding up her bare skin, right up under her shorts to grab her ass and pull her tighter against him. His lips left hers and trailed along her jaw, down her neck, whispering her name against her skin, all while still pulsing a slow grind between her legs. She felt the groan leave her throat as she tangled her fingers in his hair, needing more, feeling like it would never be enough.

"Quinn," he breathed. "God, baby—"

They had to—they had to stop. Something in her knew that. But this—nothing was better than this. Than feeling Simon's hands on her body, his mouth on her skin—she needed to touch him back, feel his skin before one of them snapped and it was over, and—she gasped as his hands moved up her waist to push her breasts up. His mouth was devouring the cleavage at the neckline of her tank top like a man starved. His thumbs raking across where her nipples were.

"Simon," she moaned into the sensation, fluttering her eyes closed and gripping him tighter with her legs. He had no idea how much she liked that, and yet there he was, finding her weakness, driving her mad with desire.

She had to touch him. She had to—she reached down between them where they were grinding together and palmed him, sending her own knuckles into herself as he pushed harder, groaning madly as she caressed the rock-hard bulge through his jeans.

They weren't going to stop. Oh, dear God, they weren't going to stop. The giddiness took her over in a wave of euphoria as she realized they were both too far gone. Quinn was shaking from head to toe with a need she'd never known in her life. All she wanted on this earth was this man, and it felt like she was going to burst out of her own skin if she didn't have him.

His face came back up to hers, his mouth sealing over hers in a kiss so deep and full of desire, it brought hot tears to the backs of her eyes. She needed him. She needed this—

"What the hell are you doing out there?"

Chapter Twenty-Two

The voice was rough and gravelly and harsh, accompanied by the sound of pipe scraping against metal.

Quinn yelped as Simon jerked away, somehow miraculously having the presence of mind not to drop her down the wall. "Shit," he muttered, his lungs burning with exertion, his head foggy with desire and lack of blood.

Bang went the pipe again, this time against the metal door, sounding like a fucking bell tower gone sour.

"Jesus," Quinn said, jumping.

"Okay already!" Simon yelled, his voice cracked and husky. "Give—" Exhaustion suddenly hit him like a wrecking ball. Not the physical kind, the mental knock-your-heart-around kind. "Give me a minute, will you?" he yelled again, pulling Quinn to him so he could pull her off the wall.

The look in her eyes as she unwound her legs and he let her slide slowly down his body—he knew it would haunt him.

It was raw. It was everything. Happy and sad. Guilty and proud. Overwhelmed and content. And wanting him. As her chest still heaved with her breathing and her fingers curled into his shirt like she wasn't ready to let him go, he saw so much need in those beautiful green eyes. And not just the kind still pulsing through his nether regions.

Simon wanted to say something. Anything. But what do you say to that? What do you do? She backed up a step to lean back against the wall like she didn't trust her legs, and he found himself moving with her. Fuck if he couldn't let go of her either.

His fingers went into her hair, falling loose and wild from her ponytail, and he closed his eyes as he pulled her close, sinking his face into her hair and breathing her in.

"Simon—" she whispered into his chest.

"Shhh," he whispered back. "Let me just feel this."

He had no fucking scruples, no logic, no functioning brain cells when it came to her. He had just about stooped to nailing Quinn Parker against an abandoned building in the middle of a crack-infested neighborhood, with a crazy old man just inside the door ready to bust both their heads open.

He could not be trusted.

It couldn't happen again.

Simon could feel the trembling in her body, and he backed off a fraction, one hand on the unhurt side of her face as he dared to look in her eyes again.

"You okay?" he whispered.

"No," she said, the word choking in her throat.

His chest tightened, squeezing his heart so hard it hurt.

"Me either."

It had been a week since Tuesday. *The* Tuesday that Simon had been the world's biggest idiot, acting like a horny high school kid on prom night. Hell, he'd been a lot classier on prom night.

Zach and Maddi were back, looking relaxed and well-sexed and happy. Assholes. The waterspout footage had been his saving grace,

Barry even saying that it might be something to consider. An auto-matic on-site reporting meteorologist for these things—*since* he'd be there anyway. The last part said exactly like that.

The conflict-of-interest clauses had to be flipping over in their little paragraphs, locked away in a drawer somewhere, but Simon wasn't going to buck it for now.

Charlie had finished up her interviewing and drama early, prob-ably figuring she had enough. And with he and Quinn being the fuel to feed that drama, and half the party not there, fifty percent wasn't enough.

Quinn hadn't been back.

She'd called in sick on Wednesday, although Hannah told him she went to her night job. Thursday and Friday were minor filming points she begged out of, Saturday nothing happened, and Sunday's segments were all about the family's history.

By Monday, exhausted from closing the shelter all weekend and carting people around, Simon was the walking dead, and by Tuesday he caved to texting her.

You okay?

The irony of the last time he'd asked her those very words wasn't lost on him, but he needed to know how she was doing. What she was doing. Where her head was.

He'd done nothing but replay everything on long loop for days. The look in her eyes. The words falling out of his mouth asking her not to leave, which was evidently all she needed to spur her on. The frenzy of need he had never experienced before. And he'd experienced plenty.

The way she tasted, the way she felt, her body responding under his hands, how she damn near lost it when he touched and kissed her breasts. The sound of her excited breathing. Of her moaning his name. The feel of her legs wrapped around him, and the feel of her hand on his dick and her ass in his hands.

None of it was healthy to think about, but with her gone, it refused to let go. And it was a welcome escape from the doom of the shelter closing.

Quinn didn't answer him, and he talked himself out of calling her. She was busy. She had a—he held his phone in a death grip—a fucking wedding to prepare for. And he was a man. Not a sappy woman waiting on a text from a lover. And they weren't even that. Although, what the hell, they might as well be.

"Screw this," he said, tossing the phone on the counter just as there was a knock on his door.

"Hey," Zach said with a grin, leaning on the door frame when Simon opened the door. "Busy?"

Just feeling sorry for myself. "No, what's up?"

"Came to tell you that Maddi's bringing the latest episode over for a prescreening this afternoon after work, instead of us going there," Zach said, tilting his head in a mini shrug. "Perks of being married to the APA."

"APA?"

"Assistant producer's assistant," Zach said, chuckling. "Do you have to work?"

Say yes. "No. But is it mandatory?" Simon asked. "I mean, it's not like they would change anything, right? And once you've seen one, you've seen them all."

"Seriously?" Zach said, slapping Simon on the shoulder on the way in. "I always see something I didn't even see when I was living it. Come on, come live it again with me. Maddi hasn't even seen it yet. She's waiting to watch it with everyone."

"Y'all get too damn excited about these things," Simon said, feeling like a grumpy old man.

Zach frowned at him. "What's up with you? You're usually the happy one. Eli's the Scrooge."

Simon scrubbed at his hair, feeling itchy all the time now, like his skin didn't fit.

"Is it the shelter?" Zach asked. "Because, man, I know that was a kick to the nuts. I know what that place meant to you and Dad."

Simon just stared forward. "Yeah. Shelter." He picked up a cup and walked around the kitchen counter to set it in the sink. "Want something to drink?" he asked, opening the fridge and pulling out a bottle of water. "I have this. That's it."

Zach laughed, straddling a bar stool and leaning on the counter. "Nah, I'm good," he said. "So are you coming?"

"Mom's or your house?"

"Mom's."

"Everyone gonna be there?" Simon asked, trying to sound subtle with that very unsubtle, very loaded question.

"I have no idea," Zach said. "I'm telling who I see. I called Eli. I think Maddi was gonna call Hannah and Quinn."

He felt the twitch in his jaw at the mention of her name. Speaking of nut-kicking, that was doing it.

"What's eating you, big brother?" Zach asked, his expression going more serious. "Something's not right." His eyes narrowed as Simon looked at him. "What'd I miss?"

Zach wasn't only Simon's brother. He was his best friend. The only other person he could say that about was Quinn, but that had all kinds of weird colors and levels to it now.

Simon leaned back on his side of the counter, holding his head back as if an intervention could happen in some miraculous way. It wasn't going to.

"Me and Quinn," he said simply. He didn't have to fancy it up or go into details with Zach. He'd get it.

"Oh," Zach said, surprise lifting his eyebrows. "Shit."

"Yeah."

"You did the deed?"

"No, but we may as well have," Simon said, picking up a wooden spoon that was only there for decoration. He needed something to twist in his hands before he exploded.

"Shit, Simon, I was only gone seven days," Zach said. "How the hell did this go down? When I left, she was engaged to St. James."

Simon blew out a long breath, feeling his knee start to twitch. "Still is."

"Fuck," Zach said under his breath, sitting back. "So she's still marrying him?"

"Seems that way," Simon said.

Zach frowned, studying him. "Quinn's not a—*fling* kind of woman."

Simon shook his head slowly. "No."

"Or one to cheat on her fiancé, I wouldn't think."

Simon clenched his jaw so tightly it hurt. "She's not like that, Zach. This just kind of—flipped. She didn't plan it. *I* didn't plan it—"

"Relax," Zach said. "I'm not saying you did."

"Then don't call her a cheater—"

"I'm saying open your eyes, jackass," Zach said. "She's in love with you, too."

Quinn popped her trunk open as she got out of her car and looked up at the pristine grayness of the house in front of her. The paint— or stain, or whatever it is you do to stone or stucco or fancy mor- tar—was literally the same color as the windows.

With xeriscape charcoal gravel in the front yard. No grass. No flowers. The only color available was if it was a pretty day and the windows might reflect the blue sky.

Today was overcast and gloomy, so it was pretty much like walking into a black-and-white movie. Maybe she'd be drained of pigment, too, once she was moved in for good.

She heard the front door and turned to see Eric jogging down the circular brick sidewalk that twisted amid the gravel.

"Hey, babe, let me help!" he said, grinning. "I can't believe you're finally bringing some stuff."

"Yeah, well, it's not much," she said. "Since you showed me the whole shelf you cleared for my books and stuff, and the extra cabinet for my mugs, I think it'll be pretty easy."

"Lovebug, I'm sorry," he said. "I know it doesn't give you much space for your things, but my things are yours, too."

Quinn raised an eyebrow. "No. And there's plenty of space. You just don't want the emptiness of it tainted with solids."

"Yeah, yeah," Eric said, nodding. "Just hand me a box."

"You know I could have done this myself today," Quinn said, pushing a box of books into his arms. "You didn't have to take off work."

"Are you kidding me?" he said, adjusting it. "It's been so nice with you here every night this week, not having to share you with a storm or a TV show, taking off the day to help you is the least I can do."

Not having to share.

Nope, there had been no sharing since a week ago, when he'd shared more of her than he knew. That had taken her guilt to a whole new level. She may have enjoyed a kiss or two before that, but what she and Simon embarked on that day had full intentions. It had been a runaway train of epic proportions, and if Harry hadn't interrupted them? Good God.

Simon had been right about taking it further and what the fallout would be. The moment she'd finally moved her feet far enough away from him to get in her car and leave, the shame over what she'd just done to Eric consumed her. She wasn't wired that way.

She had a natural attraction to Simon. That was all it was. An attraction she had no need or right to act on. So she made the only choice she could. Stay away from him for as long as possible, till the crazy could die down inside her.

If she and Eric were just dating, that would be something else. But she'd made a commitment, and that ring wasn't just jewelry to her.

Simon was a crush. Crushes faded with distance. Quinn wouldn't be able to stay away—she'd already pushed that envelope—but she could limit their time together. Use a play out of his book and push him away.

All that being said, she'd still checked her phone fifteen times a day, every day. She wanted to send him pictures of her funny portrait session in which she looked like Farmer Jane in Daisy Dukes and a veil, but she couldn't.

Letting go of your best friend was hard.

Eric's phone rang as he came back for another load, and he paused to answer it.

"St. James," he said quickly. "Henderson! Good to hear from you, man. Thanks for calling me back."

And he was gone back up the sidewalk, slowly winding his way.

Her phone dinged in her pocket and she dug it out, expecting the normal to-do list from her mother, a proposed agenda for the rehearsal dinner, or Phoebe sending her pictures of nearly naked men to pick a stripper.

What she got nearly made her drop the phone.

Are you okay?

Drawing in the shaky breath that had just been sucked out of her, she stared at the words. Remembering the last time she'd heard them. Right after—

Simon's face filled her memory, close and tortured-looking as he whispered the words.

Are you okay?

No.

Me either.

Quinn's eyes filled with tears that she quickly blinked free and wiped away, clicking her phone's screen to dark as Eric came back.

"Hey, you okay?" he asked.

An ironic laugh escaped her throat. "Question of the day," she said, swiping at her right eye. "Just got some dust or something in my eyes."

"It's a little windy," he said. "You got more up front?"

"Yeah, my mugs," she said a little breathlessly.

Don't go there. Don't think about it.

"What else do you have on the agenda?"

What else? Her brain had left her. Something. Something with her mother.

"Oh, I have to meet Mom for a—thing at the country club," Quinn said, blinking back everything and swallowing it down deep. "Checking on arrangements and stuff." She smiled at him. "You really don't want to come for that."

Eric chuckled. "I will probably bow out of that one."

"Don't blame you."

"I'm proud of you, though," he said. "Finally stepping in and working with her. You know she's doing all this for you."

Swallow. Swallow. Swallow.

Her phone rang, and her heart slammed against her ribs as there for one second she feared it was Simon. Quinn gasped at the sensation, glancing at her phone, and released the breath.

Hannah.

And why did disappointment stab her in the chest just as harshly?

"Hey," Quinn said, answering.

"Hey, stranger," Hannah said. "Sorry I had a sitting today and couldn't help. So how goes life in the concrete bunker?"

"Think it's concrete?" Quinn asked, giving the structure another look-over. "I was thinking stucco, but maybe it's too smooth for that."

Eric looked at her funny. "The house?" he whispered. "Stucco-sandstone mix."

"Stucco-sandstone mix," Quinn repeated as he carried a box of her mugs into the house. Probably to be hidden in that cabinet. Never to go out on a cute little mug tree again, showing off all the colors and smart-aleck sayings.

"Whatever," Hannah said. "I've seen prison buildings more cheerful than that thing."

"I'm thinking of doing planter boxes to set outside the door," Quinn said. "With colorful plastic flowers that catch your eye so that visitors won't worry about their vision when they come over."

Hannah laughed in her ear. "Great idea. I want to see that play out. How's your face? I feel like I haven't seen you in a month."

"You saw me Saturday," Quinn said.

"Yeah, but that was work," Hannah said. "Even when I'm shooting *you* acting like a fool in a field of daisies, it's still work."

"How did the shots turn out?"

"Gorgeous, of course," Hannah replied. "Can't see a single stitch. Want to see them?"

"Of course!"

"Come over to Mom's at two," Hannah said, making Quinn's toes and fingers go cold.

"Ummm."

"Actually it's not just for that," Hannah admitted. "Maddi's bringing the latest cut over to show us before it airs online tonight.

She hasn't seen it, either," Hannah added quickly, probably sensing the hesitation. "So she's excited to watch it with us."

"I—don't think so, Hannah," Quinn said, her mouth drying up at the mere thought of it.

"You can't hide forever, my friend," Hannah said.

Quinn let go of a disgusted sigh. "I know."

"You're still on the contract, you do have to show up eventually."

"I know that, too," Quinn said. "I just—"

"Am a big wuss?" Hannah offered helpfully.

"Needed some distance," Quinn completed.

"I have pictures from the field, too," she said. "We'll put them up on the screen for everyone to gush over."

For Simon to see.

"So, bring Eric," Hannah said. "It'll give you strength and make him feel included."

"It'll give me a heart attack," Quinn said.

"No, it won't, I'll sit on the other side of you and hold your hand," Hannah said, the tone reeking of eye-rolling. "Besides, if he's gonna be in this family of ours, he needs to see the life. All of it," she added emphatically. "He needs to see this as a real thing."

"Yeah," Quinn said sadly. "He needs to."

"Don't get too excited," Hannah said.

"Don't get too attached to your hand," Quinn quipped.

"I thought you were going to meet up with your mother," Eric said, his expression tightening when she told him the plan.

"I am, at four," she said, pulling her hair down and back up again, feeling her scalp start to sweat. She flipped on the bathroom's scented fan. "But I need to go do this first. Besides, I want to see Maddi."

Yep, that was it.

"And you need me to come?" he said, looking in the closet with disinterest.

"I want you to come," she said. "I want you to see this side of me. I go to your company parties," she added.

He turned her way. "You're comparing watching TV with going to a party?"

She gave him the look. "Yes," she said. "Yes, I am."

"Fine," he muttered.

"And just wear what you have on," she said. "This is not a business-casual thing. This is roll-out-of-bed grunge."

"Which is why you're fixing your hair?"

She stared into her own eyes and nodded almost imperceptibly. "That's because I'm a girl," she said. "And because it sucks and it's about to go through a shredder."

"Hell, no!" Eric said. "I love your hair. I fantasize about your hair."

Quinn raised an eyebrow. "You can stop there."

"I'm just saying, it's beautiful. It's hot. No shredding." He came up behind her and wrapped his arms around her middle, nuzzling her ear. "I want to still be twisting that hair around my fingers when we're eighty."

Quinn shook her head. *Swallow. Swallow. Swallow.* "Are you ready to go?"

Chapter Twenty-Three

Simon felt like he was going through the motions. Operating with those "strings" Quinn had said were coming out of her freckles the night of Zach's wedding. Different strings, different reasons, but there nonetheless.

God, that night of the wedding seemed like three lifetimes ago.

And he was as keyed up knowing Quinn was coming as a boy going to pick up his first date. Worse, actually. Because in that scenario, the girl would have probably answered his text. And he wouldn't have the endless anxiety of wondering if he'd screwed up.

That was a given. Of course he had. He'd given in to the need he couldn't deny, the very microsecond she'd reached for him. He should have stood his ground. Fought it harder.

And now she had bolted the other direction. The only things he knew for sure were from overhearing Hannah. He knew Quinn had done a photo shoot for her wedding picture and that she was staying at Eric's house more.

So either she was trying to bury her feelings by diving into life with Eric, or was so hideously turned off by their tryst that she realized what she had was better.

Neither was a great option.

She's in love with you, too.

Who said anything about love? Zach was just eaten up with newlywed disease.

Simon sat at the big table alone, running through data on his laptop instead of hanging with his family and Charlie. More comforted by numbers telling him some big cells were building to the northeast. Numbers, he could understand. They made sense. There was no gray area.

There were no decisions to make, or moral fences to ride. Numbers just were.

"Hey, antisocial," Maddi said, twisting sideways on the couch to call back to him. "Ignoring your new sister-in-law?"

"Never," Simon said, giving her a distracted wink as he stretched his arms. "As if you could be ignored."

"Hey, quit flirting with my wife," Zach said, walking in from the kitchen with a muffin of some sort.

"I love that sentence," Maddi said, leaning her face back with a silly grin as he passed behind the couch and kissed her upside down.

"Where'd you get that muffin?" Eli asked, eyeing it from the other end of the couch.

"The kitchen," Zach said, pointing.

"I didn't see any in there," Eli said.

"Mom loves me more," Zach said with a shrug.

"Wrong!" his mom sang out from her overstuffed recliner with Cracker curled up in her lap. "I dislike you all equally. Is Quinn coming?" she asked Simon.

"I don't know," Simon said. "Why are you asking me?"

She gave him the eyebrow. "Because I gave you life, Simon. That entitles me to all the questions," she said.

"Yes, she and Eric are coming," Hannah said, glancing at him. Simon did a double take on her, wondering what she knew. "They're moving some of her stuff today."

Simon's eyes met Zach's and then focused back on the computer screen and its numbers. That was that. Should have told him all he needed to know. And it didn't matter why. It was what it was. He'd fallen into this messed-up little journey and had sworn not to let it turn him into something pathetic. He wasn't about to start now. No matter how bad the beating got.

Voices in the foyer told him that might be sooner than later, and he rolled his neck to stretch out the tension. It didn't, but the popping was pretty impressive.

"Look who I found outside," said Eric, pushing Gran in front of him.

Gran was grinning ear to ear, colorful as usual in an aqua pantsuit, her white hair pulled back as though it wouldn't dare be any other way.

"Hello, my pretties," she said.

"That sounds really evil when she says that," Hannah muttered to Eli.

"I'm old, Hannah," she said, twisting one of her rings with purpose, as though it would open a secret room or something. "Not deaf."

Hannah pulled a face. "Love you, Gran."

"Mm-hmm," Gran said. "Louella, don't get up," she directed toward Louella who continued to sit, stroking Cracker. "Eric dear, would you get me some water?" she asked, as though he was there just to tend to her.

"Of course," he said, heading to the kitchen, smiling back down the hallway at something. Or someone.

"In a real glass," she added.

"Yes, ma'am."

Simon wanted to strangle Eric with the new table runner his mom had put on the table. Louella looked like she might beat him to it to strangle Gran. Then the sound of the door shutting reached Simon's ears over the chatter, and there she was.

Walking in tentatively, nervous. Very out of character for Quinn. Normally, she breezed in and out of the Chase home as if it were her own. Not today.

She stood at the edge of the room, her eyes scanning the occupants until she let out what looked like a large sigh of relief, followed by a small frown.

She didn't see him.

Simon sat back in his chair, ignoring the cardiac moment his chest was having in order to study her. She hadn't seen him. And looked relieved—and disappointed. And maybe a little irritated. Her mouth was pursed in a pouty little tell that said she'd gotten all worried for nothing.

And Simon never wanted to kiss a mouth so badly in all his life.

Shut it down.

He pushed back in his chair and stood, and Quinn's peripheral vision pulled her around. And Simon damn near lost his knees as that look slammed into him.

Shut. It. Down.

He was trying. But all he could really process was the thought that everyone should see someone look at them that way at least once in their lifetime.

Quinn had bolstered herself up. Readied and steeled herself to walk into that house and face it all. Simon. Everyone in the family surely knowing by then, including Miss Lou. Simon.

And then she went in, and everyone was talking, and not one of them was Simon, and she could let go of the breath she'd been holding. But then disappointment ripped through her heart and she was like, *What the hell?* What kind of messed-up *was* she, that she was let down that the subject of her stress wasn't—

And then there, to her right, pushing up from his laptop at the table, was everything. Just—everything. Looking at her like she was water and he hadn't had a drop in years. She had to grip the chair closest to her for grounding as the weight of realization landed on her like a blanket soaked in honey. She was stupidly, hopelessly in love with her best friend. And marrying someone else in two weeks.

You okay?

No.

Me either.

For the first time, she allowed herself the thought of *I can't marry Eric* instead of the constant *I can't be with Simon*, and it scared the hell out of her. Eric would be crushed if she did that. Their families would be crushed.

But—it was liberating, and oxygen was reaching her brain again, and—

"Here you go, babe," said Eric behind her, startling her for a second that there were still other humans in the room. "Got you some water, too."

She turned and looked up into Eric's eyes, and the love there kicked her square in the throat.

"Thanks, babe," she said, taking the glass. Relishing the cold against her palm and wishing she could pour it over her head. "How'd you know I was thirsty? That's sweet."

"Just looked it," he said, kissing her forehead. "Kind of guy I am," he added, chuckling as he poked her gently in the ribs.

"Go grab us a spot by the fireplace," she said, turning back to Simon as Eric walked away. Needing to absorb that feeling for a second longer.

Something had changed in that moment, however. That thing in his eyes was gone. He leaned over to plug in his computer, and gave her a polite smile on his way back up.

"Good to see you, Quinn," he said, moving around her to head to the kitchen.

Good to see you?

Really?

She felt her mouth fall open until she rested her gaze on Eric again. *Get it together.* Forcing her feet to move in a forward motion, she made it to the spot next to him and sank into a cross-legged position.

It was like being in a play where everyone kept switching roles. She was lost. She was confused. She watched him emerge from the kitchen with a soda, stone-faced, going back to sit alone in front of his laptop. Not looking back up.

And everything inside her twisted.

A click and flash made her blink, and she turned to see Hannah leaning sideways from her chair, taking a picture of Quinn with her cell phone.

"Just taking a picture of y'all," she said, smiling, but the speedy way she looked at Quinn and closed the photo said otherwise. "Here, y'all pose, I'll get some better ones."

Quinn leaned in to Eric as he wrapped his arms around her, trying to remember to smile and look happy and all the things you're supposed to radiate as near-newlyweds without being uber-aware of another set of eyes that may or may not be watching. She didn't know. She couldn't look.

"You two just look adorable," Gran said. "Perfect. Like Barbie and Ken."

Quinn jumped as Simon slammed his laptop closed with a thwack.

"Problem, Simon?" Gran asked.

"No, ma'am," he said, giving her a tight smile. "Everything's perfect."

"Hey, did y'all hear?" Miss Lou said. "Levi got an offer from the high school in Briartown. To come coach for them!" she finished excitedly.

"Seriously?" Hannah said. "He's coming home?"

"He's coming home," Miss Lou said, closing her eyes. "Or forty-five minutes from here, anyway. Close enough."

Quinn noticed the guys nodding. They weren't surprised. They knew.

"Heather's mom is sick," Miss Lou said. "I heard she wasn't doing too well. Heather's moving back, and with Kinley—well, you know your brother isn't going to give up his custody."

"It'll be good to have him home," Zach said.

"When?" Hannah asked. "I want to know when to kick his ass for not telling me."

Miss Lou laughed. "I don't know, Hannah. Probably the summer, when the school year's over."

"That's wonderful news," Gran said, and everyone went quiet. "Sure do miss that boy."

"Okay," Maddi said, standing, breaking the awkward moment of silence that passed after Gran's comment. "So, thanks for coming on short notice. And thank you for putting up with my assistant—that still sounds hilarious, sorry—while I was off honeymooning with your brother. I know they started some new things in my absence."

"Hate to see what they'd do if you took a month off," Hannah said.

"If I took a month off," Maddi said, "I'd better use it to hunt for a new job. So was it horrible?"

"Just—weird," Eli said. "Awkward. Putting us in unnatural places to try to act natural."

"I heard you had a little storm, though," she asked.

"It was beautiful," Quinn said. "Never seen a waterspout like that."

"And you!" Maddi exclaimed.

"I know," Quinn said, holding up a hand. *Please don't elaborate and give Eric more fodder.* "Stitches come out on Friday."

"Well, enough excitement for little while, I thought," Maddi said. "But Simon tells me there's something going on northwest of Fort Worth?"

Quinn forced her head to turn his way as everyone else's did.

"It will be," he said. "Right now it's in the Panhandle. Something to watch, though."

"Something big?" Zach asked, and Quinn had to smile. Zach lived for bad weather.

"Might have teeth," Simon said quietly.

"Chomp, chomp," Zach said, winking up at Maddi, who just shook her head in barely disguised amusement.

"Ready to be a grown-up?" she asked, head tilted.

"Oh, I'm all there, honey," Zach said.

"Get a room," Hannah muttered. "Hey, before we start, check these out." She hit a button on the remote. "I uploaded Quinn's wedding portrait pictures I took. Y'all tell me your favorites."

"Hang on, I'm not supposed to see this," Eric said.

"It's cool," Quinn said. "There's no dress."

The big screen filled with daisies, an old wooden fence in the distance.

"I like that one," Zach said, putting up a hand as Maddi swatted at him.

The next one was Quinn in her veil, green tank top, and blue-jean cutoffs. Posing cutely and laughing.

"Aw, I love that!" Miss Lou cooed. "That's adorable!"

"I thought it would be in your wedding dress," Eric said. "This *is* for the country club, right?"

"Don't be my mother," Quinn whispered at him, smiling, not moving her lips. "Have some fun."

She darted her eyes back to where Simon sat, resting back in his chair, staring at the screen with emotionless eyes.

The screen flicked from one to the other, various poses of the same basic concept, while everyone commented on this or that. Then the last one. And Quinn gasped.

There was no veil. No posed smile. Just a close up of Quinn sitting down, surrounded by the flowers, her head tilted back to the sun with eyes closed and a tiny smile of contentment on her face. One rogue daisy lying against her bare shoulder like a hug.

Quinn didn't know she'd taken that, and it gave her goosebumps. Not because it was her, but because it was exactly the kind of picture she herself would have snapped. It was photography gold. It was real. And raw. The camera doesn't lie.

"Hannah," she whispered, her eyes going misty.

"That's it," Simon said under his breath.

Quinn turned and blinked her eyes clear to see Simon leaning forward on his elbows, a look of awe taking over the stony expression of before.

"That's perfection," he added, glancing her way. "It's you."

Quinn's heart squeezed in her chest, and she had to take a deep breath and look away. She covered by laughing.

"Hannah, you're a sneaky one."

She grinned. "Wanted to surprise you."

"It's amazing," Quinn said. "You are so good."

"There's no dress, no veil, it's just a random picture," Eric said. "A *great* picture," he amended quickly as Quinn leveled a gaze at him. "But for the wedding? Really?"

"Yes," she said simply.

"Where are the stitches?" Zach asked.

"Photoshop!" Hannah said, holding her arms up like a goal was scored. "It's the bomb."

"Okay," Quinn said, blowing out a breath. "Enough of me." She took one last look at the scene in front of her. Knowing that was heaven. Simon was right. Hannah had captured her idea of the perfect happiness. One she'd probably never know again unless Mr. Thibodeaux, the old man who owned the land, would let her come visit his field on a regular basis. "Let's get to the down-and-dirty stuff now."

"Okay, I haven't vetted this yet," Maddi said, standing up. "But Nicole did. And Charlie did, too. And I hear it's *hot*."

She hit a button, and the credits started. Quinn had to admit, that part was always cool. Seeing her face and name in the opening shots, everything flashing and spinning and back and forth all set to heavy hard rock music—it was hard not to get caught up in the rush of it.

It opened with some snippets of interviews. A piece of one. A line or two of another. A cut to Hannah and Quinn being interviewed together and losing it, bleeping things out as they laughed and Hannah cussed.

It skipped to a shot of Eli looking at something in the distance, hair plastered to his head and dirt and leaves peppering his face, and saying, "God, that's beautiful."

That was from the waterspout trip in Texoma—Quinn remembered that very moment. But they didn't use it with footage from the spout; they used it as personal footage for Eli, flipping to a one-on-one with Quinn.

"Eli plays the grumpy Papa Bear," on-screen Quinn said. "But that's just part of who he is. It's like he takes on the whole world for his team every time we go out there, and somebody has to be the worrier."

The screen flashed on Eli running his hand over his face, then back to Quinn.

"He's good at that," on-screen Quinn said, laughing. "He and Simon are the practical ones, keeping everything grounded while Zack and Hannah and I—we see all the beauty. But Eli—he really does see the beauty in the beast, too. He just doesn't advertise it."

"Aw, Quinn, that is so poignant," Miss Lou said from across the room, dabbing at her eyes.

They were back to the shot of Eli in the rain, then there it was. The waterspout.

"Wait, we just shot that," Quinn said, feeling the tingle of wariness tickle the back of her neck. "Since when do they jump so far ahead?"

"Yeah, there must be a dozen other runs we've filmed before this," Hannah piped in.

Maddi frowned. "I'm not sure," she said softly as it continued to play.

Wicked and twisting and swelling gorgeously white, the waterspout pulled the lake up by its drudges and spewed it back out the sides. Slinging it as far away as where they stood. Quinn remembered the smell of mud and fish that assaulted them along with the dirt and the stinging spray.

The majesty was unmistakable. The reverence, she could feel through the screen. Where other funnels they'd encountered were careless beasts and trolls and monsters that stomped and crushed their way along, this was different. This was a queen, emerging from quiet water to merge with the clouds and roar her reign for a moment.

"Damn it, I can't believe I missed that," Zack said.

"Excuse me?" Maddi said.

"Because I had something so much better going on," he added quickly.

The shot switched to Eli again, yelling something at Simon, running against the wind to get back in the vehicle and run statistics. Then a pan of Quinn yelling over the wind at Simon, her face bloodied.

The frame froze in still-shot, and the narrator said, *"So, thirty minutes earlier . . ."*

They were in the car, and the narrator was talking about them getting prepared for what was to come, although they had no idea just how much that would involve.

Crap. Quinn knew what was to come.

On-screen Quinn was talking about anchoring, describing what she did for Charlie as she lowered the window. Eli and Simon were talking in the background, and the shot alternated between inside the car and the outside angle from the van. The rain was crazy-intense. Small hail pelted the camera, and the roar of the wind and the increased tempo and volume of the conversations got Quinn's blood pumping like she was there again.

From inside the vehicle, on-screen Quinn anchored her leg behind Simon's back, the camera zooming in on the side of his face and then hers. Quinn swallowed hard and licked her lips as she darted a glance to Eric's profile. He didn't appear to notice, thank God, although she didn't know how. It looked like a screaming beacon to her.

"And there she goes," Eli said, making the room chuckle as on-screen Quinn swung out of the window.

"Jesus," Eric muttered.

Shit.

She squeezed his knee. "Looks like a bigger deal than it really is, babe," she said. "From that angle—"

Then it switched to the van camera's perspective, which looked like Quinn was basically holding on with a toenail as sideways rain and hail battered her and the movement of the vehicle swung her around like a monkey.

"You look so badass when you do that," Hannah said.

"You were saying?" Eric said, turning to give her a what-the-hell look. He wasn't amused. He wasn't impressed with her badassery.

"You might not want to watch this next part, then," Quinn said softly.

Which unfortunately made him look back just in time for Eli to swerve hard, the camera shots cut back and forth at lightning speed to oh-so-graciously catch the thunk of Quinn's meet-up with the vehicle on repeat about twenty-seven times from every angle. Including hers, from her own camera as it then bounced to the ground.

Hannah's on-screen *"Oh, my God"* was just as pronounced, and all of it set to pounding music that didn't help Quinn's case as Eric looked back at her again with impossibly more disdain than before.

"Just knocked around the car a little?" he said. "Seriously?"

Quinn opened her mouth to say something, but he shook his head and focused back on the screen.

The next part was truly like watching someone else's experiences, since she didn't remember it very clearly. The vehicle skidded to a stop, from the outside, the inside, Simon pulling her from the window into his arms.

Into his arms.

Her head in his lap, her face in his hands, as he whispered something against her forehead.

I need you.

The camera didn't pick it up amongst all the chaos of the wind and debris flying around, and thankfully they weren't wired for sound that day, but she remembered it.

Her hand coming around the back of his neck at the same time. An intimate gesture.

No, no, no, Eric, don't watch this! her mind screamed. Why did she insist he come?

Hannah discreetly looked back at Quinn and they shared a thought. This was another camera. Hannah had worked on footage and Charlie's, making sure nothing damaging was on there. Who was filming this?

Then a cut to a snippet of an interview with Simon, talking about the intensity of the field. Then a cut back to the wind blowing them against the vehicle and him blocking her with his body.

Quinn couldn't breathe. They were going to show it. What Hannah deleted. It cut back again to another interview snippet of Simon and Quinn together, on the day where she was trying to freeze out all emotion. Not show anything. Which inadvertently showed everything.

The camera doesn't lie.

A question was asked about their on-screen chemistry, to which Simon said jokingly, "Well, I get her out there, but another guy beat me to the lifetime version."

Oh, fuck.

It was a joke. It was said to be funny. To probably lighten up and balance out her somberness. But in lieu of everything and the scene it then cut back to, with their faces nearly touching, it spun a whole new direction.

Eric didn't look back at her that time. And that was bad. She knew that was bad.

"It's not like that, Eric," she whispered, adding a chuckle. "It's—"

He held up a finger as the narrator said, "Hot enough for you? Well, let's rewind back about twenty-four hours . . ."

There was an effect of actual old-school rewinding, and then they were back in the rec room the day before, Eli sitting at the table his swim trunks and T-shirt, grinning about not getting in the hot tub while he and Hannah overenunciated their sentences and Quinn and Simon glared at each other. And by the continual back-and-forth footage between them, the camera had picked up on the tension.

Oh, no.

Casey had erased it. He had erased it.

Quinn felt her scalp begin to sweat, and her skin begin to tighten over her bones as she watched the progression of the argument between her and Simon, his storming out of the hot tub, her following—

"No," she whispered, not realizing it was out loud until Eric glanced back at her. She saw the move, but she didn't dare look at him. She couldn't. She didn't want to see the questions. She couldn't pull her eyes from the screen, watching herself storm after Simon in her white bikini that showed entirely too much ass for the camera.

Please cut.

Quinn's mouth went dry as she watched the drama unfold. The words couldn't be heard clearly, but they weren't needed. There was the towel—and the pull—

Please cut.

And then Simon's hands were on her face, pulling her in as he kissed her with all he had.

It was like time stood still. The room was quiet as the image swam before her in a watery haze. Simon kissing her. Quinn melting into him. Hannah muttering something and then yelling for the camera to stop. Everyone running at the camera, and then another camera taking over as Simon and Eli bullied Casey into deleting it. Yelling at him about her life.

Her life. Her life that was sitting next to her watching this.

The sound of a chair scraping the floor reached her ears, and there was movement to her left, but Quinn felt frozen in place. Afraid to look at the man on her right. Or the man on her left, who grabbed the remote from Maddi's stunned fingers and hit *Stop.*

Chapter Twenty-Four

Eric sat there motionless, staring at a paused video he probably didn't want to come see in the first place, having had his nuts shoved up into his stomach in front of an audience.

Simon had never cared much for Eric St. James—he always thought him a blowhard pretty boy—but no one deserved a kick like that. He also knew that once Eric got his mind moving again, he'd be coming after him. And that he actually deserved it, to a point.

Simon had decided when they first got there, after the initial shock of looking into Quinn's eyes for the first time, that the struggle he saw her having was all on him. There wasn't the dilemma of a choice for him—she was his choice. But for Quinn, it wasn't just about what man she wanted. She was raised in a different world, one of structure and rules and etiquette and obligation. All things that she balked at and rebelled against, but they were there, bred into her anyway. In her mind, she'd chosen Eric St. James years ago, regardless of some crush she had on Simon. She'd said yes when Eric asked her to marry him, and she kept her promises. Her mother was planning a wedding, and she had to follow through. It was as ridiculously simple as that.

For the past two weeks, everything had tested those values. And he couldn't be the cause of the turmoil he saw in her eyes anymore.

He couldn't be the reason. Quinn needed to love Eric if she wanted to love Eric, free and clear of any question. Or decide *not* to love him, if that was the case. But her choice—her decision—needed to be made free of Simon. Free of comparison.

So in a moment's decision, he had shut it down. Swallowed it down so deep that it couldn't possibly show in his eyes. The look of confusion on her face had been potent, but he kept it together regardless.

Now—shit, what was going to happen now was anybody's guess.

Simon stiffened as Eric pushed to his feet, bracing himself for what he would do in Eric's shoes.

"Eric," Quinn said, her voice higher than normal. She reached for his hand, but he eluded her.

"Excuse me," he said softly, keeping his eyes on the floor as he walked from the room, not looking at anyone. Not even Simon.

Quinn suddenly burst into life as she scrambled to her feet and ran after him.

"Eric, wait!"

The front door opened and closed twice, and then all eyes were on Simon.

"What did you do?" his mother said.

"I'm gonna kill that little prick Casey," Eli seethed. "He lied to us."

"Charlie had to know, too," Maddi said from behind her hands. "And Nicole. Oh, my God, y'all, I should have vetted this personally. I'll never let that out of my control again."

"What are you going to do?" Hannah asked, looking at Simon.

Simon sighed and grimaced. "Probably go let him punch me," he said, sounding weary as he trudged toward the front door.

"Need a backup?" Eli asked.

"Nah, I got it."

"I assume you can get a ride home," Eric said quietly, heading for his car, digging keys from his pocket.

"Eric—"

"Your home, not mine," he clarified, chilling her midstep.

"Please stop," Quinn said, her voice wavering. "Please look at me."

"Look at you?" Eric said, wheeling around. "What the hell did you ask me to come here for, Quinn? To rub it in my face? To humiliate me?"

"No!" Quinn cried. "I had no idea. That was never supposed to be aired—"

"That's your explanation?" he bellowed. "It wasn't supposed to be used for the *show*?" Eric stepped closer, glaring down into her face. "What about that it wasn't supposed to *happen*?"

She shut her eyes tight, hot tears squeezing out beneath her eyelids. She had to own up to it. She had to make it right. She'd loved Eric for years, it wasn't right to hurt him like this.

"I know. You're right," she said.

"Is this why you've suddenly been so interested in moving in? In our wedding?" he asked, pointing off toward nothing. "Guilt?"

Yes. "No," she lied. "Nothing happened. That was—"

"That was all me," came Simon's voice from the porch behind them. Quinn spun around, shaking her head.

"Go back in the house, Chase," Eric said through his teeth. "I'm trying to leave here out of respect for your mother's home, so just get the hell out of my sight."

"I'm telling you, it's not her fault," Simon said, crossing the space between them impossibly fast. "I did that in there," he said, thumbing behind him. "I advanced on her—she did nothing to encourage it."

"Simon," Quinn breathed. What was he doing?

"I didn't see anything discouraging it, either," Eric said. "Sure looked mutual to me."

"Don't be a dick, Eric," Simon said. "You have her. Don't throw that away—"

Quinn sucked in a gasp as she saw the flash of Eric's fist, unable to warn Simon fast enough. The smack of bone and flesh against each other was sickening as he landed his punch against Simon's jaw.

"Fuck," Simon growled, reeling back from the blow. He shook his head free of the pain. "I'll give you that. I deserve that one."

But he barely got the words out before Eric, fueled with the adrenaline that first punch set loose, rushed him, slamming him up against a porch post with Simon's shirt in his fists.

"Oh, my God!" Quinn shrieked. "Stop it!"

"Don't tell me what you'll give me or what I have," Eric seethed. "I know what I have."

In a second, Simon flipped them around, tripping Eric with a foot behind his so that he fell back against the post. Simon's arm came up against Eric's chest.

"I said I gave you *one*," Simon said. "It's not a good time to push me."

Shoving Eric to the side and away from him, Simon glanced at Quinn.

"You're a smart guy, Eric," he said. "Most of the time. Listen to her."

He walked up the porch and back into the house, brushing himself off. And that's when Quinn knew. He was making the decision for her.

Just like everyone else.

And Eric was staring at her, pissing her off and breaking her heart at the same time. Why was he pissing her off? She didn't know. Just something in his stance reminded her of control. Of her mother. Of—

"What do you think that was like for me in there?" he asked, pointing to the house.

"Horrible," she breathed. "I'm so sorry."

"Are you over it?" he spat.

Quinn blinked. "Over—over what?"

"Over him," he clarified. "Whatever prewedding crush or crap you had on him."

The earth needed to open up and swallow her. Right there.

"There was no—prewedding anything, Eric." *It was all there before.*

"Is it done?" he yelled, his face red.

Quinn took a deep breath and nodded, sure that it was, regardless of Eric. She was tired of being told what to do.

"No more storm chasing," he said.

"What?"

"No more storm chasing, or no more me," he said.

"Are you insane?"

"No, I think that's pretty fucking generous, considering what I just sat through," he said.

He was right. Quinn knew he was right. That had to have been unbelievably hideous to watch, and he had every right to be angry. Hell, to leave her ass in the driveway. To cancel the wedding. To tell her to kiss off. But he wasn't.

He was giving her an ultimatum.

"You know what?" she said, pulling her phone from her pocket. "You can both go to hell."

"Excuse me?"

She went and sat on the steps. She wasn't leaving with Eric, but she sure as hell wasn't going back in. She pulled up her texts and saw Simon's again.

Are you okay?

Yeah. She texted Hannah.

Can you bring me home when y'all are done?

Uh oh.

Yeah.

Sure thing.

"What are you doing?" Eric asked.

"Waiting on Hannah," she said. "You can go."

"What does that mean?" he asked, raising his hands at his sides. "You kiss another man and now *I'm* the bad guy to be dismissed?"

"It means I'm tired of being told how to live my life, with who, what, when, where, and why," she said, her eyes filling with tears again. "By you. By my mother. Even by my friends. I'm sorry about what you saw, Eric. I'm sorry it happened at all. But it's actually not the biggest issue."

"How can you say that?" he said.

"It's everything to you right now, because you're hurt."

"Damn right I'm hurt, Quinn, how would you feel?" he yelled.

She opened her mouth to answer, held it back, and then thought, *Hell, no—this is open-mike time. Time to put it out there.* "Devastated. And probably like maybe something's missing."

Her phone dinged. She looked down to see the picture Hannah took of Quinn and Eric. The one where she was looking off at Simon with absolute despair and longing. It took her breath away.

Pictures don't lie, my friend.

"Really?" Eric said. "And is Simon Chase what's missing?"

"No." She blinked back up and him and shook her head, and it wasn't a lie. Not completely. "Quinn Parker is."

The big storm that had stalled and dumped all over the Panhandle for almost a week was finally headed east-southeast. It promised to be a dangerous group of cells, and chasers were coming out of the woodwork like worms after a rain.

Jonah Boudreau had come by Zach's to see if his family, including his dad, Harlan, could weather it out in Zach's storm room again. Harlan's house had been destroyed in the last one, and he still hadn't rebuilt. He was living in Jonah's old hunting trailer on the land. Simon knew it had to be hard for Jonah to eat a little crow on his family's behalf, but he would give him that. He had never cared much for Jonah, both in the storm world and in his sister's. But Jonah did look out for his family, and that's how things should be. And when all was said and done, storm chasers were a family of sorts, too. Competitors, and sometimes scavengers, but still, when the chips were down, they helped their own.

And the chips might be falling down again. Soon. As Simon watched the reports, all he could do was get everyone prepared. He was working a lot, so he was able to access the big databases, gathering all the data he could. This big behemoth had done an insane amount of damage along its path, and Simon was worried. He didn't say that much, because Eli would pace and fret and Zach would salivate. But he was worried.

Quinn had gone AWOL again, but that was okay. They weren't currently filming anything, and she needed to be away. Their indiscretion had been blasted over the Internet, and the fallout for her had to be ungodly. If she and Eric were going to survive it, she needed to stay away from Simon as much as possible. Possibly forever.

That was a hard pill to swallow, but it was what it was. Hannah said she was freezing Eric out too, over something he'd said, and they needed to work it out.

Independent of him.

That's what he woke up alone every day and told himself.

Shut off the heart, and go through the motions, and eventually all would be fine.

They weren't filming anything because big brother Elijah had gone all wrath-of-God at the studio, asking for heads to roll. There was no blood yet, but there was a bit of a hiatus in the meantime. Simon wasn't even sure if this storm would be part of filming, which would be a shame if it turned out like he felt it might.

A knock on his door surprised him, and he set his laptop aside and wandered that way to open it. To a very pregnant Phoebe Parker Blackwell.

"Phoebe," he said, frowning at the first thought that came to mind. "Is Quinn okay?"

"Well, that tells me something if that's your first question," she said. "Can I come in?"

"Sure," he said, moving aside. "Can I, um—get you something? Water?" He panned her huge belly. "A chair?"

"Chair would be great," she sighed. "No couch. I'll never get up. I'm ready for this puppy to be carried *outside* my body. Give a few different muscles a chance to participate."

"Like ones belonging to your husband?" he asked, pulling out a wooden chair from the set Zach had made him.

"Exactly like those," she said. "I hear there's a storm brewing? I saw it on the news."

"Big one," he said. "Could hit this area again, might not. You were out of town for the last one, right?"

She nodded. "We were on a cruise, actually," she said. "Puking, nauseated, four months pregnant and seasick. Doesn't that sound like fun? Couldn't even drink to numb it."

Simon laughed. "Well, this time y'all need to get to Zach's house to his storm room when it's time. Your parents, too."

She blinked. "Seriously?"

"Seriously," he echoed. "You know where he lives?"

"Yeah," she said, her hands automatically rubbing her belly. Protective mode.

"It'll be crowded, but you'll be safe," he said. "When you get the word, go."

Phoebe nodded and did a weak little salute. "Gotcha."

Simon sighed. "So what brings you trekking over here?"

She caught her breath as she studied him, so different from Quinn in looks, with her auburn hair and rounder, curvier features, managing to sit very properly even with a watermelon trying to separate her legs. But very much the same in their quick wit, their wariness, and class that couldn't be missed. Breeding was breeding.

"So all that happened with you and Quinn," she said.

All that. The public didn't know the half of it, but how much did Phoebe know?

"I guess you saw the show?" Simon asked, sitting on the back of his couch.

"I did," she said, nodding. "And I know about Zach's wedding."

Simon nodded and looked at his hands, remembering them on Quinn's face. On her lips. On her body. She didn't tell her sister about the warehouse. That was good. That was probably good.

"Okay," he said. "And what's your question?"

Phoebe tilted her head. "You know, there's this thing that happened when we were kids," she said. "I was four. Quinny was six."

Okay. Any story that started with *When I was four* required a real chair, so Simon pulled out another one, turned it backward, and straddled it, leaning his forearms on the back to face her.

"We used to have a pool in our backyard," she said. "Where the big patio is? That concrete is like ten feet thick."

"Oh, wow."

"Yeah," she said, making a very Quinn-like face that had him smirking. "So we had a nanny back then. Helping Mom out so she could—I don't know—plan parties? And as I understand it, I decided I wanted to go swimming."

"Okay."

"Now, I don't know where this nanny went, or if we escaped her, or what the deal was, but Quinny in all her six-year-old-grown-up-ness went to get the floaties." Phoebe's smile started to wane as her gaze got very far away. "Here's the thing. Quinn says we jumped in without them, but I actually remember jumping in before she got back. Because I can remember the panic of realizing I was alone and that I didn't float like I normally did. And swallowing water and screaming."

Simon leaned forward on the back of the chair, not sure where she was going with this story, but positive it was important.

"Then there was this big splash, and Quinny was pulling at me and shoving me up," Phoebe said, her eyes going shiny and red. "It wasn't working. We were both sinking. And suddenly I could touch. There was something under my feet, letting me push up to the surface."

Simon felt the tingles cover his skin. "Shit."

"Yeah," Phoebe said, a chuckle escaping her throat as she blinked tears free and wiped them away. "I remember telling people there was a magical new bottom under my feet. I was a little older before I fully realized that memory. That the *new bottom* I'd felt that day was my big sister down there drowning to hold me up."

The *something that happened* when Quinn was a kid that had her terrified of water. Simon's heart squeezed, and he clenched his teeth together. Why was she telling him this?

"We don't talk about that day in my family," she said, sniffling. Simon got up to get her a paper towel and handed it to her. "Thanks," she whispered. "It's like taboo. Someone heard me, thankfully, and got us out. Saved her life. But she saved mine. I was the impetuous carefree one, even back then, and she bailed me out. Pushed me to safety. She has looked out for me and been the responsible grown-up in my life for as long as I can remember."

Simon swallowed hard, not wanting to feel. *Shut off the heart. This was their business.*

"It's time for me to return the favor," she said, looking up at him. "You love her, don't you?"

Fuck. Wrecking ball to the chest with not enough wall to stop it.

"You're awfully subtle," he managed.

"You love her," she repeated.

"Phoebe," Simon said, walking to the kitchen to get himself a water. Maybe pour it over his head. "Quinn isn't six anymore. She's a grown woman who can make her own choice. She's made it."

"She's a grown woman who's been raised to believe her choices are only valid if they conform to acceptable standards," Phoebe amended. "Essentially Adelaide Parker's. Or what won't embarrass her."

"She's marrying St. James," he said.

"Is she?" Phoebe said, that cute little head tilt again reminding him of her sister. "Because she won't talk about the wedding at all right now, says our mother can handle it, she's just going through the motions, I think, till she says *I do.*" She pushed herself to her feet. "That sound all romantic and joyous to you?"

Don't. Shut it off. Don't.

"If she shouldn't go through with it, then that needs to be about her and Eric. Not about me. I can't be part of the decision."

"Oh, for God's sake, quit with the psychobabble old-school chivalry," she said. "You two have been circling each other like buzzards for years. Of course you're part of the decision. She knows what real love *is* because of you."

Zing. Damn, that one was aimed well.

"Why are you telling me this?" he asked. "Why aren't you telling her?"

"I have," she said. "She's got all these walls up now, not listening to anyone. Has this thing about people telling her what to do for too long, she's done with it, blah blah."

"And—"

"And I've never seen her happier than when she's talking about you, Simon," she said, stopping him in his tracks. She held up her hands. "Okay, don't say anything. Let her make this mistake. I just had to tell you, in case you want to fight for her. I couldn't let her drown again."

She turned to leave and patted his arm.

"Zach's storm room," Simon said, needing work mode back in the worst way. "Don't forget."

Chapter Twenty-Five

Beethoven's something or other rang ominously from Quinn's phone. Again. She'd never been one for separate ringtones, but lately setting up one to screen calls from her mother seemed like a good plan.

Quinn didn't want to hear about how important her hair style would be, or about the caterer, or the club seating, or the seating chart, or debate whether pistachios were really a nut. She'd swallowed that crap for a full week before Eric went all pick-door-number-one on her and then the show hit newsfeeds everywhere, and both sets of parents turned into Godzillas in expensive clothing.

Somehow they'd managed to spin it to their important friends as *that film world's creative license. Reality shows are all lies. Sensationalism for ratings. Smoke and mirrors.*

Yep, that was all a big staged act.

The only person's phone call she would take was Eric's, because she owed him that, but she refused to talk about quitting anything or the ultimatum he'd given her. She'd gone back to her little brownstone for the time being, even though half of her things, her books, and her beloved mugs were at Eric's.

She just didn't want to be there.

There just seemed to be more important things to worry about than seating charts. A huge storm was rolling in, even not being around the team lately, she knew that. Hannah told her that they were loading for bear, in the same sentence she asked if her bridesmaid dress was hot.

That was why she loved Hannah.

In addition to the storm, Phoebe was having false labor pains off and on. Surely that had to trump how Quinn was planning to wear her hair with the veil. The veil she never ordered.

So, in the spirit of no arguments, fights, or lectures on how she needed to overcompensate for embarrassing the families by being seen everywhere, madly in love with Eric and gushing over the upcoming nuptials, Quinn answered her calls with texts.

You take care of the seating chart. I know you already have anyway.
You can choose the meat for the entrée.
Have the cake delivered. I don't need to see it.
Have the cursed orchids delivered too. I really don't need to see them.
Hannah is picking up the portrait. She'll bring it.

That last one was the only one that Quinn truly enjoyed sending. She couldn't wait to put that out there.

She scrolled through her recent texts to see Simon's name. His *Are you okay?* was still the last correspondence.

So many times she'd wanted to text back *No*, and wait for the possible *Me either*, but she didn't. She couldn't. She couldn't have that intimacy with him anymore. The friendship or the joking or the—definitely not that. Not the thing that made her whole insides swell with a feeling too intense to contemplate.

Hannah came in as Quinn sank into the big wicker chair.

"It's getting so thick out there," she said. "The air. It's not even moving."

"Getting close."

"I thought you had to work today," she said.

Quinn shook her head. "I asked off for all three weeks of my vacation," she said.

Hannah landed on the couch across from her. "You did what? Why?"

"Wedding preparations," Quinn said with a smirk. "Honeymoon."

"You're not prepping anything, Miss Four Days Out," she said. "And the honeymoon's only a week."

"Yeah, I know," Quinn said, scrolling back through her phone.

"What if you need that vacation time?"

"I won't," Quinn said.

"What if you get pregnant?" she asked.

Quinn glared at her. "I won't."

"And if you don't marry Eric in four days, and my brother decides to sweep you off your feet and—"

"Don't," Quinn said, ending the game.

"Mmm, touchy subject," Hannah said. "Interesting."

"No, just not realistic," she said. "Want to plan your wedding to Jonah?"

Hannah's expression clouded over, and Quinn was instantly sorry. This was her best friend, not the enemy.

"I'm sorry, that was shitty," Quinn said. "I'm so bitchy right now, ugh, I can't stand myself."

But Hannah was looking at her funny. "No, it's the same, though, isn't it?" Hannah said. "You're in love with Simon."

Those words bounced off the walls and back like anyone could snatch them up.

"Don't say that," Quinn said under her breath. "Don't say that out loud."

"Because it's true," Hannah said, pulling out her phone.

Quinn remembered the intensity that had passed between them

at Miss Lou's house. The love that had almost been palpable. Before he shut it down, anyway.

"It doesn't matter," Quinn said.

"It *does* matter," Hannah responded, her voice hardening. "You don't *want* that life, Quinn," Hannah said. "You don't want to be me, watching the man you love make a life with someone else."

She got up and went to the fridge, opening the freezer door instead, as if needing to ice herself back down. Hannah wasn't one to talk about it, and Quinn rubbed the goosebumps back down on her arms.

"And he will one day," she said, her head still in the freezer. "Because he'll get tired of watching *you*."

Her phone rang in her pocket, and she turned away from Quinn, swiping at her eyes quickly as she shut the freezer door and pulled her phone out.

"Yeah?" There were a few minutes of silence as she listened. "Okay. Bye."

"Have a secret spy mission?" Quinn asked, trying to lighten the mood.

"Better," she said, going to the desk cabinet where she kept all her gear. "That was Eli. The run is tonight. We're meeting at Mom's now." She paused, sounding like they were hitting a bank robbery instead of tracking a storm. "Are you in?"

Quinn's heart sped up in her chest, the adrenaline already kicking in. There were probably fifty-one reasons why she shouldn't go.

"Absolutely."

"First things first," Eli was saying as Simon came back in from setting his stuff in the lead vehicle. He shook his hair free of the rain that had just started to fall and shoved his favorite cap on. "We need to make sure that everyone gets to Zach's."

"Harlan's there now," Zach said, irony lacing his voice. "He's waiting for Derrie and Brax."

"Who's getting Gran?" Hannah said, clearing her throat at the mention of the Boudreaus.

"She's actually at some board function in Houston," Miss Lou piped in, breezing into the room with a tray of hot coffee. "So we don't have to worry about her chair this time."

"When are *you* going?" Zach asked her.

"When Quinn's family gets here," she said.

"Should be any minute," Hannah said. "Quinn went to get them."

As if on cue, the front door opened, and from where Simon was standing, he could see two women his mother's age, Phoebe, her husband Doug, and Eric.

Cracker took off howling, but Miss Lou scooped him up and headed off to welcome them.

No Quinn. Eric and Doug led the way in, Eric smiling tightly at Miss Lou. Simon was pretty sure this was one place he never wanted to return to. He locked eyes with Simon, then walked up to him, not blinking.

Simon waited him out and then widened his eyes in question. "What?" he said quietly. "You need another shot at me?"

Eric's jaw twitched, and Doug slapped him on the shoulder. "Come on, man," he said.

Phoebe walked next to her mother, who took one look at Simon and sent ice daggers his way. It was a banner day for the Simon Chase Fan Club.

The other elderly woman Simon pegged to be Eric's mother, as she had that same useless air of not wanting to be there.

"I have coffee," Miss Lou said. "Other drinks, if you prefer. We'll head down to Zach's place in a minute, but please make yourself at home. Where's Quinn?"

"Right here," she said, coming in last, brushing her hands off.

Simon took one look at her before he made himself look away and shut down. Too many people analyzing his every move there today. His every look. She didn't need that. So he mentally recorded her in her white cap, ponytail, tank top and khaki shorts with work boots. Same shorts he'd slid his hands under, when she'd wrapped those legs around him.

He shook his head. *Don't go there, boy.*

Phoebe came up and laid a hand on his arm. "Thank you for thinking of us," she said, palming her belly.

"Don't mention it," Simon said. "Quinn is family here." His eyes met Quinn's as he said the words, and he couldn't make them move. "And any family of hers is welcome."

"Thank you, Simon," Quinn's mother said, with not the slightest hint of actual thanks. "This is Bitty St. James, by the way," she said, putting an arm around the other woman. "She'll be Quinn's mother-in-law."

Nice move. "Nice to meet you," Simon managed with a smile as Quinn swooped in.

"All right," she said. "Y'all come sit down over here. We have to do our plan and get miked, so we probably need to get on it."

The room went quiet except for her voice, and Eli was looking at her with amused eyes.

"I mean, right?" she asked, looking at each of them in turn. "I saw the van."

"Miked?" Eric and Quinn's mother said at the same time.

"We get wired for sound," she said distractedly, looking at Eli.

"Yeah, they're filming," Eli said. "Maddi's in back giving them instructions. *Clear* instructions," he emphasized. "So you're back in my truck?"

Quinn grinned like he hadn't seen her do in a while, and Simon had to take a deep breath. Fuck if she didn't take him down.

"Unless you have a better plan, big guy?"

"Hell, no," he said, high-fiving her.

"Wait, you're going?" Eric said, getting back up.

"Yeah," she said.

He turned in order to get a more private angle. "Quinn, do you remember what we talked about?"

"What *you* talked about?" she asked, quietly. "Yes. Do you remember what *I* said?"

Wheels spun so fast, Simon could see them moving in his eyes. "Then I'm going with you," Eric said.

"No," she said laughing. "There's no room."

"Then you need to stay here with us," he said.

"No."

"Quinn," he said, jaw tensing.

"I don't interfere with your job, Eric. This is mine," she said. "Sit down, I'm working."

Oh, holy fuck, Simon had to turn around on that one, and he saw Hannah's mouth fall open as well.

"Screw this, I'm leaving," Eric said in a low tone. "Mom and I will ride this out in a house stronger than anything Zach has."

"Eric, I'm gonna blow out a human any minute now," Phoebe said, raising her voice to almost shrill, stilling the room and making Eric turn back. "And I'm stressed. You are here in a safe place. Be grateful. Please don't stress me out further by being a dick—yes, Mother, I'm sorry I said that."

"Not your business to worry about me, Phoebe," Eric said.

"No, but it is my damn business to worry about my sister," she said. "And if she's thinking about you out there, then she's not paying attention and ends up with more stitches in her face. So can you please shut the hell up and just be proud of what she does instead of bitching about it?"

She took a deep breath as Doug rested his hands on her shoulders. "Wow, Mom, there were about fifty bad words in there. Let's just do a big blanket blessing, okay?"

"Just sit down, sweetheart," she said, her smile tight.

"Can we move on?" Eli asked.

"Please," Quinn said, mouthing an *I love you* at her sister.

Phoebe raised her hands in an it's-all-good gesture and sat down.

"Wow," Zach said, clearing his throat. "Okay."

"This is a big one, guys," Eli said. "Stay vigilant."

"Stay in the car," Hannah whispered to Quinn, who smirked.

She was in rare form, Simon thought. Like the old Quinn, unfazed and untethered by propriety. It was fascinating to watch.

Not yours.

Yeah, he got that.

"We're heading northeast," Simon said. "And we may hit it sooner than expected. It's flat-out hauling ass."

"Upside of that is less damage in one place," Eli said.

"And downside," Zach added, "is the potential for skippers. Probably not big granddaddies that eat up a mile at a time. This will likely be multiples, small."

"Isn't that better?" Phoebe asked from her seat.

"No," Simon said. "Big ones, you can see, you can plan your course. Little skippers bounce around, suck up, fall back down, whip the hell out of everything. They're unpredictable."

"Think of a fire hose that gets loose and whips around," Zach said.

"In the dark," Eli said, glancing outside at the bluish-purple near-dark. "Lots of lightning kicking up, though. That's a blessing."

"A blessing," Eric muttered from the peanut gallery, shaking his head.

Maddi came down the hallway, leading the crew like she was Queen Mother, Charlie following her dutifully. "All right, let's clear the air. Charlie is sorry for the misunderstandings of before."

"Misunderstandings?" Eli said, giving her a look. "We said delete. Casey said okay, and hit a button. It wasn't deleted. Charlie was there all along and knew what was appropriate and what wasn't, and yet—"

"I got a little overzealous," Charlie said, holding up a hand. "I apologize."

Eli went back to his notepad. "As long as everyone remembers we aren't robots and we aren't actors. We're just people." He looked up and met both women's gazes. "You exploit that again, and this is over. I don't give a rat's ass about that contract."

Maddi nodded, licking her lips. "Okay, guys," she said, addressing the crew looking on with wide eyes. "You all know how to do this in under thirty seconds by now. Line up."

"Why don't we go ahead over to Zach's while they get ready," Miss Lou said, winking at Simon as she turned to the crowd on her couch graciously. "Before it gets too bad out there. Normally we could walk, but with this rain—"

"We're in the Escalade," Quinn's mom said. "It will fit us all."

Miss Lou grinned. "Sounds great."

Quinn turned as the group passed, reaching for Eric's hand, but he stepped free of her reach. Simon frowned, conflicted at the twist of mixed feelings that gave him. She looked embarrassed, irritated, a little angry. He felt for her and her pushback against being controlled, and understood Eric's anger at the same time. She'd kicked him twice in the same house, in front of people. He'd be ticked off, too. Especially to then go be herded off like cattle with the old folks.

That was a horrible thing to think, and he was always one of the first to push people to look for shelter, but deep inside he was always secretly glad he had an out. That he didn't have to burrow in.

Maybe that was his inner Chase, a little piece of his dad in there after all.

Chapter Twenty-Six

Y ou see that?" Zach yelled.

"Shit!" Hannah said, twisting in her seat, soaked from head to toe from her foray outside. "That went—"

"—right fucking over us!" Simon said, punching keys as fast as he could while still watching it live.

"Jesus, it's like being in a carnival ride," the little camera guy riding along said from the backseat, twisting from side to side.

The guy was young and green, but he wasn't Casey, and that's all that mattered to Simon. And they had the vehicle cams on, so it was all good enough.

"Better," Hannah said, slinging wet curls back from her face.

"The readings are all over the damn place," Eli said over the radio, his voice sounding tinny against the ever-increasing pounding rain. "I've clocked two for sure, but I don't think they were down. Too dark to tell."

"Three," Simon said into the receiver. "Radar confirmation only."

"Debris just stopped the network van, I think," Eli yelled back.

"They have our cell numbers," Simon responded.

"Shit, this hail," Zach yelled through his teeth. "I can't see anything. Hannah, are you in?"

"Yes, I'm not into becoming cottage cheese," she said. "This stuff's too big."

"That means the good stuff is here," Zach said.

The noise, the pressure, the relative solidity—it all was deafening as massive waves of water and debris knocked the vehicle about like it was a Tonka toy.

"There's no visibility, Zach," Eli yelled over the radio. "Let's pull to—fuck!"

The panic in the expletive plus the sound of Quinn screaming over the radio made Simon temporarily forget what his fingers were doing.

"Eli!" he yelled into the receiver.

No response. He looked at Zach's profile. "Quinn!"

His heart thundering in his ears and knowing there were deep ditches on either side of that road that were probably topped off, Simon threw the receiver down. "Fuck the good stuff, Zach. Turn around."

"Damn it. Already on it," Zach said, pulling over. "Everybody say a prayer on where the side of the road is."

Blindly, he turned the vehicle around on the two-lane road, Simon hoping like hell that Zach could thread that particular needle.

"Go slow," Simon yelled over the din.

"You think?" Zach said.

A gust slammed into their left side with so much force, they actually went up on two wheels for about a second. Hannah gasped.

"Holy shit."

"You people are certifiable," the camera guy said, looking around with wide eyes.

"Don't pee your pants, baby," she said. "Call it an adventure."

"Another one over us," Simon said, swallowing hard as he refreshed the radar on his screen.

"Kinda gathered that," Hannah said.

"I don't even see their lights," Zach said,

"Turn down the foggers," Simon said. "Less reflection off the water." He dug his phone from his pocket, trying not to think too hard on that scream.

"Pick up," he muttered, trying not to think too hard on whose number he called first, either. Not wanting to distract the one driving. That was it.

"Hey," her voice came into his ear, smooth and low and everything Quinn, blanketing his edginess. "We're okay."

"What happened?" he asked.

"A tree," she said. "Again. Like a whole damn tree. Came right between us and took out the antenna."

"Is it still in the road?"

"I don't think so," Quinn said. "I think it had other places to go."

Simon resisted a smile as they picked up Eli's car in the low light from the fogger beams, turned sideways in the road, headlight beams facing off into a ditch. "Y'all still drivable?"

"Yeah, we were just trying to get our bearings," she said. "Eli's out there getting the antenna back up, or trying to. Hard to tell which way we're facing." There was a pause. "I sure hope that's you."

Simon smiled that time. "It's us. Tell Eli to go ahead and turn it around—we're headed back the way we came."

Zach frowned over at him. "Why?" he asked.

Simon pointed at the screen. "Because that's where it's going."

It was a somber feeling, knowing the storm truly was headed homeward. Again. Even though they were smart and had gotten everyone where they needed to go to be safe, it was nerve-wracking. That excitement level changed from adrenaline to worry. Quinn had even moved to the front seat, something she hardly ever did. Just felt right.

Eli got the car turned around, let Zach pass them to lead again, and together they slow-rolled. Feeling their way through miles and what was normally a fifteen-minute stretch, till the rain lightened up and the exit for Trinity came into view. Except there was no exit sign.

"Eli?" Quinn said.

"I see," he said softly.

They exited and made the twisty turn, rain slacking to a steady vertical fall instead of horizontal.

Quinn's phone dinged with a text from Simon. *Maddi called. Network van turned back. Going by the shelter.*

"They're going by the Trinity shelter," Quinn said.

"Why?" Eli asked.

"I don't know," she said. "I guess to make sure it's still there."

"Check the radio," he said.

Quinn grabbed the receiver. "Chase Two to Chase One, you there?"

"Really?" Eli said. "You just made us the second car?"

Quinn laughed, and static crackled as Zach's voice filled the speakers. "I like being number one, Quinn."

Eli took the receiver from her. "Hey, guys, I don't trust this," he said, leaning forward to look up at the sky. "There's a weird green in the black."

"Think more is coming?" Zach asked over the radio.

"I do," Eli said.

"I know that already," Simon said back. "Unlike you two, I actually look at radar—"

His voice cut off as they pulled into the parking lot, Zach's headlights and theirs coupling to shine reality on what was in front of them.

Nothing was in front of them.

"Oh, my God," Quinn breathed as lightning helped illuminate what their headlights didn't reach.

The Trinity Outreach Center was gone. Swept away, leaving only pieces of wood and insulation and mangled furniture. Another flash of lightning showed similar outcomes for the houses around it, and Quinn felt her eyes burn. The shelter was vacant, hopefully. Closed down and unoccupied. But those homes weren't.

"Eli," she choked.

He was already out the door.

She pulled a flashlight from the door pocket and clambered out. Light rain falling down and gusting in swirls caught her in the face, pulling with it the smell of brokenness.

That was the closest way to describe it. She'd seen the destruction that went with that smell so many times, she could almost detail out what they were about to encounter without the flashlights.

Wet, rotten wood. The tar from mangled shingles. The musty smell of wet fabric, and the unmistakable aroma of burning electricity.

"Live power lines down somewhere, y'all, be careful," she called out.

"Anyone here?" Simon yelled over the wind, his voice cracking. "Hello?"

"Didn't it close?" Hannah asked.

"Doesn't mean there weren't squatters," Simon said, climbing over the mess of metal and glass in the parking lot.

"Simon, stop!" Eli yelled. "You don't know what's in all that. Wait till morning. We need to check these other houses for people."

"Hello?" Simon yelled again, ignoring Eli, his voice going hoarse.

Quinn's heart hurt for this. For the place, for the people that weren't even there anymore, for the history of it. But mostly for Simon. This was his dad in so many ways, and seeing it close was bad enough. This was—

"Help—" came the faint female voice just beyond where Simon stood.

"Shit," Simon cried. "Quinn, shine that light over here!" He kept climbing, stumbling and catching himself. "Keep talking! Where are you?"

Zach pulled out his phone and turned on the spotlight, running around to access from the other side.

"Front door," said the voice. "By the front door."

There was no more front door.

"There!" Simon yelled, pointing his beam, catching the swirling raindrops in the light. "The door's on top of that pile."

Zach was there faster, while Simon climbed over debris like a monkey. Hannah called 911.

"I'm going door-to-door," Eli said, heading off on foot. "I don't care what neighborhood it is."

"Coming with you," Hannah said.

Only Quinn stood, holding her flashlight for Simon and Zach as they hauled a thick metal door off a pile of wood. Feeling useless. Not as useless as the cameraman filming from his stand on one of the bumpers, but still.

"Oh, thank God!" came the voice of a little old lady, looking up at them from a fetal position in a nook formed by the wood pile.

Zach sucked in a breath and stood straight up for a moment, digging his thumbs in his eyes and shaking his head.

"Fuck," he muttered.

Simon glanced up at him and nodded. "I know, bud," he said. "Come on, let's get her out."

And then Quinn realized—that's how she'd heard Zach found Maddi once upon a time. Curled up in a fetal position. Protected by the grace of God and two bookshelves.

Pulling wood away carefully, they extracted the woman, and Simon gave her a once-over.

"Mrs. Tanner, what are you doing here?" he asked, hugging her gently.

The woman was thickly wrinkled and snaggletoothed, covered in dirt, with a cut on her cheek. Tears streamed paths through the dirt on her face.

"I heard about the hole," she said, her voice quivering.

"What hole?" Simon asked, helping her over to sit on a flat wooden beam.

"The hole by the air conditioner," she said. "Some of the young ones were talking about it. About how we could still get in out of the rain if we climbed through that hole."

"Oh, my God," Simon said under his breath.

"It wasn't easy," she said. "And it was so dark in there, I wanted back out, but I figured I'd just unlock the door." Mrs. Tanner shook her head, her eyes shiny. "Then it got so loud, and then the door just—went away."

"Is anyone else in there?" Zach asked.

"No," she said, sniffling, rain mixing with her tears. "I was surprised it was just me." She looked over at what was once her haven. "I'm sure glad no one else was here."

If the shelter had still been open—Quinn knew what was going through Simon's mind. It would have been packed to bursting in weather like that.

"Simon," Quinn said, making him turn her way. "Harry."

Simon only had to look at Zach for him to get it.

"Go," he said, looking at the sky and rolling his shoulders. "Hurry. You feel that?"

There was a sharpness to the air again, as if just being out there in the rain should be jolting.

"Yeah," Simon said. "Taking Eli's," he added, running for it. "Mrs. Tanner, an ambulance is on the way. My brother will take good care of you!"

He opened the door and slid in, pushing away the gut-wrenching sickness he felt. It was gone. Not just closed. Not just waiting. Gone. Ripped to the foundation. But he didn't have time for that right now.

Feeling around the steering column with his fingers, he scored. Big brother left the keys. The passenger door opened then, and in jumped Quinn.

"What are you doing?" he asked, turning the engine over.

"Going with you," she said, raising her eyebrows.

He paused, then looked forward, trying to separate things. He could smell her. Even soaking wet and working, she smelled of sweetness and salty mixed together. She smelled like he knew her skin tasted.

"You should stay here," he said.

"Well, there's *should*," she said, fastening her seat belt, "and there's what I'm going to do."

Simon bit back a smirk. "I don't even have it in me to argue with you. If you're feeling rebellious, so be it."

"I'm just doing my job," she said. "Part of that is not letting you go out there by yourself. Let's go."

He shrugged. "Yes, ma'am."

The back door opened just as he put it in reverse.

"Where do I go?" the camera guy asked.

"Stay here," Simon said. "Film Mrs. Tanner. Ask her about the shelter. About her life."

"Will do," he said, slamming the door.

Simon sighed and hit the gas. Sadly, that story would probably boost ratings. Going looking for a recluse in an abandoned warehouse who may or may not want to be bothered—that wouldn't. The vehicle cams and their sound mikes would be enough, and the powers-that-be could decide if it was worth it.

"I'm sorry about the shelter," Quinn said.

Simon clenched his teeth together.

"Let's not talk about that," he said. "I'll deal with that in the—harsh light of day tomorrow." He blew out a breath. "Eric doesn't seem too happy," he said, maneuvering around a small tree when they turned the corner.

"We aren't talking about that, either," Quinn said.

"Oh, is he not-to-be-named again?"

Even in the dark, he could see her smirk.

"No, I'm just not talking about him with you."

He nodded. "Works for me." He picked up the receiver on the dash and flipped on the radio. "Chase Two. Trinity took a bad hit," he said into the mike. "We're good. Checking on multiple buildings now."

He knew Harlan brought Zach's radio in the room with him, he wouldn't go in there otherwise. So at least he could let everyone in there know all was okay so far.

"So did Llano," said a voice undeniably Boudreau. As in the Jonah variety.

"Damn, that's two counties over," Simon said.

"Yep," Jonah said. "Big skippers. Cody's negative, though."

"Thanks."

Well, that was something, anyway. He knew that was meant for Zach more than him. Jonah's way of letting Zach know in their weird little truce of understanding that Maddi was okay.

A loud clap of lightning shook the vehicle.

"That was close," she said. "And look, it appears okay," she added, pointing.

Simon rolled across the mud and gravel, eyeballing the giant structure through the swirls of rain reflected in his low beams.

"Stay here," he said, leaving the car running.

"No," she said, unbuckling.

"Quinn—"

"Give it up, Simon," she said, getting out.

"Jesus," he muttered. "It's getting worse again." He looked around him, feeling the charge on his skin. "You're safer in here."

"Mr. Harry!" Quinn yelled, her voice carrying off with the wind. "Mr. Harry, it's Quinn and Simon!"

"Well, at least he knows there are two throats to slit," Simon said. "Harry!" he yelled at the top of his lungs, in his deepest voice.

"Shit!" Quinn exclaimed as lightning struck a tree in the nearby grove at the end of the building, setting it aglow.

The rain came harder, and then the pellets, and Simon knew. He knew like Zach always knew. He felt the presence even before his other senses could pick anything up. Then there it was. The ear-popping.

"Harry!" Simon yelled, banging on the door. "Let us in! We need—"

Two clangs sounded, and then the door pushed open.

"—shelter," Simon finished as a hand grabbed his arm and yanked him inside. Simon just barely had time to grab Quinn's hand and pull her with him before the door scraped shut again.

"Imagine hearing you two again," Harry said, the noise getting louder by the second. "What the hell are you doing?"

"What I do," Simon said, shoving him forward as he pulled Quinn behind him. "The shelter's gone, Harry. We were just there."

"What?" Harry asked, stopping short.

"It's gone."

Harry stared at him, emotions traveling over his dirty face. He might not have been able to go there anymore, but it still meant something.

Simon pushed at him, unable to go down memory lane right then. "We gotta get someplace low and under—"

"Come on," Harry said, opening a large trap door in the floor, revealing a rushing water way below. Water from the creek. "There's a ledge under the floor. Safest spot."

"No way," Quinn yelled, staring down at the rushing blackness.

The sound of twisting metal and cracking stone reached their ears, roaring toward them like a speeding, merciless freight train.

"It's taking the house!" Harry yelled, eyes wide, looking more normal under absolute pressure and talking about his "house," than Simon had ever seen him. "Get down there—now!"

Simon climbed down quickly and reached a hand out for Quinn as the roof opened up over her head and nothing but a gray mass revealed itself.

"Jump!" he screamed, pulling her.

"No!" she yelled, teetering on the ledge before Simon yanked her down, shoved her under the floor and pressed his body against hers.

"Harry!" she cried as the trapdoor ripped off the hinges, pulling parts of the boards up with it. The sound was almost unbearable as boards peeled up like Popsicle sticks and concrete bricks hurtled around the room as if they were sponges.

"Simon!" he felt Quinn scream in a long wail against his chest, but all he could do was press her against a wall of support beams he hoped would hold while the floor over their heads came apart strip by strip.

"Shit!" he yelled, gripping a beam as everything they stood on twisted and a large sink came bouncing end over end around the room, smashing everything in its path. "Keep your head down!" he yelled, holding her whole head in his arms, shielding her as best he could.

"Oh, my God," he heard her cry as she pulled back to look.

This was no skipper. This beast wanted them. It already had Harry. Fuck, it had Harry. Simon swallowed that pain down as he tried to hold on to Quinn and a structure that was twisting underneath him at the same time. Boards, nails, tools, food, boxes, chunks of bricks—all of it was one big swirling, catapulting mess, raining down on top of them. Ripping their clothes, bludgeoning them with debris.

It was yanking him away from her, and he groped for her hand, slippery in the dark.

"Simon!" she yelled. "No! Don't let go! Take my hand!"

"Hold on!" he yelled, grasping for a beam as the one he held went away.

"Take my hand!" she repeated, reaching out for him.

He couldn't reach her anymore, but he could hear the water below, taunting, angry. All he could think of was keeping her out of that water. "Quinn, hold on to someth—"

A strike to the side of his head, and everything let go.

Chapter Twenty-Seven

S imon!"

Her shriek sounded foreign, even to her ears. "Simon!" she sobbed in absolute terror and devastation, blinking desperately to adjust her eyes to the darkness below, to try to see him.

She did! He wasn't floating away! The water wasn't as far as she thought—it was right there—about twelve feet down, she could see his white shirt.

"Simon!" she yelled. "Please—please hear me—look up!"

But her voice was hoarse and her words were drowned and useless in the noise, and then—the white shirt went under.

"No," she croaked, shaking violently, "No!" Images of him sinking mixed with the image of Phoebe sinking, and she screamed his name, screamed to hear her own pleas, screamed to God as she jumped.

The spring-fed creek was shockingly cold as the dark water swallowed her, closing over her head like it had one other time. Like death. But she had more important things to worry about as she flailed wildly with her arms, her fingertips begging to touch him. Searching blindly for where she saw him last. It wasn't deep, she could push off, and just as she did, her hand met with fabric.

Screaming underwater, Quinn pulled with all she had, pulling, pushing him to the surface, her lungs burning. Her fingers found his face and brought it up with her. Pushing him up. Crying, sobbing, sucking in water and gagging. All she could hear were the bubbles in her ears and her own yelling underwater, making them. Then there was air.

Hot, dirty, thick air, but Quinn gulped it in before her face went under again with his weight. *Kick!* Swimming was foreign to her, but survival was not. Terror licked at her brain, making her suck in a mouthful of foul. *No! Kick!* She broke the surface again and gasped as a large chunk of something solid splashed down next to her. Debris was raining down everywhere. There was a post within her reach and she lunged for it, shoving Simon up against it, holding him up by the collar of his shirt as she wrapped her leg around the post underwater to anchor herself.

"Simon!" she choked. "Simon!" She slapped his face, shook him, felt for a pulse, but her hands were so cold, she couldn't feel anything. "Breathe, baby," she sobbed, her limbs tired and burning with exhaustion. She kneed him in the stomach, pulling him to her at the same time. And he coughed.

"Oh, my God," Quinn cried, watching him choke and gag and never seeing anything more beautiful than that. Her hat had long since taken its leave, and she laid her forehead against soggy, splintered wood, not caring if it drove stakes into her head.

Finally catching his breath, wincing as he held the side of his head, Simon looked around them, then at her.

"Are you okay?" he asked.

Quinn laughed, a chuckle at first that tickled her and grew from sheer exhaustion and delirium.

"Am *I* okay?" she echoed, her eyes filling with tears on the end of the laugh that captured her. She wrapped her free arm around his neck and pulled him to her as near as she could get, feeling the rush come down and the emotion with it. "Are *you*?" Feeling him close to her again, feeling his arms come around her in response, protective, loving, she didn't have the strength to maintain walls. She clutched him tighter, shaking from cold and emotion, letting the burn burn. "It took Harry," she choked.

"I know," he said hoarsely.

"Are you hurt?" she asked, trying to pull back to see the side of his head.

"I don't—I'm fine," he said. "Did you fall?"

"You weren't fine!" Quinn cried, the sobs about to overtake her. She could feel it. "You weren't—you weren't breathing."

She saw him blink and take that in. "Did you jump down here?"

"You sank," she whispered, barely hearing her own voice over the sound of the water rushing around them. "I couldn't—" Sobs caught her breath, and she pulled his forehead to hers. "I love you."

Quinn heard his sharp exhale, and his hands came up her body to her face, pulling her to him.

"My life doesn't work without you in it, Simon," she said against his lips.

"I can't believe you did that," he whispered against her mouth. "I can't believe—"

He kissed her. Not hungry this time. Not taking. Slow-kissing her, giving her every ounce of all he had, telling her all he couldn't say. Savoring her. Loving her.

"You two gonna fuck all over my building, or get the hell out of here?" said a voice over their heads.

"Harry!" Quinn cried, nearly going under when she jolted back. Simon grabbed her around the waist and held her up, and she lunged for her post again.

"Damn it, Harry!" Simon yelled, pressing a fist to his forehead as if in prayer. "I thought you were gone, man."

"Shit," Harry called down, sounding like he was moving something. "I been through worse. And you will, too, if we don't get you out of there."

Simon frowned. "Why's that?"

"Because that's not the creek down there," Harry yelled. "That's overflow trapped in what used to be a cellar of sorts. It's been leaking out as fast as it leaks in, but this floor's about to go," he said. "There ain't much left holding on up here."

"Then get out, Harry!" Simon yelled. "Car's outside. Get on the radio and yell for my family. They're at the shelter!"

"How about you shut up and let me try to get you out," Harry said. "If you die, I'll worry about telling people then."

"That's encouraging," Quinn said, wishing she could scale the damn beams. She couldn't pull herself out from water high enough for her comfort, no matter what she grabbed.

"I have some rope and a chain I'm throwing down," Harry yelled. "Don't be looking up."

Simon pulled Quinn to him, covering her head with his arms, and her heart wanted to reach out and sprout roots into him.

A length of chain tied to two lengths of rope came splashing down, and Quinn suddenly realized how long she'd been floating or holding herself out of the water, with it up to her shoulders. That chain looked as good as a snowcone on a summer day.

A sickening groan, however, froze her midreach, and she retreated back to her post, trying to separate herself from the water to no avail.

"What was that?" she asked. "The tornado coming back?"

"That was—" Simon began.

The groan became a chorus of splintering wood and twisting metal as debris rained down on their heads in chunks of wood and concrete and dust. It was like Quinn imagined an earthquake might feel, everything trembling around her. Even the water.

"Keep your eyes shut!" Simon said, tugging at her hand. "Let go of the post, I've got you."

"No offense," she yelled, gasping as a large brick landed in the water next to them with the finesse of a hippopotamus, "but this post is keeping me sane right now."

"Shit!" Harry yelled. "We have to hurry, it's—"

The sound of the floor and the support beams and everything they were connected to giving up filled their ears. Quinn suddenly had the odd sense of traveling as the beams overhead and the posts holding them gave up the fight.

"Duck!" Harry yelled.

But it wasn't so much caving in as it was moving over. Like Hercules himself was shoving on the building, everything leaned to the right. Then something snapped.

"Get down!" Simon shouted, lunging to her and her post, shielding her again.

Something broke above them, bringing a section of floor down on them and breaking the beam Quinn held in half. Yelping, she went tumbling into the water.

"Si—" she screamed, but her cry was cut short by the next round. Two big underwater beams shoved forward in the move, causing the new wave of falling objects to pin her at the ankle between them. "Ow—fuck!" Water sprayed in her face as something was opened up in the shift, sucking more water in from the creek. She flailed, panicking, sending pain radiating up her shin. But she couldn't reach the edge. She couldn't reach anything. She was trapped. The water had her.

She could feel the last vestiges of her sanity, of her calm, of her keeping-her-shit-together-ness slipping the bounds of earth.

"Simon!" she shrieked.

"Quinn!" Simon yelled, working his way through the debris in the water to where she was. "You okay?"

"I'm stuck!" she yelled over the angry rushing water hitting her in the face, her voice shaking. "My ankle," she said, her breath catching. "It's got me by the ankle."

Simon dove down into the cold as she screamed for him to come back. He could hear the muffled noise, but he couldn't waste time. They had to get out of there. He felt along her legs, to the ankle that was pinned—really in a triangle of sorts, planting her firmly in a mangle of debris.

Shit.

He pushed back up to find her crying, holding her face away from the spraying water, eyes wide and terrified. This was her worst nightmare. Being burned alive would be welcomed over this for her.

"Baby, I've got you," he said, inserting himself between her and the spray, giving it the back of his head. "I'm here."

"How do I get out?"

Good question.

"I'm going back down."

"No!" she screamed, sobbing, her fingers clutching his shirt. "Please don't leave me alone!"

"Look at me," he said, grabbing her face, pressing his forehead to hers.

"I can't," she sobbed silently, her eyes shut tight. "You don't understand."

"Yes, I do," he said. "Phoebe told me. Now, listen!" he yelled as more debris rained down. "I have to go back down to try to free your foot. You'll feel me the whole way. I will not leave you." He gripped her face tighter and shook her to make her look at him. "I will never leave you."

A pause and then she nodded, and he was down, not wasting

a second. He worked his hands down her calf till he found the top beam. The one rammed against her shin. Using one of the other beams as leverage, he tried pulling them apart. *Come on, I only need a couple of inches.* Nothing budged.

Simon bolted back up and nearly lost his stomach at what he saw.

The water level was rising, and the debris wasn't. What was at her chest level before was now lapping at her chin, and she looked frozen, as if the dilemma of the situation had set in.

She was shaking violently, her teeth chattering as the spring-fed cold water surrounded her body and poured onto her head. He was cold, too, but he didn't have time to think about it.

"Hey!" he said. "You stay with me!" he yelled. He kissed her lips, her nose, anything to make her blink, look at him, look alive.

More of the flooring above was falling, more groaning was happening.

"You need to get out of here," she said, her words hiccupped and choppy. Tears filled her eyes.

No. No.

"Stop that," he said. "*We're* getting out of here."

"Simon, go," she said. "Before the whole building falls on us!"

"I'm not leaving you!" he yelled, blocking the spray.

"You'll die here!" she yelled back, breathing hard, her voice hoarse, the water high enough that she had to lift her face. Trying to be brave. "Shit!" she screamed, shutting her eyes as another board fell and splashed the water over her head. She gasped as her face broke the surface again. "Go!"

Simon felt the hot burn of tears he hadn't felt in many, many years.

"My life doesn't work without you either, Quinn," he said. "I'm not leaving!"

The chain.

"Fuck!" he yelled. "Hold your breath!"

"Simon!" she gasped as her mouth filled with water and she choked.

He lunged back at her and pulled her up by her neck, stretching her into full air access. "Don't you dare give up on me!" he said. "Hold your fucking breath!"

One blink and she sucked in as much air as she could hold and he spun around, feeling blindly in the low light for the chain. Was it even still there? Did the debris pull it down?

"Harry?" he screamed.

Nothing. *God, please.*

His fingers closed on chain links and he turned back around. She was underwater.

Screaming through his teeth, he dove down, scraping his hands and face on pieces of concrete and wood, feeling the beam at the junction where it held Quinn captive. He wrapped the chain around the top one, planted his feet against the bottom one, and pulled with all he had.

Bubbles streamed from his mouth as he yelled, filling his ears with nothing but terror and watery prayers.

She jumped in here to save me.

Don't let her die this way.

Don't let her die.

He felt the groan of the wood through the vibration in the water, and then there was movement. There was movement. It was Quinn, kicking free.

Dropping everything, he bolted to the surface, where she was gulping in air and croaking out screams that sounded an awful lot like his name.

Nothing in his life ever sounded better.

"Right here," Simon yelled.

She spun to her right and flung herself at him, wrapping herself around him and crying. The chain tied to the rope floated next to him, not attached to anything. What the hell? How—

It didn't matter how.

"Jesus," he mumbled into her neck, clinging to her. Holding her like she was his to hold. His to love. "Thank you, God," he cried, the adrenaline crash rushing in on him. He was treading water for both of them, holding them both up by the grace of a miracle, and none of it mattered. She was alive. He kissed the side of her face, her hair, everything he almost just lost, as hot tears spilled from his eyes.

"Don't let go," she said, sobbing, shaking, winding her arms tighter. "Ever."

It all became very simple.

"Marry me," he said.

She let go just enough to look into his face. "What?" she asked, teeth chattering.

"I love you, Quinn Parker," he said, his voice catching from exertion and the tears. "Life's too short, and you're all I want in it. You said something the other day about this not being real." He squeezed her tighter. "Baby, it doesn't get more real than this."

He felt her crying and saw the tears, but the look on her face was incredulous.

"Marry me in that field of daisies," he said. "With the sun on your face looking just like you did. That's enough for me."

"Simon! Quinn!" came a thunderous voice that wasn't always associated with good things, but that night it was like rainbows and butterflies. Even interrupting his impromptu proposal.

"Eli!" Simon yelled with relief, his voice cracking. "Be careful up there, it's not stable."

Quinn continued to look at him, tears streaming down her face to join the other water rivulets. She hadn't said a word.

"Throwing a line down," Eli said.

Chapter Twenty-Eight

It was a large blur of crazy from the moment of *throwing a line down* to sitting in a hospital exam cubby in a backless gown, waiting to be checked out.

Harry had stepped outside his box after all, running outside to beckon Simon's family on the radio. Everyone else back in the storm room would have heard it, too, unfortunately, but hey, it worked. He and Quinn got out alive. And the ambulance that came for Mrs. Tanner called one out for them, just in case. Which Eli made them take, to get checked out with all the scrapes and cuts and general banged-up-ness. And Simon *had* been knocked unconscious, after all.

But he and Quinn hadn't been alone for even another second since—well, since.

The words still echoed in his head, words so foreign to him he never expected to utter them.

Marry me.

Yes, it had been a highly emotional moment, but the kicker was, he'd do it again. Right now. Or a week from now. Or a month and three days from now.

He was that in.

He had glimpsed a moment of what life would be like with no Quinn, and it was enough to know that standing back and being the bigger man—telling her that he couldn't be the reason for her choices, or watching her take another man's name—was all total bullshit.

Life was too short. She might still say no. But at least he took the chance.

"You look pensive," said Stacey as she entered the room.

"Concentrating on whether there's a draft back here," Simon said, pointing to his ass.

Stacey leaned behind him, and then glanced sideways up at him. "Definitely a draft," she said with a wicked grin.

"You're having too much fun back there."

"What can I say?" she said. "Your ass was born for backless hospital-wear." She picked up his chart. "Out playing dodge-the-flying-object again, I see?"

"More than one," he said. "But I think I scored higher."

"You were knocked out?" she said, flipping on a little penlight and shining it in his eyes.

"For a minute," he said, downplaying it.

She picked up his hand and assessed the cuts on his skin. "You look like you've run through a shredder."

"Flying rocks'll do that."

"And Quinn?" she said, making him cough on his own spit.

"What about her?"

"Is she okay?" Stacey asked. "I saw her name on the board. I swear I've seen her more lately than I used to see you."

"Yeah, I think so," he said. "Her ankle got pinned under—hey, Stace," he redirected, remembering. "We went to the shelter."

She nodded. "I know. Barney called me. And I saw Mrs. Tanner. Thank God you came by or she'd have been there for Lord knows how long."

"Stacey," he said, looking her in the eyes. "If it had still been open and running. On a stormy night—"

He let that thought ride through her mind, watching it hit her eyes. It kept hitting him. All the old men that came in and played cards at night. The families that maybe were too proud to come in decent weather who came in to protect their kids in bad weather. Laura, who he'd played jacks with, and her mom. How much of a blessing the closing had actually turned out to be.

"Oh, my God," she whispered.

"Yeah."

She finished examining him in silence, checking his head, deciding he was as normal as he was going to get.

"So—you and Quinn?"

"I wish I could tell you," he said.

"Progression?"

"I proposed."

Stacey nearly dropped her stethoscope. "Shut up."

"I know."

She gaped at him. "Isn't she already engaged?"

"Yep."

She chuckled. "And she said?"

"We got rescued at that very moment," he responded. "So, nothing."

Stacey shook her head. "Holy shit, Simon, you sure like to keep things complicated."

"Yeah, that's me," he said wearily. "Can I get my clothes back now?"

"I don't know," Stacey said. "I bet if you go find Quinn like that, she'll pop out a yes a lot faster."

"You're messed up, you know that?" he said. Stacey laughed, but Simon had to ask something else. Something eating at him. "So, you've met Eric. Rich, successful, good looking—"

"—boring, controlling, wants to put her in a pretty display

cabinet," Stacey finished. She leaned over and kissed his cheek. "You're the grand prize, baby. She's an idiot if she turns you down."

Quinn felt like she could climb right out of her body and run around the hospital fifteen times, she was so antsy. Yes, there was just a series of tornadoes that had ripped through the area, and yes, there were probably a lot of people needing medical attention, so why not let her be on her way so they could be seen faster?

She had a bruised ankle and some cuts and scratches. So she looked a little rough—her mike pack definitely had it worse. It was cracked and drowned, and part of it was so tangled and messed up, it had to be cut off of her with scissors. Quinn was surprised when she was undressing that it was still even attached. But lots of other people out there in the waiting room were in worse condition, and she had things to do.

Like finding Simon.

Marry me.

All the blood left her head again as she remembered his mouth saying those words. His voice shaking, his eyes crying, his arms holding her so tight that she couldn't catch her breath.

Marry me in that field of daisies.

"Jesus, John, and Alice," Quinn said, running her hands over her face.

The nurse came in. Finally. "Sorry?" she asked, eyes questioning.

"Nothing," Quinn said, smiling politely. "Listen, I'm fine, I just hurt my ankle a little but it's okay, I just need to go get hold of some people and my phone is gone—"

"Just relax," the nurse said. "Let me check you over, it'll only be a minute."

Quinn sighed. "Okay."

"But if you'll hang tight for a second, I'll be right back," she said. "I have to get something."

"Seriously?" Quinn said to the once-again empty cubby.

She got up from the exam table she was perched on and tested her ankle, putting a little weight on it, then more. It was a little unhappy, but not screaming at her. She could walk on it. She caught sight of herself in the glass cabinet's reflection and winced significantly more at that.

Her face was scraped, the scar from her stitches was reddened, she had a cut above her left eyebrow, and her hair was a matted mess. Dried mud and debris from the water had taken residence, and the ends had stiffened up like dreadlocks.

Quinn pulled loose what she could see and feel and tried combing her fingers through it, but it wasn't much help.

And it wasn't important.

Marry me.

There hadn't been a moment alone. Eli and Hannah kept talking and she kept trying to catch Simon's eye, but he was too busy fielding statistic questions and thanking Harry, and then they were here and ushered into separate rooms.

And with no phone to call him or anyone, and not even Hannah showing up for moral support, all Quinn could think about was finding Simon. She needed to look into his face. See his eyes. See if it was real.

"That's it," she muttered, yanking off the gown, walking to her clothes buck-naked. "I'm out of here."

Her clothes were still wet and didn't smell all that great, but they'd have to do. She'd have given just about anything for a pony-tail band, but that was out of the question.

She was slipping on her wet boots when the noise assaulted her ears.

"I don't care about your policy," her mother was saying, her voice getting louder as it got closer.

"Oh, no," Quinn said under her breath, closing her eyes midlace.

"Ma'am," the nurse said.

"I'm her mother and this is her fiancé."

Quinn wished for an invisibility spell. Then the curtain swung aside, and there stood Adelaide Parker, Phoebe, Eric, and Eric's mother. Very much seeing her.

"Well, good thing you weren't about two minutes sooner," Quinn said. "You would have an eyeful of more than you want."

"Oh, my God," her mother said. "Are you all right?"

"I'm fine," she said.

"Excuse me," the nurse said. "You haven't been examined yet."

"I'm waiving my need," Quinn said. "I'm fine."

"You look horrible," her mother said dramatically.

"Thanks, Mom."

"Oh, don't get smart," her mother said. "Look at you," she said, pointing up and down. "Your arms are all scraped up, your face—"

"Quinn," said Eric as he came forward, looking like he'd been chewing metal. "We were listening."

Suddenly her weary and addled brain wasn't sure what they were listening to. Was there anything incriminating?

"We heard y'all chasing. We heard you stop at the shelter. We heard the whole insane thing."

"I don't think you got anywhere near the most insane part of it," she said.

"It was intense," Phoebe said, rubbing her belly, breathing fast.

"Are you okay?" Quinn asked.

She gave a thumbs up. "Peachy."

"Quinn, you're a Parker," her mother said. "You're a lady—about to be a married lady—not someone gallivanting around in the mud. You're thirty years old. Don't you think it's time to grow up?"

"Grow up?" Quinn echoed. "We saved an old woman from being buried under rubble tonight, Mom. We went to check on a recluse who ended up saving *our* lives. Simon nearly died tonight, Mom. I nearly died." Phoebe gasped. "Is that grown up enough for you? Or is my appearance right now really eating you up that badly?"

"Come here," Eric said, pulling her into his arms. "Jesus, Quinn," he said, holding her close and then backing out of it a smidgen when he realized how wet her clothes were. "You scared us, is all. Next thing we know, Maddi gets a text that you're at the hospital."

Quinn took a breath to calm down. "I know, I'm sorry."

"Well, now maybe you'll listen to me," he said.

"Oh, you had to ruin it," she mumbled.

"Seriously, Quinn," he said. "This is no life for us. No appropriate life for my wife. Do you know how many times you've been to this hospital in the past three weeks?"

"Twice."

"And look at you!" her mother piped in, Eric's mother nodding next to her like a bobblehead doll. "Here you are, all beat up again, with the wedding just days away!"

Quinn stared at her in awe.

"Did you hear what I said about saving a woman?" Quinn asked. "About me nearly dying? It was in a hole full of water with a building falling apart on top of me, yet the wedding is your big worry?"

"I heard you, Quinn," her mom said. "And of course that makes my stomach turn. I've lived it before, too, remember?"

Quinn bit her lip. "But?"

"But I'm also evidently the only one of us thinking practically. You are getting married at the end of the week," she said emphatically. "Can you manage to be female for that long? Your hair alone is—"

Quinn wheeled in place, marched to where she last saw the scissors, and grabbed a handful of hair.

"Quinn, no!" her mother shrieked.

Freedom landed in her hand in the form of probably twelve inches of dirty matted blonde hair. Half her head. Phoebe sucked in a breath and then clapped a hand over her mouth. Eric looked on in horror.

"There," Quin said, throwing the hair in the garbage. She looked in the cabinet glass and grabbed the other half, pulling it over her shoulder and severing it as well. "No more worries about my hair. Can we go now? I'd really like a shower."

"That was so—" Eric said, looking like he couldn't find his tongue, he was so mad.

"Inappropriate?" she offered.

"Reckless," he said. "You have to stop this. Acting out just to piss people off. It's beneath you. You may be a Parker, but you're about to be a St. James. It's time to put this behind you and do something sensible with your life."

"Sensible?" Quinn said, her voice cracking with delirium.

"Normal," he said through his teeth.

"I would rather die a hundred times in holes like tonight than live that kind of life," she said. "I would wither on the vine in that kind of mundane existence."

"That's my life," he said, narrowing his eyes.

"And that's why I can't marry you."

Chapter Twenty-Nine

Everyone gasped. Phoebe grabbed her belly. Eric just stared at her.

"What?" he breathed.

Oh, holy hell, Quinn thought as the weight of a million anchors released their hold on her. All the strings dissolved. It was like being on a lifeboat cut free from the mother ship. A ship that wasn't necessarily sinking, but it was going to Hong Kong. And she wanted to go to Australia.

She could breathe. But the hurt in his eyes made that air feel thick.

"I'm sorry," she said, her eyes filling with hurt for him. But not for herself. That told her volumes.

"Wait," he said, reaching for her hand. "Don't do that. I know what all this means to you. But you can still do your photography."

"Eric—"

"I was going to surprise you," he said quickly. "But I'm having a darkroom contracted out for bids. Your own, all for you, in the backyard."

"A darkroom?"

"So after working all day, you can come home and nurture your creative side," he said.

"Stop, Eric," she said, her voice catching.

"Quinn."

"Eric, I just said I can't marry you," she said, her chin trembling as hot tears burned her eyes. "If you think a *darkroom* will swing my decision, then what would that say about our marriage?"

"Why are you so against change?" he asked. "How can you pick this over me?"

"How can you ask me to completely change who I am?" she said. "You wouldn't be marrying me, Eric. You'd be marrying the person you want me to be."

"I don't believe this," his mom said.

"Bitty, I'm so sorry," Quinn's mom said, hands to her flushed cheeks. "Quinn has clearly lost her mind."

"No, I found it, actually," Quinn said. "Mrs. St. James, I realize you already had our nursery picked out, but that'll have to wait."

"Three years he wasted with you!" she spat.

"Mom, stop it," he said.

"I have to go, y'all," Quinn said. "I have to—"

"I'll move," Eric said. "We'll look for a house of our own, like you wanted."

Quinn reached up and kissed him softly on the lips. "It's done, Eric," she said. "I love you. But it's not enough."

"This is about Simon Chase, isn't it?" he seethed, his eyes red and raw.

"No," she said, knowing it was the truth. "It's about us. I want someone who wants *me*. *This* me. The dirty, smelly, inappropriate, unconventional, sometimes crude and outspoken person who wants to hang out a window in a hailstorm and run wild in a field of daisies." Tears streamed down her face. "That's not you, Eric. And it's not fair for me to expect that of you, either."

"Oh, my God!" Phoebe cried.

"It'll be okay, Pheebs," Quinn said. "Now, I really have to go."

"No," Phoebe said, looking at each of them with a panicked expression. "My water just broke!"

Simon was too tired to even care about the wet and rancid clothes he had to put back on. All he wanted to do was go home and take a shower. But he needed to find Quinn first. Look in her eyes. See where her head was. Convince himself she really told him she loved him. That there was actually the slightest iota of a chance.

"Honey! There you are!"

Simon turned as he left the cubby to see his mom hurrying his way.

"Mom, what are you doing—" he started to ask, but it dawned on him then. The radio. "Oh, you heard about it probably."

"Well, some, and then Hannah texted Maddi, and it just—" she said, wrapping her arms around him.

Simon chuckled and hugged her back, knowing how close he came to not doing this again. She didn't need to know that, but he knew. If Quinn hadn't jumped in to save him, he'd be gone right now, and this mother would be short a son. He was aware of his blessings.

"I'm okay, Mom," he said. "Have you seen Quinn?"

"She's down another hall," she said. "Her family is with her, so I came to find you."

"Her family—and Eric?" he asked.

She gave him a look. "Yes. Simon, you're playing with fire there."

"Oh, I'm way past playing, Mom," he said, sinking onto a nearby chair. His legs didn't even want to hold him up anymore. "I'm burned, toasted, and fried."

She sighed. "You could have any woman you wanted, baby."

"And she's the only one for me," he said.

His mother tilted her head curiously. "You're in love with her."

Just three weeks ago, he would have thought those words sounded crazy. But after everything he'd said out loud earlier, that sounded frighteningly accurate.

"Afraid so."

"Oh, my Lord," she said, lowering into the chair next to him. "My Simon, finally in love," she said with a shrug. "With one of my favorite people."

"So you'd be good with it?" he asked.

She laughed out loud. "Oh, I'd be fantastic with it," she said. "Her fiancé probably wouldn't be, though."

Hannah went running by, skidding sideways as she caught sight of them.

"Hey, you okay?" she asked.

"I'm good," he said. "Where you running to?"

"Baby department?" she said. "Neo-something or other?" she added, pointing up. "Quinn texted me her sister's water just broke, she's in labor."

"Oh, my God!" Miss Lou exclaimed, laughing. "What a night!"

"Yeah—and—" Hannah paused, and Simon narrowed his eyes. "What?"

"Apparently she broke up with Eric."

He couldn't believe what he'd just heard. Simon wanted to lie down on the floor and just breathe. He felt like he hadn't taken a full or easy breath since the night of Zach's wedding, and that news—

His mom leveled a look at him, bringing him back to earth. "What did you do?"

"Why do you always assume I did something?"

She raised an eyebrow.

He looked away, his insides doing a dance his body had no energy to do. "I might have asked her to marry me."

"What?" Hannah shrieked.

"Joseph, Mary, and John," Miss Lou said.

"Simon Chase proposing?" Hannah said. "Holy hell, what's the world coming to?"

"So what did she say?" his mom asked.

"We didn't get that far," he said. "Hannah, I have to see her."

"Well, come on, lover boy," she said. "Let's go find a pregnant woman in labor, with a sister that smells as bad as you do."

"Where's Doug?" Phoebe said through her teeth, breathing like a marathon runner. "He should be here."

"He's coming," Quinn said, holding her sister's hand, ignoring the French sculpts digging into her flesh. After nearly being eaten by a tornado, what were a few fingernail marks?

"*Go on and see Quinn,* he said," Phoebe huffed. "*Bond with the family, I'm gonna go swim a few laps.*"

"That's okay," Adelaide said, flanking Phoebe's other side, pushing her hair out of her face. "He's just working off a little stress."

"Stress?" Phoebe said, eyes wild. "Stress?! What the fuck does he have to stress about?" she screamed. "He doesn't have a small person trying to kill him from the inside."

"Okay, little momma," Quinn said, squeezing her hand. "Let's try to channel some of that adrenaline into bringing baby Wellie into the world."

"Exactly," her mom said. "Doug is coming. Eric went to find him."

"Eric just got dumped in a hospital exam room, Mom!" Phoebe grunted. "Do you really think he gives a flying fuck about us right now?"

"Let's dial that back, honey," her mom said. "You don't want the baby's first words heard to be—"

"Fuuuucccckkkk!" Phoebe wailed at the top of her lungs, her head thrown back in pain.

"Then again," her mom said, grasping Phoebe's other hand, "give it all you've got, baby. I know it hurts like hell."

Quinn's eyebrows raised in amusement and surprise, and she couldn't resist a chuckle as she met her mother's gaze.

"Fifteen hours of labor with you," she said, looking at Quinn. "Nine with this one. There's no class in childbirth. It's all brutal."

"Fifteen hours?" Phoebe said, her voice wobbling. "Is that supposed to be a pep talk?"

"You won't be seeing fifteen hours of this," the doctor said, walking in and lifting the sheet. "This baby wants out. Prep for delivery," he said to the nurse.

"What?" Phoebe said, her face red and sweaty. She struggled to get up on her elbows. "Now? But Doug isn't here yet!"

"I don't think your son or daughter cares one way or the other," he said.

"No!" Phoebe yelled. "He had to have fucking sex, he can sure as hell fucking be here to see the outcome!"

Quinn winced as her thumb was bent backward, and she glanced at her mother just in time to see her bite back a laugh.

Well, well. The ice queen of propriety was a real woman, after all.

Simon could hear the shrieked obscenities from the elevator.

"Ten bucks says that's Phoebe," Hannah said.

They jogged toward the cursing, rounded a corner, and there she was.

Not Phoebe—although yes, she was there, too. Latched on to her sister's and mother's hands for dear life and looking ready to murder someone.

But there was Quinn. Scraped up and dirty and looking absolutely stunning, laughing and talking her sister through her breathing.

"Are you the father?" a nurse said, appearing in front of him with a panicked expression.

"No!" Simon said. "Most definitely not."

Quinn looked up at the sound of his voice, and that—right there—nearly buckled his knees. The intensity of her whole heart lit up on her face like a neon sign.

"Then I have to ask you to leave," the nurse said, trying to turn him around. "Only males past this point are the daddies."

"Wait, Doug's not here?" he asked. "Do I need to find him?"

"Yes!" Phoebe screamed. "Tell him to get his ass here or he'll never use his dick again!"

"Wow," Hannah said.

"It's normal," the nurse whispered.

"Looks like a blast," Hannah whispered back.

"Eric went to find him at the club," Quinn's mother said, turning around. "But yes, any help would be appreciated. They're getting ready to—"

"It's cominnnnnnnggggg!" Phoebe screamed, her top half rising off the bed like she was possessed.

"On it!" Simon said, taking off for the elevator. But just as he hit the button, the door to the stairs flung open.

Out came a wet and flushed-looking Doug, running the wrong direction, clothes sticking to him, shirt inside out.

"Doug!"

The guy nearly busted his ass skidding to a stop and turning around at the same time, putting a hand down to catch himself.

"This way, man!" Simon called. "Was just coming to look for you."

"Swimming," Doug huffed, unable to catch his breath. "Phoebe?"

"She's about to deliver, bud, come on!"

"Oh, my God," Doug said, sucking air. "Where is she?"

"Where's my fucking husband?" came Phoebe's hoarse scream, echoing through the corridor.

"Three guesses," Simon said, slapping him on the back.

He went running in. Phoebe started to cry. And Quinn and her mother stepped out.

"Done," he said.

Adelaide laughed sarcastically, then focused on Quinn.

"Thank you for staying," she said. "I know you want to get home."

Quinn looked at her oddly. "Mom, I wouldn't be anywhere else. I never leave my sister in a crisis. Neither would she."

Adelaide Parker blinked rapidly and pressed her lips together, laying a hand on Quinn's scraped up arm.

"I know," she whispered.

Quinn opened her mouth to say something but closed it again in stunned silence.

"I'm going for coffee," her mom said, taking a deep breath before walking off.

"Um," Quinn said, crossing her arms, watching her mother walk away, "okay."

"Breakthrough moment?" Simon asked.

"Odd . . . moment," Quinn said, tears touching her eyes. She shook it off and smiled up at him. Nervously. "Hey there."

"Hey. Are you okay?" he asked, pointing down. "Your ankle?"

"Oh," she said. "Yeah. Just, you know—"

"Bruised up?"

"Yeah."

Okay, the small talk was painful. He touched her hair and watched her breathing quicken. God, he loved that she reacted to him like that.

"Nurse go crazy on you back there?"

Her hand reached up to touch her hair, and she let go of a breath as she chuckled.

"No, that was me. Had a little point to make with my mom."

Simon nodded. "I'm sure you'll rock it."

She tilted her head. "Why, thank you."

He looked at her more seriously, holding her with his gaze. Wanting to pull her to him more than he wanted to breathe.

"You okay otherwise?" he said softly.

She didn't blink, just nodded, the hint of a smile on her lips. The tinge of worry in her eyes. Nervousness. Questioning.

Was it real? Did you mean it?

It was all over her face.

He spoke slowly, emphatically, his voice just above a whisper. "Every word."

Quinn gasped and her eyelids fluttered, her cheeks pinking as she realized he'd read her thoughts. He needed to walk away, let her be with her family right now, *not* lay the kiss on her that he wanted to. Not there. Not then. Not yet.

"I'm gonna go," he managed to push out. "Do you need anything? Clothes? Food?"

She was shaking her head as the words left his mouth, and before he knew what was happening, she walked straight into his arms.

"Just this," she said into his chest. His hands came up her back as hers wound around him. "Just for a second."

Nothing in his life had ever felt that good. The best sex in the world couldn't beat the way she felt fitted against him.

Simon kissed the top of her head and closed his eyes, resting his face there.

"I'll give you two," he said.

"We smell hideous," she said, her voice muffled into his chest.

Simon laughed and rocked her. "Yes, we do." He pulled back and held her face in his hands. "Hey," he said again.

Those incredible eyes sunk right to his rawest places. And he saw hers, too. It wasn't as simple as yes or no. She had things to process, a relationship to let go of. Business to take care of.

"Hey," she whispered back.

"You do what you have to do," he said. "Come find me when you're ready."

The relief and gratitude mixed with the love in her eyes was enough to carry him for days.

"Deal."

"I'm gonna go take a shower now," he said.

"I'm envious."

Simon grinned, unable to resist it. "Like I said, come find me when you're ready."

Quinn smirked, but he saw it. The darkness that changed her green eyes as her pupils dilated with desire.

One eyebrow lifted.

"Deal."

Chapter Thirty

Five days. Simon had counted them, one long-ass day at a time. Five long days of work, cleanup at the shelter site, and thinking. Too much thinking. It was clear at the hospital where her head was, but they'd just come off a roller coaster night of hell, she'd broken up with her fiancé, and her sister had been passing a human. Maybe she changed her mind. The wedding date had come and gone, so that was over and in the past, but maybe she decided she didn't want anyone.

Maybe he was just delirious from lack of sleep.

The shelter—or what was left of it—had been god-awful to see in the daylight. Like God himself had stepped on it, flattening it like a pancake and scattering the crumbs. Nothing was really salvageable. A sink. A few chairs. He and Stacey and the others went through the rubble the best they could and finally determined it was a total loss.

Except for one thing he'd found the next morning. His dad's sign. Still intact. It had brought tears to his eyes for the second time in two days.

And that was more crying than he'd done in years.

He stopped at his mom's after the night shift at the station, having endured yet another ass-chewing for not filming anything for the news. To which Simon finally told his boss that they needed to send a camera of their own next time because when his family was out there, they were busy staying alive, not worrying about footage. The reality show worried about that. The news station could worry about that, too. Leave him the hell alone.

He was going to lose his job. He knew he was only still there because Raymond couldn't work around the clock. Eventually they would find someone willing to put up with their bullshit, someone new and hungry and without a reality show pulling them another direction. It was just a matter of time.

Simon chewed on that all the way home, stopping at his mom's because she'd asked him to. And when he pulled in the driveway, he saw why. Gran was there. He loosened his tie. Joy.

Then the front door opened before he reached it, and Hannah was pushing Gran out.

"Hey," Simon said.

"Hey, yourself," Gran said. "Heard you had quite the adventure the other night."

"That's one way to put it," he said.

"Well, you're late and I have to go, so I'll give you the rundown," she said as Hannah rolled her eyes behind her.

"I just got off work," he said. "How can I be late coming to my mother's house?"

"Boggles the mind, doesn't it?" his mom said, walking out to the porch.

"Yeah, keep mouthing off and I'll change my mind," Gran said as they approached Hannah's car.

"About what, Gran?" he asked.

"About rebuilding that shelter of yours," she said.

"About—" Simon shook his head, not understanding. "What?"

"You heard me," she said. "Rebuilding. The right way. With everything up to code and state of the art."

She was kidding. She was messing with him.

"Why?" he asked.

"Why?" She looked amused.

"Yeah," he said, standing with hands in his pockets. "The other day, you didn't want to throw good money after bad, jump on a sinking ship—I think there were a few more metaphors in there. I don't remember."

Gran laughed. "All true, but there's one difference now."

"What, that it's gone?" he asked sarcastically.

"Yes," she said. "Exactly." She wheeled away from Hannah, toward him. "Simon, now there's no history to fight, no permits to get redone, no climbing out of a hole. It's a lot easier to start from ground zero than from ten miles underground, in the red."

His heart started pumping a little faster, but he had to wait. He couldn't get excited just yet. Gran did nothing for free.

"This is nonprofit, Gran," he said. "Why would you want to do this?"

She looked at him as if he wore her out. "I have charities, Simon. Not everything I'm involved in generates coin."

"You didn't answer my question," he said.

Gran sighed. "Because you told me my son loved it," she said. "And so did you, and you did it together." She blinked away for a moment. "Okay? So call me a sentimental old fool, but I'd like to keep that kind of bond in the family."

She was good.

"And the catch?" he asked.

"What catch?"

"There's always a catch," he said.

"Oh, whatever," she muttered. "You call it a catch. I call it opportunity."

"Okay, elaborate on that opportunity, then," he said.

"Here in the driveway?"

Simon smiled. "Sure."

Gran took a deep breath and let it out. "I've set up a foundation for it," she said. "To be run by a person I'd like to hire to oversee—"

"No," he said. "I have a job. Two, actually."

"I wasn't offering it to you," Gran said.

He blinked. "Oh."

"I'm hiring Stacey March," she said.

"Oh," he repeated.

"Is that a problem?" she asked.

"No," he said. "Just—"

"Why?" she asked. "Because I recognize tenacity," she said. "And passion. She's killing herself to work two jobs and feed the fire of the one that drives her." Gran shrugged. "She's a nurse at her core, so she can still do that, but she'll have the income to let some of that go and focus on what she loves."

Simon didn't know what to say.

"Speechless?" Gran asked.

"A little."

Gran chuckled. "That's always worth it." She turned back, and then stopped and held up a finger. "Oh, and it will be called the Josiah Chase Outreach Center, and you'll be on the board. We'll meet once a month."

"And there it is," Simon said under his breath, pointing.

Yet the wheels started moving in his head. Yes, Gran had pulled her normal moves to keep her family close as usual, but having a say-so on the board—that could be a good thing.

"Also, smart-ass, it's being built partially by some of the homeless folks themselves. Giving them a part of it," she said, wheeling up to the passenger side of Hannah's car. "And one of them—someone named Harry Smith—is running that. Donated his services.

"Harry Smith," Simon said.

"You know him?" Gran said.

Simon chuckled. *Wow.* "I think I do."

Quinn showered and shaved everything to within an inch of its life, and looked at herself in the mirror. It had been five days. Five days since the apocalypse and the meet-up at the hospital.

Come find me when you're ready.

She'd been ready for four and three-quarters of those days. Yesterday was the day she would have married Eric, so she felt it only appropriate to wait to discuss another marriage proposal until that one was over.

It was over. She was a free woman. With options. And still living in her brownstone. With short, cute, kicky hair that she'd had repaired, but she loved.

And now it was time. Time to go look into Simon's eyes and see the score. He'd been busy, and she knew from Hannah that he'd worked last night, so he'd probably be tired, but she couldn't wait anymore.

She had to see him.

Quinn walked into her living room as Hannah strolled in, tossing her keys in a bowl.

"You look cute," she said. "Your hair is perfect like that."

"I know," Quinn tilting her head. "I love it."

"I like the little minidress look on you. Since when do you wear dresses, though?" Hannah stopped and clapped a hand over her mouth. "You're dressing for sex!"

"I am not!"

"Yes, you are," Hannah said. "Easy access—oh, my God, easy access for my brother! Ew!"

"It's not *my* brother, so it's not *ew*, you big twelve-year-old," Quinn said. "But yes, I'm dressing for him. I want to look good. I want him to forget how to breathe when he sees me like I do when I see him."

"I think you already have that covered," Hannah said, scrolling through pictures on her phone. "I sent this to myself to show you one day when you'd need to see it."

Hannah held out her phone, and Quinn put a hand to her chest.

It was a photo Hannah had taken on Zach's wedding night, with Simon and Quinn looking at each other longingly. It was sad and haunting and brought tears to Quinn's eyes.

"God, you're good at that shit," Quinn said, dabbing under her eyes and taking a deep breath. "Why am I so nervous?"

Hannah hugged her. "Because this is the real deal, grasshopper. Now, go get yourself engaged and lucky." She held up a hand. "And I only want to hear about the first part."

Simon walked into his condo, put his keys on a side table, and yanked off his tie. A shower was calling his name, but an apple was calling louder. Or pudding. Or the cookies still in the package in the pantry. He was hungry, tired, and so antsy he could hardly be still.

He unbuttoned his shirt and opened the fridge, deciding the apple sounded too healthy and going for the pudding. Three mouthfuls. That's all the little pack offered. He sucked it down, tossed it in the trash, and was about to hit up the cookies when his doorbell rang. Scrubbing fingers through his hair and assuming it to be the little boy from down the street again, selling magazines, Simon pulled the door open unceremoniously.

To Quinn.

Knocking the air right out of his chest.

"Hey," she said, looking like heaven in a short little dress that instantly took him to about four different scenarios without having to even think on it.

"Hey," he said.

"Bad time?" she asked, pointing at his undone shirt.

"Oh!" he said. "No, just got home, and—" He lost his words as he looked at her. As he took her in and landed back on the eyes he'd missed like crazy in a face he'd been dying to see on a body he'd been jonesing to touch. "It's really good to see you," he finished.

She pressed her lips together nervously.

"So can I come in?"

Simon took a deep breath and let it go slowly.

"As long as you know that if you come in here," he said softly. "I'm gonna have to touch you." His voice lowered. "And once I do, I won't want to stop."

Her eyes went impossibly dark.

"Can I come in?"

Chapter Thirty-One

Everything in Quinn's body went to liquid the second he opened that door, shirt halfway off, hair a little rumpled. She forgot how to speak for a moment and *hey* was about as profound as it got.

Then he said *that*.

John, Mary, and Jennifer.

Quinn didn't remember him stepping back to let her in, or her taking the steps to get there, but suddenly she was standing there. Door closed. Looking into the blue eyes she hadn't been able to quit thinking about for the last five days. Hell, the last three weeks. Screw it, be honest, the last ten years.

And now— now they had no forbidden walls, no moral restraints, nothing keeping them apart. Now she was free to do what she wanted. And all she could do was stand there, sprouting roots into the rug.

"So, how's Phoebe?" he asked, looking for something to fill the awkwardness. "How's the baby?"

"Miss Chloe Louise Blackwell is absolutely perfect," Quinn said proudly. "If not loud."

"Like her mom," he said.

"No shit," she said, chuckling. "And Phoebe is fantastic. And Doug still owns his dick."

Simon laughed. Stopped. And then laughed again at the silence as they just stood there.

"What?" she asked.

"Us," he said. "Standing here like fifteen-year-olds at a school dance."

Quinn smirked. "Very true. Except I was much less awkward *then*."

"Really?" he said, taking a step forward.

"Mmm," she said, interlacing her fingers with his when he got close enough, her fingertips tingling with the touch. "I scared most of the boys."

"I can see that about you," he said, pulling her hand up between them and looking at the union. "You scare the hell out of me."

She gazed at their hands, too. "You know, we've never even done this. Held hands."

"We are now," he said, his voice pulling her gaze back up to his.

The look there broke her. So much *everything* looked back at her, shattering every defense. Knocking down every wall. Dissolving every doubt and every reason not to be there. Suddenly she knew she was exactly where she was supposed to be, and she couldn't get close enough.

Her free hand moved up his chest at the same time his traveled up her arm, to her neck, to her face.

"I really need to kiss you now," Simon said under his breath, his eyes on her mouth.

"About damn time."

His mouth claimed hers as his hands went into her hair. She expected the fire of every other kiss from him, but it was different. He made love to her mouth in a slow, sweet sizzle that rode the fence between having all the time in the world and needing crazy unhinged sex against a wall. It was intoxicating. She could kiss this man this way for days if the rest of her body didn't need attention so badly. And as if he knew that, his lips left hers to travel down her jaw, down the side of her neck. She felt the sigh escape her throat as his hot breath on her skin lit a fire in its path.

Her hands slid up over his face to twist her fingers in his hair, pulling him in, pushing herself deeper into him. Needing to feel him wrapped around her. His hands began to roam, toying with the edge of her dress until there was no more toying. Until his need to touch her won out and his hands were sliding up her ass while his lips were kissing the tops of her breasts.

Quinn's toes curled and she moaned at the sensation, arching into him.

That was her weak spot. The one thing guaranteed to buckle her knees, and it was about to take off like a freight train if his mouth inched any lower.

"What were you about to do when I got here?" she breathed.

"Shower," he said, lifting her dress over her head in one movement, his eyes taking her in like he'd never get another chance.

She shoved his shirt off his shoulders and let her hands travel slowly down the taut muscles of his arms, then back up his chest to his face.

"Sounds like a great idea."

Simon could say he'd had some pretty amazing sexual moments in his life. Some majorly memorable ones, even. But watching the woman he'd fantasized about and loved for a thousand years step into the shower with him—there would never be words to do that moment justice.

And not just because she had the most beautiful body he'd ever been blessed to see. Seriously.

It was the look on her face. The absolute surrender. Commitment. The giving of all she had, stripped and naked and bare and laid out there just for him. It shone from her eyes, and in the seconds it took for their eyes to lock, hers filled with emotion.

"I love you," she said in a whisper, as if she was afraid he might not say it again.

Oh, he most definitely planned on saying it again, but the rawness in her eyes, the vulnerability in her stance, so different from the bravado out in the living room—it broke him. He'd never wanted anyone as badly as he wanted her, and he'd never loved like that—ever. That thought rocked him.

All his previous carnal nasty ideas washed away with the water, and he reached for her.

"Come here, love," he whispered, turning them so that she was under the spray. He soaped his hands and intertwined them with hers. Then he started at her neck, washing her lovingly, slowly, intimately, moving his hands down her body as she moved hers across his chest. The feel of her slippery hands on his skin was intoxicating, but he had a mission. A mission to reach her heart and put her nerves at ease.

He kissed her forehead, her nose, her closed eyes, her cheeks, working his way to just under her ear, where he whispered, "I've loved you since the first day I saw you."

Those eyes flew open, blinking free fresh tears with a look that he thought might take him down.

"Please tell me those are happy tears," he said, whisking them away.

"So happy," she said, her voice wobbling as her hands slid up his chest to his head, bringing him down to her mouth.

It was her answer. He felt it. They hadn't even mentioned the question, but he felt her answer as she kissed him like she was trying to reach the other side of him. With her entire body. As if all doubt had been cleansed away with his words. She never had any cause to doubt. Ever.

The feel of her breasts pressed against him, however, and her belly cradling his aching dick as she kissed him hungrily made Simon realize he had to change things up or it was going to be over before it started.

He tore his mouth away from hers with a growl and turned her around, running his hands along her arms as he dragged his mouth along her neck.

"Let me love you," he said against her skin. He drew her arms up over her head around his neck and pulled her tight against him as he groaned. Fuck if her ass didn't nestle him perfectly. Still, his pleasure needed to wait. He had other things to do.

With one hand, he cupped one of her breasts, rolling the nipple as she gasped and arched her back, grinding her ass into him and nearly buckling his knees.

"Quinn," he moaned against her skin, letting his other hand slide down her belly to find her.

"Oh!" she cried, the sound almost guttural as her hand fisted tightly in his hair and she moved on his fingers.

God, it was hotter than he could have ever imagined, watching her let go like that, and it was all he could do not to lose it as she gyrated against him and his hand alternately.

"Baby," he growled, barely holding it together. Unable to believe he was about to blow from just this. Just touching her. Just watching her.

"Simon," she forced out through her teeth, tensing up like a plank as his fingers worked her hot flesh. "Oh, fuck—Simon!" she screamed, as her body convulsed, and primal moans escaped her throat.

All he could do was hold on to her as she rode out the waves, trying to think of things like weather forecasts and anemometers and ugly dogs and anything he could think of to keep from coming.

Breathing hard as she came down, she rolled her head back against his chest.

"I'm so sorry," she said. "I can't believe I did that."

"Are you kidding me?" he said, sliding his hands up to dig his fingers into her hips, pulling her harder against him. "That was over-the-top hot. I'm dying here."

"You did it," she breathed. "The way you touched me. The nipple thing."

"Good to know," he said as she pivoted in place. "What's next?"

Quinn took him in her hands, holding him against her abdomen as she worked him slowly. "Your turn."

Simon planted a hand against the tile, wishing he could sink his fingers into it. He pressed his forehead against hers.

"I need you," he said, his voice husky with desire. "I wanted to love you so slowly, but you just killed that guy."

Quinn giggled and kissed his lips, his chin, his chest. "Well, if that guy's gone, then maybe a little something-something for this guy first," she said, lowering slowly, dragging her lips down his belly. "I'll just be a minute."

"Killing me," Simon said, somehow staying on his feet as he watched her. Watched her tongue taste him as she looked up at him from under her lashes. Her mouth kiss him. Take him in. His woman. *His woman.*

"Come here," he said hoarsely, lifting her back up. Holding her face. Kissing her like his life depended on it. Pulling her so tightly against him, there wasn't room for air.

"I love you, Quinn Parker," he said against her lips when he pulled back.

"I love *you*, Simon Chase," she whispered back, wrapping a leg around him. "Why don't you take me out of here and show me how much?"

He grinned as the growl of desperate need and desire rumbled through his chest.

"Killing me," he repeated, picking her up.

It didn't matter that they were soaking wet or still had soap dripping in places. The bed would dry.

The look on Simon's face as he laid Quinn down and hovered over her, his muscles taut and popping as he held himself up—oh, God, he was beautiful. Her mind flipped to all the other times he had looked at her like that. Through the camera. When he kissed her. She'd never get enough of that. She didn't want to get enough.

His mouth dropped onto hers, kissing her with so much love, so much desire, making love to her mouth as he pushed himself between her legs, teasing her with the movement. She wrapped her legs tight around his waist and moved with him as his hands loved every inch of her they could reach.

Quinn had never felt so one with another person. Not Eric. Not anyone. It was if they'd met ten years ago for this moment.

"Quinn."

She met his eyes, hearing it in his tone. The need, the everything that was rocketing between them. It was a question, but there was only one answer.

"Please," she breathed.

In one stroke, he pushed inside her, making her arch into the bed with a sound of primal ecstasy that matched his.

Simon played with her fingers as they lay face-to-face on their sides, spent and heavily satisfied and sated after round two.

He knew that there had to come a day when this would seem normal. Commonplace. Real. But right now he couldn't imagine ever taking this scene for granted. Quinn. In his bed. In his life. Loving him.

And on that note, it was time to address the dancing elephant. Or maybe it was just dancing for him. It might be over in the corner smoking a cigar for Quinn right now. She had just come off a two-year engagement—she might not be ready to jump back into that again, in love with him or not.

It was a possibility.

"So," he said.

"So?"

"Yeah."

He looked into her eyes and ran a finger along her cheek, making her eyelids flutter as she breathed in quickly. God, that was sexy.

"Oh—*so*," she said emphatically. "*That* so."

"Well, you know," Simon said. "The other so's were busy."

Quinn giggled. "So—I seem to remember a question—I don't know, there was a lot of water at the time, my brain might have been a little sloshy."

"Or you were just waiting to see if I was any good in the sack first," Simon said.

"Well, you know," Quinn said, making a *duh* face.

"Damn, and I threw it out there on blind faith," he said.

"And now?"

"Now I'm really hoping you say yes, or else doing it for the next several decades might be awkward," he said.

Quinn's chuckle grew into a full-out tickled laugh, and Simon had to hold his heart down.

"So were you serious about doing it in the field of daisies?" she asked, an innocent look on her face. "The wedding, I mean."

"Absolutely," he said. "Wear shorts, even. Eat cobbler. And short ribs."

Quinn pushed up on an elbow. "How did you know about the short ribs?"

"I didn't," he said. "*I* want short ribs."

She sighed and shook her head. "See? This is why I love you."

Simon let a slow grin pull at his mouth. "So, is there an answer in the near future, or do we need to have sex again just to be sure?"

"Hmm," she said flopping on her back.

"Hey," he said, rolling to lean over her. "In all seriousness, Quinn, I want you to know it's okay to say *hang on*. Or even *no*." He moved a lock of hair out of her eyes and let his finger trail her cheek. "I know you just left a long engagement, babe. It's okay to be leery." He took a deep breath at the seriousness that had entered her expression. "I know you love me. I'm not going anywhere."

Quinn's eyes filled, and a tear leaked out of the corner into her hair. Panic filled his gut.

"Crap, baby, I'm—"

"No, no, no," she said, laughing and wiping them away. "You just—you have no idea how you keep surprising me."

Simon narrowed his eyes. "Is that good?"

"You had me at *marry me*, Simon," she said. Simon blinked, goosebumps traveling down his back. He didn't get goosebumps. He was a guy. But damn if she wasn't doing it. "When you said you wanted me to be like I was in that picture—my answer was already yes."

"You were still with Eric," he pointed out.

"Yeah, well, I didn't say there weren't obstacles," she said.

"You're serious?"

She widened her eyes. "Well, if you're still asking."

"I'm gonna smother you with that pillow," he said.

Quinn giggled again but took his face in both hands, looking into his eyes. "Baby, I'd marry you a hundred times over."

Simon kissed her, needing it. Needing to seal it. His woman. Hell, his—fiancée. Good God, he'd never had one of those, and now he did and it was Quinn. Someone needed to pinch the hell out of him.

"I have a fiancée," he said softly.

"Ehh," she said.

"What?"

"I kind of wore the finish off that word."

He pointed at her. "True."

"How about wife?" she said, rising her eyebrows tentatively. "I've never been one of those."

His eyebrows raised too. "Like—now?"

"How scared are you?" she asked.

Simon looked in her eyes and was surprised to find that he wasn't. At all. *Interesting.*

He touched her lips. "I'm in. *You're* not scared?"

"I think I've loved you so long," she said, laughing, "that it doesn't feel rushed at all."

He took her hand and kissed it. "Let's do it, then," he said.

"In the field."

"With the shorts."

"Well, of course with the shorts," Quinn said, smiling, pulling his body down to hers, wrapping herself around him. A feeling he'd never tire of. "I'll call sweet old Mr. Thibodeaux," she said, pulling back to look at his face, pure joy on hers. "Are we crazy?"

"Does it matter?"

She laughed, a beautiful, husky sound that was now his to hear forever.

"Not even a little bit," she said. "I love you, Simon. You know, I lied about my bucket list."

"I wasn't on it?" he said. "Don't break my heart now, Little Bit."

"Oh, no, the kiss was on it," she said. "But the line under it said *Marry Simon Chase.*"

Simon held his head back to look in her eyes. "You're making that up."

She held up a hand. "On my coffee cups, I swear."

"Why did you tell me it was just about a kiss?" he said.

She made a face. "Because even drunk, I wasn't a complete idiot. Besides, that gave me the courage to kiss you, and that was the best kiss ever."

"Kiss heard 'round the world," he said against her lips.

Quinn chuckled, sighing against his. "You know, it's good to keep improving, though."

"Mmm, I'm all for practice," he whispered, sealing his mouth over hers.

Blackberry Cobbler That Quinn Wants
Almost as Much as Daisies...

Dough
3¼ cups all-purpose flour
¾ teaspoon salt
1½ Crisco
1¼ cups milk

Filling
4 cups fresh blackberries
1½ cups sugar
1½ cups water (you may need less if your berries
  or other fruit are really juicy)
½ teaspoon cinnamon (optional)

For The Top Crust
6–7 Tbsp butter
½ cup sugar to sprinkle on the top crust
Optional: cinnamon or nutmeg to sprinkle on the top crust

Plus
Pam spray
Wax paper

Directions:

Mix the flour and salt. Using a pastry cutter, cut the shortening into the flour. Once it becomes a meal texture, add the milk and stir together. Mix the fruit, 1½ cups sugar, and water in a saucepan and bring to boil. Turn down to simmer while you roll some dough into dumplings.

Begin with about a quarter of the dough. On a floured surface, roll the dough to about quarter-inch thickness (or less). Cut into 1-inch pieces and drop into berry mixture. Allow to cook a minute before stirring down and adding more dumplings. You may need just a bit more of the original dough for dumplings. Once you have a good mixture of dumplings and juice, remove from heat. You want this to still be a little juicy. Please remember that your bottom crust will absorb some of the juice.

Split the remaining dough into near halves. (If one side has slightly more, save it for last.) Roll out the first half. Spray Pam into the bottom of a glass 9-by-13-inch pan. Place the rolled-out crust into bottom of pan. (Don't cover the sides.) If the crust tears, it's okay—you can piece it together for the bottom of the dish.

Pour the berry mixture on top of the bottom crust.

Roll out the remaining dough into a rectangular shape larger than the glass dish on floured wax paper. Once the dough is large enough, use the wax paper to turn the top crust onto the cobbler. If an area tears, you can use some of the extra to cover the tear. If some areas go beyond the dish, press them back into the dish. The top crust is yummy, flaky goodness, and extra is always a good thing.

Preheat your oven to 350 degrees F. Cut up the butter and spread out pieces all over the top crust. Sprinkle with sugar and cinnamon or nutmeg. Bake for 30 to 35 minutes or until nicely browned.